A Day in the Life of
LOUIS BLOOM

Previous Titles

McCusker Mysteries:
Down on Cyprus Avenue

Detective Inspector Christy Kennedy Mysteries:
I Love The Sound of Breaking Glass
Last Boat To Camden Town
Fountain of Sorrow
The Ballad of Sean & Wilko
The Hissing of the Silent Lonely Room
I've Heard The Banshee Sing
The Justice Factory
Sweetwater
The Beautiful Sound of Silence
A Pleasure to do Death With You

Inspector Starrett Mysteries:
The Dust of Death
Family Life
St Ernan's Blues

Other Fiction:
First of The True Believers
The Last Dance
The Prince Of Heaven's Eyes (A Novella)
The Lonesome Heart is Angry
One of Our Jeans is Missing

Factual:
Playing Live
The Best Beatles Book Ever

www.paulcharlesbooks.com

A Day in the Life of
LOUIS BLOOM
The Second McCusker Mystery

by Paul Charles

Dufour Editions

First published in the United States of America, 2018
by Dufour Editions Inc., Chester Springs, Pennsylvania 19425

Cover photos by Paul Charles

ISBN 978-0-8023-1362-1

2 4 6 8 10 9 7 5 3 1

Library of Congress Cataloging-in-Publication Data

Names: Charles, Paul, 1949- author.
Title: A day in the life of Louis Bloom / by Paul Charles.
Description: Chester Springs, Pennsylvania : Dufour Editions, [2019] |
    Series: McCusker mystery ; book 2 | "First published in the United States
    of America, 2018"--Title page verso. | Includes bibliographical references
    and index.
Identifiers: LCCN 2018017808| ISBN 9780802313621 (hardcover : alk.
paper) |
    ISBN 0802313620 (hardcover : alk. paper)
Subjects: LCSH: Murder--Investigation--Fiction. | GSAFD: Mystery fiction.
Classification: LCC PR6053.H372145 D39 2019 | DDC 823/.914--dc23
LC record available at https://lccn.loc.gov/2018017808

Printed and bound in the United States of America

Thanks are due and offered to:

The Dufour fab four: Duncan, Christopher, Miranda and David.

Also Gary Mills, David Torrans, Clair Lamb, Lindsey Holmes, Jeff Robinson, Lucy Beever, Adrienne Armstrong, my magic wife Catherine and, my hero, my father, Andrew.

CHAPTER ONE

THE DAY: THE THIRD THURSDAY IN OCTOBER

This is not the beginning of the story; it is just where we join it.

'Guess what the last thing I said to Louis Bloom was?'

McCusker clearly must have felt that wasn't a real question, because he didn't attempt to answer it.

'"Oh Louis Bloom, you'll be the death of me, you will,"' Elizabeth Bloom volunteered, in answer to her own question. 'He'd left the door wide open and the wind was angry last night, so that's why I called out after him as he scooted out through the front door. All I heard in return was him laughing back at me. That was the last I heard of him. He just disappeared into the night.'

McCusker sat opposite the woman in the cosy living room of her Edwardian house on the corner of Colenso Parade and Landseer Street. The living room was tidy yet littered with photographs, paintings and ornaments. The spick-and-span house overlooked the glorious Botanic Gardens in the campus area of Belfast.

Lily O'Carroll was off somewhere else in the house brewing up, no doubt, a sugar-generous cup of tea.

'Mrs Bloom,' McCusker started, only to be interrupted by:

'Elizabeth, please call me Elizabeth – everyone calls me Elizabeth.'

'Right, Elizabeth, okay,' McCusker started back up again slowly, 'what time did Louis run out the door at?' McCusker was not as conscious of his Ulsterism as he was of making sure he followed her lead by pronouncing the "s" as an "e" in her husband's Christian name.

'It was at 8.55,' she offered immediately. 'The reason I'm so convinced of that is because we were just about to start to sit down to watch *The Fall* – we both just love that programme. Never miss it, and that starts at 9.00 on BBC. The BBC shows always start sharp as scheduled; I suppose that's something to do with their no-adverts policy.'

McCusker looked at his watch. It was coming up to 01.00 a.m. Just four hours since Louis Bloom had gone missing. Normally a Misper (missing person) wouldn't be treated as an official missing person until forty-eight hours had passed. Not every Misper, though, was a lecturer at Queen's University, whose wife had a sister named Angela, who had married an RUC man called Niall Larkin, who was now a superintendent in the PSNI and, subsequently, the boss of both DI Lily O'Carroll and McCusker – the very same Grafton Agency cop currently looking at his watch.

Elizabeth Bloom, wife of the aforementioned Louis Bloom, was usually the most relaxed and self-confident of women but had now confessed to being, 'at my wit's end' since her husband hadn't returned from dumping their daily rubbish in one of the bins in the (very) nearby Botanic Gardens. She had waited a good three hours before ringing her sister, Angela. Angela, keen to return to her slumber, immediately nudged her husband, Superintendent Niall Larkin, awake and successfully passed the baton on to him. Larkin nearly dropped the baton at that point, feeling the Misper, husband of his wife's sister or not, could wait until the morning. He eventually showed that behind every great man is an even greater wife. Consequently he thought better of his first instinct to return to slumber-land, choosing instead to ring O'Carroll. Larkin conceded to overtime for her and agency-cop McCusker before turning off his bedside light. He then drifted off into a nightmare where he reviewed the Grafton Recruitment Agency's invoice for McCusker's time on the case, only to find his entire annual budget for the year had been blown on this Midnight Hour Case.

O'Carroll, in turn, called in-person to McCusker's student-style accommodation in University Square Mews, just off Botanic Avenue.

Maybe O'Carroll was hoping to catch out McCusker and her sister, Grace… as in catching them in, and together, which only went to prove that both McCusker and Lily O'Carroll were thinking about her sister at the exact same moment. And no, Grace O'Carroll had not been in McCusker's rooms when Lily came calling. Whatever had been on McCusker's mind as he enjoyed – as in *really* enjoyed – his early morning mind-set and coffee, disappeared by the time DI Lily O'Carroll had given his quarters a quick, but thorough, once over. O'Carroll was hyper and fidgety during the very short drive from University Square Mews to Botanic Gardens.

As a Grafton Agency cop, and unlike O'Carroll, McCusker could have refused the overtime and returned to his slumber. This wasn't an option he even considered due mainly to the fact that both Superintendent Larkin and DI O'Carroll had gone out of their way to make him feel very welcome at the Custom's House over the past year or so. This most certainly wasn't always the case with agency personnel. If anything the rank and file of the PSNI went out of their way to make them feel inferior and unwanted. Larkin though was a good friend of Superintendent Thomas "Tommy" Davies, McCusker's ex-boss in Portrush. When McCusker had found himself in an awkward predicament 18 months previously, Davies had contacted Larkin and called in a favour to secure McCusker, via the Grafton Agency in the Customs House, a job. The fact that in the intervening year McCusker and O'Carroll had formed a very successful team had undoubtedly helped his situation. But the unescapable simple fact was that he was still an agency cop. So when O'Carroll came calling in the early hours of the morning as the behest of Larkin, McCusker was happy to be there - and not just to be there – but, to be there with bells on.

'It's okay for you, McCusker,' she began, carelessly, noisily, shoving her car into gear. 'If we don't solve this case quickly, you'll just be replaced, but I'll have to stay on in the PSNI in deep humiliation, watching every other fecker who started after me fly past me on the promotion ladder.'

'Praise seldom comes to those who seek it,' McCusker said, as much to the raindrops on the side window as to his rattled colleague.

'Ah man… pleazzzze… I'm really in no mood for your beer-mat philosophy.'

'Okay, okay,' McCusker started, desperately seeking for a direction, 'let's not worry about solving the case just for now. Let's just get stuck in with collecting as much information as we can and see where that takes us.'

'Now that works big time for me, McCusker,' she said, relaxing into her seat like she'd just taken a greedy first drag on a much desired ciggy, 'that's what I needed to hear.'

Two and a half minutes later they were in Mrs Elizabeth Bloom's handsome three-bedroom period house and the owner's anxiety immediately washed away all of McCusker's early morning concerns.

CHAPTER TWO

McCusker and O'Carroll worked well together. On paper, as McCusker was an agency cop – also unaffectionately known as a Yellow Pack – O'Carroll was senior, but they worked happily as equals. In real terms that usually meant that the senior member of the partnership was gracious to a fault. For McCusker's part, he never stood on O'Carroll's toes or tried to upstage her. He wouldn't really know how – his singular priority was to solve the mystery of the crime. That was his one and only drug, well, apart from the occasional pint of Guinness.

As he looked around the lecturer's comfortable house, he pondered whether Louis Bloom had perhaps done a midnight-flit – as in done a runner from his wife – or perhaps he had been kidnapped, assassinated, murdered or terminated? He then wondered if assassinated, murdered and terminated could be considered to be one and the same.

'Mrs Bloom...'

The missing lecturer's wife nodded her head negatively from side to side.

'What did we agree?'

'Sorry?'

'We agreed you...

'We agreed I was going to call you... Elizabeth?' McCusker replied, just before he imagined a big gong was about to go off.

'Correct,' she replied, quite feisty for someone an hour after midnight, and like she didn't have a care in the world.

'Elizabeth, was your husband wearing a jacket when he went out to dump the rubbish?'

Elizabeth rushed out into the hall and nearly bumped head-on into O'Carroll, who was making her way into the sitting room with a wooden tray, laden with tea, milk, sugar and maybe even, if McCusker's nostrils were not deceiving him, several slices of toast.

Mrs Elizabeth Bloom's voice returned to the sitting room a few seconds before she did. 'Yes, he took his black Barbour jacket and his New York Yankees baseball cap. It's not that he supports the Yankees, or any baseball team for that matter, it's just he feels the Yankees have a proper-shaped cap with a solid peak. He really hates the local style of baseball caps, which are nothing more than bad copies of flat caps.'

'Does he have his wallet, credit cards, or money in his pocket all the time, or does he take them out of his pocket when he comes home?' McCusker continued, as O'Carroll poured the tea.

'Always in his trouser pockets, cash on the left, credit card wallet on the right, keys in his jacket pocket.'

'Mobile phone?' McCusker suggested.

'Certainly not,' she replied, immediately.

'Really?' McCusker pushed.

'No, my husband is forever saying that sometime during the day all humans should be, uncontactable… no sorry, that wasn't the word he used… yes that was it. Louis said that humans need to be unconnected for part of their day. We all need space to breathe and to just… to just… be humans.

'Would you know what credit cards he has?' O'Carroll asked in an effort to return to the original thread, as she passed over a cup of tea to both Mrs Bloom and McCusker.

'MasterCard credit card, Visa debit card and that's it,' Mrs Bloom replied, as she insisted on sugaring her own tea, choosing just the one spoon-full.

'What age is Louis?' McCusker asked.

'Fifty-three at his last birthday.'

'Did your husband have any illnesses?' McCusker continued.

'Oh, let's see now,' she started off slowly, as she returned her tea cup to the saucer, 'he has bad eyesight; sciatica in his left leg; a bad back; lack of hearing in his left ear; he is prone to catching a bad cold if anyone so much as looks at him – Louis is convinced that each and every cold he catches will develop into full-blown pneumonia.

Oh, and arthritis in his left hand. In addition to all of that, he's a terrible patient. He used to say, "I'm not looking forward to this dying malarkey. I think the trauma of it all will most likely kill me." He's a habitual hypochondriac but generally he's a lot healthier than he thinks he is.'

'But there's never been any sign of Alzheimer's?'

'No!' Mrs Bloom said, shooting up out of her chair. She then seemed to freeze in thought, 'Oh, you think that when he went out he forgot who he was and he's wandered into someone else's house and just sat down with someone else's wife to watch *The Fall*?' she added while keeping a poker face.

'Well, it would be an explanation,' Lily O'Carroll offered.

'Oh, don't be a silly moo,' Mrs Bloom chuckled.

McCusker couldn't work out if she was presenting a brave face or that she genuinely wasn't worried. But, if she genuinely hadn't been worried, then why had she rung her sister – the wife of Superintendent Niall Larkin – in the middle of the night, thereby setting up the process of stirring others from their nocturnal slumbers?

McCusker imagined from Mrs Bloom's glazed eyes that she was on some kind of medication, some form of mother's little helper. Physically she was clearly trying to be friendly, upbeat, even, and all in an attempt to be of help to her husband. But her eyes told a different story. To the detective Mrs Bloom's eyes betrayed not so much a story but more a nightmare of someone whose insides were screaming in quiet desperation.

McCusker was impressed by O'Carroll; she'd probably been woken from the middle of a deep sleep, yet here she was, looking a million dollars in her fresh make-up, dark red trouser suit with a pink, polo-necked, woollen jumper and her outfit complete with her sensible fawn Birkenstock laced shoes. For his part, McCusker had enjoyed a little more notice than O'Carroll, in that she had to drive over to him to pick him up, so he'd a shower and a very quick electric shave to go. He found electric shavers very unrewarding in that they could, with a lot of effort, remove the physical signs of your stubble, but they never, ever offered you the refreshing and cleansing feeling of a blade and shaving cream. McCusker had several suits that he rotated through; today's was a dark blue, smart, non-designer label number, which was his current favourite. He wore a fresh shirt every day, currently a blue and white striped one, with a bottle green tie. He wore a pair of Prada sports-like black shoes, but the regular use had betrayed their main flaw in that the leather toecap scuppered just a wee bit too easily. To complete the picture of a modern-day Ulsterman, McCusker's solid frame was topped by straw-like hair, which had made do with its early morning finger-comb.

'Is Louis a religious person?' he asked.

Elizabeth Bloom smiled a large, gentle smile, clearly reflecting before answering the question.

'Well all I can tell you is that Louis passionately believes that Heaven is what we have today, here and now on Earth. He believes this is Heaven. He thinks that life is perfect and we should all slow up and enjoy it more, before it's over.'

'What does Mr Bloom do for a living?' O'Carroll asked, as McCusker considered the Heaven on Earth concept.

'He's a lecturer at Queens University.'

'But of course he is,' O'Carroll replied, remembering how the investigation had started.

'Does Louis have a study in the house?' McCusker cut in, proceeding to look around the room as though he had X-ray eyes and he could see through the internal walls of the house to where a study might be. As he studied the room, O'Carroll gave him the briefest of nods in acknowledgement of the fact that he'd successfully distracted Mrs Bloom from focusing too much on her own minor gaffe.

'Yes,' Mrs Bloom gushed, 'he only went and commandeered our spare bedroom upstairs, the one at the front with the brilliant view of the Botanic Gardens. He doesn't have a phone up there, nor internet or even television. I have occasionally heard what I imagine to be the sounds of Radio Four coming out from behind his frequently closed door.'

'Can you show us where the study is?' McCusker asked.

'Of course I can! But it wouldn't do you any good.'

'Oh?' McCusker offered, in relatively harmless shock.

'Yes, he always locks his room and keeps his key on his key ring.'

'Would there be access by a window?' O'Carroll asked, appearing to grow a little frustrated with Mrs Bloom's apparently unproductive cooperation.

Mrs Bloom shook her head.

'Do you have a cleaner who comes around?' McCusker asked, trying another angle to open the door not just to Louis' study but also to their faltering investigation.

'Do we heck as like. Can I remind you we're talking about Queens, in Belfast, and not Harvard, in Cambridge?'

'So does Louis clean out his own study?' O'Carroll asked, sounding like she was preparing to give up with this line of questioning'

'Oh yes,' she conceded. 'In fairness to Louis, we could easily have afforded a cleaner, but he just hated strangers around the house, around his space.'

'Have *you* ever been in Louis' study?' McCusker asked, feeling like it was a game of table tennis where the PSNI team had the advantage of an extra player.

'Well,' Elizabeth replied, slowly drawing the word out, 'it's not that it's officially out of bounds but I can tell you that the only times I've ever been in there, Louis has always been present.'

'So would it be fair to assume that the study is the place that Louis would do his research and keep his diary, for instance?' McCusker asked, again playing the part of the dentist.

'And things like that,' Mrs Bloom eventually agreed.

When PSNI didn't return the ball, Mrs Bloom continued with, 'Look, you don't think the silly bugger has gone off and gotten himself into trouble do you?'

'Oh, we don't even know if he's missing yet, let alone in trouble,' McCusker offered, trying to reassure Mrs Bloom while not appearing to succeed.

'Do you have any children you'd like to come and stay with you, that you'd like us to contact on your behalf?' O'Carroll asked.

To McCusker, O'Carroll sounded like she felt they had nearly progressed as far as it was possible to go for now.

'No... just me and Louis.'

'Okay...'

'We both agreed on it and planned it that way,' Mrs Bloom stated, before O'Carroll could continue. 'There's just too much heartbreak involved. Either they break your heart or you break your own heart over them.'

'Friends?' O'Carroll asked.

'Yes, lots of friends.'

'No, sorry I meant are there any friends who could come over and stay with you?' O'Carroll suggested.

Mrs Elizabeth Bloom thought for a good few seconds. However, she looked not so much that she was thinking which friend she should or could invite over. No, she looked more like she was deciding if she would admit to the name of the first person that had sprung into her mind. Eventually she said, 'Yes, I'll give Al a shout.'

'Okay good,' McCusker said, feeling that they were making some progress at last, in that at the very least they would be able to leave Mrs Bloom and start their investigation. 'Is Al a friend of yourself and Louis?'

'No, no, not at all!' she countered. 'He's Al Armstrong – I met him at Surrey University and *we've* been good friends since.'

'Right,' McCusker offered, hoping he wasn't sending out any judgmental signals, when in fact he wasn't meaning to. 'Can we ring him for you?'

'Oh that's alright, I've already rung him,' she admitted, a bit sheepishly. 'He's on his way over.'

CHAPTER THREE

The very same Al Armstrong rang the doorbell about ten minutes later, just as the third hour of the day was about to complete its circuit of the clock. During the intervening time, neither McCusker nor O'Carroll learned anything interesting or even valuable. In fact all they learned was what had happened in yesterday's evening's episode of *The Fall*, which Mrs Bloom had already admitted she'd enjoyed in her husband's absence. McCusker felt this too might have been part of the upbeat facade Mrs Bloom was trying to project

Al Armstrong was a tall, slim man, who even at 3.00 a.m. was dressed most dapper in his tan slacks, brown leather slip-on shoes, brownish tweed jacket, country-style checked shirt, red V-neck woollen pullover or sleeveless jumper (McCusker couldn't really tell until such time Armstrong removed his jacket) and a blue and gold cravat. His stubbled face was flushed, and his green eyes were slightly bloodshot. To McCusker he looked like someone who had just been on the pull at an old fashioned dinner-dance. Armstrong had a very strong Belfast accent with a raspy voice that sounded permanently hoarse.

'Gosh Elizabeth, are you okay love, you poor dear, what's he gone and done this time?' was Armstrong's opening line, as he walked through the front door.

Al clocked the two police officers and seemed to put the brakes on, both physically and mentally. McCusker got the impression that if they hadn't been there, Al and Elizabeth would have run straight into each other's arms. But that was just a hunch, one he didn't even share with O'Carroll.

'Mr Armstrong,' O'Carroll started, taking Mrs Bloom by the hand and guiding her towards the kitchen, 'could my colleague here have a quick word with you while Mrs Bloom and myself go and make a fresh pot of tea and prepare some more toast.'

O'Carroll's tone made it clear it wasn't a question.

'Gosh, yes, of course,' Al croaked, as Lily and Mrs Bloom positively glided out of the room.

McCusker started straight in with: 'You've known Mrs Bloom a long time?'

'Oh gosh, yes, we met in Guildford, at Surrey University, back in the late seventies, maybe more like 1976. I'd started the year before – I was taking engineering and she medicine. When she arrived we just hit it off immediately. She was local, I was an exile, so that was our bond I suppose.'

McCusker wondered if they had been boyfriend and girlfriend back then.

'Did youse start dating then?' McCusker heard a voice he recognised as his own ask. He hadn't intended to ask; the question had just popped out of his mouth, as personal questions had a habit of doing with him.

'Ha!' Armstrong offered with a nervous laugh, which, with his voice, sounded like a death rattle. 'Well, if I'm to be honest with you, we kinda did.'

'Kinda did?' McCusker repeated.

'Yes, you know, we hung out, we dated, and we went to the flicks. She's a girl, I'm a boy, so we occasionally kissed a bit, but that was the sum total of our romantic fumbling.'

McCusker couldn't be 100 per cent sure but he guessed from O'Carroll's tell-tale, over-rattling of the china that she was departing the kitchen shortly, which also meant that he wasn't going to have Armstrong exclusively to himself for much longer. This troubled McCusker because it compromised his questioning of Mrs Bloom's male friend of long-standing.

'You know,' McCusker started, 'I wonder if you could do me a great favour and accompany me on a quick dander around the Botanic Gardens, just to double-check nothing obvious happened to Louis Bloom. DI O'Carroll and I meant to do it, but we wanted someone to be with Mrs Bloom. I'm sure you're more familiar with the layout.'

Armstrong surprisingly agreed immediately. 'You're not from Belfast then?' he asked the detective.

'Ah no, I'm from Portrush,' McCusker admitted.

'Gosh, I see they've just been listed in the Sunday Times Best Places to Live in the UK, 2018,' Armstrong croaked, in clear envy, 'how'd you end up down here then?'

'It's really a long story, excuse me a second,' McCusker replied, before turning and walking into the kitchen. He immediately noticed a tell-tale box of Xanax, the top discarded and with a few of the light blue pills spilt carelessly on the work top. Close by was a glass with just a few drops of water remaining. He managed to wink at O'Carroll behind Mrs Bloom's back, 'Mr Armstrong has kindly agreed to accompany me on a quick dander around the Botanic Gardens to see what we can see.'

'Okay, good idea,' O'Carroll replied, while Mrs Bloom totally ignored him.

'Keep the tea and toast warm for us,' McCusker said, as he stepped into the hall via the living room.

'Take him in by the Sports Centre entrance, Al, all the other gates will be locked,' Mrs Bloom called after them, proving she did know what was going on behind her back.

A few minutes later he and Armstrong were out of the front door and taking a right at the front gate and down Colenso Parade, a left into the entrance to the Queen Sports Centre, and then a very quick left through the small entrance to Belfast's famous Botanic Gardens, or the Royal Botanic Gardens, as the 28 acres were known when they opened in 1828 (although they hadn't actually opened to the public until 1895).

It was a breezy, moonlit night, making it possible to see almost everything most of the time, although occasionally the clouds would block out the Moon and the resultant light to such a degree that it would fall almost pitch dark.

'So you would see Mr Bloom a bit socially?' McCusker asked, resuming his questioning and consciously omitting as to how he'd landed up in Belfast.

'No, not really,' Armstrong admitted. 'Mostly I'd see Elizabeth just by herself. Louis would be secure in his wee room, enjoying his great thoughts. Elizabeth, on the other hand, loved to go to lots of events, flicks, just like in the early days, and shows at the Opera House, and I'd always be her preferred plus one.'

'Oh right,' McCusker replied in an "I see" kind of tone. 'But you saw Louis sometimes?'

'Some of the time, but not all of the time,' Armstrong conceded.

'When was the last time you saw him?'

'Gosh, oh let's see now,' Armstrong posed, as they walked on.

McCusker noted that as Armstrong walked, he folded his arms in front of himself in a very lady-like manner.

'I was here two nights ago… but ehm… no, Louis wasn't here then, so probably it would have been at Sunday lunch. Yeah, that was it – I was here for Sunday lunch. Sunday past – that would have been the last time I saw him.'

By which point they'd reached the bin that Mrs Bloom had re-ported as being the very same that her husband used to deposit all his nocturnal, nostril-offending deposits.

The bin in question was a heavy-duty, black plastic wheelie bin, which was strapped to one of the Garden's many archaic, circular black bins, which had (from top to bottom, and painted all in silver) "LITTER" in capitals, two hoops that stretched around the bin, an inch apart, Belfast's official logo (a seahorse, a reference to the city's maritime history), and "BOTANIC GARDENS", again in all caps. The bin itself looked to be fixed securely into the earth.

McCusker took a photo of the bin as it currently was. The detec-tive gloved up and dipped his hand into the three-quarters full bin, re-moving the plastic bags one by one and taking a photograph of the remainder after each removal.

'The camera's a better version of a notebook,' Armstrong observed. McCusker didn't reply so Armstrong continued. 'I'm a songwriter and I used to use only a notebook on my walks, but now I seem to get as much information from photos as I do from my notebook.'

'This one seems to be like the bag Mrs Bloom described… it's the only light blue bag in the bin.'

'Oh gosh, yes, that's definitely one of Elizabeth's blue bags,' Arm-strong croaked.

'I'd like to leave these three and the one beneath back at Mrs Bloom's before we continue our walk, if you don't mind?'

'Totally fine with me,' Armstrong replied, 'but why would you want to bring four bags back and not just Elizabeth's?'

'Well, whoever dumped the top two bags, one black and one grey, obviously did so after Mr Bloom, and the yellow one at the bottom was deposited just before Mr Bloom. Now that we know the sequence of the bags, the Scene of Crime team can go through the bags' contents and hopefully discover the owners.'

'Gosh, okay,' Al chuckled, 'that's both very clever and very simple at the same time.'

'So you write songs?' McCusker asked, as the deposited the rubbish bags in the Bloom's front garden behind the hedge.

'Yes I do.'

'Do you write under your own name, Al Armstrong?'

'Gosh yes, it's much too much like hard work to give credit to someone else, even though they might even be a *non de plume*.'

'And would I know any of your songs?'

'Yes, well, at least I hope so,' Armstrong replied, through another nervous throaty laugh.

'Oh, I don't know, I wouldn't be a good example of "the man on the street". Now, DI O'Carroll – she'd be a much better bet for you. She and her sister Grace are both very big on their music,' McCusker replied, wondering exactly why he'd (again completely unconsciously) included Grace O'Carroll in his conversation. He just had a habit of opening his mouth and not knowing what was going to come out.

'What about 'Causeway Cruising'?' Armstrong offered, with a lot of confidence.

'Why, yes of course, everyone knows 'Causeway Cruising'. I mean, as I said, I'm from the Port and that was the big song two summers ago. But you didn't record that under your own name, I would have recognised it. It was a band name. What was the name of the band now, don't tell me… yeah that's it, Zounds!'

'Gosh, yes, that's the name, well remembered,' Armstrong replied, positively beaming.

'So you're a member of Zounds?' McCusker asked, while thinking Mrs Bloom's best friend looked too old to be in a pop group.

'No, no, the record wasn't by me. I gave up recording years ago.

Yes, I wrote the song, but it was recorded by Zounds, and they'd a huge hit with it.'

'Goodness, that is a great song,' McCusker started, 'it sounds a wee bit like the Beach Boys.'

McCusker had meant it as a compliment but the creased lines of Armstrong's forehead gave the impression that the detective had just shot the songwriter through his heart.

Although McCusker was impressed to meet a real-life songwriter, he was trying desperately hard to get the questioning back on course. 'On a different matter, why do you think you and the husband of your best friend don't get on better?'

'I think in the early days Louis had thought there was more going on between Elizabeth and I, than there actually was,' Al replied instantly.

Two things struck McCusker: one, if ever there was an answer that should have started off with Armstrong's trademark "Gosh" right there, that surely should have been it; two, it seemed to the Ulster detective that the answer had come from the "here's one I prepared earlier" production line.

'Do you really mean to tell me that you don't have a good friend, a very good friend who's female?' Armstrong offered, when it appeared that McCusker wasn't buying into his reply, sounding like he still hadn't forgiven the detective for the Beach Boy remark.

'But of course,' McCusker replied, picking his words very carefully. 'Equally I'd be very surprised if their partner wasn't also a good acquaintance of mine as well. It seems to me that the simple fact is that both you and Louis Bloom were giving each other a wide berth.'

'Are giving each other...'

'Sorry?'

'You know, you said "were giving each other", as in past tense. As in you think he's dead, when, in fact, surely he's just a missing person or, in PSNI speak, a Misper?'

'Sorry, of course – you're 100 per cent correct.'

'But going back to your last statement; the fact is that Elizabeth never seemed to be bothered about it,' Armstrong continued, 'and maybe if she had been, I'd have made more of an effort in trying to be a better friend to Louis.'

'And there's definitely no "baggage" between you and Elizabeth that prevented you and Louis becoming better friends?'

'"Baggage" between us, is it? You're such a romantic, Inspector,' Armstrong croak-chuckled.

'Just McCusker will do,' the detective added, barely resisting sighing through having, once again, to follow PSNI procedure and make it clear to all members of the public that he – an agency cop with the Grafton Agency – came into contact with while on duty that he was not, in fact, an official member of the PSNI and as such did not have a rank. 'So, Mr Armstrong, did you and Mrs Bloom ever share any romantic moments at University or even afterwards would have prevented you and Mr Bloom becoming better friends?'

Al Armstrong grimaced for a bit as if considering that very thought. They walked on in silence towards the original rubbish bin they'd examined. Armstrong still had his arms folded in front of him. Eventually, under the cloak of darkness offered by another cloud blocking out the moonlight, he admitted: 'Well, if I'm being 100 per cent honest, I suppose I'd be pissed at someone who spent as much time with my wife as Elizabeth does with me.'

Some kind of progress at last, McCusker thought. 'What does your wife think of your relationship with Mrs Bloom?'

'Sorry, that was a hypothetical answer I just gave you. I'm not married.'

'Currently or never?'

'Never ever.'

'Gosh,' McCusker replied involuntarily. The response seemed to bite a bit at Armstrong.

'The big thing about Louis though,' Armstrong began, sounding like he was very keen to change the subject, 'is that all his students positively love him. All that adulation, and he's only a lecturer for heaven's sake.'

'But Al, you surely went through all of that in your pop star days?' McCusker offered trying to make amends for his earlier backhanded compliment via the Beach Boys.

'Oh Gosh, now there's a thought,' Armstrong replied, clearly still deep in his state of envy, 'me and every pop star who ever graced the airwaves of Radio Ulster can only but dream of the commitment of Louis' fanatics. But yet…'

'But yet?' McCusker prompted picking up the pace of their walk if only to generate some body heat.

'And yet he seemed so unaffected by it all,' Armstrong concluded wistfully.

Just then another thought came into the detective's mind. 'Tell me this, Mr Armstrong: if I wanted to get out of the park from here without going back again past the Bloom's house, what would be my best way to go?'

'Oh, that's easy, we'd cut down there, bearing left between the back of the Ulster Museum, on our left, and the Conservatory to the right, which would take us out just above the Whitla Hall, you know, diagonally opposite the Students' Union building. At this time of the night the main gate will be closed but I know a way at the back of the Whitla Hall that we can get out on to the main road by.'

'O-kay,' McCusker said, as he quickened his pace somewhat, 'let's walk that way.'

The only action on University Road was the changing colours of the traffic lights, which, without their usual queue of vehicles, made them appear quite eerie. The streets were sodden from an earlier shower, and empty.

'Do you often have to work this late at night?' Armstrong asked, breaking into McCusker's mood.

'Usually not,' McCusker replied, remembering he hadn't actually been on a graveyard shift since his days up at Portrush. 'Where would the nearest taxi rank be?'

'Either on Botanic Avenue or down outside the Europa Hotel on Great Victoria Street,' Armstrong replied. 'If you definitely wanted to be assured of getting one, I'd say outside the Europa would be your best bet, but...'

When Armstrong didn't complete his answer McCusker leaned his head and shoulders towards the tall thin man, while continuing their walk, keeping his hands in his pockets as he did so.

'Well, I was going to say that if you wanted to be more *discreet*, if you see what I mean, then perhaps Botanic Avenue would be a better option.'

'Right! Yes. Good point,' McCusker gushed, 'tell me this Mr Armstrong: did Mr Bloom drive, did... *does* he have a car?'

'Yes, Louis drives an elegant ice blue Jaguar S Type, possibly the last classic car to come off the UK production line. On the other hand Elizabeth drives a black VW Golf, and they were both parked outside their house when I arrived earlier.'

Al Armstrong and McCusker stood on the pavement just outside the beautiful Queens University red-brick Lanyon Building, across the green in University Square. McCusker found himself mesmerised by the grandeur of the building.

'Maybe we should be heading back to the house,' McCusker said, as he looked back up University Street, in the direction he clearly wanted to go.

'Gosh, I suppose Botanic will be teeming with PSNI at first light?' Armstrong offered, seemingly totally comfortable, with his arms folded in front of him as he walked along.

'That'll be the plan,' McCusker replied, as they passed the spot they'd exited a few minutes previously and continued on up Stranmillis Road, past the front of the Ulster Museum, then past Friar's Bush graveyard. McCusker had never noticed the graveyard before and went to open the gate.

'It's always locked,' Armstrong offered. 'There is too much vandalism going on these days. You have to make an appointment to gain entry.'

McCusker returned his hands to his pockets and continued up the gentle slope, to where they took the next left into the quaint Landseer Street, which looked like it was a stage set for a period drama.

Something was troubling McCusker and he couldn't work out what it was. It was 03.50 a.m., and he felt a real need to return to the Bloom household, which was at the other end of Landseer Street. He wasn't quite sure if he'd be rescuing Mrs Bloom or DI Lily O'Carroll.

Fifteen minutes later, tea and toasted up, McCusker had another thought. 'Where did Mr Bloom keep his passport?'

'In his office, love,' Mrs Bloom quickly replied.

'And his office is still locked and you don't know where the key is,' McCusker said, not so much as a question, because he knew the answer, but more to draw a line under yet another dead end.

'I know where he keeps the key to his study,' Armstrong offered, like a pupil keen to score Brownie points with his favourite teacher.

'Really?' Mrs Bloom offered, in what appeared to be genuine shock.

'Gosh yes,' Armstrong said, a little more self-consciously this time, 'I didn't realise it was such a big secret.'

He walked out of the kitchen followed by (in order) Mrs Bloom, DI Lily O'Carroll and McCusker bringing up the rear.

On the first landing he walked straight over to the door immediately in front of them and raised his left hand up, his fingers blindly working their way across the top ledge of the door frame. Not a difficult feat for someone of his height, but a clear impossibility for someone of Mrs Bloom's stature.

'Yes… here we are,' Armstrong eventually, and largely, croaked as he handed a Yale key, not to either of the police but to Mrs Bloom, who stared at it in disbelief for a full minute before handing it over to DI O'Carroll.

CHAPTER FOUR

McCusker wasn't even sure if he was expecting a dark and dusty, book-laden study but when they eventually unlocked the door, he was shocked at how bright, airy and uncluttered it was.

Mrs Bloom and Al Armstrong rushed right into the study ahead of the two members of the PSNI (one official, one via Grafton Agency). Mrs Bloom seemed beside herself in her excitement at being able to gain access to her husband's private space. She had to be physically restrained (quite literally) by O'Carroll from sitting behind her missing husband's desk.

'Sorry, Mrs Bloom, we need to leave everything in here exactly as it is.'

'You can't stop her looking through her husband's papers,' Al protested loudly, 'matrimonial rights!'

McCusker shook his head and rolled his eyes.

'Yes, of course,' Armstrong croaked, 'what's hers is his, but equally what's his is hers.'

'Well sir,' O'Carroll started off, patiently enough, 'at the moment Mr Bloom has officially been reported as missing and so as there may be vital evidence in this room, we really need the both of you to please leave with me now so that my colleague can search this room for evidence that suggests where Mr Bloom may be.'

'Yes, Al, she's correct isn't she,' Mrs Bloom offered quietly. 'Let's not get in their way. The sooner they discover what happened to Louis and find him, the better.'

With that Mrs Bloom meekly led the way out of the study. McCusker overhead her saying to Armstrong that she needed to take a nap, and would he be a dear and stay around to watch the place.

McCusker assumed the Xanax had just reached full effectiveness in her blood stream.

McCusker figured that the reason why the study and the adjoining conservatory – which was built out over the entrance hallway below them - was so sparsely furnished and airy was so that Louis Bloom would have no distractions to his research, writing or whatever else it was that the lecturer did up there.

The walls were painted off-white and totally free of attachments. The desk, Captain's Chair, easy chair, bookcase and filing cabinet were all American Arts and Crafts design. On second glance McCusker figured that the Captain's chair may not have been an American Arts and Crafts item. What looked like the original floorboards had been expertly sanded and stained, and the fact that the planks ran the full length of the room and extended into the conservatory proved that the glass structure was not the add-on that McCusker initially guessed it to be. The conservatory itself was totally item-free apart from some red and green stained glass on the back wall of the conservatory. The same pattern flicked across the translucent-walled room in red and green shafts of light.

'No, there wasn't a single item of furniture in the conservatory,' McCusker repeated to himself, just under his breath. So, clearly, Louis Bloom was going for the Zen look in his study and he was using what looked like a greenhouse, which had just been plonked on the top of his hallway, exclusively as a light source.

The desk drawers – three on one side, a pair on the right and co-joined by a longer, thinner drawer across the knee-well – were all unlocked apart from the one on the bottom left. McCusker imagined that the key would be secure in one of the remaining drawers.

The top middle drawer was neatly – very neatly, it has to be said – filled with pens, pencils, erasers, rulers, paperclips, a few batteries, some coins in a red fingerbowl, and some plain but classy comp slips, with black embossed "Louis Bloom, QUB" in pleasing old-fashioned, courier font across the top. In the top drawer to the left was an inch stack of personalised (same style) foolscap, bonded, high-quality paper with matching envelopes. Next drawer down was empty except for a Perspex cylinder containing four green and white juggling balls. The bottom left drawer contained several bulbs; a small electric fan; a Roberts Radio & CD Player (2 in 1); copies of The Beatles' *Abbey*

Road, Revolver and *Rubber Soul* CDs, some Apple dongles, (charging leads, and two Apple charging plugs) all in matching white. The top drawer on the right contained half a dozen QUB prospectuses and about two-dozen Phil Coulter vinyl records. The stash of singles was from Phil's long-gone days at QUB when he fronted Phil Coulter & the Gleemen on their one and only single, 'Foolin' Time'. All copies were perfectly mint (1963) on the UED (Ulster Electronic Development) label, and protected in a Perspex box.

The next drawer down on the right was locked. Try though he did, McCusker could not find a key to that bottom right drawer. When O'Carroll returned to the study about 30 minutes later, McCusker complained about not being able to find a key.

'Well, it must be here somewhere,' she offered, starting on a bit of a shufti.

'Or it's on his key ring,' McCusker said, in his own defence.

'No, I don't think so,' she said, through an apologised yawn, 'the door key was too obvious.'

O'Carroll took the Phil Coulter singles and the QUB prospectuses from the top right-hand drawer and then tried to remove the drawer totally from its runners. It would only come out about 80 per cent of the way and then wouldn't budge any further. O'Carroll got down on the floor on her hands and knees and used her right palm to feel all around the underside of the extended drawer.

'Here's my wee beauty,' she said gleefully, as she removed a key, which had been taped to the underside of the top drawer.

McCusker couldn't wait to open the drawer and then seemed simultaneously shocked, surprised and disappointed when he discovered about two-dozen vintage *Playboy* magazines.

* * *

'Did you find his passport yet?' O'Carroll asked, tut-tutting her way through one of the *Playboy* mags.

'Nope,' McCusker replied. 'Where's Armstrong?'

'He fell asleep on the living room sofa,' she replied, still distracted by the magazine. 'Not a pretty sight. He sleeps with his mouth open, catching flies, every raspy breath sounding like it would wake a herd of elephants.'

McCusker examined the three-drawer filing cabinet. The top drawer was locked, the middle drawer unlocked. He tugged on the bottom drawer expecting the same, but although it didn't actually open he could feel it give a little. O'Carroll walked over to him, still engrossed in the mag. She gave the bottom drawer a solid Birkenstock-assisted kick. McCusker, just to humour her, leaned over and tugged once more at the handle of the drawer, and was pleasantly surprised when it opened to a gentle tug.

'You know,' O'Carroll began, as McCusker started to investigate the contents of the drawer, 'they had some really cool underwear in the nineties. I wonder where I could get any of this today?'

McCusker was too distracted by the contents of the bottom drawer to pick up what she had said.

'Sorry?'

'Nothing, nothing,' she said, quickly closing and returning the *Playboy* to the desk drawer they'd found it in, 'I was just thinking out loud. What's in there?'

'Just a lot of paperwork in files – seems to be either his research or lecture material. I'll leave it for DS Barr; he excels at this kind of stuff…'

'On top of which, he loves doing it.'

McCusker was about to complain about not being able to open the top two drawers of the filing cabinet when he remembered her trick from earlier and hunkered down and slid his hand in the bottom drawer space and along the bottom of the middle drawer. Just like O'Carroll and Tom Thumb, he too was rewarded by discovering not a plum, but a key taped to the bottom.

The middle drawer seemed to contain more files just like those below, but McCusker figured they must be more important, due to the fact they were under lock and key. Again he decided to leave them for DS Willie John Barr.

The top drawer, to McCusker's eyes, most definitely contained top-drawer material: journals; diaries; passports, for both Mr and Mrs Bloom; letters (still in their envelopes and addressed to Mr Louis Bloom c/o of a Belfast PO box number); postcards addressed to the same PO box; bank statements; credit card statements; phone records; National Insurance details; pension statements; job records; education certificates; sports diplomas; medical records; dental records and insurance policies. All fodder for DS Barr.

McCusker locked the door to Louis Bloom's very private office space. Just in case either Armstrong or Mrs Bloom might have been watching him, he pretended to replace the key back on the top ridge but instead palmed it into his pocket. He wandered down the stairs believing that butter wouldn't melt in his mouth. McCusker thought this was one of the many really silly sayings; why on Earth would anyone want butter to melt in their mouth?

CHAPTER FIVE

McCusker used the excuse of "freshening up" the fly-catcher's tea in order to wake him.

'So tell me this, Mr Armstrong: who are Louis' friends?'

'Gosh, let's see now,' Armstrong sighed, through a stifled yawn, 'gosh, that I know of, there would be: Sophie and Harry Rubens. Then there was the formerly elegant (some say *escort*) Mrs Mariana Fitzgerald. Then there's a friend of hers, Mur... Muriel, no not Muriel, Monica maybe... no, not Monica either... sorry, I forget her first name, but she's best friends with Mariana and she's married to this big player about town – we (that is, Elizabeth and I) don't exactly know what it is that he does. There would also be a couple of lecturers at Queens – Elizabeth can give you their details, but they'd have a better handle on Louis' friends than Elizabeth or I would have. I only know about Mariana because I was sitting next to her once at a dinner party. She's difficult to forget; she had jet-black hair the whole way down to her backside. She was quite interesting looking, in an Eastern European kind of way. There's someone Louis...'

McCusker tuned out of the conversation at that precise moment. He was worrying about whether or not this Mr Louis Bloom was really missing or not. Maybe he'd only gone AWOL and the only reason O'Carroll and he were still spending time on this was due to the fact that Elizabeth Bloom, *née* Kavanagh, on discovering that her husband, apparently a man of very defined habits, had disappeared. She had immediately rung her sister, Angela Larkin, *née* Kavanagh, who in turn woke her husband, Superintendent Niall Larkin, who in turn woke Detective Inspector O'Carroll, who once again proved the theory that ordure always runs downhill and rang McCusker. There'd be an even bigger palaver in the morning when Louis Bloom returned home safely and Larkin would be buzzing about Customs House, complaining about overtime bills. McCusker was on double time but he didn't think O'Carroll was. He'd thought DIs in the PSNI didn't get overtime until O'Carroll had claimed Larkin had okayed overtime for this case; maybe she meant he'd okayed it for everyone else bar the DIs. It was most certainly at times like these that the DI Cages of the Customs House pointed the finger of PSNI resentment at the greed of the Yellow Packs, the Grafton Agency boys. Even the girls at the Grafton Agency were referred to as boys. But that was another rant he wanted to avoid. He felt terrible after he realised he was in a way wishing that something really bad had happened to Louis Bloom, and that Bloom was still genuinely missing.

'What does Louis Bloom look like?' he suddenly asked.

'Oh gosh, now that just very well may be *the* question of the morning,' the lanky Armstrong replied, as he awkwardly climbed out of the sofa. He reminded McCusker of a baby giraffe struggling to its feet; you always felt that the legs just were not going to be strong enough to support the rest of the body in their endeavours. Not only did Mrs Bloom's bestie make it to his feet, he also scurried, hips swinging from side to side, out into the hall and returned a few seconds later with a framed ten-by-eight.

When the camera had happened to catch Louis Bloom, it looked as though he'd been unaware that his image (or part of his soul, as the Native Americans claimed) was being stolen. He clearly hadn't had time to prepare for his close-up. He'd a full head of fine, copper coloured hair, which was absolutely shinning from the light of the flash of the camera. He wore his hair in a pageboy style, more John Denver than the Beatles on 1965's *Rubber Soul* album sleeve. He had half-moon eyebrows, which were darker than the fringe they protruded from. Louis Bloom had a cherub face, flawed only by a feebly grown, droopy moustache. His skin was winter white. He looked younger than McCusker expected him to look. Or, at least, he looked a lot younger than he expected any husband of Mrs Bloom to look. The camera (or the resultant crop) had caught him only from the neck up, a neck

completely hidden behind a black QUB scarf with its legendary dou-
bling up of green, red and blue stripes. McCusker had always thought
you could tell a lot from a man or a woman's neck and ankles. Louis
Bloom looked like a man who might have difficulty with the smiling
process. Maybe he felt it was unbecoming for someone such as a lecturer to be behaving frivolously in public.

McCusker found himself deeply drawn into Bloom's clear, very
healthy-looking brown eyes. Due to the angle of the camera, it looked
like Louis Bloom was questioning him, questioning the detective. Mc-
Cusker had been searching for something in the photograph, something that would call out to him, but had discovered only a challenge
from the subject.

Just then McCusker got the shivers. He told himself not to be foolish, it wasn't anything, or anything other than the cold winds of the
Glenshane Pass still haunting him.

He thought of Grace and about how lucky he'd been, that last night
hadn't been one of the nights she'd slept over; hadn't been one of the
nights they'd spent chasing the butterfly. Again, he accepted he was
being foolish. He was aware that O'Carroll knew he and her sister
were regularly sharing intimate moments, of course she did. But she
was still very protective over her sister, and it would have been very
awkward if she'd walked in on them that morning. Maybe it would be
different if he and Grace were living together. Perhaps then, if that
ever happened, Lily would finally be convinced that he wasn't taking
advantage of her sister.

McCusker and Grace had never discussed moving in together. His
place was cosy, but certainly not big enough that he'd ever subject
her to living with him there. Her place was even "cosier". He was just
getting back on his feet again after his wife and their nest egg disappeared (together). He and Grace certainly weren't teenagers, so he
couldn't expect her to wait around for him, like teenagers would, until
they worked their way up the property ladder. McCusker was 15 years
older than Grace O'Carroll, but she wasn't as conscious of the age
difference as McCusker knew her sister, Lily, would be. It felt good
to be with Grace, it felt right. He knew that above all else. He shook
his head to leave his thoughts behind and concentrated once more
on the photograph.

'What were your dreams, who did *you* love?' McCusker whispered.

All he got in reply was Louis Bloom's still-questioning eyes.

The doorbell rang.

McCusker knew it would not be good news.

CHAPTER SIX

DS WJ Barr was usually the first police officer into the Customs House. He didn't make a fuss over it; he was just always first in and last to go. Some thought he never left the place. He loved his work as a detective sergeant, and was ambitious. But not in a bad way – not in the way, say, the Customs House resident a-hole DI Jarvis Cage was.

Cage didn't like hard work – strike that, he didn't like work *full stop*. He coveted the glory though. Not surprisingly, he wasn't very popular with his colleagues. He once went to Superintendent Larkin and quoted a regulation, which stated that members of the PSNI were not allowed to wear anything that could be taken as an offence by a member of the public. Cage claimed that WJ Barr's Manchester United tie contravened that particular regulation. Larkin's hands appeared to be tied, but he turned the immature action against Cage by addressing Barr in front of the entire team. He said that he had just received a complaint from a member of the public who claimed that Barr wearing the Man United tie while on duty had offended him. He asked Barr to remove the tie immediately. When Barr took it off (in front of the team) he handed it to Larkin who in turn immediately handed it to Cage saying, 'You're a Man United fan, aren't you?'

'No not at all, I'm a Liverpool supporter,' Cage had replied, cagily.

'Oh, you didn't make that clear when you made your complaint,' Larkin had continued, as he took the tie back again from Cage. 'Your complaint, as a member of the public, is therefore not valid because you have a vested interest.'

He'd handed the tie back to Barr and added, for the benefit of the team, 'and if you, DI Jarvis Cage, ever waste police time again, I'll have DS Barr here investigate you for attempting to impersonate a police officer.'

There'd been howls of laughter as Cage was then sent to the basement to measure the sinkage since the last time he'd been down there. DS WJ Barr had worn his Man United tie every single day since.

In fact, he was wearing the now-famous black, red and white tie when he rang the doorbell of Mr and Mrs Louis Bloom's house that morning.

He advised O'Carroll and McCusker that he'd been at his desk when a call came in from the gate lodge at the historic Friar's Bush graveyard. The tenant of the lodge – a Miss Emmylou Holmes – had taken Bertie, her brown and white King George Cocker Spaniel. (Barr was a stickler for the details), out for an early morning comfort break. The usually well-behaved dog had scooted down to the overgrown, yet still groomed, pathway leading to the Botanic Gardens' eight foot high walled border to the graveyard. The pup had taken a quick left up a gentle incline, and there, lying by a chained gate, among ruins that were in danger of being so overgrown that they'd soon disappear from view altogether, Miss Holmes had come across a spread-eagled body. She'd remained very calm, checked for a pulse and on finding none, "only ice cold skin," had returned to the lodge immediately to call the PSNI.

Barr had been endeavouring to contact DI Lily O'Carroll, his direct senior, to report the discovery when the duty desk sergeant, Matt Devine, advised him that O'Carroll and McCusker were out on a VIP Misper in the same area and perhaps there might be a connection. He directed Barr towards the Bloom residence on Landseer Street.

O'Carroll claimed that she should stay at the Bloom household while Barr and McCusker went off to investigate Friar's Bush graveyard. McCusker knew that this had a subtext – O'Carroll really didn't trust Armstrong.

The rain of the previous evening had cleaned the air and McCusker felt more like he was about to head out for one of his favourite walks past the remains of the Strand Ballroom in Portrush and on to the East Strand Beach. The sky was a true blue and the extra early morning sun, though not hot – or even warm, for that matter – was lighting the scene as spectacularly as if it was a David Lean film, or "filum", as McCusker insisted on pronouncing it.

They arrived four minutes later at the arched gothic, yet cute, gate lodge, which had been built by the Marquis of Donegall in 1828. A uniformed PSNI constable was on guard and opened the gate for Barr and McCusker taking them through the cobble-stoned entrance. There was a ginger cat snoozing on the window ledge on the inside of the arch.

McCusker wondered, as he walked along a grass-covered pathway, if the luscious blues, greens and wonderful sunlight were orchestrated so that all of those visiting graveyards might feel that their dear-departed were perfectly comfortable in their current surroundings.

The feel-good factor disappeared at the top of the slope as McCusker spotted two feet, through the growing and ever-moving limbs of the Crime Scene Investigators – in the graveyard. The soles of the two feet, a half a metre apart, faced McCusker, and he marvelled at just how unused the light tan rubber soles appeared. Unfortunately, the bedroom-slippered soles were attached, via feet and legs, to the remainder of a body, which was lying by the locked, iron gate of the ivy-covered Lennon Family Mausoleum.

McCusker walked carefully up the length of the body, and once he'd confirmed it was the remains of Louis Bloom, he walked on around the ruins, allowing the CSI – Crime Scene Investigators to busy themselves about the corpse. Mentally he still thought of them as SOCO offices but each time McCusker mentioned that particular acronym, O'Carroll glared at him until he corrected himself.

Louis Bloom's big, brown eyes were as wide open and demanding in death as they had been in the photograph that had so troubled McCusker earlier that morning. That's why he'd been happy enough to get away and busy himself with a search of the locale.

The Grafton Agency cop reckoned there wasn't a lot of the original Mausoleum left standing and without the ivy, various trees and bushes, it would either be a public safety hazard (he did notice the sign attached to the gate back at the lodge, which stated that visits were strictly by appointment and always to be accompanied by a member of the dedicated council staff) or it would have collapsed altogether by now. Although the Mausoleum had been built in the 1860s, members of the Lennon family were buried in this particular location since 1760. McCusker wasn't a history buff specialising in 18th- and 19th-century burial grounds. No, he gleaned the information from one of the several durable information cards helpfully peppered about the graveyard in strategic locations.

He also discovered that a disputed legend had it that St Patrick had built a church on this graveyard site and that Plaguey Hill, a mount to the left of the entrance, contained a mass grave of hundreds (some say thousands) of souls who had lost their lives as a result of cholera ravaging the community in the 1830s and the famine of the 1840s.

McCusker wondered what, if any, significance could be attached to the fact that Bloom's remains were left by the Lennon Family Mausoleum. He wrote "Lennon" and "1860s" in his notebook. Who were the Lennons? A Belfast family? This modest-sized tomb was certainly no Taj Mahal but, in its day, it would still have been as magnificent if not as majestic as its counterpart in Agra, India. The Lennons would surely have been a family of considerable prosperity, but the structure might not have been a show-piece of their wealth (and perhaps even affection) as much as a way to protect the recently buried from the Resurrection Men (aka grave-robbers) intent on an equally lucrative, if not legitimate, profession.

The pathologist was considerately going about his work as McCusker gingerly concluded his circumference of ruins. He paused to acknowledge McCusker's arrival.

'Our victim…' Robertson offered.

'Mr Louis Bloom,' McCusker interrupted, in a whisper.

'Would that be pronounced Louis or Louie?'

'Pronounced Louie, spelt Louis.'

Oh, you knew the man?' Robertson said, sounding like Billy Connolly's older brother but with the patter slowed way down by at least 50 percent.

'We've just come from his house. His wife reported him missing, last evening,' McCusker advised Robertson, who was writing away as they talked.

'Well, all I can tell you is he didn't put up a fight. There are no signs of a struggle.'

McCusker moved his attention back to the corpse. The black Barbour jacket that his wife had reported him wearing was open, revealing a red, logo-less, sweatshirt and black chinos. His New York Yankees baseball cap was missing, though. He was dressed in more of a "lounging around, watching TV outfit" than a QUB lecturer on downtime.

'He didn't meet his end here,' Robertson continued, to an audience his eyes avoided.

'Good to know,' McCusker offered in acknowledgement of what the pathologist had said, while not admitting he understood.

'Your Mr Louis Bloom has lost a lot of blood. I'm imaging he was stabbed, and from behind. I bet when we turn him over we'll find a wound or wounds in his back. You'll notice there is no blood in the ground around the body. So, my inference is that he was stabbed elsewhere and brought here afterwards.'

'Okay,' McCusker said. 'I'll be back in a few minutes.'

McCusker needed to find the crime scene, and soon. Before they knew it, the local workers and students would be flocking through Botanic Gardens and the surrounding streets, and, unless diverted, would destroy potentially vital evidence. McCusker needed to do too many things and immediately. He requested WJ Barr to take a couple of officers and search the Botanic Gardens everywhere, from the graveyard back to Bloom's house. It had to be a request, rather than an order because, technically speaking, Barr, as an official member of PSNI, was McCusker's senior. Barr wasn't one to stand on ceremony, and he was as good spirited as ever and off like a shot.

'Keep a lookout for a New York Yankees baseball cap, if you can find it – the scene of the crime won't be too far away. Please cordon off the area immediately. If you can't find it in the next half an hour we're going to have to close the Gardens.'

McCusker needed to delay his examination of the victim. But he also needed to distract himself first. He found it very difficult to deal with what humans are capable of doing to each other. He needed to get beyond that point before he could start to attend to the "who did it, how they did it, and why they did it" section of the investigation. But once it reached the point where he became preoccupied with the mechanics of the mystery of the crime as opposed to the loss of life, he was okay. Totally okay. O'Carroll, on the other hand, would just breeze in there as if she'd just come from the set of *The Sound of Music*. She managed to separate the two big issues before she even arrived on the scene. McCusker sometimes wondered how she dealt with it. He'd asked her once.

'Well, it's very simple, McCusker,' she'd replied, 'I can either be preoccupied with that which I cannot change, that is, the loss of life, or I can be preoccupied with that which I can change, that is, finding those with criminal intent and ensuring they are never in a position to repeat their offence, and...' she'd added when McCusker thought she'd finished, 'I can spend some of the time I've managed to save, chasing for Mr Right.'

'Okay. And how's that currently going for you, O'Carroll?'

'Oh I've only recently heard that Jenson Button has retired from F1. Jenson's fit, but I'd never had him on my A-list. F1 is just too dangerous, but now that he's retired – well, he's pretty much shot up to the top of my wish list.'

'Good luck with that,' McCusker had replied, while thinking they had both found different ways to deal with what they did for a profession.

McCusker set about studying the remains of Louis Bloom and for the second time that morning he asked an image of Bloom's former self, 'What were your dreams? Who did you love?'

McCusker had already registered all of Louis' clothes but the detective forced himself to go through the procedure once again, just so he could get started in earnest this time. Once again he noted that Louis Bloom was dressed in a black Barbour zip-up jacket, which was currently fully unzipped to reveal his red sweatshirt and black trousers. Louis Bloom looked like his life had been interrupted. His life *had* been interrupted – McCusker knew that for a fact. He had nipped out of his house to dump some rubbish. He had intended to return, most certainly within minutes, to watch a TV show with his wife.

But someone felt they'd had cause to steal the life from this poor cadaver lying before McCusker.

There was nothing more to be learned from the body and so McCusker agreed to allow Robertson and his assistant to slowly turn the body over.

As the pathologist had predicted, there was a single stab wound, mid-back and south of the shoulder blades. The lack of blood around the cut in the Barbour and sweatshirt was a testimony to just how effective and lethal the assailant had been. Robertson drew attention once more to the fact that there was no blood visible around the flattened grass.

'I can't tell you much more until I get him into the lab,' Robertson said quietly.

McCusker hung on to the *much* from Robertson's statement in the hope that there would at least be *some* more right away.

Robertson quickly picked up on this.

'I'd say he was killed around,' and he paused here to physically count off some hours on the fingers of his right hand, 'no earlier than 9.00 and no later than 11.00, yesterday evening.'

Without even knowing that Superintendent Niall Larkin was on scene, let alone directly behind him, McCusker heard: 'Everything under control Mr McCusker?'

Larkin acknowledged in front of the team how he understood the team seniority to be in O'Carroll's absence.

'All good, Sir,' McCusker said, self-consciously. 'You knew Louis Bloom?'

'Yes, he'd be my brother-in-law,' Larkin replied, taking the afforded opportunity to turn away from the remains of Bloom, 'his wife Elizabeth is a sister to my wife Angela.'

'Tell me this, Sir,' McCusker replied, preparing to take advantage of his superior's insider knowledge, 'do you know this Al Armstrong character?'

'Not a lot I'm afraid,' Larkin replied, stroking his moustache as was his wont when he was keen to move on from where he currently was. 'He's a friend of Elizabeth's, although I can't for a minute see a reason why he would be.'

'Would Mrs Larkin know Armstrong?' McCusker asked.

Larkin looked at McCusker as though he was overstepping PSNI boundaries of decorum. 'No more than I, McCusker, no more than I. But let me do a bit of checking for you and see what I can find out from my contacts.'

'I'm on my way round to join DI O'Carroll at Mrs Bloom's and break the news to her. Do you want to be there?'

'She might get more emotional with me around,' Larkin said, putting on his brown fedora. 'On top of which, I've got to get back home and break the news to Angela, so she's prepared when she gets the call from Elizabeth.'

Superintendent Larkin tipped the rim of his fedora as a goodbye and started to walk away. A few steps later he turned on his brilliantly polished black leather shoes and walked back towards McCusker.

'I just wanted to say, McCusker, that Elizabeth rang Angela, a short while after you and DI O'Carroll arrived in Landseer Street,' he said, stroking his moustache again. 'She said you were both extremely nice to her and were treating her seriously. Thank you both for that. I appreciate that.'

'No problem, Sir.'

'On top of which, you don't know how happy I am that I didn't follow my initial instincts when we got the call and (8 changed order of words) just turn over instead and to go back to sleep.'

McCusker grimaced slightly.

'But believe you me, I've an even bigger nightmare than that,' Larkin continued, 'my first instinct was a budgetary-biased one, which had been to wake DI Jarvis Cage and put him on the case.'

McCusker unconsciously grimaced even more.

'Aye, you're correct, McCusker,' Larkin continued, pulling energetically on his moustache, 'you and O'Carroll and I most certainly would be up to our necks in the smelly stuff by this stage if I'd gone for that option.'

Larkin casually sauntered back towards the exit at the gate lodge, looking like he was Colonel Custer and had just managed to rewrite the history of Little Big Horn and escape with his scalp intact.

CHAPTER SEVEN

'Was it my Louis?' Mrs Louis Bloom, nee Elizabeth Kavanagh, exclaimed, the very second McCusker walked through the door.

She was flanked to the left by Al Armstrong and to the right and forward three feet (because she'd opened the door) by DI Lily O'Carroll. A phone continuously rang somewhere in the background.

'I'm afraid…' was as far as McCusker managed with his reply.

Mrs Bloom reacted like someone who had wished with all their might that something they dreaded might not happen. But now that she knew her wish was not about to be granted she seemed… she actually seemed to have been resigned to the fact she had seen the last of "her Louis" at five minutes to nine on the previous evening.

Al Armstrong reacted like someone who felt self-conscious about how they were reacting, knowing that all eyes were now on him. Not so much a "Who, me?" as an "Oh gosh, well of course it wasn't me" look.

Mrs Bloom moved to leave Armstrong behind and join McCusker and O'Carroll by the door. She grabbed one hand of each of them and squeezed both with all her might. Then she said, in a very quiet voice, 'I don't care what the silly bugger did, but I want you both to promise me that you will find the person who did this to my Louis. No matter who they are, I need you to promise me. Louis certainly had his faults, but he didn't deserve this.'

CHAPTER EIGHT

Armstrong, arms-folded across his chest, chased McCusker and O'Carroll out to the front gate.

'Aren't you forgetting something?' he said.

'Sorry?' O'Carroll replied.

'The key to Louis' study,' he croaked, 'it's gone. The Yellow Pack here was the last person up there?'

'McCusker, do you have the key?' O'Carroll asked.

'No, certainly not,' McCusker replied.

'I thought not,' O'Carroll said, sighing, 'and I don't have it, nor in my pocket, so Annabella... Annabella, who's got the key?'

And McCusker and O'Carroll turned on their heels and left, closing the gate after them, leaving Armstrong with a dumb look of "Who the hell is Annabella?"

'Okay, McCusker,' O'Carroll said, as they headed off down Landseer Street in the direction of the Lisburn Road, 'we need to get organised, so let's nip into Café Conor, have a bite of breakfast and get our system together.'

It turned out that they did a lot of eating but not a lot of talking, but at least for O'Carroll it was mission accomplished, in that she'd managed to get McCusker's nose bag on before the hunger set in. Now she had his undivided attention, well at least until lunchtime. On the way past the Whitla Hall a ticket tout approached them, displaying his wares like they were a deck of cards.

'Fancy a couple of cheap tickets to take the Mrs to see Mickey Bubbles this evening?'

'Who's Mickey Bubbles?' McCusker asked, distracted for a second.

'You ask him who's Mickey Bubbles rather than tell him I'm not your wife?'

'Don't worry Mrs, I won't tell anyone, and when the lights are low, no one will even know you're there,' the tout sniggered, and gave O'Carroll a pantomime wink. 'Surely you know Mickey Bubbles? He does a great version of Van the Man's 'Moondance',' the ticket tout shouted, as he rushed along after them, loud enough for the early morning students' to have their heads turned. Some, thinking the tickets were for Sir Van Morrison, started to gather around the tout, allowing McCusker and O'Carroll a chance to escape.

'Mickey Bubbles?' McCusker tried again.

'Michael Bublé, you daft ejit.'

They walked on in silence for three minutes, cutting across the green outside the majestic, red-bricked Lanyon Building.

'You've never heard of Michael Bublé either, have you?'

'No,' McCusker admitted, 'but I have heard of Sir Charles Lanyon, and he designed not only this building but our very own Customs House, the home of the PSNI.'

'Hopefully this one isn't going to sink when we're in it,' O'Carroll said, as they walked through the door and visited the reception desk in the middle of the university shop. They asked, as Superintendent Larkin had advised them to, for a Mr Ron Desmond, the head of the University Administration and Commercial Enterprises Department.

Before they knew it and McCusker had a chance to examine the QUB scarves in the shop, Mr Ron Desmond was by their shoulders with extended hand, ready, willing and able for an energetic shake with both of them.

Ron Desmond smelled nice. Why? How? Admittedly it was only the beginning of his day but, McCusker thought, really he shouldn't smell *that* great. How did he do it? McCusker uncharitably wondered if the administrator topped up his cologne throughout the day.

Desmond led them through the shop, back out into the hall they'd entered by and up a flight of stairs. He had time, a smile and generous words for all the students they met on their way up to his first-floor office. The students appeared to be as fond of him as he was of them.

McCusker really loved this legendary building. He'd been dying to view the inside of it since he'd arrived down in Belfast from his native Portrush. It was most definitely his kind of old-world building, where you got the feeling that the wood-panelled walls retained all the secrets of their one-hundred and sixty-eight years. It wasn't as big on the inside as McCusker had imagined from the outside. But he really felt that this wonderful 1849 building had successfully enabled them to leave the hustle and bustle of the outside world behind them. Even though students were coming and going, it still felt tranquil, peaceful and the ideal atmosphere for a house of learning. Gothic was a word that sprang to mind. It clearly wasn't really Gothic, but parts of the building definitely had that Gothic feel.

Desmond's office was a bit of a let-down until he explained his real office was part of the wing currently under refurbishment, 'in the best possible taste, you understand.' They struggled to find seats and Desmond had to move files, papers and pamphlets around so the three of them could sit at the same time. No sooner were they seated than he jumped to his feet.

'Pray forgive me, my bad manners. Coffee? Tea? A couple of Danish perhaps?'

Before O'Carroll had a chance to say they'd just had breakfast, McCusker beat her to it with, 'That would just be perfect, I'm absolutely famished – coffee for the both of us please.'

Ron Desmond bore not a great head of grey hair. On the positive side it was long, thick on back and sides, sparse on top, but it looked expensively cut, styled and groomed. He was dressed in what appeared to be his usual 'uniform' of wine-coloured, crew-neck styled jumper (although bottle green or Royal blue would also have suited him), with the dazzling white collar of his shirt protruding by an inch all around. McCusker would bet that he always wore corduroy trousers (today they were blue – green would also have worked, but never ever brown or tan). His look was completed with stunning, highly polished, brown and white brogues, with loud, multi-coloured socks. All his clothes looked expensive, very expensive. This fact alone didn't annoy McCusker. No, what *really* annoyed McCusker was that so new, fresh and well-laundered did Desmond's clothes appear, that the detective would have sworn that the university administrator never, ever wore his clothes more than a couple of times.

McCusker liked to look good in his clothes, liked to feel good while wearing them – that much was clear. But no matter how hard Mc-Cusker tried, he could never pull off that new clothes look unless he actually wore new clothes, and even then he could only get away with the look for the first day. In McCusker's case, should he add one item of old clothing into the mix then his entire outfit suffered visually from the same fatigue.

Ron Desmond didn't like to be interviewed. Rather, he clearly preferred to 'chair' proceedings.

O'Carroll soon put him right.

'What we're looking to do here is get as much information on Mr Bloom in as short a period as possible.'

'A fact-finding mission it is then,' Desmond replied instantly, while carefully potting some of the pens and pencils scattered around his desk. 'I'm sure his PA, Miss Leab David, will be much more beneficial to you.'

'All in good time, Mr Desmond,' O'Carroll replied, 'we're hoping you'll give us a better overview and then we can focus more on the individuals.'

'I'm not so sure that Miss David wouldn't be a better place to start. But anyway, here we are, so here we'll start. Shoot.'

'How long had you known Louis Boom?' McCusker asked, filling the void left, intentionally, he felt, by his colleague.

'I seem to have known him all my time at Queens. I came here from The Sports Council of Northern Ireland in 1998. I was their chief bottle-washer and fundraiser. In those days there were jobs that needed to be done and, regardless of titles, we all mucked in.

'I seem to remember,' he continued expansively, 'it was all very hand-to-mouth but, more importantly, I never had the feeling I was doing anything that would leave a lasting legacy. Yes the craic was great. For about a year I'd been thinking if I wasn't careful, I'd be with the Sports Council forever and I'd have done absolutely nothing. Then I got a call from a friend of mine, Gary Mills – I'd actually gone to Queens with him and been a member of his team, helping him out in organising the Students' Union shows.

'Anyway, Gary had stayed on at Queens and become one of their players, and he was looking for someone to come in to work in his administration team with particular responsibility for fundraising and seeing various projects to fulfilment. It appealed to me immediately; I felt, now here's something with which I could make my mark. I could leave something...'

O'Carroll gave a long and noisy yawn. She immediately apologised, claiming (correctly) that she and McCusker had been working on the case half the night. More importantly, she'd, in an unspoken way, reminded Desmond that she didn't need to be reminded how he had invented the wheel, but in fact that they were here to talk about Louis Bloom.

'Yes, I know how you feel...' Desmond sympathised, 'at some of the fundraisers of ours, you find yourself getting home when its daylight... Sorry, where was I?'

'You were about to tell us about Louis Bloom?' McCusker offered as a prompt.

'Yes, yes, of course. So, Louis had studied at Queens, qualified at Queens and immediately joined the English Department at Queens as a lecturer. And he was already one of their major players by the time I joined.'

'As part of the administration, would you have been his boss?' McCusker asked.

'Ah, that would be a no to that one,' Ron Desmond offered very theatrically, he spoke every word as though he felt Shakespeare had written it for him. 'Totally different department, although we do... sorry, of course that should have been... we *did* sit on a few common fundraising committees together.'

'Fundraising for what exactly?' McCusker first wondered and then asked.

'Oh, research, field trips, campus restorations, renovations, repairs, even new builds like the new library,' Desmond replied and physically shifted into a different gear. 'Let's see now, the new library project cost over £40 mill, and whereas the Northern Ireland Executive took responsibility for £10 mill of that through the government-led Reinvestment and Reform Initiative, we – Queens Foundation – had to find nearly £30 mill from the private sector.'

These figures seemed to spike O'Carroll's interest for the first time since the start of the interview with Desmond.

'Did you work on that project?' O'Carroll asked.

'Ah, that would be a big yes on that one,' Desmond replied, with a smile expensive enough to pay for the naming rights.

'And Louis Bloom?'

'No.'

'What projects did you work on together?' McCusker asked.

'Oh, mostly raising funds for research and then some for refurbishing buildings.'

'Any of these projects come in over £40 million?' O'Carroll asked.

'No, certainly not – well, not on a single project.'

'What about over several projects?' O'Carroll pushed. McCusker knew she was slipping into one of her traditional crime motivations. She worked on the theory that where there was money, there was greed, and where there was greed, there was crime, and where there was crime there was (occasionally) loss of life.

'I've honestly never thought about that,' Ron Desmond admitted largely.

'Could you maybe get us the details of the projects you worked on together and the figures involved?' O'Carroll asked, looking like she was having trouble believing that answer.

'But of course.'

'Did you see Louis Bloom a lot?' McCusker asked.

'Well, I'd see him around, but we weren't exactly drinking buddies.'

'Who would he have come into contact with the most here at Queens?'

'Sophie and Harry Rubens were good friends of his,' Desmond replied, as O'Carroll furiously scribbled away in her pink notebook. 'Louis' PA will get you their details. They are both on campus.'

'Anyone else?' McCusker asked, desperate to get a bit of pace in the proceedings.

'Louis has a brother – Miles,' Desmond offered, 'I don't believe they get on,' he continued, sounding like he knew just exactly how well they didn't get on.

'What can you tell us about Leab?' McCusker asked.

'Former student of Louis',' Desmond smiled, 'and no, I know for a fact that there is… sorry, there was nothing going on between them.

She was totally devoted to him, though. She's a funny, but effective way of working.'

'How so?' McCusker asked, as O'Carroll continued to scribble away.

'You'll see when you meet her. I've already spoken with her and told her to make herself available to you after our meeting.' Desmond paused to look at his watch. 'Talking of which, I'm running a bit late for my next meeting – are we nearly done here?'

'Not quite,' O'Carroll said, still writing in her pink book, 'we've two more questions for you. Do you know of anyone who might have felt they'd a reason to kill Louis?'

'You know, I've been thinking of nothing else all morning. Firstly, I don't think there was ever a QUB lecturer murdered before. Secondly, it starts you thinking doesn't it? You know, that there could just be a crank around, someone without a motive, just indiscriminately killing people. You know, just like that chap in *The Fall*? In fact,' and he stopped to look at his watch again, 'I'm about to chair a meeting on campus security. But I'm not aware of anyone with a reason to kill Louis, no.'

'So you weren't aware of any trouble Louis was in?' McCusker asked.

'Trouble?'

'You know, gambling, drugs, womanising, taking advantage of students who've an angry father?' McCusker said, starting off strong and then floundering.

Ron Desmond just laughed, rose from his chair and said, 'that's not the Louis Bloom I knew.'

'My final question for now,' O'Carroll began, as she pocketed her book and stood up, 'what were you doing between the hours of 9.00 p.m. yesterday and 1.00 a.m. this morning?'

'Well, I was travelling up from Dublin from 8.00 yesterday evening and I arrived back in Belfast at 10.40. Then I'd a light super, watched *Sky News* and retired for the evening.'

'Anyone travelling with you?'

'That would be a no to that one.'

'Were you at a meeting?' McCusker kept on pushing, 'you know, can anyone confirm that you left Dublin at 8 o'clock?'

'No, I was just down on personal business.'

'Stop off for petrol or a quick snack?' McCusker asked, trying really hard to sound helpful.

'You know,' Desmond started slowly, 'how should I put this... well, let's just say your final question seems to have as many parts as one of our examination questions.'

'And did you?' O'Carroll asked innocently.

'That would be a no to that one.'

'Okay, Mr Desmond,' O'Carroll said, awkwardly making her way through the files towards the door, 'that'll do for now, but we will be back to see you later today – please ensure you make yourself available.'

* * *

McCusker felt that O'Carroll would be impressed with such a well-turned out and perfectly groomed male.

Not so.

'Your man doesn't like women much,' she offered, as they made their way back down the wood-panelled walls of the staircase – the wood-panelled walls that so far had continued to retain their 167 years' worth of secrets

'Sorry?'

'Well, he might have female friends but he certainly hasn't any female lovers.'

CHAPTER NINE

When O'Carroll and McCusker came calling to Bloom's office, they encountered a stray student seemingly stealing some precious solitary moments in reception. She was sitting on a small, hard sofa with her Ugg-booted feet hunkered up underneath her, tapping away on her mobile screen as quickly as a mouse on the run with a piece of prized cheese. At the end of each message as she hit the send button, the fingers of her right hand flapped off into the air to the right of her mobile, just like the flapping wing of a bird, signifying to herself that the message was now making its way through the air to an unsuspecting recipient.

The secretary's desk was unwomanned and so O'Carroll asked the Ugg girl if she knew where Miss Leab David was.

Without looking up from her industrious endeavours, the girl replied, 'I am she.'

'Oh,' said O'Carroll, looking quickly from the Ugg girl to the desk where she expected to find her, back to her current location. Leab David was a thirty-three-year-old woman who acted and dressed like she was a teenager. 'I thought you were Mr Bloom's PA?'

For the first time since they'd entered her reception, Leab David looked up at O'Carroll. Her eyes were bloodshot, as if she'd been crying. Most likely she had been crying, McCusker figured. Leab continued working on her mobile with her left hand as she used her right hand to remove the hood of her black Nike hoodie from her head, letting her straight, fine blonde hair spill out over her shoulders. She was free of make-up and looked all the better for it. She appeared to continuously try to bite off a bit of annoying skin on the inside of her bottom lip. Her right hand automatically returned to its work with its life's partner. She wore black baggy slacks, the legs of which were tucked into her fawn Ugg boots.

'You've come about Louis?' she offered, eyes back on her screen again.

'You've heard that...' O'Carroll started awkwardly.

'Ron Desmond...'

McCusker couldn't be sure if Leab had paused or had completed her reply. It sounded complete, in a texting shorthand way.

McCusker figured that although, yes, her eyes made her look like she'd been crying, she didn't really look like she was upset. He also figured that, at about that precise moment, O'Carroll would have loved to have taken the offending mobile phone and chucked it through the nearest open window. No doubt it would be rescued by a student, who would have cleaned the screen on their jacket sleeve and continued working the keys as though it was their own.

'I know this is difficult for you,' McCusker started, 'you don't know how to feel about Louis Bloom...'

'Mum's just said,' she started in her beautiful County Down accent, and nodding in the direction of her screen, 'it's too early to feel anything real. She also said you'd be here and that I should help you as much as I can, so,' and she flamboyantly signed off, 'so you now have my undivided attention.'

'Leab – that's an unusual name, not from around these parts,' Mc-Cusker replied, picking a topic as far away from the death of Louis Bloom as he could.

'Ah,' she said, tightening and relaxing her jaw a few times, 'you see, my mum and dad were – are still – big fans of U2.'

'Right. So is that one of their hits?' McCusker asked, as O'Carroll rolled her eyes.

Leab smiled. 'No one has ever got it.'

McCusker and O'Carroll just looked at her blankly, waiting for the U2 link.

'Larry – Edge – Adam – Bono,' she offered.

'What is that, another group?'

'Ah McCusker,' O'Carroll hissed, 'don't ever let people hear you say that stuff. If you take L for Larry, E for the Edge, A for Adam and

B for Bono, what do you get…?' she paused as if she was waiting for him to answer her, but she clearly thought better of it and answered her own question with, 'Leab'.

'Yes indeed,' Leab confirmed, 'that was quicker than most attempts.'

Her phone pulsed but she ignored it. O'Carroll nodded to Mc-Cusker, acknowledging that he had achieved the distraction he sought with his merry little song and dance routine with Bloom's PA.

'How can I help you with Louis?' she asked, her voice sounding like she was close to tears.

'We need to build up a picture of Louis and his day, so we can figure out what happened,' O'Carroll offered gently.

'You mean, as in a day in the life of Louis Bloom?' Leab asked.

'Well yes,' McCusker replied, thinking that the day he really needed to know about was the final day in the life of Louis Bloom. But a typical day would do for now.

'Okay,' Leab started, biting the inside of her lip furiously, 'let's see now. I get in here around 9.00 a.m. Sometimes Louis is already in, but mostly not. I'll start to check my overnight emails and deal with them. They can be a pain – there are so many of them and they all have to be replied to… no matter how inane they are. Louis insists everyone gets a civil reply. The problem I find is, when you give someone a *polite* no, they seem to take that as an invitation to start a dialogue and negotiate. You know, "Can he come another day?" Or, "I know I said we didn't have any money to offer towards his expenses but if we did, would that help?" Or, "What about if he didn't have to talk about our chosen subject and he picked one of his own?"'

All the time, O'Carroll furiously scribbled away once again in her pink book. McCusker figured she didn't want to interrupt Leab's flow, so she was jotting down questions for later.

'And all the time I just want to reply: "No, and just bog off!" But no, Louis wants all of them treated respectfully. He says you never know where some of these people are going to end up. "Politeness costs nothing," he'd say, "and if some of these people end up involved in funding, we don't want our requests going straight to the dustbin, or they may have friends, or relations, involved in some of the speaking engagements we would want to do." Well…'

'Politeness costs nothing,' O'Carroll added quickly, maybe proving that patience was a much more expensive commodity.

'Then around 10.00 I'll nip down to Kaffeo, who do the best cof-fee on campus, and get us two cortados and a croissant for him and a Danish for me. That would be the latest he ever gets in. He always pays, and out of his own pocket, not from QUB expenses. I deliver his coffee and nibbles to him at his desk. I always close the door after me; he likes peace and no interruption in order to write and research. He'll have no meetings or callers, or phone calls, between 10.00 and 12.00. Even if we spotted Sir Charles Lanyon walking around this building again, it wouldn't matter: Louis was not to be disturbed. When I close the door after I deliver his coffee, until he opens it, he's not to be dis-turbed. And that's under any circumstances. The earliest he will emerge is 12.00 and the latest I have known was twenty-past-two. When he does eventually open his door, he'll nip out for a "wee scoot around to get some air and exercise", and he'll end up perhaps with Harry Rubens and they'll pop into Café Conor for a brief bite or he'll just get some fruit on his travels.

'If he has any lectures…'

'If?' McCusker felt compelled to ask. 'Did he not give lectures every day?'

Leab David, just laughed – a knowing, insider's laugh.

'Lecturers rarely take classes,' she advised. 'The teaching – I think that's what you're referring to – is either self-taught or sometimes post-grads will take classes. The priority is not so much teaching as re-search.'

O'Carroll glared at McCusker, who didn't ask the question on his lips.

'If Louis has a lecture he always gives it in The Emeleus Lecture Theatre. Louis loved it in there. It's very old word and he felt com-pletely at home there. It's named after Emeleus, a Finnish professor who was a bit of a superstar himself back in the day at QUB. Emeleus' chosen subject though was maths.'

McCusker worried that O'Carroll was going to yawn again. She didn't.

'Louis' talks are usually great fun and well attended,' Leab contin-ued, 'and I always try to sneak in, under the auspices of taking notes. If he's not giving a lecture he's taking or attending meetings, *lots* of meetings. He usually meets up with the Vice-Chancellor once a day.

That's Louis… sorry, that *was* Louis' power base, the fact that he ge… sorry, *got* on so well with the Vice-Chancellor. A Vice-Chancellor wouldn't usually hang out with a lecturer but Louis told me that something just clicked between them the first time they met.

'I'll work away, answering emails, organising his travel and accommodation. When he returns to his office, late afternoon, but always before I leave at 6.00, he briefs me on his meetings and dictates any emails or letters he needs me to send. Mostly when I leave, at 6.00, he'll still be here. His door will be open and we have our wee routine where I'll say "Anything else you need me to do?" and he'll always reply, "No, that's it for today, Leab, thank you – have a nice evening."'

'And are you aware of what time he would go home?' McCusker asked.

'Mostly apart from Thursdays he won't. He'll go to meetings, dinners, public functions, talks, films, the Opera House, concerts…'

'And on Thursdays?' O'Carroll prompted, as she concluded writing in her pink book.

'Thursdays he'll always be home by 7.00 for dinner with his wife; he claims it's the best night for TV programmes and he will not accept invitations for a Thursday night.'

'Okay Leab, that was very insightful for us,' O'Carroll started. 'What we'd like to do now is go back to yesterday and build up Louis' actual day. For instance, was he already in when you got here at 9.00?'

'Yes.'

'Yes, good. And then you did your emails and he did his emails until just before 10.00 and you fetched the coffee and a croissant for Louis and a Danish for you.'

'Yes.'

'Then he locked his door…'

'No, he doesn't lock the door,' Leab corrected O'Carroll firmly, 'I shut the door after me so that he can have peace to do his work and not be interrupted.'

'And then he worked, wrote, researched until noon at the earliest.'

Leab nodded yes.

'What time did he emerge from behind his closed door for his dander, as McCusker here would call it?'

'Yesterday it was just before 1.00, when he went out for his daily walk to clear his head.'

'Good, good,' O'Carroll enthused, jotting away in her pink book, 'and did he have a lunch date in his diary for yesterday?'

'Yes, he'd lunch with Harry, that's Harry Rubin, at 1.30. They went to Café Conor.'

'So you don't know what he did between 1 o'clock and 1.30?'

'He might have just dandered…' Leab paused and looked in consideration at McCusker before continuing, 'over to pick up Harry and then walked back up to Café Conor. Louis loved the work of Neil Shawcross – you know, the English artist who lives in Belfast – so much, that sometimes he would go and sit in Café Conor for an hour or so by himself just to soak up his dramatic, soulful paintings exhibited on the walls.'

'How long would his lunch have lasted?'

'Probably no longer than an hour, because he'd a walk-in meeting with the Vice-Chancellor at 2.45.'

'Yes, you said he met with the Vice-Chancellor every day,' O'Carroll remembered. 'Could you explain the exact meaning of a "walk-in meeting" please?'

'It's either a one topic meeting, where they would share information they'd gathered on a topic since their last meeting, or it could just be a quick, general catch-up.'

'Would you ever accompany Louis Bloom on any of these meetings?'

'Rarely, and certainly not on the walk-ins.'

'Okay, good, good.'

O'Carroll, McCusker figured, was just stalling while she remembered where exactly she was up to with her questions.

'So what was his next meeting after the 2.45?'

Leab had already scrolled up the info on her iPhone. 'He'd a quick walk-in with Ron Desmond at 3.'

'Okay,' O'Carroll said, encouraging Leab to continue.

'And Prof. Best at 3.30.'

'Right, got that – and then?'

'And then he'd a personal meeting down in his diary from 4. until 5.30. Then he was back here for our daily debrief and he'd dictate a few emails he needed me to send out.'

'So who was the 16.00 meeting with?'

'I haven't a clue.'

'How many of these personal meetings would he have during the week?'

'Two or three,' Leab replied.

'Two or three a week and you hadn't a clue where he was?'

'They weren't to do with QUB or his professional talks, so they were none of my business,' Leab protested. 'On top of which, it certainly wasn't two or three *every* week – some weeks there would be none in the diary at all and some weeks there might just be one in.'

'Okay,' O'Carroll conceded, not even trying to hide the fact that she was surprised, 'but you really didn't have a clue who any of these meetings were with?'

'Hand to God,' Leab replied sweetly, actually raising her hand to the heavens, or at least the ceiling of the reception area.

'I've got a few questions here for you as a result of some information you shared with us earlier. Did Professor Bloom get many emails from nutters?'

'Well doesn't everyone? Like a few. I don't really mean *real* nutters – more like harmless nutters, if you know what I mean. There might have been a few that scared me but Louis just laughed them off.'

'Which ones scared you?'

She looked like she was scrolling the inside of her eyelids as she tried to remember examples.

'You know, let me look at them again,' Leab offered, as her fingers danced across the screen of her iPhone, inserting a reminder, and using her signature fluttering of fingers into the ether to show the task was successfully completed.

'You mean you've still got them?'

'Yes. Louis told me to bin them all but I felt I should keep them. Mostly I just wanted to see if any of the senders would fulfil their prediction and become important people we needed to deal with.'

'Can you send me a copy of them please?' O'Carroll continued.

'I don't see why not, but let me just run it by the Vice-Chancellor,' and her fingers returned to the screen to scoot off another email, requesting the same.

'Did Louis get any threats via email or letter?' O'Carroll asked, as she ticked off another of the questions in her pink book.

'Not that I'm aware of.'

'Did Louis have his own separate email account?' O'Carroll asked, leading McCusker to believe she'd been expecting Leab's previous answer.

'Why yes, of course.'

'Do you have the details?'

'I have the address, but not the password.'

McCusker jotted something down. 'When he gives these talks, what does he talk about?'

'You know he never prepares them – he just gets up, put his hands in his pockets, starts to walk around the platform or stage and words come out.'

'And he gets paid to do that?'

'It seems to work for Michael McIntyre – and former Queen's student - Patrick Kielty…'

'But they're comedians,' O'Carroll protested, looking at McCusker.

'Louis held the belief that comedians are the free-thinkers of the modern world. He would frequently quote Sir Ken Dodd and William Shakespeare in his talks to prove his theory… and get a few laughs into the bargain,' Leab added, proving she'd successfully studied timing herself.

'How does he decide which speaking engagements to accept?'

'Familiarity, local places and people of interest, ease of travel, quality of hotel, honorarium, securing the services of a great speaker to visit QUB in return, and not necessarily in that order.'

'How much did he receive for these engagements?'

'From FOC to £5,000.'

'FOC?' O'Carroll asked.

'Free of charge,' McCusker replied.

While her eyes flashed McCusker a "trust you to know that one" look, her mouth gushed, '£5,000?!'

'That would be the average,' Bloom's PA replied. 'The most he received in my time with him would have been in the UK. He received £9,999 + expenses for a corporate motivation speech in the City in London, down in the old Whitbread Brewery complex by the Barbican.'

Funny fee, McCusker thought, and then said so out loud.

'He was trying really hard to get ten grand and the Henry he was dealing with said he couldn't possibly pay that and Louis said, okay, he could understand and accept that as long as Henry would understand and accept that unless he, Louis, received £9,999 then they better look for someone else. The fee was much higher than the majority of people on the circuit received. The absolute most he ever received was $30,000 + all expenses including two first-class return flights for a speaking engagement in Boston, USA.'

'Did you accompany him on that engagement?' O'Carroll asked.

'No I didn't,' she replied, sounding a wee bit embarrassed at the suggestion.

'Mrs Bloom?'

'She never travelled with him for his speaking engagements.'

'Who was his plus one then?'

Leab worked on the screen of her phone and scrolled through some files, then she looked at O'Carroll, who had asked the question, and then glanced to McCusker before saying, 'I don't have that information.'

'Earlier you told us what Louis did for lunch, but you didn't say what you did or when?'

'Oh, I'll bring something in, or a mate will bring me something here, or I'll nip out for a while.'

'Are you aware of anyone who might have threatened Mr Bloom?' McCusker asked.

'No,' she replied, shaking her head furiously and sounding like she was annoyed he'd even think Louis had enemies.

'Did he owe money to anyone?'

She repeated her 'No' with the same annoyed emphasis, but this time she qualified her displeasure with: 'Louis was well off, you know. He was also very generous. He paid me a percentage of his fees for his speaking engagements. He said it was above and beyond my duty. He didn't need to do that for me, you know, and over the course of the year it was, as my dad would say, "a good chunk of change."'

'Please don't be alarmed at this question, Leab,' O'Carroll said cautiously, 'but we really do like to rule out as many people as possible from our investigation as early as possible – saves us so much time later on. So could you please tell us what you were doing yesterday evening from say 20.30 to 01.00 this morning?'

'Washing my hair.'

'Sorry – for four hours?' McCusker said in disbelief.

'No, of course not. I meant it as a clichéd figure of speech, you know, the bachelor girl's lament: "What were you doing last night?" "Oh nothing, I just stayed in and washed my hair."?'

'A partner with you?'

'I live alone.'

'Okay, Leab,' O'Carroll started, 'that'll do us for now; we're going to look around Mr Bloom's office.'

Before O'Carroll and McCusker had made it as far as the dividing door separating the PA's reception space from Bloom's office, Leab's fingers were once again dancing across the screen of her phone, ten to the dozen.

* * *

McCusker was shocked by Louis Bloom's office, his principal workspace. It was as sparse as his home office, in that there was a desk – glass top, on silver metallic triangles – a healthy-looking chair, two matching wooden chairs and a matching sofa, all positioned on a boring, hard-wearing grey carpet and absolutely nothing else. No filing cabinets; no drawers; no pictures, paintings nor posters adorning the walls; and no windows. None of the above – just the aforementioned desk, desk-chair, two easy chairs and a sofa occupied the room. There wasn't a fridge, nor even a fan for the traditional 17 days of summer. There was, however, a fridge-freezer in Leab's reception area.

'This is strange?' O'Carroll whispered. She whispered half from shock and half because they could see Leab David's shadow float past the door every now and then, her silhouette betraying her deft fingerwork, busy as a bee on speed, at her phone.

'No distractions,' McCusker whispered back, 'absolutely no distractions for someone who wanted to just think and write.'

* * *

'Do you have a key to this office?' McCusker asked, as he closed the opaque glass door behind him.

'Of course, I lock it every night.'

'Can I have the key please?' O'Carroll asked.

'Why yes, of course,' Leab answered nervously, seemingly shocked by the request. Maybe even as though the reality of what was happening was slowly dawning on her.

'The Vice-Chancellor said we should be okay with me giving you that file of nutter emails but he needs to check first with the university lawyers.'

'So Mr Bloom has no computer in his office?' O'Carroll asked.

'No.'

'Nor files, nor paperwork.'

'NO.'

'So how did he do his work?'

'He had one of the large iPads he was always hammering away on. He also had a journal he frequently wrote in.'

'And where is his iPad?

'So you've found the journal then?' Leab said, catching the DI out.

O'Carroll had the grace to smile before repeating, 'And where is his iPad?'

'He has a brown-leather shoulder bag he always carries with him. It's well worn – even when he nips out of here for a few minutes on one of his many sojourns he'll take his shoulder bag. His iPad and his notes are contained therein. He never leaves them on campus.'

'Tell me this,' McCusker asked, quite quietly, as though he too had been hit by a realisation from the visit to Louis' inner office, 'what was Louis Bloom's chosen subject?'

'Oh, sorry, I thought you would have already known that one,' Leab David replied. 'The Politics of Love.'

CHAPTER TEN

By the time McCusker and O'Carroll returned to Louis Bloom's house on the borders of Botanic Gardens, Sgt WJ Barr (O'Carroll's crime scene bag-man of choice) had the Crime Scene Investigators team at full steam.

Barr had also discovered (and secured the surrounding) scene of Bloom's missing New York Yankees baseball cap. He took McCusker directly there, while O'Carroll got up to speed with the results of the house search. Barr had actually discovered the Yankees baseball cap not too far from the original rubbish bin where Bloom had deposited his plastic bag of domestic refuse. It was a couple of minutes' walk away, back towards Bloom's house, just to the right of what would have been Bloom's entrance to the Gardens. The cap had become entangled in a bush in a picturesque laneway created between the hedge that bordered the Gardens with Colenso Parade, and a hedge that ran parallel, 12 feet across.

Perhaps a caring walker had discovered Bloom's cap lying on the ground and had placed it higher up in the bushes, in the hope that it wouldn't get damp or trodden on, and in order to catch the owner's eye should they return in search of their missing lid.

'Maybe the cap was placed here,' Barr offered hesitantly, on a slightly different tangent, 'in order to make us believe it was a random attack.'

'Good point, WJ, and very possible, very possible.'

'We're continuing to search the Gardens, and we're doing a H2H of all the houses in the area,' Barr continued, as he glanced back in the direction of Bloom's house. Due to the hedgerow, only the roof was visible from where they stood.

McCusker returned to the Bloom residence. Mrs Elizabeth Bloom had been taken away to the house her sister, Angela, shared with Superintendent Niall Larkin.

Al Armstrong was trying in vain to take charge and prevent the SOC officers from doing their work. McCusker heard him say: 'This might be a crime scene to you lot, but after you're all long gone, this will be Elizabeth's home again.'

O'Carroll nodded to McCusker as she said to Armstrong, 'Mr Armstrong, we'd like to continue our interview with you.'

'Oh gosh, would you now?' he croaked. 'Well, as you can see I'm very busy here, so you're just going to have to wait.'

'Well here's the thing,' O'Carroll began, her hackles certainly rising. 'We can either do it here an' now, or I can ask one of these nice officers you've been haranguing to take you down to the Customs House, and McCusker and I can officially interview you when we've finished here.'

'Well gosh, wouldn't you know it,' Armstrong started, breaking into a large, fake smile, as he folded his arms about himself again, 'but a window of opportunity has just become free in my diary, so I'm all yours for the next...'

'Until we're finished,' O'Carroll interrupted, her usual good humour clearly gone the same way as her previous night's sleep.

'I wanted to talk to you about Louis' habit of taking to nipping out to one of the bins in the Botanic Gardens,' McCusker started, as they strolled into the kitchen.

'Oh yes, Louis' over-active nostrils.'

'How frequently does Louis get rid of the rubbish this way?'

'Gosh, nightly. He's fastidious about smells around the house – sometimes he'll dump twice on Saturday and same on Sundays. And if he's not around, Elizabeth will have me dump the bags on her behalf.'

'And is it always at the same time?' McCusker asked.

'When I'm here it's always just before 9 o'clock. Louis is always at home on Thursday evenings so he'd always do the rubbish-bag duty to get back to the house, to see whatever was on the telly at 9.00.'

'Did he always use the same route to the bin?' McCusker asked.

'Elizabeth said that if their usual bin was full we were not allowed to just leave our blue bags just by the bins, as some people do. We would have to find another bin that could accommodate the rubbish.'

'Did a lot of people know that Louis dumped his rubbish in Botanic Gardens?'

'His over-active nostrils were not a secret,' Armstrong croaked. 'I think his circle knew about it; I've seen him excuse himself from a dinner party table to go and dump the rubbish.'

'But he'd always take out the rubbish on a Thursday evening, just before 9 o'clock?' McCusker continued.

'I'd say most definitely.'

'What can you tell us about Louis' brother, Miles?' McCusker asked, before the three of them had finally rested their weight on the chairs around the kitchen table.

'Gosh that was quick,' Armstrong said.

McCusker wasn't sure if the "quick" referred to the speed by which he delivered his second question or that Armstrong already had Miles Bloom in the frame for fratricide.

McCusker and O'Carroll both took out their notebooks and, pens primed, glared at Armstrong.

''Well, I can tell you,' Armstrong started, sounding more like an aproned-up fishwife at the clothesline than a songwriter, 'he's a piece of work is that Miles one.'

'How so?' O'Carroll asked, her interest piqued.

'Well, he absolutely hates Louis, I mean, gosh, you guys are certainly onto number one suspect very quickly, fair play to you.'

O'Carroll was about to ask another question when Armstrong leaned over the table, and dropped the volume of his croak in a conspiratorial manner. 'You see the problem is,' again he paused and looked around him, 'Miles is a lazy sod. Louis has never been scared of hard work and... well, he's not preoccupied with money the way Miles is. Their auld man, Sidney Bloom, was a self-made man. He did very well for himself at a time when the general store sold absolutely everything from nails to napalm. Auld Sidney built up his business until he had a general store, a chemist, a restaurant, a pub, an undertaking business, a trucking business and, let's see, there was also a travel agency. He ran them all phenomenally successfully. He knew it took a lot of time, a lot of hard work and dedicated staff to make a fortune. He also knew it would take a little time and an argumentative, spoilt, lazy brat to squander the same fortune. Elizabeth said that Sidney had once told her, "I've always felt that people are less careful with money when they haven't worked for it." Sidney was a cute man all right, and he was certainly wise to Miles. So he left each of his businesses to his staff and he left all his money and his property to Louis.'

'And Miles?' McCusker felt compelled to ask.

'And to Miles he left his original set of tools and a *How To Be A Handy Man About The House* DIY book.'

'No?' McCusker offered, barely containing a snigger.

'100% the truth,' Armstrong replied, looking genuinely hurt. 'Ask Elizabeth if you don't believe me,'

'Unbelievable!' McCusker offered shaking his head in disbelief while looking at O'Carroll. 'And what did Miles do?'

'He went absolutely balsamic.'

'I think you mean ballistic?' O'Carroll suggested.

'No, I mean balsamic,' Armstrong replied very definitely. The problem was he meant it. 'Jesus was crucified on the cross,' he continued, 'then he was speared a few times. But that wasn't enough either, so the soldiers poured vinegar on a sponge and put it on a hyssop plant and offered it up to Jesus' lips, so he could drink it. That was literally the straw that broke Jesus' back. Just after that he gave up. So I've always felt balsamic was the stage after ballistic.'

'O-k-a-y,' O'Carroll said, drawing the word out but not long enough to betray her feelings that she felt Armstrong was behaving "in character." 'So what did Miles actually do?'

'He contested the Will, he sued, he came around to Elizabeth and Louis' several times after the funeral and after the Will had been read, and threatened Louis with physical harm. But auld man Bloom had written an unbreakable Will.'

'How long ago was this?' McCusker asked.

'Gosh, I'd say eight or nine years.'

'And have they communicated since?'

'Mostly, through solicitors. Although I have to say, Louis seemed more bemused by Miles's behaviour, than annoyed by it. Elizabeth said that Louis admitted he and his brother had never ever been pals.'

'Was that because the father favoured Louis?' McCusker asked.

'Well, that's the really strange thing…' Armstrong croaked, 'until the Will was read no one, including Louis, had a clue that the father preferred Louis over Miles.'

'Really?' O'Carroll asked. 'Something must have happened.'

'Elizabeth thought it might have been because Louis was always very respectful of his mother, Terry, and his auld man, Sidney. She thought it might have been as simple as that. On top of which, Louis never caused them any grief. They never had to nag at him to get on with his studies, or homework or chores around the various stores. Louis was always up for doing anything. Equally, when the chores were being dished out, it wasn't that Miles wasn't first in the queue, or even last in the queue, for that matter. He wasn't even in the queue in the first place.'

It was clear that Armstrong had more to say and so McCusker and O'Carroll left him to it.

'Elizabeth felt that Louis never had any desire to take over the family business but he acknowledged how hard his father had worked at making the family business a success, and he respected that.'

'Did Louis ever offer to give Miles any of the inheritance?' McCusker asked.

'Actually, I asked Elizabeth that very question at the time and she said that Louis had only discussed it with her once, and he had said if only Miles hadn't made such a song and dance about it, he most certainly would have shared his good fortune with his brother. But Louis was really scundered with Miles dissing auld man Bloom in public after his death, with all his lawsuits and the crap involved. Miles's problem was that he'd didn't want *just* a share of the estate. No, he felt entitled to the whole shebang.'

'What does Miles do now?' McCusker asked.

'Someone told me that on his passport he listed his occupation as 'House Husband.'

'You mean he lives off his wife?' O'Carroll asked.

'I don't think that man has ever worked a day in his life,' Armstrong replied, not exactly answering the question.

'What does his wife do?' O'Carroll asked, sounding like she was itching to meet up with Miles Bloom.

'We – Elizabeth and me – always refer to her as the *Other* Mrs Bloom. She's an independent head-hunter. Apparently, according to Elizabeth, she's very, very good at her work. Yes, the Other Mrs Bloom is phenomenally successful, has two PAs and is always on a plane to somewhere or other.'

'Where do they live?' O'Carroll asked.

'Oh they've got a big pile up on Cyprus Avenue.'

'McCusker immediately thought of Ryan and Larry, the O'Neill boys and the first case he'd worked on with O'Carroll a little over a year ago.

McCusker also noted that Armstrong wasn't backwards about coming forward with information. The secret seemed to be in knowing which question to ask.

'Tell me this,' McCusker started, closing his eyes as he threw the dice, 'did Miles Bloom ever attempt to hurt his brother in any way?'

'You mean in a physical way?'

'Well yes,' McCusker replied, hopefully.

'I've been wondering about that myself all night,' Armstrong replied. To McCusker, he sounded like he was growing hoarser by the minute. 'I asked Elizabeth the same question when Louis was discovered in the graveyard and she kind of laughed, but then she, too, seemed to grow concerned. She seemed to be thinking about something she didn't want to share with me. To be quite frank with you, if you tell me in a few days' time that you'd discovered Louis was murdered by Miles, then I, for one, wouldn't be shocked. I wouldn't bat an eyelid.'

'What is your own line of work?' O'Carroll asked.

'He's a songwriter,' McCusker offered, on Armstrong's behalf, 'remember that song 'Causeway Cruising'...'

'Yes, of course – a big hit for Zounds,' O'Carroll replied, before McCusker had even asked the question. 'But wait: you're not a member of Zounds – I saw them during the summer at the Ulster Hall...'

'No, no, but he *wrote* the song,' McCusker advised his colleague, as Armstrong beamed in the background, basking in his own little unexpected moment of glory, 'Mr Armstrong himself actually wrote 'Causeway Cruising'.'

'Run up the wall and tiddle the bricks,' O'Carroll gushed, but then reverted to a Colombo moment that McCusker hoped Armstrong wouldn't notice: 'Well, that's very impressive.'

'Oh gosh, thank you.'

'My sister, Grace, and I really love that record,' O'Carroll said. 'So that's how you make a living, you write songs?'

'Yes,' Armstrong replied, his face now frozen in a permanent beam of pride.

'And how long have you been doing that?' O'Carroll continued.

'Well, ever since my university years. But I've only been able to make a living out of it since… well, really since I gave up playing with my own group and started to concentrate on writing.'

'And a decent living?' O'Carroll asked, continuing to stay in the driver's seat.

'Augh you know, I get by,' he said, with a modest shrug of the shoulders.

'That's great, Mr Armstrong…'

'Oh, you can call me Al…'

'Okay, Al – can you tell me what you were doing between the hours of 9.00 yesterday evening and 1.00 a.m. this morning?'

'Oh gosh, where did that come from?' he moaned. 'How have I been promoted to a suspect?'

'Here's the thing, Al,' O'Carroll started patiently, maybe even sincerely, 'really everyone is a suspect until we can rule them out. You'll never know how much we just love to rule people out. It means we can concentrate our resources on who might have committed the crime rather than those who definitely didn't.'

'Well, actually I was at home working on a song,' Armstrong started off, enthusiastically. 'Did you ever wake up in the morning and feel that the dream that was just ending wasn't in fact a dream, it was a scene for your real life?'

'Ah, no to that one,' O'Carroll replied, immediately. 'Were you with anyone else when this was happening?'

'What, you mean when my dream was ending? Isn't that just a wee bit too personal, even for a police *person*?' Armstrong shot back. When he was trying to be ironic his hoarse croak sounded even more pathetic than normal.

O'Carroll grimaced as if that was the image she most wanted to keep out of her mind.

'NO!' she protested. 'I meant does anyone help you with your songwriting endeavours?'

'Oh gosh, now that really was a funny moment.' Armstrong's resultant grin betrayed all the lines and crow's feet in his face. He looked like an Egyptian calligrapher had been set loose on his forehead.

'So no one helps you write your songs,' O'Carroll started back up again. 'Don't all the famous songwriters have co-writers, like Lennon & McCartney, Simon & Garfunkel...'

'Actually, Paul Simon wrote the songs and Art sang them.'

'Okay right. So you *don't* have a co-writer?'

'No, I've tried a few times to write with other people but I've never found it to be a satisfactory process.'

'So the long and the short of it,' O'Carroll said before physically sighing, 'is that there was no one with you last night when you were writing your song?'

'Gosh, that's right, but I could sing it for you now to prove I wrote it?' Armstrong offered.

'Yes, but then surely myself and McCusker here wouldn't know if you wrote it last night, or last week, or even last year?'

Armstrong seemed to consider this theory for a while but before he could come up with another excuse to play his song, O'Carroll continued with, 'Ah, did you speak to anyone on the phone, during that period?'

'No, you see when you're in that zone, well, when *I'm* in that song-writing-zone, it's a truly blissful state and times flies by, and before you know it, it's the next day. The only person I spoke with during the entire evening was Elizabeth, when she rang me up in the early hours of the morning and asked me to come around.'

CHAPTER ELEVEN

'Do we go and see Miles Bloom now?' O'Carroll asked.

'I'd favour getting some more information on him before we interview him,' McCusker replied.

'Okay, let's head back to the Customs House and see how they're all getting on.'

When they returned to the sanctuary of her battered, metallic yellow Mégane, O'Carroll said she thought McCusker, for some reason, looked gutted, and unusually down, even to the point that she felt she should bring up the subject of what was troubling him.

'So why are you so down today? It's not due to the fact that you lost your beauty sleep is it?'

'Nagh.'

'And if it's to do with my sister, I *really* don't want to know. It's just that it's not like you – you're usually chipper. I mean, yes, you're certainly antediluvian, but mostly chipper.'

McCusker shrugged, conceding she wasn't wrong in her assessment. 'You won't laugh?'

'I'll try not to,' she said, a little concerned.

'Promise you won't laugh?' McCusker pleaded.

'Oh, don't tell me, I know what it is – you've worn out the last pair of your Royal & Awesome plus-fours and you can't find a draper in Belfast who still stocks them?'

No reaction.

'Okay, McCusker – I'll really try not to laugh.'

'Well Rory…'

'Rory?'

'Rory McIlroy.'

'Oh… that Rory, okay… go ahead,' she encouraged.

'So Rory plummeted from third to thirteenth in the World Rankings in the space of a sand bunker yesterday.'

'Right, I'd hate to see what mood you'd get into if you gave the refugees equal consideration. You don't even know him – R O R Y – and you're behaving as if he's your best mate.'

McCusker just looked at her, he'd nothing to say.

'McCusker… come on, you've not been hiding anything from me have you? He's not a mate? Is he? If he's a mate and you haven't introduced me to him… he's right fit, you know. And then if he's still with that tennis girly-type… well, at least he could introduce me to his fellow professionals, some of them look… well, okay, you know, I mean a few beers makes all the difference.'

'Ah, O'Carroll, TMFI.'

'TMFI?'

'Too much 'eckin information,' McCusker replied, sounding like he was waiting for a drum roll and the crash of a cymbal to finish off his sentence. 'And no, I don't know him, but it doesn't make it any easier.'

'Why McCusker, why?' she asked, sounding sincere.

McCusker knew that when she sounded sincere, that was when she was at her most cynical and lethal, so he continued cautiously. 'I really don't know, the only thing I can figure is that he's from the wee North, and like George Best, Alex Higgins, John Watson and Eddie Irvine, he's one of the five world-beaters in their chosen sport that we've ever produced, so when you see him underperform I find it very depressing.'

'So you'd much prefer he was the cock-of-the-north and won everything?'

'No, it's not that!'

'It seems to me, McCusker, that you should consider how bad it feels when your team loses. Right? Next you should think about how you feel when they win. The balance of the intensity of the feeling is very heavily in favour of the loss. So can I just say that in any of the sports you've just mentioned, there can only be one winner and that means there have to be lots of LOO-SERS!'

'No, I don't mind him losing, it's just when he underperforms you get annoyed on his behalf, because you know he can do better, you know the games he could have won.'

'Really,' O'Carroll replied, just the slightest hint of boredom creeping into her voice. 'So you know how he *could* have won?'

'Yes, of course.'

'Really?' O'Carroll replied, just the slightest hint of intrigue creeping into her voice. 'So pray, tell me how.'

'Okay, I will,' McCusker said, looking around him as if he was about to reveal a state secret. 'When Rory talks about his game of golf before and during a match, you know, when he tries to justify his play, well eight times out of ten he will lose the game. When he keeps himself to himself before and during the game and doesn't get drawn into anything deep during the required and, most likely, contracted sponsor interviews, well, that's when he wins. That's when he's playing pure golf and not preoccupied with fulfilling his own soundbites.'

'Right. Good to know, McCusker, thanks for that,' she said, appearing to glaze over about halfway through his theory. 'How are you getting on with fixing up the appointment to visit the graveyard guide?'

'I'll chase her again when I get to my desk.'

CHAPTER TWELVE

When they entered the iconic building that was the Customs House, the one-time workplace of Anthony Trollope and currently home to the Laganside section of the PSNI, there was a message for them to go and see Superintendent Niall Larkin immediately.

'Oh goody, bickies,' McCusker gushed, Rory's woes clearly an issue of the past.

'McCusker, how many times do I have to tell you,' O'Carroll hissed, as they waited outside Larkin's door, 'you're not a teenager anymore and they're not called bickies, they're called...' Just then, Larkin's PA, Sheila Lawson – aka Wee Sheila – opened the door.

'He's expecting you. Go on through and I'll be in with tea and bickies in a couple of minutes,' she said, by way of greeting, and winked at McCusker. She was always winking at McCusker. O'Carroll just rolled her eyes.

'So, any progress to report?' Larkin asked, without inviting them to sit down.

'Well, no one seems to have an alibi,' McCusker offered.

'Do you know Miles Bloom, Sir?' O'Carroll asked.

'Ah, you've heard of the crazy brother already.'

'Do you think he might be involved?' O'Carroll asked.

'That's why PSNI pay you both the big bucks, so you can answer those kinds of questions for me.'

McCusker felt like they'd just been shot down in flames.

'Look, FYI,' Larkin continued in a gentler tone, 'my barber is on the way up, so we need to be brief. The reason I asked you up here is because you really should have a chat with Mrs Larkin. But if you don't mind, I don't really feel comfortable bringing Angela in here for her interview, so she said that I should just invite youse over to the house later for a bite. She said McCusker here looks like he could do with a bit of decent food. So how does that sound?'

'Count me in,' McCusker offered, enthusiastically.

O'Carroll looked somewhat less enthusiastic, but Larkin glared at her until she agreed.

They met Wee Sheila on the way out. She had a tray with tea and a plate of Larkin's favourite Jaffa Cakes.

O'Carroll headed on out of the office without stopping, but Mc-Cusker milked and sugared up a cup of tea and helped himself to half a dozen Jaffa Cakes as Sheila stood there. He worked on the theory that the Jaffa Cakes were so small you could get away with eating half a dozen a time.

'Brilliant, Sheila, a lifesaver,' McCusker said. 'I'll bring the cup back up later.'

'Shoot,' O'Carroll grunted as they walked down one storey to their floor.

'Are you just practising, or were you aiming for "shit"?'

'I was meant to see a prospect for the future Mr Lily O'Carroll tonight,' she groaned.

'Oh, who's tonight's lucky contestant?'

The DI was actually so shamefaced that she took a piece of paper out of her inside pocket and read out, 'A Mr Chris O'Donnell, an entrepreneur in the music business.'

'How did you meet him?' McCusker felt compelled to ask.

'Don't ask,' she replied, in a whisper, as they walked through the doors into their open plan office.

DS WJ Barr had certainly been a busy bee. He'd got the four plastic rubbish bags, including Elizabeth Bloom's distinctive light blue one, back to Customs House and by the time he'd returned himself, the team had been through each one (including Bloom's). They'd discovered, thanks to some discarded Amazon packaging, that the bag beneath Elizabeth Bloom's bag was owned by Mr T Husbands, who lived three doors away from the Bloom residence. The owner of the rubbish bag, which had been found languishing on top of Elizabeth's own rubbish bag, was proving more difficult to pin down. The only incriminating evidence they could find among the smelly refuse was a plastic bag containing the logo of Kampus Korma, an Indian restaurant that clearly did deliveries as well. Barr had rung the restaurant and discovered that they had delivered: 2 onion Bargees; 1 x Bombay aloo; 1 x Peshwari naan; a chicken korma and a lentil dish; 1 x plain rice, all to a house in Stranmillis Gardens. And the final bag – the bag Mc-Cusker, under the watchful eye of Al Armstrong, had removed first from the rubbish bin in Botanic Gardens – had belonged to a Miss Elaine Gibbons from Elaine Street. You couldn't make that stuff up, but nonetheless, McCusker asked for the proof of address evidence, and he was presented with an evidence bag with not one, but *two* envelopes (a reminder for an electric bill and a handwritten envelope) containing the name of Miss Elaine Gibbons of Elaine Street, Belfast, BT9 5AR.

McCusker volunteered Barr and himself to nip up there straight away. He wanted to leave O'Carroll in peace for a while, in order to give her a chance to rearrange her blind date, perhaps for even later that evening. On top of which, he was very happy to meet some of Louis Bloom's neighbours. Neighbours get to see into people's back gardens and also perhaps to hear things they aren't meant to hear.

McCusker decided to visit them in the order they'd deposited their rubbish. That would be:

Elaine Gibbons, Elaine Street (2 x envelopes)

Stranmillis Gardens, Name unknown (Kampus Korma delivery bag)

(L Bloom)

T Husbands, Same street, Landseer Street (Amazon packaging)

Miss Elaine Gibbons was surprisingly in residence when Barr and McCusker came calling. Unsurprisingly, the QUB second-year student thought that she was in trouble for dumping her rubbish in Botanic Gardens, albeit in a rubbish bin and, as she went to great pains to point out, at least three other people had got there before her.

'You're not in trouble,' McCusker said, 'on top of which, I'm not even sure dumping rubbing in a rubbish bin is illegal.'

He intentionally left just that wee bit of doubt hanging in the air in the hope it would encourage her cooperation. Nonetheless, she didn't invite the two detectives in, and so they conducted the interview on her doorstep. After she'd complained, in her defence, that the bin men didn't call often enough, McCusker asked what time Elaine would have dumped her black rubbish bag.

'Let's see,' she offered impatiently, 'around 8.00. I was settling down for the night. I was all cosy and didn't really want to go out, but equally I didn't want to do it in daylight just in case people clocked me. So I kinda forced myself to do it. I wasn't really dressed appropriately, but then again, who was I going to bump into other than other people dressed inappropriately?'

'And did you meet any inappropriately dressed people?' McCusker asked, as DS WJ Barr attended to notebook duties.

'Yes, there were people, but I didn't clock them for fear they'd clock me,' she started, stopped, then seemed to think for a few seconds. 'There were a couple in the shelter across from the bandstand. I was happy enough to look at them – they were sucking so much face, they'd never have noticed me even if I'd been in my birthday suit.'

McCusker knew the shelter well. It was about twenty steps away, down a gentle incline from the bandstand. It was an octagonal rain shelter with a pitched felt roof, resting on red poles and containing two rows of double-sided, black and white seats, which looked like the spokes of a crazy wheel.

McCusker, on one of his many getting-to-know-Belfast walks, had actually sheltered there from a shower and sat in the same seats while viewing the once elegant bandstand, before continuing his dander through a few trees to the nearby rose garden. The Portrush detective remembered actually seeking out the bandstand because he heard somewhere or other that it had been featured in a promo film clip of Van Morrison performing Celtic Swing there in the 1980s.

'Were they still there when you were on your return journey?' McCusker continued.

'Yes, they were, and still snogging. Must have been a first date; you never snog in public unless it's a first date. I felt like telling them to get a room at the Europa or they'll scare the animals.'

'Oh, were there people out walking dogs too?'

'Just a figure of speech,' she said, now hopping from foot to foot and keen to return to the warmth of her flat. 'Look, yes, there were other people around but I ignored them in the hope they would ignore me.'

'So, tell me more about the couple?' McCusker asked, realising he was about to lose this one.

'I didn't see much, I've told you that already,' she protested.

'We all see a lot more than we think we see,' McCusker started off, patiently, 'please just do me a favour and close your eyes, and go back to last night and think your way through your walk to the rubbish bin and back.'

She humoured him, but only for a few seconds: 'Nope… no good, all I remember is trying to walk with my bag as inconspicuously as possible, you know, trying to give off the air of: a bag? "What bag? This is not a bag, this is my laundry…" or something similar. I saw the couple in the shelter and, other than that, a lot of the tarmac footpath.' She stopped talking and closed her eyes even tighter. 'Okay… the guy was dressed in a dark blue zip-up windbreaker, black trousers. He looked cold. She was much better dressed for the outdoors, grey hoodie under a black duffle coat. YES… yes… the boy was wearing a scarf; it was a yellow and black scarf, which I thought were weird colours for Belfast.'

'Okay,' McCusker said in praise, happy with the minor breakthrough.

But Elaine from Elaine Street wasn't quite finished.

'There was something else I've just remembered,' she offered, before Barr had a chance to consider putting away his notebook. 'Yes, the other thing I thought was unusual is that they weren't kissing in the way you kiss…'

Either she'd lost her confidence, or her thread – or her patience.

'Yes?' McCusker persisted.

'Well, they weren't kissing like a couple kiss when getting ready to… to…' she stuttered to a halt, before catching her second wind and continuing with, 'yes, of course that's it, they weren't kissing like a couple who were about to make love, they were *just* kissing, and seemed very happy to be doing so.'

'How old were they?

'He was probably a first-year; she was definitely older than me, maybe a third-year?'

'Look, we appreciate your time,' McCusker said, handing her a card. 'Here's our details – please give me a shout if you remember anything else.'

McCusker and Barr were just about to walk out of her gate when she called out after them.

'Hi!'

When they turned round she was looking at McCusker.

'You were right, you know,' she said.

'Sorry?'

'You said I'd seen more than I'd remembered I'd seen, and you were right,' she offered through a smile, as she waved his business card at him and closed the door.

* * *

'So let's assume that the kissing couple would have been there for a while; perhaps they saw Louis and maybe his assailant?'

'But goodness, how are we ever going to find them?' Barr asked, to the mid-air as much as McCusker.

'Well, the boy was wearing a scarf and the boy will lead us to the girl,' McCusker said and then stopped mid-step.

'What – you've thought of something?'

'No, not really,' McCusker started, 'it's just when I was growing up we had *girl*friends and girlfriends had *boy*friends, but in modern society when you think of a couple engaging in the overtures to sexual activity... well, the words "boy" and "girl" seem highly inappropriate to use. Young men and young women would seem more politically correct these days.'

'I see what you're saying, but at seventeen, you're hardly a man or even a *young* man?' Barr offered.

'Unless of course,' McCusker said, smiling as he opened the gate at the address in Stranmillis Gardens, which had been opened by the delivery boy (McCusker felt that "boy" was a safe word in this instance) something like fourteen hours previously, 'you're seventeen!'

* * *

McCusker rang the doorbell, which produced a ding-dong sound somewhere in the depths of the house, for a good few minutes before they could hear mutterings and footsteps in the hallway.

'What kind of fresh hell do we have here?' a man said, before he'd the green door fully open.

The man, all five foot of him, in a cloth cap, was friendlier in person than his opening had been.

Barr, as the official member of the PSNI, introduced them both and, introductions over, McCusker got straight into it.

'Did you, Sir, by any chance order an Indian takeaway meal from Kampus Korma yesterday evening?'

'Ah jeez, don't tell me they're using dog meat in the restaurants again?'

'Even if they did, we understand you'll be okay, because you'd either chicken or lentils,' McCusker replied.

'Jeez, you guys have definitely upped your game since *Z-Cars*,' he replied, clearly betraying his late-sixties age.

McCusker got it, Barr didn't.

'Well, now we've ascertained you're not from the Inland Revenue, you're welcome to come in. My mum always told me never to talk to the police on the doorstep; it just brings the neighbourhood down.'

The Stranmillis Gardens' resident, George, got them settled in and offered them fresh coffee and Paris buns. McCusker was beside himself as he polished off his own bun and started into Barr's as well, but only on Barr's insistence.

'I'd much prefer to entertain you for a day rather than a week,' George said, as he scooped up his own crumbs. 'So tell me all about Kampus Korma – what have they been getting up to?'

'Well, the takeaway was really just the way we tracked you down,' McCusker admitted. 'You threw a green rubbish bag into a bin in Botanic Gardens.'

'Jeez, it's come to something when the council get the PSNI to do their dirty work for them. You can tell them from me, if they sent their bin men around more often, the community wouldn't need to use the Botanic Gardens' bins.'

'No, no, it's nothing to do with that, Sir,' Barr said, 'other residents did the same last night and in fact the immediate one before you, well he…'

'Oh you don't mean Louis Bloom do you?'

'Well yes.'

'That's so sad, what happened.'

Barr looked to McCusker, clearly surprised the news was already out. McCusker was quite happy, the H2H had been effective. It meant he could expand his line of questioning.

'We don't know yet,' McCusker began, 'but it would appear that Mr Bloom deposited a rubbish bag in the same bin. His was-'

'A black one,' George interrupted, as though he just had a visual flash.

'No,' McCusker sighed, patiently, very patiently, 'you see Mr Bloom would have put his bag in after you because his bag was found on top of yours.'

'Jeez, so whose was the black bag?' George asked, appearing disappointed.

'That was another of your neighbours. But what time did you dump your rubbish?' McCusker asked.

'It's just that with Indian food, it's brilliant, you know. I love it – I do pay for it a wee bit during the night when it repeats on me, but... the even bigger negative is that it does pong the house out a bit if you don't get rid of the leftovers and the containers immediately. So, let's think here for a wee minute. I can work this out for you quite accurately. I ordered the food at 7.15, it hadn't arrived by 7.45 so I rang them. They said it should be here any minute and no sooner had I set the phone down than the doorbell rang and there it was. I would have tucked in immediately, washing it down with my favourite white wine, Blue Nun. I would have been finished and on the way to the bin by, say, 8.30/35. I would say that I planted my green bag on top of the black bag at around 8.40.'

'Okay,' McCusker said, pausing for a wee bit, because Barr was still writing furiously away. 'Now this bit is very important. Can you tell me if you saw anyone else on your way to the bin and on your way back home please?'

'Jeez,' George wheezed, 'let's see now; there was a couple on one of those black and white bench-seats – you know, the ones under the wee shelter near the main bandstand?'

'Yes, we know it.'

'Yes… and then there were two old dears, standing by the band-stand. They were enjoying an eyeful of the couple on the black and white seats, who were kissing away ten to the dozen. I don't know who was enjoying it the most, the kissing couple or the two old dears watching on, obviously reliving their teenage years.'

McCusker nodded back to Barr's notebook.

'What do you remember about the two women? How where they dressed, for instance?'

'Well, I seem to remember they had long coats on – I couldn't tell you the colour of either.'

'Is there any chance they could have been men?' McCusker asked.

'No, definitely not,' George quickly confirmed, 'I noticed their bare legs beneath their coats.'

'Did they have hats on? Scarves? Long hair, short hair?'

'I don't think they'd hats… but yes… I can see them now. They both had long, dark hair, one darker than the other. But I suppose for me to remember the contrast in the hair colour could mean that maybe one of them was actually blonde.'

'So let's get back to the kissing couple: what can you tell me about them?'

'There were two of them,' George said, in a feeble shot at a joke.

McCusker laughed, because, in different circumstances, it was a crack similar to one he would have attempted himself. George sounded like someone who was trying to sound like he wasn't nervous. It wasn't even that he was nervous; it was more that he didn't want to *appear* nervous. It was probably more a social thing than a guilt thing.

'And how are you spelling "too"?' Barr asked, pen nib doing an imaginary, repeated figure-of-eight, about a quarter of an inch above the page, probably because he didn't want George to think that the humour had been out of place.

'Well, they were very close to each other. One of them had a QUB scarf on, I think it was the boy. They both had sporty kind of gear on. In the light, it was difficult to see where one started and the other finished.'

'Were they doing anything rude?' McCusker asked.

'Jeez, no, not at all, they were just kissing,' George guessed. 'Do you not remember when you were young, kissing until your face hurt?'

'And then did you see anyone or anything interesting on the way back to your house?' McCusker asked, totally ignoring the question.

'Well, here's the thing; I always go around the long way on the way back, a bit of a constitutional, you know, to walk off my meal. And as usual it was heaving with students, but I didn't come across anything or anyone suspicious, if that's what you mean.'

'Okay, George,' McCusker said, changing direction, 'tell me this; did you know Mr Louis Bloom at all?'

'Aye, well the Blooms have been there a good few years, and the word is that they're a very nice family. Neither Elizabeth nor Louis had airs or graces – they'd speak to you if they saw you in the street, or if you happened to come across either of them in the Botanic Gardens, but we never really mixed with them. But they were kind to me recently there.'

'So never any trouble or anything?'

'No, never,' he said immediately, but then paused in consideration, 'you'd mostly meet them separately, aye.'

'And did you ever notice anyone suspicious, hanging around the streets or near their house?' McCusker asked, nodding in the direction of George's window.

'Oh goodness, no!' George said, smiling. 'Nice area, this. We've been lucky here. Nice people and we're off the beaten path a bit, even though it's so close to Queens and the city centre is only a stone's throw away.'

'Is your wife in?' McCusker asked.

'Sorry?'

'Your wife – is she not in today? I noticed the order was for two last night.'

'No, sorry, no, I order that out of habit,' George started, trying to smile, 'my wife and I would have that same order when we had our usual Thursday night ruby.'

Barr looked up from the page in doubt as to what to write.

'Ruby?' George guessed. Barr nodded yes. 'A ruby, a curry? You never heard that before?'

'Never.'

'Aye, after Ruby Murray, a wee girl from the Donegall Road here in the city, who'd a beautiful husky voice and was absolutely massive in the fifties and sixties, with lots of Top Ten singles in the UK. Ruby would have been what Madonna is today, but she could actually *sing*. Anyway, during her success, and thanks to Cockney rhyming slang, a curry became known as a Ruby. A Ruby Murray, a curry,' he offered, sing-song style.

'Okay, right,' Barr replied, as the three of them shared a genuine smile.

'So, the Mrs and I would have a Ruby on Thursdays and we'd always have that order, which was meant for two but was certainly enough for us, and we'd share all or dishes and we'd always something left over. My wife passed last year.'

'We're so sorry for your loss,' McCusker offered, immediately.

'Jeez, I still miss her, but, augh… well, she suffered so much during her last six months…' George had dropped to a whisper and was struggling to keep his composure.

'We understand, George, we do,' McCusker offered, quietly.

'Silly auld bugger, me. She'd be so upset with me, doing that in public,' he said pulling himself together in his wife's memory. 'Anyway I just keep ordering our meal, so there.'

'Look, we've probably already taken up too much of your time,' McCusker said, 'but look, if you ever remember anything else from that night or just fancy a wee chat, please give us a ring.'

'Aye, I will right. And equally, if you ever fancy another of my wee Paris buns, don't wait for an invite, just drop in.'

'Oh, you can bet your bottom dollar I'll do that,' McCusker said, and meant it. 'And thanks a million, George, you've been very helpful.'

* * *

Two doors away from Louis Bloom's house in Landseer Street, lived a man by the name of Mr T Husbands – well, at least that was the legend according to the Amazon packaging, discovered in the grey rubbish bag found on top of Louis Bloom's blue bag in the bin by the signpost, close to the border of the rose garden and closer still to the bandstand and the shelter in the nearby Botanic Gardens.

Mr T Husbands was a member of the relatively new consulting community, a workforce that had forsaken the rent and overhead of an office for the price of an iPad, an iPhone, a dedicated room in their home – or even just a coffee table in the living room – an address book and three daily cappuccinos. They had also – by choice or necessity, when necessity was instigated by redundancy – forsaken a regular salary for as many monthly consulting invoices as their particular part of the marketplace could take.

For all of that, Mr T Husbands was bright and breezy when Mc-Cusker came calling that autumnal morning. His skin and hair enjoyed the hue of one that had recently showered and shaved. Where Mc-Cusker might have expected a member of this community to be still in their dressing gown, slippers and unshaven at this time of the day, Mr T Husbands was dressed and turned out to a standard that would have shamed most of the community over at Stormont, with his crisp, clean white shirt, and tie, and all.

'I can explain the parking tickets,' Mr T Husbands said, laughing, by way of greeting when McCusker and Barr flashed their identity cards, before adding a cautious, 'just kidding.'

Mr T Husbands, as his accent testified was not from these parts, but he sounded like he had acquired an Ulsterised version of English in order to disguise his Brummie roots.

'Com'on in?' he said, proving the point. 'Is this about Louis Bloom?' he began, 'I heard he died last night.'

'Yes, Mr Husbands,' McCusker replied softly, 'we've come to talk to you about Mr Bloom.'

'But you know my name, so you're not just doing a door to door, or cold-calling as we say in our business.'

'Correct Mr Husbands,' McCusker continued, as they were led through to the kitchen where Mr T Husbands had his desk/office spread out over the entire kitchen table and seemingly used salt and pepper cellars and other such condiments containers as paperweights for his various files, invoices and receipts.

He quickly removed the detritus from the table. 'It's Tommy – people call me Tommy,' he said, not before McCusker clocked that his chequebook appeared a lot busier than his paying-in book. No doubt O'Carroll would have thought that his use of cheques was so yesteryear.

'We believe that last night, sometime after 9 o'clock, you deposited a grey refuse bag in a rubbish bin out in Botanic Gardens?' McCusker started, as they all took a seat around the table, refusing Mr T Husbands' offer of mineral water.

'My goodness, I didn't think they had CCTV cameras in the Gardens.'

'No, in fact they don't. But, you see, Mr Bloom did the same thing, just before 9 o'clock, and as his bag was just under yours we knew you'd come after him,' McCusker said, as Barr took notes.

'It's not illegal is it?' Mr T Husbands asked, 'I mean a lot of people do it and the bin men don't come around often enough. Unless it's Christmas and they're knocking on doors looking for their tips.'

'Not that we know of,' McCusker began, 'no, we're much more interested to hear what time you left your rubbish bag in the bin.'

'I'd say I was there about 9.15, maybe 9.20 at the latest.'

'Okay,' Barr said, as he jotted that information down.

'Did you notice anything, or anyone suspicious in the Gardens yesterday evening?' McCusker asked.

'Well, I met Wee George from Stranmillis Gardens – he was just coming back as I was heading out. He nodded at my bag and said "Mum's the word". And he went off home I assume.'

McCusker thought this was slim pickings but didn't say so. 'Anyone else?'

'I mean, there were people around, but I usually try to keep to myself. I didn't notice anyone doing anything suspicious or looking suspicious.'

'On your way to the part of the Gardens where the bin is, did you pass the shelter?'

'I didn't actually pass by it, but I did see it.'

'Was there anyone in the shelter?'

'No, no one – sometimes there'll be a bunch of kids hanging out there, but last night it was totally empty.'

'After you dump the rubbish, what route do you take home?'

'I nipped down to the Crown and had a pint with a couple of former workmates,' Mr T Husbands said, as if it was the highlight of his day

Barr's pen looked as dejected as McCusker felt.

'Did you know Louis Bloom very well?' the detective asked, crossing his fingers and hoping the pickings wouldn't be as slim on this topic.

'Louis was friendly enough,' Mr T Husbands began, 'I mean, he'd never invite me around to any of his dinner parties. That seemed to me more of an alumni crowd than I'd usually mix with. Neither of us was

big on our gardening, so we'd never lean over the fence for a chat
about our rhododendrons while taking a break from weeding. I just
leave the vegetation to grow and then whack it down when it gets too
embarrassing. Mrs Bloom got different people in to do theirs regularly.
Looked like students to me. Louis seemed to travel a lot, I mean by
himself – he seemed to always be away somewhere and she always
seemed to be around the house. I suppose you could say they led separate lives.'

'You don't mean that they were separated do you?'

'No, I don't think I do, but at the same time they never came across
as a "couple" couple. I know through a friend that she'd have dinner
parties and he wouldn't even be there. That man Armstrong would be
there, though; he was always hanging out with Elizabeth – they
seemed to be besties.'

'You don't mean you think there was anything going on between
them, do you?' McCusker asked, as Barr bolted upright in his chair.

Mr T Husbands just laughed.

'What, sorry?'

'There's always going to be *one* too many in any relationship he's
involved in,' Husbands claimed.

McCusker wasn't even sure he knew what that meant. But he let it
lie, and soon he and Barr were off. He'd got slim pickings from Elaine,
George and Tommy, but at least they got something.

CHAPTER THIRTEEN

McCusker considered going back to see Mrs Bloom, but returned to the Customs House instead. DI O'Carroll would want to be with him for that interview. When he and Barr entered their open-plan office on the first floor, O'Carroll was at her desk, busy on the phone. She certainly seemed happier than earlier, when she'd discovered she had to reschedule that evening's blind date. Barr headed straight to his desk and dived back into his attempts to compile the complete picture of Louis Bloom's last day, based on the Leab David interview details, which were neatly written up in O'Carroll's pink notebook, and chasing down Bloom's credit card receipts and phone records.

Cage was complaining as usual and still referring to Bloom as a "missing person". His regard in the office was betrayed by the fact that none of his fellow workers put him right.

McCusker spent some time thinking about the couple on the bench. Both Elaine Gibbons and Wee George had witnessed them. Elaine said the boy was wearing a black scarf with yellow stripes and Wee George said it was a QUB scarf. McCusker put more credence in Elaine's eyesight. But by the time Mr T Husbands was there at 9.20, the couple had disappeared. They were definitely there at 8.40, when Wee George spotted them. So were they there at 9.00, when Louis Bloom deposited his garbage? Did Louis Bloom spot them? Had he been as interested in the "sucking face" couple as the others had been? Had the kissing couple spotted Louis Bloom at 9 o'clock, and had they spotted what had happened to him? Had they been scared by what they saw? Was that the reason they weren't there at 9.20, when Mr T

Husbands came along? McCusker then remembered the men's magazines stashed in one of Louis' locked drawers. Could the kissing couple have actually caught Louis Bloom acting as a peeping Tom? Maybe even with them as the object of his interest? Could that be the solution to what had happened? Maybe they'd caught him. What if the boy had confronted Bloom and a fight had broken out? Had they fallen to the ground and continued their fighting there? McCusker always thought how ungracious and ungainly fighting really was: a bit like two bad swimmers in action, only one of them is on top of the other. But in the melee, had Louis banged his head on the solid ground? Had the couple panicked and dumped Louis Bloom's remains over the wall, into the Friar's Bush graveyard? Then McCusker remember two vital points that disproved his theory. One: the body was found not just dumped over the wall, but quite a bit up the graveyard, by Lennon's Mausoleum. McCusker was sure he could have found a solution to that wee discrepancy, but the second point was a more difficult problem to explain: Louis Bloom hadn't died from a head injury. No, Mr Louis Bloom had been stabbed in the back.

All McCusker had to go on was this fact of a young male in a black and yellow scarf. The rest of the office was in such a buzz and so he felt guilty for not having something to do while he waited until O'Carroll was ready to pay another visit to Mrs Elizabeth Bloom.

So he set himself a task.

Twenty minutes later, he was in O'Carroll's battered, metallic-yellow Mégane, telling O'Carroll what he'd been up to, and she said, 'Colour me impressed, McCusker – how did you manage to discover that?'

'Well, I started off doing what everyone in the office does first…'

'What, make a cup of coffee?'

'No,' he said, laughing, 'I Googled it.'

'Wait! What!' O'Carroll screamed, as she nearly drove into the back of a bus, 'you what?'

'I Googled it…'

'But McCusker, they didn't have Google in the Seventies, so how did you manage to catch up with it so quickly?'

He went to say something but O'Carroll continued, 'it must be the positive influence of my sister.'

'WJ uses it all the time – I spotted him at it and so I nicked the idea.'

'That's genuinely brilliant, McCusker. You know, I didn't tell you this before, but I was starting to get quite worried about Grace dating such a complete Luddite. But here you are, proudly stepping into the 21st century.'

'Just one tiny problem,' McCusker admitted, reluctantly.

'And what's that?' O'Carroll said, still buzzing with excitement at the news.

'Google didn't work,' he deadpanned, 'it wasn't there.'

'What wasn't there?' she replied, appearing not to hear him properly.

'The information I was seeking – it wasn't there.'

'Of course it was there, you fool – everything is on Google.'

'Well, I can testify here and now that "Which school or college or university in Northern Ireland has a black and yellow scarf?" is very definitely *not* on Google.'

'But so how did you find out?' she said, disappointment dripping into each and every syllable.

'Oh, good *old-fashioned* police work,' he offered, to the sound of a roll from the imaginary snare drum and a crash of a cymbal. 'I remembered a constable up in the Portrush nick, who spent all his spare time taking his sons to football matches all over Norn Iron. He knew the colours of every opposing team his boys ever played against. So I rang him up and asked him who had black and yellow shirts, and he knew immediately: Magherafelt High School has chessboard black and yellow shirts, and he confirmed their scarves were black and yellow as well.'

'You know, McCusker,' she said, as she pulled up outside the gate to Louis Bloom's house, 'I did mean it when I said I was really quite worried about Grace dating a complete Luddite such as yourself. But not anymore.'

'Oh really,' he said, puffing himself up for a bit of praise.

'No, I've very recently discovered that there's something much worse than being a Luddite.'

'Really? That's progress coming from you,' he said, waiting for the inevitable bit of back slapping. 'And what exactly is worse than being a Luddite?'

'Oh,' she said, opening the car door and starting to get out, 'a smart Alec McCusker, particularly when my sister is dating the fecking smart Alec in question. Yes that is so *much worse!*'

CHAPTER FOURTEEN

By the time O'Carroll and McCusker had entered Louis Bloom's house on Landseer Street, O'Carroll was all sweetness and light again. Like McCusker, she enjoyed their banter, if only as a way to distract themselves from the faithful departed.

Al Armstrong had retired to his accommodation to, in his words, freshen up, and Elizabeth had just returned from her sister, Angela Larkin's house. She seemed quite at peace with herself – not really the way McCusker imagined a very recent widow would behave. She certainly wasn't being disrespectful, though – in fact, she was now dressed completely in black. McCusker figured that perhaps she felt she'd lost Louis quite a while ago. From what they had gathered so far, they seemed to live quite separate lives, so in practice it wasn't really that he was there fully one day and then gone the next. Give it a few weeks, McCusker thought, and the realisation that she would never, ever see her husband again would sink in.

'So I see your friend Mr Armstrong is a successful songwriter,' McCusker said, as they all sat down in Elizabeth's lounge for a cup of tea.

'Sorry?' Mrs Bloom said, as she let O'Carroll sugar her tea.

'Mr Armstrong – he told us he makes a living as a successful songwriter,' McCusker offered by way of explanation.

'The big Jessie! He converts flats for a living. His biggest hit would have made him thruppence ha'penny.'

McCusker and O'Carroll had to laugh.

'No, seriously!' Mrs Bloom continued. 'Yes... he got some airplay for 'Causeway Cruising' on Downtown and Radio Ulster, and it made the Ulster Top Ten. But all that means was it sold 345 copies. And, yes, the group who recorded the song, Zounds, would have made some money from personal appearances and television, but my Louis reckoned that Al would have made 78 quid from the publishing, as the writer of the song – and that's if he was lucky, very lucky.'

She'd a wee chuckle to herself before she continued with, 'you know, Al lives in his own wee fantasy world, and he's got a recording of every DJ on the radio introducing that song. And he'll bring the cassette over here with him and insist on playing it – not the song, you understand, but what all the DJs said about it. You know, he'll say, "Listen, listen Elizabeth, here's Ivan Martin saying how great the song is." But then Ivan will come on and say something like, "And here's another great wee home-grown group", and not even mention the song. But I do like Ivan; he's got a great wee show on every Sunday morning.'

'So you say he converts flats?' McCusker asked.

'What, Ivan does that as well?' Elizabeth said, sounding shocked, 'I wonder does Al know.'

'No, sorry,' McCusker offered quickly, 'I meant Mr Armstrong. Mr Armstrong actually makes his living converting flats?'

'Well, he's very handy. He's always doing things around my house, always mending things, doing things a husband should have done, but then Louis was always very busy, wasn't he?'

McCusker couldn't read O'Carroll. Equally, he didn't know if he should pick up on the Louis tangent and see where that would lead.

'So did Mr Armstrong work on a lot of properties?' he said, his voice making the decision his mind seemed incapable of.

'Well, you see it started off many years ago. He'd always buy a dilapidated flat for peanuts, but then spend a couple of years doing it up. Then he'd want a new one and so he'd sell the original at a great profit, buy another decrepit one and then do the new one up. Pretty soon he was successful enough to finance his lifestyle. Then he found a wee house he loved, and so he kept that as his home and would do up an additional flat one at a time to earn his keep.'

'Can we talk about Louis?' O'Carroll asked.

'Oh, my Louis, of course we can talk about my Louis,' Elizabeth said, sinking in to her comfortable armchair. 'Let's see now, where should I start? Well, he'd only eat his foods individually. For example, he can't eat meat and potatoes and/or vegetables at the same time. Hates food mushed up – likes visible, separate portions of his food and his bites. He hates wearing new-looking clothes. He needs to always sleep on his side of the bed. He hates eating cold food, unless it's rice pudding. He hates people who cough in public without using their hand or handkerchief or Kleenex to keep their germs to themselves. He hates people talking in the cinema, says it doesn't allow him to get lost in the movie. He hates how at the end of the trailers the credits flash by so quickly that he doesn't have time to read any of them. He hates people in classes, asking questions only for the purpose of drawing attention to either themselves or their self-perceived intelligence; he usually shoots them down in very public flames. He hates people throwing rubbish on the ground in Botanic Gardens – "That's what the bins are for", he says. He hates it when other people – me included – read his newspapers first. He hates people who serve the public who clearly *hate* serving the public; they transparently feel it's beneath them and should leave it who people who genuinely want to do it, the people who the former group of people are doing out of a job. He hates the new "entitled" generation, whose children grow up never knowing any other way to behave. But Louis would put his spin on all of the above by presenting it a different way. He loves people who live by the rule that "coughs and sneezes spread diseases, so trap your germs in a handkerchief". He loves waiters who clearly love their job. He loves people in the Botanic Gardens, like himself, who take their rubbish to the rubbish bins. He loves people in classes who ask a question because they really want to know the answer, and he will usually start his response to the same with "Good question, Williams…", or whomever. He loves genuinely humble people who never use the word "humble". He loves wearing comfortable, non-eye-catching clothes. He loves people who keep quiet in the cinema, although surely he's always totally unaware of them because…they don't talk in cinemas.

'He was a funny wee man,' Elizabeth concluded, with a large smile, 'you know, when he was young he was in the Boy Scouts and he has lived his life to their motto: "Be prepared". Being Louis, though, he always had to take it quite literally to the extreme. Like, for instance, he would always re-fill the kettle just in case the water would be turned off at the mains in the middle of the night.'

She stopped and laughed out loud.

'Do me a favour, DI O'Carroll, go over there to that sideboard and open the door on the left and tell me what you see.'

O'Carroll did as she was bid and she too laughed out loud when she opened the door to discover a stack of candles, boxes of matches and a few torches.

'And he has a stash at the ready in every room in this house,' Elizabeth claimed proudly. 'But we did have our problems, and our Angela says I have to tell you all about that side as well. She says other people will tell you versions of it, but it would be best if I told you the facts, rather than you hear the rumours first.'

'Okay,' McCusker said, hoping he was sounding encouraging, 'and your sister is 100 per cent spot on.'

'And she speaks very highly of you and DI O'Carroll here,' Elizabeth said, taking a sip of her tea, before noisily replacing the cup in the saucer, sighing and continuing: 'I'm a lot older than Louis. When we got married it wasn't an issue, and perhaps the age gap itself wasn't the issue. No, the biggest problem we ever had was that Louis didn't want any kids, while I did and so... because he wouldn't let me get pregnant, I eventually stopped sleeping with him. By the time we'd put that major difference aside he'd... well, hadn't the silly bugger only gone and gone off me in that... well... ah, shall we say, in the physical department.

'Now, in all of this there were never any raging screaming rows or fall-outs. He's always been... well, *we've both* always been very fond of each other. It's just – and Angela says I have to spell this out for you because it might be very important in your investigation – that we've never had a physical relationship since the very early days. And you know what; after a time, it's never been an issue. I didn't know if he ever went anywhere else for those particular needs, and I never really wanted to know, to be honest. But we've lived as man and wife, in all other senses, all this time. We get on very well, always have. Now he's always very busy and not around as much as most husbands, but he always sleeps here in our bed with me when he's in Belfast. He's always home for dinner and TV on Thursday nights and here for our traditional Sunday lunch, sometimes with friends and sometimes just the two of us.

'You know, the thing I've found about being together as husband and wife is, if you get to stay with each other for long enough, like Louis and I did, sometimes – not because you want to, but because people don't know anything else to do – friends start to celebrate these big anniversaries for you. Then, before you know it, the fact that you're going to stay together forever seems to be taken for granted, and not just by everyone around you, but also by yourselves too.'

Mrs Elizabeth Bloom seemed to reach a natural end to her thought.

'Well look, Mrs Bloom, er… Elizabeth,' McCusker started to a big smile which immediately washed away her earlier pensive look, 'we want to thank you for being so honest with us, and if any of our questions are too troubling we can leave them for another time.'

'Angela said that time is of the essence,' Mrs Bloom offered confidently, 'let's do it now.'

'Okay, please just remember, we're really just looking for information,' McCusker started off hesitantly. 'Do you know if Louis saw other women?'

'He was a randy wee sod in our earlier days so it was always my impression that yes, he did see other women. But he was too much of a gentleman to rub my face in it.'

'But you didn't know who any of these other women were?'

'No, nor did I want to,' she offered quickly, 'I mean with all his travels he would have had an abundance of opportunities. Equally, Louis was very private; he wouldn't have wanted anyone knowing his business. And he would have been very careful. As I told you last night, he was a hypochondriac, so he'd have… he'd have taken all the necessary precautions.'

'Okay Mrs B…' McCusker began, 'of all Louis' friends, do you think there is anyone in particular he would have shared this information with?'

'Don't you mean boasted about it?'

McCusker really wanted to respect her willingness to go down this road so early in the investigation that he wanted to be seen to be giving her and Louis the benefit of the doubt. They were two ordinary (and on the surface) nice people who were only doing what everyone tries to do: live their lives the best they could. But perhaps Louis, either knowingly or unknowingly, had done *something* – maybe even as simple as having an affair with the wrong woman – that had triggered a chain of events, which in turn had led to his untimely and violent death.

'No, no, not really that,' McCusker suggested, 'I suppose I was wondering if he had a friend who he could talk to about his personal issues?'

'I suppose he would have been good friends with Harry Rubens and his wife, Sophie, too, but he was never the kind of man who would go down the pub, have a few pints with a bunch of mates and boast about what he'd been up to the previous evening.'

'Anyone else?'

'Well, the Vice-Chancellor and Louis were always thick as thieves.'

'Okay,' McCusker said, as O'Carroll sat back and wrote in her pink notebook. 'I understand Louis didn't get on very well with his brother, Miles.'

'Chalk and cheese, oil and water, Borg and McEnroe, Paisley and Adams.'

'Was there a particular reason,' McCusker asked, 'a reason they'd fallen out?'

'Have you met Miles yet?' she replied.

'Not yet.'

'Let's see if you still need to ask me that question after you meet with him.'

'Anyone else he liked?'

'Well, Louis always got on very well with women,' Elizabeth started off tentatively. 'Angela always said it was because he knew how to act like a true gentleman and there were never any undertones. If he liked a woman, he was genuinely interested in her as a person and not an object of desire or a possible conquest. Like Al, for instance; he's always trying it on with the women he comes into contact with, but I think it's because he feels he should. I also think if any of them said "Yes, come on, follow me I'm the Pied Piper" he'd run the whole way up to Napoleon's Nose without once looking back.'

'Could he be doing it to make you jealous?' O'Carroll asked, when the three had stopped laughing at the image of Armstrong running up Belfast Mountain in fear of a woman, 'he seems very fond of you?'

'And I him,' she replied, just a beat too quickly for McCusker. 'He's been a good friend to me and, I hope, I to him. But really he's as interested in all that stuff as I am.'

'Is he gay?' O'Carroll asked, as McCusker's eyebrows nearly flew off his forehead.

'I'll tell you this, DI O'Carroll, if a man came on to Al he'd get to the Isle of Man quicker than Finn McCool did.'

O'Carroll looked confused at that one.

'You know, Finn McCool the legendary mythical Ulster giant?' McCusker offered.

'Well, I know you're always going on about him but I figured it must have something to do with your lads up on the North coast. Okay, I'm biting, so how did he get to the Isle of Man so quickly?'

'Well, legend has it that he was looking for his true love, Sadbh, who'd fled to Scotland. Anyway, Finn McCool lifted a sod of earth out of Mid-Ulster and flung it into the Irish Sea so that he could use it as a stepping stone to get across to Scotland. Now, because he was a giant, the sod of earth was a big sod, so big a sod, in fact, that it became known as the Isle of Man...'

'...and the hole in Mid-Ulster created by the missing sod, filled in with water, became Lough Neagh, the biggest freshwater lake in Europe,' Elizabeth added seamlessly.

'Youse two should go on stage,' O'Carroll suggested.

'Oh, I only known about Finn because Al wrote a song about him and he went on and on about all of Finn's legendary feats for nearly a year. I can tell you, I was quite relieved when he finished writing that song; I was beginning to feel like I'd lived every single line of the lyrics. It must be very tiresome living with a giant – I can see why Sadbh fled to Scotland.'

'I imagine you've already been thinking about this one,' McCusker started back up again, worrying that they'd gone so far off-topic that none of them would remember what the original question was, 'but do you know anyone who Louis fell out with in any way, or anyone who wished him harm?'

'The full truth is, from the part of his life that I shared with him, I can't think of one single person who wished him ill. As for the rest of his life – his other life – I just wouldn't know.'

'What about Miles?'

'But sure, Miles, for all his faults, was still his brother,' Elizabeth Bloom said with such conviction that she clearly considered it an impossibility that one brother would kill another.

McCusker felt that the interview had reached a natural conclusion. O'Carroll clearly felt the same, because she put her notebook away. There were certainly other topics McCusker wanted to discuss, but he was happy to leave them for another time. The three then went up to Louis' study. McCusker already had the key in his hand and palmed it from the top of the door ledge, pretending to have to search around to secure it.

'That daft apeth couldn't find that key anywhere up there,' Elizabeth said, as McCusker opened the door.

The two detectives packed away all the stuff they needed, including Louis' journal, while Elizabeth seemed very content to just sit in Louis' space and try to soak up what remained of his aura.

Just as they concluded their task, Elizabeth Bloom, looking out at the spectacular view of the Botanic Gardens, sounded like she'd started to talk to herself. She mumbled something, which ended in her saying 'I'm sorry'.

'Pardon?' McCusker asked, fearing he'd failed to pick up something important.

'I mean, I don't want you to give the wrong idea and think was I speaking ill of Al. He's been a good friend to me and great company for me over the years. He's always been loyal to a fault.'

'We got that impression,' O'Carroll said, as they packed Louis' stuff into two box files they'd brought with them.

'A totally different man to Louis,' Elizabeth continued, as much to herself as to the detectives.

Then a few seconds later, as if hit by something she'd very quietly recalled, she said: 'I told you I was older than Louis, quite a bit older, in fact. I'm in my mid-sixties now. My parents disapproved of me marrying him. They had great plans for me and clearly wanted someone better, someone of our own station and breeding. When I wouldn't give in to their demands to dump Louis, they totally washed their hands of me. They both advised me that they wouldn't be attending the wedding. My mum actually said, although she often protested that it was an unintentional slip of the tongue – me, I'm still not so sure –

but the actual words she used were: "Your father and I won't be attending the *funeral*." My mum gave me £500 to buy my wedding dress, on the quiet, behind my father's back. I believe to this day it was her final way of insulting me and my husband-to-be. I'd always dreamed of a perfect wedding and I was determined my parents' mean-spiritedness would not get in the way of our happy day. I couldn't ask Louis for extra money for the wedding dress; he was already paying for the wedding. On top of which I was too ashamed of my parents to ask Louis. He would have just laughed a little, got out his chequebook and wrote me a blank cheque, but you'd never, ever know what he really thought. And who uses chequebooks these days anyway?'

'Oh, I believe we'll find McCusker here is not a stranger to that particular antiquated system,' O'Carroll cut in.

'So I found myself getting rather down about all of this and my best friend from university days, who had married well in London, sent me over a British Airways return ticket and invited me over for the weekend. That was the time when a weekend trip was rather a big thing, *the* thing, if you will. She was six months pregnant and claimed it would be her final night on the tiles before the birth. I went over on a Friday and the next day we went to the movies in Leicester Square – saw this great period drama, and I forget who the actress was, she was stunning. Anyway, she was at this ball, in this amazing backless, off-white gown and we immediately looked at each other, nodded and silently mouthed the words, "that's the perfect wedding dress."

'After the movie we'd quite a late liquid lunch. I was quite squiffy from all the white wine and she was high from the bubbles of her Pellegrino, and she pulled me into Simpsons as we were passing, and for a lark we went to look at their wedding dresses. We were fooling around, searching in vain for the £200 bargain-basement item, when we came across a gown almost identical to the one in the movie. We couldn't believe it. She said "You're just going to have to try it on", and following a brief faux protest, five minutes later we were both studying me in the wedding dress from the movie, in a full-length mirror. Then I came down to Earth with a bump as the realisation of my situation set in. My friend nipped off to check the baby department, to give me time to take off the gown. I was sitting there in the demo room, still with the gown on, elbows on knees, staring at myself in that mirror. But not *really* looking at myself. I was still a little drunk. I was feeling extremely sad about my plight and the fact that my parents didn't want me to marry Louis, and what a big disaster my wedding was going to be because everyone would notice that my parents weren't there. Then the manageress of the wedding department returned and brought me back down to Earth with an even bigger bang.

"'And what does madam think of the dress?" says she.

"Oh it's wonderful," says I.

"And will you be taking it?" says she.

"Oh but I wish that I could," says I.

"But *surely* you can," says she.

"I could never afford this," says I.

"But surely you can," says she.

"How much is it?' says I.

"£950," says she.

"Oh I'm really very sorry," says I, "I have to admit, I knew I could never afford it, but I saw the exact same dress in a movie earlier today and I fell in love with it, but I really should never have put it on."

"But surely, your father or husband?" says she.

'So I explain the whole situation to her about my mum and dad not approving of Louis, and them disowning me.

"'But surely you must have some budget?" says she, as if she'd been the recipient of an entire book full of "surelys" to distribute in that week's sentences.

'£200," says I.

'She looked me up and down. She looked around the demo room and then she came and sat down beside me and put her arm around my shoulder.

"Well then, it's your lucky day," says she. "This store is closing down shortly. It's not going to be announced until next week, but we're having a massive clearance sale starting on Monday next, so I can let you have this dress for your £200 budget and I'll just ring up the transaction on Monday morning."

'Well, I just burst into tears. Not over my plight, but more because I was so happy that it didn't matter how big a bunch of shits my parents were being to me, something bigger than that, than them, than all of us, wanted me to have that dress. Something more powerful than all that stupid domestic immaturity had brought me to London, to that movie, into that store, on that very day, with this particular, special shop assistant, to ensure that I would have my wedding dress,' Elizabeth Bloom said, then paused to draw a very large sigh before concluding: 'You know, when I think about that day, and I have to admit that I still do, and often – like this morning, for instance – that was most likely the happiest day of my life.'

O'Carroll was very quiet on the car ride back to Customs House.

'Don't be getting all gloomy on me,' McCusker eventually said to her, if only because he could not bear the silence between them.

'No, I wasn't,' she claimed, shaking herself out of whatever it was that had preoccupied her thoughts.

'There'll be someone…' McCusker said in a whisper, and cut himself short before mouthing "for you".

'No, no, that's not what I was thinking,' she said, nearly as quietly. "I was thinking how little distance we've come, where every wee girl has been brain-washed into thinking that their wedding day will be the most important part of their life and of what they will do with their lives. Total B.S.'

'Hymm.'

'Yeah, and I bet you were thinking that just because you've met my Grace, that you're all right Jack, and so now I'm the one to be pitied?'

'No, no, not at all,' McCusker protested, 'I was thinking it was painfully sad that Mrs Elizabeth Bloom had claimed that the day she got her wedding dress was the happiest day of her life.'

CHAPTER FIFTEEN

Back at his desk, McCusker set himself the task of discovering the name of the kissing student from Magherafelt High School. He doodled on his notepad, searching his brain for an idea.

O'Carroll, as ever, was working away diligently at her desk. Everyone else seemed to be able to get straight back into desk-work when they returned to the Customs House, but not him. He was still not as comfortable there as he'd been up in the Portrush nick. He liked to be out of the office talking to people – live, in person. He needed to look them in the eyes and see how they reacted. He felt he progressed far more quickly out on the street, rather than stuck at his desk, drowning in paperwork and research.

Then he started to think of Elizabeth Bloom and her sad wedding dress story. Elizabeth had also told O'Carroll (during their chat when McCusker was out walking around Botanic Gardens with Armstrong) how she and Louis had first met.

Elizabeth had been over in Belfast to stay with her sister, Angela, for a summer. She'd been to the Ulster Hall to see The Waterboys, who turned out to be Louis' favourite group – in fact, he liked The Beatles and The Waterboys, and that was really it. Angela also loved The Waterboys, and that was why Elizabeth was there. Elizabeth had accidentally dropped her ticket in the foyer and Louis had tapped her on the shoulder to reunite her with it. Angela had kept the conversation going and before Elizabeth had known it, she'd been deep in conversation with this charming younger man. They'd made a date to see each other the following week and, with said date, had set themselves off on the natural flow of their life path together.

McCusker started to really focus on the victim again, honing in on "a day in the life of Louis Bloom". He considered a typical day in the lecturer's early life, maybe around the time he first met Elizabeth.

McCusker tried to comprehend all the worrying Louis would have gone through – exams; girlfriends; family; finding employment to see him through university; securing his current job; making ends meet; his lecturers; his clothes; his look; his health and his money. Now all that mountain of worrying had just turned out to be a complete and utter waste of time. A waste of time, due to the simple fact that his life had been suspended – well, more like terminated, really – mid-season. Some person or persons unknown had upset the flow of the seasons to the extent that, in Louis' case, spring would no longer follow winter. And by ending Louis' rhythm of seasons, a person or persons unknown had put paid to all of Louis' energies, thoughts, dreams and worries. Not only that, but you could also say the same person or persons unknown had put paid to all the thoughts, energies, dreams and worries of several generations of the numerous branches on Bloom's complicated family tree, whose side of the bloodline would end with Louis. Surely that was why he and O'Carroll and the PSNI owed it to someone, or something, to remove the person or persons unknown from society so they may never, ever interfere with the essential rhythm of an unsuspecting person's seasons again.

Just as he was about to concentrate on tracing the pupil with the Magherafelt High School scarf, O'Carroll set her phone down.

'That was the Superintendent – he'll be down in ten minutes so that we can all have a catch-up session.'

* * *

'So where are we?' Larkin asked, the moment he strode into their office, looking quite dapper in the black, pin-striped trousers and waistcoat of his suit, with his clean, white shirt and one of his several multi-coloured striped ties. McCusker figured if he put enough thought into it he could most likely work out which day of the week it was solely based on Superintendent Larkin's tie.

McCusker was closest to the Perspex noticeboard that showcased the team's current notes, photographs and names, so he started re-calling the facts of the case as they currently stood.

'Okay. We still need to talk to Louis Bloom's brother, Miles, plus Professor Vincent Best, Harry and Sophie Rubens, and the Vice-Chancellor.'

'How are you getting on with piecing together the rest of Louis' day?' Larkin asked DS WJ Barr.

'Yep, making good progress, Sir – here's what we have so far.' Barr nodded at a section of the Perspex board beside McCusker.

<u>Louis Bloom's Thursday.</u>
07.30 Woke up, got out of bed, dragged a comb across his head
08.00 Breakfast at home
08.30 Left home
09.00 Already in his office when Leab David arrives
10.00–12.55 Louis working undisturbed in his office
12.55–13.30 ???
13.30–14.30 Lunch with Harry Rubens
14.45–15.00 Brief meeting with the Vice-Chancellor
15.00–15.15 Brief meeting with Ronald Desmond
15.30–15.50 Brief meeting with Professor Vincent Best
16.00–17.30 Personal meeting with ???
17.30–18.30 Back at office (18.30 estimate)
19.00 Home for dinner with Mrs Bloom
20.55 Takes rubbish bag out to bin

'We hope to have more info in by the end of the day,' Barr added, when it looked like Larkin had finished reading the list.

Barr was looking a little uncomfortable. McCusker wondered if he wasn't now having second thoughts about using The Beatles' lyric for the 7.30 entry. But Larkin most likely would be well aware that the entry wasn't due to a lack of respect; it was just one of the little things they all needed to do to deal with the darkness of the situation, yet still be able to function as humans.

'Any clues as to the ninety minutes he was missing yesterday afternoon, as discovered by DI O'Carroll and McCusker?' Larkin asked, proving he certainly wasn't dwelling on the merits of a Beatles lyric.

'Sorry, no,' Barr admitted, 'there's nothing showing up on Mr Bloom's credit card or iPad, Sir. I'm still trying to uncover the password to his email account. Hopefully there'll be something there.'

'Good, good,' Larkin offered in praise, 'going through our tried and tested procedures, that'll produce dividends for us.'

McCusker had the impression that Larkin knew it was much too early for results but was checking in with them just because he'd told someone – his wife, for instance – that he would. The detective felt he should offer something, anything.

'I don't think I've ever worked on a case before where the first three people we've interviewed – Armstrong, Desmond and Leab David – didn't have an alibi.'

'Taking anything from that?' Larkin asked, seeming happy at the scrap.

'No, not yet, but DI O'Carroll and I feel we do need to check out Al Armstrong some more.'

'Good, good, keep me posted – see you both at 7.00 for that other meeting,' Larkin replied, but this time addressing O'Carroll.

As Larkin walked out through the swinging office doors, DI Jarvis Cage bounced in, full of beans.

Three minutes later, Cage barked 'How do we even know he's missing?' on receiving what he felt was an unreasonable request from O'Carroll to partake in more than his fair share of his chores – that is to say, having to ring up the QUB Students' Union to check if Louis Bloom was a regular visitor to their building. Cage was still unaware that Louis Bloom had in fact been discovered, and was even dead. So unpopular was the lanky detective inspector that no one, including his immediate senior, DI O'Carroll, had seen fit to update him.

'Oh, just pretend that you're in a detective novel where you don't have to justify your actions,' O'Carroll snapped back, sounding like she was clearly running late for one of her legendary blind dates.

'What? What?' Cage perked up, looking like he felt he might have picked her up incorrectly. 'You mean this guy, Louis Bloom, is so famous they're going to do a cop TV show on this case?'

'But of course, sweetie,' O'Carroll replied, reeling Cage in slowly but securely.

'EX-CELL-ENT!' Cage replied, doing up his top button and tie.

'Sadly, at this stage the only part they've left to fill is one of the smelly corpse…' The end of her sentence was drowned out by the guffaws around the office.

'That was very unlike you,' McCusker offered five minutes later, when they were in the privacy of her Mégane.

'You don't mean to tell me that you feel sorry for that prat?'

'No, not that,' McCusker replied, aping the perfect timing of Ken Dodd, 'I mean using the word "sweetie".'

Just then McCusker's mobile phone chimed in with its unique war cry. McCusker claimed it was Finn McCool, although O'Carroll was convinced it was Tarzan. The detective went as white as a typical bed sheet on an Ulster clothes line. He made no replies excepting the initial, 'Yes.'

O'Carroll grew distracted at his silence.

Eventually he disconnected after saying, 'Okay.'

'Goodness, McCusker – you look like you've just seen the Grey Lady from Stranocum's Dark Hedges.'

'Worse than that,' McCusker whispered, 'I know this ghost – it's Anna Stringer!'

CHAPTER SIXTEEN

O'Carroll instinctively knew not to ask McCusker about his conversation with his ex-wife. Well, she wasn't officially his ex-wife yet, in that they'd never divorced – more like she'd just completely disappeared off the face of the Earth. He'd always, even during the years that they were together, referred to her as Anna Stringer, never as Anna McCusker.

Thankfully, McCusker didn't find it difficult to completely block her from his mind as he walked up the driveway to Superintendent Niall Larkin's humble, but stylish, home on the Bangor Road, just out past the George Best Airport.

He'd never been to the Super's house before. Yet, he figured that for some reason or other, Mrs Angela Larkin had decided that she was going to like McCusker in advance of meeting him. He didn't quite know why; maybe something to do with her husband (he hoped), but he was happy for it to be true, mainly due to the simple fact that sometimes in his life, the complete opposite was true. In fact, such was the case with Ethel Stringer, the mother of his estranged wife, who most certainly felt that her daughter was too good for McCusker. Mrs Stringer, in her defence, had always held that opinion. Equally at the opposite end of loath and love, and right from the get-go, Angela Larkin was fussing over him like a mother hen reunited with one of her own after a forced absence.

Mrs Larkin was equally warm to Lily O'Carroll; they clearly got on well and had an established banter that started off immediately with, 'So how are you getting on with your manhunt?'

'You mean Mr Louis Bloom's murderer?'

'No, actually I meant your enduring search for Mr Right?'

'Well, I'm just trying to make sure I get it right first time like you and the Superintendent did.'

Niall Larkin basked in the glory of that for a few seconds before his wife continued with 'So how come you allowed your sister to steal your boyo here from right under your nose?'

'Now, now, Angela,' her husband said, clearly trying to cut off Angela's subtle attempts at matchmaking at the pass. 'You promised me that the officers' personal lives would be out of bounds tonight.'

Angela smiled a "We'll let it go, for now" smile and then started to busy herself bringing out various dishes.

'We thought we'd have a light supper, just in case either of you were on the way to somewhere else,' she said, as she winked at O'Carroll and proceeded to set the dishes on the table.

The promised "light supper" fast became a mini feast as she carted out plates filled with: halloumi, fresh from the oven, baked crisp and nicely browned on top; slithers of hot toast with smashed avocado spread generously on top; hummus and hot pitta bread; and a generous supply of cocktail sausages, well-cooked to perfection, or at least to McCusker's taste. The Larkins enjoyed a glass of wine each but O'Carroll and McCusker politely declined, winning the desired Brownie points from their senior.

'Do you know this Armstrong fella?' O'Carroll started, as everyone seemed to have eaten their fill.

'What? That long, croaky, pipe-cleaner-like drink of water?!' Angela Larkin replied, without a moment's hesitation. 'He's nothing but an excuse for a human.'

'Now Angela… I don't think the phrase "long, croaky, pipe-cleaner-like drink of water" actually assists our two detectives in their investigation.'

'Okay, then how about a pothead, a dope dealer, a man who has never worked a day in his life. He's been on the dole for as long as I can remember and he's still never paid taxes and… and he's always scrounging off my sister.'

'Okay,' Larkin replied slowly, 'let's consider those, item by item. Have you ever actually seen him smoking pot?'

'Oh, he's much too cute to let me see him; he knows I'm much too loyal to you not to report him.'

'Has Elizabeth ever seen him smoke pot?' Larkin said, continuing the interrogation of his wife.

'Not just that, Niall, she also said he's actually *shared* some with her! She claims it helps her lumbago!'

'Sadly, that's just hearsay.'

'Has he actually been done for dealing dope,' O'Carroll ventured, seeing a possible angle.

'No,' Larkin admitted.

'But he did tell Elizabeth he was thrown out of his beat group because he was supplying his *friends* with pot, and the band manager was scared of unwanted attention from the drug squad.'

'Okay, next point,' Larkin started, 'admittedly he's been on the dole for a while–'

'For... ever...' came Angela's hasty interruption.

'I'll give you that...'

'Says his asthma means he can't get a proper job,' Angela chipped back in, with all the perfect double-act timing of Morecambe & Wise.

'But...' O'Carroll said, willing onwards.

'But yet he makes an absolute fortune from doing up those properties and selling them on. And he boasts that he never pays a penny in taxes.'

'If he registers them as his prime residence then he's allowed to sell them without paying taxes,' Mr Larkin offered.

'Yes, that was fine when he was buying them as a wreck, moving into them, doing them up, selling them on at a profit, buying another dilapidated house and doing it up, and on and on,' Angela protested. 'Actually, Elizabeth claims he's very, very good at it. Says he's a real handy man and is always doing thing around Landseer Street for her... where was I...?'

'You were about to climb up on your soapbox and give us one of your "if every person who didn't pay taxes, paid their taxes, then the rest of us wouldn't have to pay anywhere near as much tax" rants, Angela.'

'Oh yes, I remember,' she said, completely ignoring her husband, 'but then he got that wee house over in Camden Road.'

'Bigger than our house,' Larkin cut in on his wife, in good humour.

'I won't move from here, Niall, you know that by now. So, Armstrong moves into Camden Road, to all intents and purposes makes it his permanent home, yet he still continues to renovate properties for great profit.'

'Again, Angela, he can nominate any of his properties.'

'I know, I know, Niall,' she admitted, 'I just get so annoyed at scroungers, people who scrounge on the country yet they're the first to complain about it! If I ever find out that he's scrounging off our Elizabeth, I'll, I'll…' Angela stumbled over her answer, 'I just can't think of anything severe enough to do to Mr Al Armstrong.'

'I'd say by the pitch of his voice someone has already beaten you to it and done the obvious,' McCusker offered.

There was much laughter from around the table.

'Do you think now that Louis has passed, that Elizabeth and Mr Armstrong will resume their university romance?' McCusker asked, clocking what looked like relief on the Superintendent's face and hoping it meant he was happy with the change in direction.

'You don't mean to say you think that could be the motive?' Angela asked, as she seemed to consider this for a moment. 'No, our Elizabeth isn't that daft.'

'Did Louis and Elizabeth have a regular place they visited on their holidays?' McCusker asked, still searching, for something, anything.

'They never went on holiday,' Angela said regretfully, 'Louis, with all his travels, didn't have time to take *his wife* on holiday.'

'Did–' McCusker started, without having thought through his question properly.

'Elizabeth and *Armstrong,* however, did like their wee Ulsterbus trips – you know, weekends all over the South and Scotland. She loved them – separate rooms, of course,' Angela added, going to great pains to point out the sleeping arrangements.

'Do you know a Miss or Mrs Mariana Fitzgerald?' McCusker asked.

'I've heard the name – how does she fit in?'

'Who is she?' Larkin asked his wife.

'Augh, you know, Niall, she's the one with the really long hair…'

'Oh yes, I remember that night at the Queens fundraiser for the new library.'

'Yes, that's the one. She knew Louis. I don't know how she knew him.'

'She has a friend,' McCusker tried, 'her name might be Muriel – do you know her?'

'No, we were never even properly introduced to Mariana. I think she's a Mrs, not a Miss. Yes, in fact she is. I remember her husband now – a much older man. He was there with her that night. He's in banking or investments – family money apparently. I'd be very surprised if Louis and Ronald Desmond weren't trying to tap him up that night for a few bob. Oh yes, that's right, Niall, you remember that was the night Louis and Ronald also tried to tap you up for a few bob for the library?'

'Oh yes, of course,' Larkin said, as he and his wife broke into a fit of the giggles.

'Oh go on,' Angela encouraged her husband, 'you tell them.'

'Well, they asked me – at the table, in front of everyone – if I was going to make a donation to the library,' Larkin started, as Angela was now absolutely roaring with laughter. 'So I said, yes, that I felt libraries were a very worthy cause and I would definitely like to make a donation. And they both got excited and asked me – again, in front of everyone – what they could put me down for. Clearly the intention was to, you know–'

'… to try to embarrass Niall into keeping up with the Jones's by matching the other donations,' Angela explained, on behalf of her husband.

'So I considered it for a few seconds and said, "Well I've thought about it and I feel it should be something substantial, something worthy of a great library…'

'All this time Desmond and Louis were growing increasingly excited about the prospect of reeling in another donor,' Angela continued. 'And so Niall said…'

'…and so I said that I would like to donate my complete set of 46 paperback editions of all the Dick Francis books.'

More joyous laughter around the table – mostly, it had to be said, from Angela.

'Now that was funny,' Angela offered, clearly proud of her husband, 'and well Louis, God rest his soul, saw the funny side of it and had a great laugh with the rest of us, but Ronald Desmond, well, let's just say he wasn't best pleased at all.'

'Fair play to you,' McCusker offered, still chuckling. 'Angela, did Elizabeth ever share any worries she had about Louis with you?'

'For instance?'

'I'm thinking of him having a bad falling out with anyone? Money troubles? Owing anyone money, you know?' McCusker was fishing around as best he could.

'No, they were always fine for money. One thing about my sister - and this has always been the way between us since our pre-teens - she would always reach out to me if anything were troubling her. Like when Louis went missing last night – she didn't sit stewing in her house, worrying all night long. No, she rang me pretty quickly. And she knows I'd always rely on her in the same way.'

'Did, say…' McCusker began, before he'd a proper question formulated, 'did Louis ever invest in any business or in any friend's start-up projects?'

'Louis would often tell me he'd no time for investing; he saw it as a form of gambling,' Larkin replied. 'We discussed it quite a bit over the years – the way he told it to me, it had nothing to do with risk. No, he always said that his father had worked too hard for him to come along and just waste it.'

'Please forgive me for asking this…' O'Carroll started.

'Please, ask away – Niall has already advised me you're only going to ask very personal questions. He also said you would only ask questions you feel you need the answer to.'

This gave O'Carroll the confidence to continue. 'Did Elizabeth ever confide in you that Louis had an affair?' She looked relieved to have got it all out in one go.

'No she didn't, but…' Angela paused, 'she said they hadn't lived as man and wife for years, and she wouldn't be surprised if he needed to. But she really didn't want to know and for Louis' part, well, there was never, ever any gossip about him and other women.'

'What about Elizabeth, did she ever–'

'No, I don't believe she did and I also believe if she did, she'd have a very difficult time not telling me about it. Perhaps that's why she and Armstrong are such great chums. You know, he ticks all the friendship and companionship boxes without having to…'

'Tell me this, Mrs Larkin: do think that Elizabeth and he ever…?' McCusker said, hoping he was sparing his senior's blushes.

'Let me tell you this, boyo, if Elizabeth – or any woman, for that matter – ever came on to Armstrong, he'd have been out of there quicker than a pink balloon rising from the bottom of the swimming pool.'

'Do you think Armstrong is gay?

'If any man ever said to Armstrong "Come on, babe, follow me I'm your Pied Piper", he'd have set off out of there like a bat outta hell and wouldn't have stopped until he was at the top of Napoleon's Nose.'

No laughs from the four, but hints of a smile. What McCusker did find funny though, was the fact that both Angela and her sister had used the same simile. Obviously it was something they'd discussed before.

'Do you really think there's a chance that Al Armstrong could be involved in Louis' disappearance and death?' O'Carroll asked.

'Personally speaking, I would bet money that it would be an impossibility for him. So, if he was involved it would only be if he'd hired an assassin,' Larkin replied.

That was pretty much as far as they got discussing the case. They went around the houses with different topics for about half an hour or so and then proceedings came to a natural end.

On the doorstep as they were saying their farewells, Angela Larkin invited McCusker to 'Return soon, in the not-too-distant future, with Grace, for a more relaxing evening'. Hoping to avoid a potential faux-pas she added quickly, 'And you should come too, Lily.'

'That would certainly be entertaining,' O'Carroll replied on the doorstep, while ninety seconds later, in the security of her car, she belatedly added, 'what, and have me play the part of a gooseberry?' She paused before adding sing-song style 'I don't think so!' Another pause while she started the car before offering 'Which reminds me; Grace said if we were done by 10.00, I was to drop you off at her place.' O'Carroll looked like she was going to say something else but she laughed instead.

'Sorry, what?'

'Actually, what she really said was: if we were done *by midnight*, to drop off, but you see that just created too visual a scenario for me and maybe even showed her off in a bad light.'

'Meaning?'

'Well, you're hardly going to go around to her flat at midnight just to lament Trump and Brexit or even watch the Stephen Nolan show, now are you?'

'Okay... I got you now,' McCusker said, back-pedalling as fast as he knew how. 'Actually we wanted to watch *Newsnight* together, you know, just to catch up with current affairs.'

'Yeah right,' she said, grinning at herself and muttering something under her breath that sounded like, 'more like *carnal* affairs if you ask me.' Whatever it was she said, it caused her immense self-amusement.

CHAPTER SEVENTEEN

The thing McCusker found about Grace O'Carroll, and he'd admitted this to no one but himself, was that she inspired unquenchable lust in him.

They ended up in bed quite quickly – actually, more like *on* the bed. Grace loved to lie on top of the bed talking, chatting about anything and everything that came to mind. The upside for McCusker was that he got to view her for ages in her delightful, sensible, but equally sensual underwear. The other thing about Grace O'Carroll was that she really didn't realise how beautiful she was. Nor did she realise how big a turn-on it was to be so physically close to her. McCusker had never really experienced these sensations before.

Tonight's topic was looks, and what attracts men to women and equally women to men. Grace playfully asked McCusker what it was he thought he possessed that might attract women to him.

He thought long and hard, for he was desperate to find something that could delay their inevitable (he hoped) encounter.

'The only thing I can remember is from my high school days, when this girl said to me that she thought I had beautiful long eyelashes. I wasn't even confident enough to know if she meant the eyelashes were both "beautiful" and "long", or if the word "beautiful" referred to the word "long", in that my eyelashes were "beautifully long".'

'Awwh' she said, as she climbed over him to get a better look at his eyelashes. She said something that he couldn't quite make out. She looked deep into his eyes. He couldn't believe that he could be so close to this beautiful, wholesome being. The absolutely tangible, physical charge of her body made him shudder with pure, unbridled lust every time he was close to her. Sometimes he didn't need to be so close; late at night, the memory of her was enough to make him involuntarily tremor as he tried to fall asleep.

She leaned over McCusker and kissed him on his eyelids and in doing so released the beautiful elusive butterfly of their passion. They mutually set off to chase it – never quite catching it, but ecstatic when it managed to escape them, so they could set of on another chase, until… eventually, the butterfly would willingly surrender.

Another major thing about Grace was that McCusker found she was equally attractive and appealing *after* they'd chased the butterfly, as she had been just before.

Something very special had just happened between them, but he was too reserved to talk about it.

Grace, still breathing heavily, said 'That was just so good, most likely due to the fact that you weren't performing – you weren't pre-occupied with your performance. Neither was I. We were just so… together. It was wonderful. I have never before felt what I just experienced. It was always just "sex". And before you get too big-headed, can I just say that there was some fantastic sex, too, but… that was something altogether entirely different. What we just did, it's not that it was different… maybe it was spiritual. I don't know, but I do know that most certainly the mechanics of the process were missing from my mind… maybe that was… I don't even want to say it.'

'I… I…', McCusker started hesitantly. He couldn't remember ever expressing these feelings before, but after their experience, he felt he needed to. 'I never, ever felt anything like that before… it was like…'

'Don't you ever tell our Lily about any of this,' she interrupted, before he'd a chance to properly articulate what was in his heart. 'In one way, it's quite embarrassing.'

'Why on Earth–'

'No, no, nothing like that,' she tried to reassure him. 'It's because it came out of nowhere. I wasn't expecting anything as wonderful or as beautiful as that.'

McCusker visibly relaxed.

'I… I don't feel…' she continued, 'oh…'

They stopped talking and clung on to each other like their lives depended on it, and woke up in the exact same embrace the following morning. Instead of being embarrassed about the precious thing they had been through with each other the previous evening, they were comfortable with it – so much so, in fact, that they embraced it once more.

Chapter Eighteen

Day Two: Friday

McCusker, at Grace's suggestion, had some stuff – as in fresh shirts, clean underwear, toiletries etc. – stored at her flat, mainly because she didn't want McCusker going straight to his office any morning and her sister seeing that he'd stayed overnight.

'But more importantly,' she'd added, 'I don't want you not staying just because you feel you can't get straight to the office from here.' Besides, it wasn't a major problem because the majority of times they slept together, it was at his quaint "student" accommodation up on University Square Mews, just off Botanic Avenue.

O'Carroll was already in the office by the time McCusker arrived. As usual DS WJ Barr, was also in residence and hard at work.

'So, McCusker,' O'Carroll started, 'how was *Newsnight*?'

'Sorry?'

'My mother always used to tell Grace and me that if we were going to tell lies we needed to make sure we had perfect memories.'

McCusker just looked at her, the question mark still large upon his face. She'd distracted him somewhat by mentioning Grace's name.

'Come on, man,' she smiled, 'I dropped you off at Grace's yesterday evening so you could watch *Newsnight* with her?'

'Oh yes, sorry – by the time I got there she was already watching a movie.'

'Yeah, she loves those old black and white classics, doesn't she?'

'Yeah, but there's something quite charming about them,' McCusker offered, happy he'd pulled it off.

'Agng nagh,' she puffed, sounding like a foghorn, 'wrong answer.

Grace hates black and white movies with a passion! She's always saying when these so-called stylised directors insist on shooting their new films in monochrome, someone should point out to them that, even before colour TV and movies existed, the world still existed in *full colour*. So Grace's point was that these directors should do us all a big favour – keep it real and shoot it in colour!'

McCusker hoaked around in his bottom drawer, if only in the hope that O'Carroll wouldn't catch him grimacing.

'So, let's get stuck into this. I need to get off early tonight,' O'Carroll said, thankfully now bored of her ribbing.

'Who's the lucky candidate?'

O'Carroll actually shocked McCusker by pulling out a five-by-three cue card from the inside pocket of her jacket. She brazenly read the card details:

'Name: Sean Niblock

Age: 38

Description: 5-foot 10-inches tall, black hair, own teeth

Status: Single

Children: None

Accommodation: Own flat

Mortgage: Not known

Employment: Freelance Consultant in the package-holiday business

Salary: Don't know but see "Car" details below

Car: Jaguar F-Type

Interests: Cars

Recommendation: He's my hairdresser's brother.'

'As you would say, "Colour me impressed!" You've got this auditioning process down to a fine art now, haven't you?' McCusker offered, in praise at the conclusion of her enthusiastic delivery.

'Yes, but of course. Well, you have to, don't you,' she replied, tapping the card against her chin before replacing it in her pocket again. 'I have a good feeling about Sean, he seems… well, let's not tempt fate, eh?'

'And if you come in one day and your hair's a mess, I'll know it didn't work out.'

'And if I don't come in one day, you'll know I've gone off with Sean on one of his package holidays!'

'I'll be rooting for you,' McCusker offered, genuinely meaning it.

'Good. So let's get into this,' she continued seamlessly, clearly throwing small talk into touch. 'What's on our board for today?'

'I thought a good starting point would be Harry and Sophie Rubens,' McCusker offered. 'They seem to have been good friends to Louis. Then I need to visit Ron Desmond again, then Professor Vincent Best, then the Vice-Chancellor. Hopefully we'll fill in a bit more of the picture on Louis from those interviews and will be in a better position to meet the "troubled brother". How do you want to divide it up?'

'Well, you and I can get stuck into that together, and WJ and the team can hold the fort here. The autopsy results should be in soon and WJ wanted to revisit the scene of the crime.'

'Yep, I'm on it,' Barr agreed, 'but you both realise, don't you, that DI Jarvis Cage is in fact my senior?'

'Yes, of course,' O'Carroll agreed, 'but no one seems to have told him that yet, so let's keep that as our little secret, shall we.'

* * *

When they walked into his office in the Neo-Georgian, David Keir Building on the Stranmillis Road, the first thing that struck McCusker about Harry Rubens was how young he was. It was just something about the names *Harry* and *Sophie Rubens*, and maybe even that they were always mentioned together, that led McCusker to assume they were going to be an old couple. But Harry Rubens looked so sharp, so cool, so young and so hip, he could have made the wallpaper turn around and sneak a peek at him.

'I've been expecting you guys,' Rubens said, as he shook both their hands enthusiastically.

McCusker had a theory that everyone – especially professionals – seemed so well groomed these days. It was as though before they even ventured out of their homes in the morning, they prepared themselves for a possible TV appearance. Harry Rubens proved McCusker's theory in spades.

'Shall I text Sophie to meet us here?' he asked, still clearly buzzed.

'It's probably better we see her after you,' O'Carroll said, making it sound like a request rather than a demand. 'From what we've been told, you were both very good friends of Louis', so we'll probably pick up more if we talk to you both separately.'

'So shall I get her to come here in half an hour, say 10.30?' Harry Rubens continued, undeterred.

'Sounds good,' O'Carroll said, 'but maybe have her meet us at Louis' office at 10.45.'

Rubens' office was a complete contrast to Louis' office. While Louis office was very Zen and uncluttered, Rubens' office, like the man, was very buzzy, busy and packed to the rafters with stuff. He'd a kind of a den area in the back, with no windows, dim lighting, a brown sofa and two mismatched easy chairs.

Harry Rubens, in his ultra-back-supported, desk-chair-on-wheels propelled (with feet power) his way over to a small fridge and shouted back, 'What's your poison?' He then whizzed back to them even more quickly, with a still mineral water for O'Carroll, a Perrier for McCusker and a chilled Coke Zero for himself. 'Since they,' he continued, nodding at his bottle, 'sponsored our Belfast Bikes, you feel obliged to support them don't you?' he offered, by way of justification.

Neither McCusker nor O'Carroll felt obliged to agree.

'How long had you known Louis Bloom?' O'Carroll asked, after a polite sip.

'I met Louis and Sophie on my first day here, eight years ago, September 27th past.'

'Oh,' O'Carroll started in surprise, 'so Sophie and Louis already knew each other?'

'Yes they did,' Harry replied, through a large smile, 'yes they did.'

'Okay, let's see now; if I understand this correctly,' McCusker interrupted, 'Louis and Sophie were an item before you and Sophie were married?'

Harry laughed out loud, and warmly.

'No, Louis and Elizabeth were already married when he met Sophie. Sophie started here a year before me. She and Louis met on a music department committee to rename the McMordie Hall. I think she met him very briefly at one of his talks, but the first time they worked together was on that committee.'

'Did Louis introduce you to Sophie?' O'Carroll asked.

'Yes, he did,' Harry offered in agreement, 'yes, he did.'

'Do you remember how youse all came to meet?' O'Carroll continued, appearing keen to follow this thread.

McCusker figured it was most likely research for her ongoing dating venture.

'Yes, of course. The Vice-Chancellor suggested I call in with Louis – he said he thought we'd get on well and that Louis knew all the short-cuts around the campus, geographically and politically speaking.

'When I happened to drop by his office that first morning, Louis, Leab and Sophie were all enjoying a morning coffee and a catch-up. They were all very sociable and shared a little of each of their coffees with me. They admitted they were being selfish, saying it would make it my turn next time.'

'So you and Sophie…' McCusker struggled, but he knew O'Carroll really wanted to know, so he spared her the embarrassment, 'hit it off?'

'Well, actually what happened was, about half an hour later Louis was about to start his morning session, which he's very precious about, and so Sophie – as she'd some spare time, and to save having Louis throw us all out – offered to show me around campus. There was something about her that I liked from the first moment I saw her. She's a very special person; you'll see when you meet her later. Gary Mills had already given me a tour of the campus, but I never let on about this to Sophie, in order that I could spend some time with her. So off we went on our tour, walking and talking. And we've been walking and talking ever since – actually, there's been quite a bit of laughing thrown in as well.'

McCusker knew that O'Carroll was dying for him to ask Harry Rubens what it was about Sophie that had attracted him so much. But he couldn't find a comfortable way to go there, so instead he said, 'so the three of you became good friends?'

'Yes, we did,' Harry said, smiling, 'yes, we did.'

'Have you met Al Armstrong?' McCusker asked, deciding it was about time to get into the interview proper.

'A few times,' Harry said, the permanent smile definitely ebbing a little. 'Mr Armstrong is more of Elizabeth's friend than Louis'.'

'Did Louis ever talk to you about Armstrong?'

Rubens' hesitation confirmed that he probably had.

'Look,' he began, 'I know you have to ask all these questions to try and find out what happened to Louis, and Sophie and I will certainly do all we can. We're agreed with each other that we're going to be very candid with you in all of our answers. But, I'd like your assurance our information won't be used maliciously.'

McCusker wasn't exactly sure what the lecturer meant, but O'Carroll must have fully understood, because she gave an immediate agreement.

'Okay,' Rubens started, clearly assured. 'Al… it's my understanding that Al smokes a lot of pot. I don't really understand what exactly goes on between Elizabeth and him. Louis was convinced that there was nothing physical about the relationship. But they are as inseparable as Harland and Wolff were. When I spoke to Elizabeth yesterday evening – Sophie and I dropped around to express out condolences – we asked her if there was anything that we could do to help and she said that she was fine and that her sister and Armstrong were looking after her. Louis did voice his concern that Armstrong might be trying to fleece Elizabeth. He was always doing odd jobs around the house for her, but he charged her, and Louis felt he was charging top dollar. He asked Elizabeth to get receipts from Armstrong for his work.'

'And did she?' O'Carroll asked.

'No. I mean she certainly asked Armstrong the next time she paid him in cash for a job for a receipt, and she reported to Louis that Armstrong had complained "That'll take all the good out of it". Meaning, I assume, that he didn't want to declare it.'

'We believe that Armstrong is on the dole and he doesn't pay tax on his refurbishment work?'

'So I believe,' Rubens replied, 'but surely in this day and age he can't get away without paying taxes? You know, could it maybe just have been the idle boast of an armchair socialist?'

'Surely a socialist is willing to pay tax?' O'Carroll cut in.

'I believe socialists *are* willing…' Harry offered, through a smile he, McCusker guessed, had perfected in front of his students, 'for other people to pay taxes.'

O'Carroll reluctantly let it go.

'You don't believe that Armstrong murdered Louis, do you?'

'Do *you*?' McCusker quizzed, in return.

'I can't think of a motive,' Rubens replied, slowly, as if he was genuinely searching for a reason. 'I can't think of a motive. You know, unless Louis caught him out on something…'

'Something like…?' McCusker ventured, intrigued by Rubens' reply.

'Well, there was some talk of Armstrong dealing pot, but "just for his friends".' As he said this, he used a finger from each hand to signal quotation marks.

'But wasn't that years ago when he was in a group?' O'Carroll suggested.

'Ah no, apparently not – apparently earlier on this year.'

'Does Armstrong have many friends?'

'I don't really know, to be honest, but Louis was convinced his only real friend was Elizabeth.'

'So how could he then be meant to be dealing dope for his friends?' O'Carroll asked.

'Well, that was kinda Louis' point,' Rubens said, and paused in consideration before starting back up with 'let's assume that Armstrong and Elizabeth are really good friends; could it have been in his interest – I'm talking financially now – to get rid of Louis? Louis, as you have probably discovered by now, was a man of considerable wealth. Will all that wealth go to Elizabeth and might that wealth cause Armstrong to be interested in being *more* of a friend?'

Even if Elizabeth was considering a scenario like that, McCusker was convinced that Angela Larkin, not to mention her husband, would aggressively council against it.

'Did Louis ever confide that he was worried about anything, you know, personal threats?' McCusker asked.

'No nothing like that at all.'

'Did he have any enemies?' O'Carroll asked.

'Oh, I'm sure there would be a few fellows on campus who would have been jealous of Louis' position, where he could pretty much get any projects he wanted green-lit,' Harry Rubens said and laughed. 'But that would be more of an Agatha Christie plot, wouldn't it? I think we're most likely looking at more of a Morse-type subversion, aren't we? Please forgive me,' Rubens pleaded the moment the words had left his mouth, 'I didn't mean, in the circumstances, to be so frivolous.

To be quite honest with you, I'm having a problem accepting that he's gone. I still find myself expecting Louis to, quite literally, walk through my door at any minute.'

'You had lunch with him yesterday?' O'Carroll asked, flicking back through a few pages in her notebook.

'Yes, I did,' Rubens confirmed, 'yes, I...' That was as far as he got. He tried to get more words out but he just couldn't. His eyes welled up. He bit his lip, he tried to stop the emotion rising up inside of him but he just couldn't. He slowly walked back over to his desk and took some tissues from a box and, keeping his back to the detectives, dabbed his eyes. 'I'm sorry...' he started, but again his emotions proved to be his master.

'It's okay, Harry,' O'Carroll offered, sympathetically.

Rubens walked back over to them and sat back in his chair. His eyes were very teary. He blew a large gasp out when he clearly felt those tears coming again. This time he kept them at bay by using his tongue to do a couple of circumferences of his lips.

'I'm really sorry,' he said slowly, as though testing himself. 'I'm really sorry.'

'It's okay.'

'It was just, when you said I had lunch with him yesterday I suddenly realised that was the last time I was ever going to see him, and that's the first time I'd harboured such a thought. I didn't think I'd be so emotional with the PSNI here – I expected to do that with my wife but not the PSNI.'

'You know, we can break for a while if you'd like?' O'Carroll offered.

'Oh no, no,' he protested, 'no, really, I'm happy to continue; I know how important it is you get as much of this background information as quickly as possible.'

'Right,' McCusker said, accepting how difficult it was for a man to cry in front of another man and thinking everyone seemed so willing and keen to give them as much information as they had and as quickly as possible, 'what time did you meet?'

'He came by here at 1; we chewed the fat for about twenty minutes, walked down to Café Conor together, had lunch between 1.30 to 2.30.'

'How did he seem at the lunch?'

'He really seemed fine. You know Louis – fussy eater, complained about too much salt on his meat, that he couldn't find a *Tele* that wasn't creased.'

'What did you chat about?'

'You know, just a couple of good mates chatting. I told him what I'd been up to. Sophie and I are heading off to Dublin for a long weekend and he'd tipped us off on what he felt was the best room in the Fitzgerald Hotel. You know, just stuff like that. He told me what he'd been working on that morning.'

'What had he been working on that morning?' McCusker asked.

'Well, he was a bit excited. He'd had a bit of a breakthrough on his work that morning. He… he, even at his age, was still trying to figure out what it was that attracted people to each other. The "beauty is only skin-deep" rule didn't apply to him. He maintained that some of us simply have the ability to see the true beauty in others, whereas others are blinded by certain predetermined prejudices. He also believed that we subconsciously know when someone else is attracted to us and that, in itself, is an attraction. He still had work to do on it, but he'd broken the back of the task that morning.'

O'Carroll was still scribbling away a minute or so after Harry finished talking.

'Miles Bloom,' McCusker announced to break the silence, 'what can you tell us about Louis' brother, Miles?'

'Well, we talked about Miles quite a bit over the years,' Rubens admitted, 'and I sometimes thought the big thing with Miles was that Louis wasn't so much intrigued that someone would want to walk up Slieve Gullion on a daily basis. No, Louis could kind of get that. What he couldn't get his head round, though, was the fact that Miles not only wanted to do the climb on his hands and knees, but that he'd also insist on doing it with a boulder strapped to his back.'

'So are you saying there was no strife between them?' McCusker asked.

'Oh, there was strife between them all right. Miles most likely had a wee doll dressed up to look like Louis, and my guess is that it wasn't so much he was sticking pins in it, but more that he was hammering nails right through it.'

'Do you know what was behind the hatred?'

'Oh yes, everyone did,' Harry said. 'It wasn't a big secret, everyone knew about it.'

'And it was?' O'Carroll prompted.

'Basically it all stemmed from the fact that Louis' father, Sidney, left all his money and property to Louis.'

'Was the hatred mutual?' McCusker asked, taking up the questioning again.

'No, Louis felt sorry for Miles.'

'But not sorry enough to redress the balance and gift Miles some of the money?' O'Carroll asked.

'He did think about it, believe me,' Rubens said, with a gentle smile, 'but he didn't want to go against his father's final wishes and, more importantly, he knew Miles would blow it all in a matter of months and be back looking for more.'

'Why would Miles think he was entitled to some, if not all of his father's estate?' McCusker asked.

'Miles was the older brother, and the eldest son usually–'

'-usually gets the majority of the estate,' McCusker said, finishing Rubens' line for him.

'Was Miles equally at loggerheads with the staff his father had willed all his business to?' O'Carroll asked.

'Oh, he spent a considerable amount of money in the courts with that one as well. But the father had foreseen such an outcome and had made everything watertight. But to answer your original question, he seemed to reserve all of his personal hatred and anger for his brother.'

'Could Miles' anger have been severe enough that he could have done harm to Louis?' McCusker asked.

'Well, that's the question everyone is asking.'

'And what do you think?'

'Candidly?'

It was a weird question to ask a policeman investigating a murder.

'Yes, of course, we'll be discreet,' O'Carroll agreed.

'Well, I certainly think he was unhinged, and Sophie and I always cautioned Louis to be careful. But at the same time, I've always thought that if Miles had done anything to harm Louis, then surely it would just put the family money even further away from him.'

'Fair point,' McCusker said. 'And before we leave Miles Bloom for now, are you sure there is nothing that happened or that you are aware of which would point a direct finger at Miles?'

'Well, Elizabeth would be a better person to speak to about that, as she witnessed several of the incidents.'

'Okay,' McCusker said, hopefully signalling they were going to draw a line under that for now. 'Do you know a lady by the name of Mariana Fitzgerald?'

'Yes I do,' he replied with a smile, 'yes I do.'

McCusker nodded at Harry Rubens in a, "Yes, and?" kind of way.

"Well Sophie is the real connection; she is a friend of Mariana's husband.'

'What can you tell me about her?'

'That's probably a better question for Sophie – she knows her better.'

'What about another friend of Mariana's? A lady who might have been called Muriel, or maybe something similar?'

'That would be Murcia.'

'O-kay,' McCusker replied, very happy to at least now have her proper name. 'Was she also a friend of Louis'?'

'Again, that's a good question for Sophie. I believe she, Mariana and Murcia have enjoyed a few girls' nights out.'

'That's nearly it,' McCusker said, feeling that he already knew the answer to at least part of his final question of the session. 'Finally, what were you doing last night, between the hours of 9.00 p.m. and 1.00 a.m.?'

'Let's see now,' Harry Rubens started slowly, 'let's see now. I was here from about 7.00 until about midnight.'

'Really?' McCusker said involuntarily, expecting that Harry and Sophie would be each other's alibi.

'Yes, what's so strange about that?'

'You were here, that whole time?'

'Yes… sorry, I mean no. I nipped out at about 8.00 to Smokey Joe's, you know, the chippy on Camden Street?… for one of those treats – a fish supper, fish and chips by another name, the fish in really crispy batter, forbidden, unhealthy and quite possibly, necessary indulgences. You know, you really should avoid the calories but sometimes they're purely irresistible. I got back here about twenty minutes later with my fish supper and I'd a wee glass of Sancerre – I keep a bottle in the fridge for such occasions.'

'So you would have got back here around 8.20?'

'Maybe, I wasn't clock-watching – could have been a bit earlier, could have been a bit later?'

'Did anyone see you en route?'

'No one I recognised.'

'Tell me this, Mr Rubens,' McCusker asked, 'do you use that particular chippy a lot?'

'Well, hopefully not a lot, but yes, I do occasionally go there.'

'Do you go there often enough that some of the staff would recognise you?'

'I would imagine so,' Rubens replied, 'I would imagine so. It's a family business. Ernie's the guv'nor – he always says hello to me and I believe at least a couple of them would know me.'

'So you left here around midnight,' McCusker said, 'then where did you go?'

'I went home.'

'Which is where?' O'Carroll asked.

'We live on campus in the Elms Village.'

'And was Sophie awake when you arrived home?'

'No, she wasn't,' he replied, 'no, she wasn't. I went to bed and when I woke up this morning she was already downstairs preparing our muesli.'

'Okay,' O'Carroll said, putting her pink notebook away, 'that'll do us for now.'

CHAPTER NINETEEN

As they were walking down Stranmillis Road, past the chunky Ulster Museum, on the way to the Lanyon Building and Louis Bloom's office, McCusker said: 'You know, Harry Rubens was walking down, or up, here at around a similar time as Louis Bloom was taking his rubbish out.'

'Yes,' O'Carroll replied, in a tone that suggested her mind was elsewhere. 'You know, Harry Rubens was perfectly turned out, don't you think?'

'I suppose it's all a matter of taste,' McCusker replied, fearing where this was going.

'You know, you could do worse than adopt the new casual dress sense, whereby it isn't necessary to wear a suit and tie every day.'

'But I like wearing suits and ties,' McCusker complained. 'I'm not really a fan of the way people wear wrinkled clothes these days.'

'Be quiet, will you, for heaven's sake, we're in public,' she hissed, 'sure they're designer wrinkles, and very expensive at that.'

'And you call me weird!' he said, as they arrived at Louis Bloom's office.

O'Carroll let McCusker go in by himself, while she remained outside the door so she could make a call on her mobile.

'Ah, Inspector McCusker, your sergeant said you'd be by,' Leab David offered the second he walked through the door. She appeared very happy to see him.

This time he took pains to explain to her that he wasn't exactly an officer of the PSNI, but was hired from the Grafton Agency on a freelance basis. So frequently did he need to point this out, as per PSNI regulations, that he really was thinking of getting the information printed up on a wee card that he could hand out to people.

'I've a wee favour to ask you,' McCusker continued, knowing from the blank look on her face that he'd lost her at "officer": 'I wonder if you would have access to a student register?'

'Yes indeed, who are you looking for?'

'Well, I don't know his name but I know he came from Magherafelt High School?'

'Okay, I wouldn't have that information to hand but I think I know a way to uncover it – can you give me until this afternoon? I've got a pile of stuff I need to do.'

'Perfect,' McCusker replied, just as a proper member of the PSNI, DI Lily O'Carroll, walked through the door with a strange looking girl-woman.

'This is my colleague, McCusker,' O'Carroll started off, by way of introduction. 'McCusker, this is Mrs Sophie Rubens.'

Mrs Sophie Rubens looked like she was too young to be a Mrs. She was unsymmetrical and her crow-feathered hairstyle looked like an artist had drawn it on her head. She wore a long, bottle green neck-to-ankle smock-cum-habit affair, which was waisted with a pencil thin, shiny black leather belt.

'Was your husband okay when you stopped by to see him on your way over here to meet us?' McCusker tried, punting a long one. 'He was quite upset when we left him.'

She paused for a second, thereby confirming that, in fact, she had quickly been to see her husband for a catch-up before proceeding to her own interview.

She winked at McCusker, who quickly came to realise that Sophie always winked at you in place of nodding agreement or saying yes.

'He was okay,' she said, 'he's going through a bit of a bad tine at the moment.' Then, after a pause, she quickly added 'We all are.'

'My partner thinks I should dress more like your husband,' Mc-Cusker offered, as an alternative ice breaker.

She rewarded him with a high-pitched shriek of a laugh. Mc-Cusker couldn't figure out if she was amused that her husband's clothes would allow themselves to be inhabited by someone as un-cool as himself, or if she thought McCusker was aware that he had just made a very funny suggestion. Whatever the reason, she couldn't get it out of her mind because she let fly with another shriek.

'*My* partner,' O'Carroll offered, perhaps in an attempt to balance the books, 'still feels that Nike should make trainers that look exactly like brogues.'

This elicited another raucous laugh from Sophie Rubens. McCusker realised that Sophie liked to fly her sharp, cutting laugh into every available gap in the conversation, humorous or not. It's like her laugh was pre-recorded onto a tape machine, which she replayed on cue, so identical were her emissions in duration, pitch, crackle and insincerity. Perhaps, McCusker thought, the laugh was based more on nervousness than insincerity.

Eventually they settled down in Louis' office. Leab David closed the door behind them. McCusker wasn't sure if it was intended to give them privacy or to retain the privacy and quietness for herself.

'Oh this is terrible, isn't it?' Sophie started, 'who would do such a thing? Could he just have been mugged in Botanic?'

'Are there many muggings in Botanic Gardens?' O'Carroll asked.

'There were a few – perhaps all by the same gang, back in 2010', she replied, appearing to focus all of her concentration on the history of muggings in Botanic Gardens. 'I don't believe any have been reported since.'

'Harry told us that you and Louis were already friends when he met you?'

'Yes, Louis and I met Harry on the same morning, in this very room in fact.'

'How did you and Louis meet?' McCusker asked, O'Carroll seemingly keen to let him take the lead in these chats.

'A friend of mine brought me along to one of the talks he was giving outside of campus. I thought he was great, as he always is when he's freefalling. I went up to him after his talk and told him how much I enjoyed his chat. When he discovered I'd just started to lecture at QUB he told me to ring up Leab David and fix a time to come in to see him. I think he did it this way so I would know he wasn't trying anything on with me. That's one of the things I loved about Louis; he was always very straightforward. He always wanted everything to be transparent.'

'Did you know he was married?' O'Carroll asked.

'Why yes, of course,' she agreed, this time both with the words and her characteristic wink.

'Did he tell you?' O'Carroll pushed further.

'My friend really liked him from afar and she knew all about him, on top of which he was wearing a wedding ring the first night.'

'Did she get to meet him that night as well?' McCusker asked.

'No, no, it *really* was like hero worship for her. She had actually worked out in her mind what she was going to say to him if she met him.'

'What was she going to say?'

'She'd spend hours working this out but she was going to use that famous quote from the movie *Casablanca* – "Louis, I think this is the beginning of a beautiful friendship." But on the actual night when it got down to it, well… she was absolutely petrified. When I suggested we go up and introduce ourselves, she chickened out and did a quick body swerve at the last possible moment.'

'I believe you introduced Louis to a friend of yours, a lady by the name of Mariana Fitzgerald?'

'Yes, actually I was more a friend of her husband before they got married.'

'And Mariana and Louis remained friends?' McCusker continued, on the same theme.

'Yes, indeed,' Sophie replied.

'When you introduced Mariana to Louis, was she already married to Mr Fitzgerald?' McCusker ventured, not really thinking.

'No.'

'But you said that you met Mariana because you were friends with her husband?' O'Carroll said.

'Ah yes, I can see what you mean,' Sophie replied slightly awkwardly. 'You see, when I met Mariana, she and Francie were just dating. Francie was a good friend of my older brother's when we were growing up, and we've all remained friends. Francie and Mariana got married after I introduced her to Louis.'

'Was she still playing the field at that stage?' O'Carroll asked.

'Good heavens, no!' Sophie Rubens replied immediately, 'I mean, they went through a couple of tricky patches before they eventually married. To be very candid with you, it was so on-off, on-off, on-off, that I was really surprised when they announced they were going to get married.'

'So how did you come to introduce Mariana and Louis?' McCusker asked.

'Well, it was in one of Mariana and Francie's down periods and she rang me up one night saying she was bored and did I want to go out for a drink. So we went out, had a few vodkas on an empty stomach, then a few more, then we got a bit squiffy, as one does. She poured her heart out to me. She was annoyed at Francie because he wouldn't commit to her and, in her words, she didn't want to waste her life on him only for him to run off with a younger filly when… well, the actual words she used and I remember them well, were, "When everything starts to go south". As part of the same conversation, she said she'd just like to have some fun again. She wanted life to be fun again like it had been when she first met Francie. She asked me if I'd any friends who liked a bit of fun. I immediately thought of, and suggested, Louis…'

'But he was married,' McCusker complained.

'Yes, and it's 2018 and men and women and boys and girls can go out with each other and still keep it uncomplicated and innocent.'

'You'll have to forgive my partner; he's still stuck in the sixties,' O'Carroll protested, 'but an even bigger problem might be, it's the 1860s he's stuck in.'

Sophie Rubens let fly with another wild shriek of laughter, staring intently at McCusker, 'Louis is a loyal husband to Elizabeth but… sorry, not but… and – yes "and" is the word. Louis is a loyal husband and they have become more like companions. I'm not swearing here that he never ever…' again she paused to stare at McCusker, 'slept with another woman. I just don't know, and I really didn't want to know. All that I can tell you is that before Louis introduced me to Harry, Louis and I went out several times, and it was never, ever, anything other than fun and social – and in that order. He never once even tried to land a brotherly peck on my cheek, you know, just to see how I'd react.'

'So Louis and Mariana met up… and became friends…'

'Yes indeed. In fact,' Sophie said, and winked, 'I do remember a couple of times when I went out with both Louis and Elizabeth, and there was never anything weird or awkward. There was even a fundraiser that Louis and Elizabeth, Mariana and Francie and Harry and I all attended together.'

'Right, so,' McCusker replied, accepting that he'd just been put back in his box; nonetheless, there were still questions to be asked. 'So Louis and Mariana became friends, and they continued to be good friends even after she and Mr Fitzgerald were married?'

'Yes, they still go out for an occasional drink or meal, you know, for a catch-up. I know she cared immensely for Louis and she will be very upset... as we all are.'

'What does Mariana do?'

'She's married,' Sophie said, flying in another laugh.

'And you're married,' O'Carroll said, 'and you work here.'

'Okay, fair point,' Sophie replied, 'Francie did not want his wife working – she doesn't need to.'

'Okay,' McCusker started quickly, 'tell me this, Sophie: what did Mariana do for a living when she met Louis?'

'Ah... okay,' this time her laugh was more of a nervous one, 'Mariana was an escort when she met Francie – yes, in fact, that is also how she met her husband.'

'So Mariana was an escort when she first met Louis?' McCusker asked. 'He needed it spelling out.'

'Well, yes and no really.'

'Sorry?'

'Well, I introduced them both as good friends of mine and not as an escort and a potential client, if you see what I mean. But at the time they met she was still in the escort business.'

'As an escort, what would have been expected of her?' McCusker asked, feeling this point also needed spelling out.

'Well, you know, I suppose we could all be guilty of hearing the word "escort" and thinking "nudge, nudge, wink, wink, I know *exactly* what that means". But I can tell you this: Mariana is nobody's fool and all I would say is she was never going to do anything she wasn't comfortable doing. I know her company takes a very large deposit and it's made clear to their clients that the service provided is companionship. You know, some men really are satisfied just to have some great company for an evening, and they're equally keen to be seen with a beautiful girl on their arm.'

'Okay, that makes sense,' McCusker said, happy with the information. She perhaps did "protest too much." There was perhaps more valuable information to be gained on the topic, but he wasn't going to get much more right now. On top of which, if he continued with the direct questions he really wanted to ask about Mariana, there was a good chance that Sophie, and perhaps even his own partner, were going to accuse him of being un-gentlemanly.

'Have you ever met a friend of Mariana's called Murcia?' he asked, deciding to move on.

Sophie Rubens looked a little uncomfortable. She looked like she was going to give another of her "yes" winks but didn't. The problem for McCusker was that she had looked uncomfortable in so many different ways since the start of the interview.

'Yes, I know Murcia; I've met her a few times, solely through us both being good friends of Mariana's.'

'And Murcia was also a good friend of Louis'?'

'I don't know if I would use the word "good" to describe their friendship but, yes, they knew each other.'

'And would you say that Murcia and Louis–'

'I wouldn't really be qualified to answer that question; you should ask Mariana, or, better still, Murcia herself.'

'But from your knowledge, would you say that was Murcia and–'

'Look, I'm sorry,' she said, semi-glaring at both of them, 'I really don't know a lot about that and I feel it unfair to speculate.'

'Okay,' McCusker said, thinking that's also one he might need to leave for another time. 'Did Mr Fitzgerald and Louis get on okay?

'Yeah, I mean when I saw them at social events, mostly fundraisers, Francie, Louis and Ron Desmond always seemed to be thick as thieves.'

'But not Harry?'

'Not Harry what?'

'Well, you just said that when you saw Francie, Louis and Ron together at fundraisers, they seemed thick as thieves?'

'I didn't actually mean they were thieves, Mr McCusker,' she said, and shrieked.

'No, I know, I got that,' McCusker conceded, 'but my point was that if you saw them all at fundraisers, then there was a good chance that you would have been there with Harry, yet you didn't say that Francie, Ron, Louis *and Harry* were always thick as thieves…?'

'Goodness, I believe we've just enjoyed a Columbo moment,' Sophie shrieked, as she checked her extremely large wristwatch. 'Yes, you're correct. But, you see, my Harry isn't part of that fundraising set, so he's never off working the room.'

'What about Al Armstrong, what can you tell me about him?' McCusker asked.

'Okay, time out,' Sophie Rubens called. 'Can you guarantee me that anything I tell you won't get myself and Harry into trouble?'

'For instance?' McCusker asked, now totally intrigued.

'For instance, hypothetically speaking, of course: if, say, I wanted to tell you that I saw Al selling say… am, oh… what could we be talking about now… oh, yes I've got it… what if I said we saw Al selling weed,' she said, making "weed" sound like a revelation she'd just experienced. 'Could that get Harry and me into any trouble?'

'No,' O'Carroll replied, as the official member of the PSNI, 'you wouldn't get into trouble.'

'And what if say, I said, I mean wildly out of character here, I know, for Harry and I…' and her shriek of laughter was even wilder than normal, 'but say I said that Al sold Harry and I some weed– what would your position be then?'

'As long as you were only using it personally and in the privacy of your home, we would have no issue with that at all. As you said to my colleague earlier, it is 2018 after all.'

McCusker wanted to high-five O'Carroll on the spot – the only problem was that neither of them were high-fiving kind of people.

'Okay then,' Sophie braced herself and proudly announced, 'we regularly bought very expensive, but consistently high-grade marijuana from Al Armstrong.'

That got the pen squeaking noisily in O'Carroll's wee pink notebook.

'Did he sell to Louis?' McCusker asked.

Sophie let out another perfectly timed shriek. 'You've got to be kidding,' she said in a whisper, as if someone was listening in. 'Louis was the poster-boy for people who were naturally high on life! He liked an occasional glass of expensive red wine, but that was it for him.'

McCusker was about to raise his next question when she continued with, 'Mind you, Louis did say that there were a few evenings when he went home and Armstrong had clearly been around, and Elizabeth was stoned out of her brains'

'Did he sell to other people?' McCusker asked, still somewhat shell-shocked from Sophie's last revelation.

'Yes, of course, and he used his property refurbishments as a way to launder his money. Every time Armstrong had a property sale, Louis would always say, "I see my wife's bestie has just got rid of another shipment of weed".'

Okay, McCusker thought – this is the type of progress I like. Could Armstrong have a supplier, who he in turn owed money to, and either Louis found out about it or Armstrong saw getting rid of Louis as a way to getting to his money through Elizabeth? The other image he was having a hard time with was the one of the Superintendent's wife's sister sitting in her wee house up on Landseer Street stoned out of her Christmas tree.

'Did you ever meet Louis' brother, Miles?'

'Never did, no. But Louis and Harry used to talk about him,' Sophie said, and then released another of her laughs, which McCusker was convinced rattled each and every one of his and O'Carroll's dental fillings. 'He certainly sounded like he was out there. Way out there! Harry can probably fill you in better on Miles' background.'

'What can you tell us about how Louis was, the last time you spoke to him?'

'Do you remember when you were young, and you felt that time used to pass really so slowly? Later, of course, you come to realise that it's because you only had a few things on the horizon, like summer holidays, birthdays and Christmas. As we get older we have lots more special events to fill up our lives with – adventures, career highs and lows, new books, new albums, new movies, TV programmes, the theatre, concerts, trips, holidays, special meals, friend's weddings, the birth of friend's children, friend's children's weddings, and on and on. Well, you have to know the everyday of Louis' life was like a birthday or Christmas Day to him. I've never known a man or woman whose life was filled with so many wonderful things, and equally I've never known anyone who enjoyed their life more than Louis did his.'

'Tell me this, Sophie,' McCusker started, and paused, 'you know the woman you went to see Louis with that first night?'

'Yeah?'

'What ever happened to her?'

'She also met her true love, a farmer's daughter from Randallstown, and they run a very successful garden centre up just outside Randallstown.'

'Excellent,' McCusker replied, 'could you give me her details please?'

Sophie seemed very put out by that, but passed the information on anyway.

'For ruling-you-out purposes only, Sophie, could you please advise what you were doing last night from 8.30 until, say, 1.30 this morning?'

'I was at the Mac Theatre seeing Eric Bibb.'

'Were you with Harry?' McCusker asked, feeling quite foolish, not to mention guilty, because he knew, he thought, exactly where Harry had been at that time. He was equally convinced that a husband and wife would never contradict each other, particularly a married couple that had managed a quick catch-up between police interviews.

'No, Harry was working last night.'

'Were you with a friend?'

'Nope, just by myself.'

'Did you buy anything by credit card – tickets, coffee or even a snack? They have a really nice café on the second floor there,' McCusker said, knowing it was on the ground floor.

'Nope, I paid for my ticket, in cash, went upstairs to the café, had my coffee, wine and quiche, all paid for with cash,' she replied, fumbling around, like she knew she'd made a mistake. She looked at her watch again.

'Okay,' McCusker said, taking the hint, 'we've probably detained you long enough for now, so let's leave it there.'

Sophie got up to leave, said her farewell with a 'Cheery-bye', but just before she opened the inner of Louis Bloom's office door, she turned and added, 'I suppose Harry told you about Louis' worry over Elizabeth?'

'Oh,' McCusker replied, completely caught unawares, 'and what worry was that?'

'Well, Elizabeth Bloom frequently used to make this mysterious drink for Louis, but she'd never say what it was she put in it. She'd always say it was all very healthy stuff for him. Like an energy drink. So, about a week ago, Louis brought the remains of one of the drinks to Harry and asked him to analyse it to see exactly what it was she was giving him.'

CHAPTER TWENTY

As they were entering Leab David's reception space outside Louis Bloom's office, seconds after Sophie Rubens' departure, Leab looked like she was about to give McCusker some information. However, O'Carroll's mobile went off with its distinctive Stevie Wonder '*I Just Called To Say I Love You*' ring tone. It was Superintendent Larkin instructing them to go immediately, without further delay, to Louis Bloom's house, where a disturbance had just been reported.

They did as bid.

'Who invented the wheel?'

'What are you on about now, McCusker?'

'No, it's just that your wheels caught my attention just as we were about to climb on board,' he said, as they fastened their seat belts and she noisily engaged the gear stick and headed back up towards the busy Stranmillis Road, 'and I was just thinking that, you know, as an invention, we rather take the wheel for granted and really, when you think about it, it's such a marvellous invention, isn't it?'

'Sometimes, I mean like now for instance - I'm really so sorry I ever mentioned you to my sister.'

'No *seriously*,' McCusker protested, 'just think about it; let's forget all about the Industrial Revolution – where would we be without the wheel? In fact where would the Industrial Revolution be without the wheel? Take another instance; just now, if we needed to run up to Landseer Street, well... we'd arrive severely out of breath and hardly be in a position to deal properly with a disturbance of any kind. So every now and then, you know, I'd really just like us to stop for a few seconds and celebrate the person – man or woman – who invented the wheel.'

'McCusker...'

'I'm serious, Lily,' McCusker interrupted her interruption, 'think of where Henry Ford's motor car would be now if someone hadn't invented the wheel. All these vehicles scooting all around and about us would all be parked by the side of the road, rusting.'

'McCusker,' she started again, this time as she took a quick left into Landseer Street, 'I think Grace does have the measure of you. She claims that there is method in your madness. She says if I, or we, or she, or whoever only stopped to think – like just now, when you asked "Who invented the wheel?", we'd realise that there was always a point behind your tangents or, maybe to put it more bluntly, a method in your madness. Like, for instance, we're here, and due to our preoccupation with your tangent, we're relatively stress-free and neither did we endanger either ourselves or, more importantly, other people on the road in the process.'

As they hopped out of the car and ran towards Louis Bloom's blue, Victorian, front door, McCusker was saying, 'I still maintain we couldn't have done it without wheels!'

* * *

McCusker and O'Carroll had to wait for ages outside the door. They could hear screaming and shouting and effing and blinding like it was going out of fashion from beyond it. Eventually the door opened up and Al Armstrong appeared. The majority of his snow-white T-shirt, or what used to be his snow-white T-shirt, was covered in the rich, crimson life force, known as blood. He'd a towel with some ice cubes held to his nose.

'What on Earth is happening?' O'Carroll asked, in a surprisingly calm voice.

'Miles has gone loopy again!' Armstrong managed to croak, rolling his eyes and nodding his head in the direction of the kitchen.

O'Carroll headed off in that direction as McCusker, supporting Armstrong by the elbow, peeled off into the lounge and succeeded in managing to get the casualty to lie down on the sofa (minus cushions, so that he was totally horizontal). McCusker removed some of the ice cubes from the towel, placed them in one of the napkins Mrs Bloom had on the sideboard and put the ice pack underneath the quivering Armstrong's neck.

'Keep it there,' McCusker advised, 'it'll cool down your blood, which will, in turn, slow down the flow.'

'Elizabeth,' Armstrong managed to mutter, and McCusker immediately headed off in the direction of the screaming and shouting in the kitchen.

'So where's the Will?' a stranger shouted at the recently widowed Mrs Bloom. The stranger, McCusker assumed, was Miles Bloom, and he was screaming at the top of his lungs, about 2 inches away from the face of a sobbing Mrs Bloom.

'I don't know, Miles, I keep telling you I don't know,' Elizabeth cried out in utter desperation.

'Step away, Sir,' O'Carroll commanded repeatedly.

'What's in the fecking Will?' Miles demanded, totally ignoring O'Carroll. 'Do I get my money back? I have a right to that money, it's mine.'

'I don't know how many times I have to say this, Miles,' Elizabeth pleaded, wiping her eyes and nose with a soggy tissue. 'I don't know and I don't care.'

'Step back.'

'It's none of your fecking business, get out of here,' Miles screamed at O'Carroll, before returning his attention to his sister-in-law. 'You must have discussed it. You must know if I'm getting my birth-right back.'

'Step back,' O'Carroll ordered, for what sounded like the final time.

'You take care of Mrs Bloom,' McCusker suggested, as he ran in, 'the thing I find is when you're dealing with a spoilt child, you have to treat them as a spoilt child.'

With that, he opened the kitchen door out into the garden, simply grabbed Miles Bloom in a bear hug from behind, trapping his arms, and then surprised everyone by yanking him off his feet and marching the shocked, denim-clad man – who looked and sounded like he made a habit of stamping his feet and getting ugly in mixed company – out into the garden.

Now Miles was incensed to the nth degree.

'I'll have you for GBH! This is police brutality! I'll have you!' he screeched in an inhumanly high-pitched whine. 'I've got witnesses! Elizabeth you're a witness to this,' he called back into the kitchen.

'No, Sir,' McCusker started, 'when you calm down, I believe you'll find that I'm not in fact brutalising you, but I am in fact restraining you for your own good.'

Miles struggled with all his might and couldn't break free of McCusker, who by this time was gently whispering in his ear: 'Shame on you for terrorising a poor woman who's just lost her husband.'

There was more screaming and shouting and frustrated effing and blinding from Miles.

'Can I just say, Sir, that I can comfortably restrain you like this – for your own good, you understand,' McCusker continued, in a very soothing and even tone, 'for quite possibly the remainder of the day, but most definitely until you calm down.'

Just like a spoilt child, Miles Bloom eventually settled down a few minutes later. By which point O'Carroll had a brew-up going for all of them.

'So I suppose you have to take me to jail now,' Miles inquired, after a few more minutes of silence.

Elizabeth didn't betray relief at the suggestion; if anything, she looked particularly concerned.

O'Carroll took her lead from Mrs Bloom and said, 'Well, this seems to me to have been a domestic dispute and in such instances we have to give a warning...' she paused to glare at Miles, 'the first time. The incident with Mr Armstrong seems to be another matter entirely – he seems to have been assaulted and if he wishes to press charges_'

'Assaulted?!' Miles cried, dropping his volume considerably mid-word.

'No assault, I can assure you, DI O'Carroll,' Elizabeth said, gently through a compassionate smile, 'no, assault at all... the silly apeth simply ran into the back door in his haste to get out of the house when Miles started shouting.'

McCusker and O'Carroll left the three of them to it and made arrangements to see Miles at the Customs House that afternoon at 3.00 p.m.

'That was quite bizarre, McCusker, even for you, your spoilt-child routine. Where did that come from?'

'Well, it wasn't so much a spoilt child really,' McCusker started off slowly, 'but did you ever see that movie *The Horse Whisperer*, you know, the one with Robert Redford? Well, this stallion is uncontrollable and Redford just keeps whispering in its ear until it eventually settles down.'

'McCusker, you know you really do talk the biggest load of crap sometimes – I suppose that'll be the culchie in you.'

CHAPTER TWENTY-ONE

Professor Vincent Best, another of Louis Bloom's colleagues on the Senate, was what could officially be termed as old. Or at least he looked old – very old, like a grandfather. He was tall, slightly stooped, and anaemic-looking. He didn't suit having long hair, yet that is what he had – long, grey, dense, fluffy hair, with a parting that appeared as though someone had taken a knife and sliced a 45-degree wedge out of an Afro. His clothes were old, but clean. He wore a shirt that, quite simply, had been dry-cleaned just once too often – clean, but in a dying-kind-of way, where the life had been completely washed out of it. It had probably been white at one point but the original colour was now almost imperceptible. His trousers were grey, a bit too long and very creased – creased in that they looked like he had slept in them, and for several nights at that. He was wearing a wine-coloured button-up cardigan, probably the newest item in his wardrobe. The buttons and holes were one space out of sync with each other, but the top button-holes looked so under-used it appeared that he never undid them and instead used the cardigan as a pullover. His fingernails were overly long, but clean. His hands were an unpleasant combination of withered and red-peppered, and the dark blue of his veins was visible and protruding, making the back of his hand look like a 3D map of mountain ridges. He smelled of a combination of tobacco and a strong yet pleasing deodorant.

McCusker and O'Carroll had the impression from the get-go that they were lesser beings being tolerated by an audience.

'They say Bloom was stabbed in the back,' Best said, after brief introductions. 'What I'd like to know is, was he stabbed just the once or several times?'

'We're still awaiting the autopsy results,' O'Carroll replied.

'You mean members of the Royal Ulster Constabulary no longer use their eyes?'

'It's the PSNI these days,' McCusker replied.

'It'll never be anything but the RUC to me, dear boy,' Best started, paused and when O'Carroll started to say something, he closed her down with, 'but my point was going to be that if someone stabs someone else, it's not that they just want to kill their victim, it's that they want to hurt the victim too. And if they stab the victim, several times, well they *really* want to hurt them. Period.'

'Louis Bloom came to see you yesterday around 3.30 – how did he seem?' O'Carroll asked, wanting to change direction.

'He seemed in a big hurry to get away.'

'Did he say what for?'

'He didn't even say… we passed a bit of daily time, neither of us had anything important to discuss with each other. On reflection, if either of us had known it was to be our last time together, I know it would have been different. Period.'

'Do you know anyone who would have wanted to hurt Louis Bloom?' McCusker asked.

Professor Best tended to squint a lot, and what with the squinting and his demeanour, at that precise moment he looked as interested in the PSNI representatives as a music publisher who used to be an accountant would be, in listening to a songwriter talking about his music. Best, through lack of speech, just point blank refused to answer McCusker's question.

Working on the theory that Best was old and might possibly be losing his hearing, McCusker made, in Best's eyes, the faux pas of repeating his question.

'I heard you first time, dear boy,' he said. 'What you're actually asking me to do is to use my imagination to guess what might have happened?'

'Well, yes,' McCusker ventured.

'As Stephen King once famously said, "Imagination is not something you can put in a box; it's never a tamed animal", you know.'

'Nonetheless, Professor Best,' O'Carroll cut in, 'all McCusker was asking you to do was to think of the people you knew who were in Louis Bloom's life and surmise if there were any who had a reason…'

'Very diplomatic, Miss O'Carroll,' Best, who had a habit of letting his facial expression predict a negative before his voice actually did, replied.

As McCusker and O'Carroll were waiting for Best to complete his sentence, McCusker thought that no one starts off old, which is why a lot of their (old people's) mannerisms must come from their youth, which is why the old may sometimes unintentionally appear younger, childish even. Like just now, for instance: instead of Best adding to the sentence he signalled that he had already finished it by offering himself a large "what a clever boy I am" grin.

'Actually, it's Detective Inspector, Professor,' O'Carroll said.

'Sorry?'

'It's not Miss, Professor, it's Detective Inspector. I'd never address you as anything other than Professor as your deserved title, so I'd like the respect to be reciprocated.'

Again Best offered another large smile and quite a bit of squinting.

'Good on you, Detective Inspector, I love people who are never scared of speaking up for themselves.' Professor Best nodded towards O'Carroll. 'You know, I reached the age of 78 on my last birthday. I have discovered there are two things in particular about reaching 78: one, you're now officially old enough to die. You've finally reached the status of years that when you die, people will no longer discuss your meaningless illnesses in great detail for hours, but will merely state "Oh, he'd a great innings" and still have sufficient time left to go on to discuss your achievements at length.'

When it was clear he'd omitted something, O'Carroll prompted, 'and the second thing Professor?'

'Pardon…? Oh yes… ah, let's see now what was it? Oh yes, it might have been: once you're over 78, it's *cool*, as my students have a habit of saying, to forget shit.'

McCusker took that as, hopefully, a thawing of the ice. He was starting to feel despondent though. They weren't really making progress with the case. He accepted the fact that he pretty much always thought they weren't making progress at this stage in a case, but the thought didn't comfort him. He couldn't even think of a single question to ask the professor, apart from maybe: "Did you murder Louis Bloom?"

'Look dear boy,' Professor Best started, this time addressing and trying through his squinting to make eye contact with McCusker, 'I went to see Bloom address his students a few times, he was quite the orator, I can tell you – very passionate. The students absolutely loved him, nay, worshipped him. But the point I want to make to you is that he was passionate about his topic, LOVE. But he wasn't interested in writing poetry about it. I remember him instructing his students at the top of his voice:

"When it comes to love,
Don't write about it
Do it.

When it comes to love,
Don't dream about it
Live it.

When it comes to love,
Your only regret should never be,
You missed it."

'But the thing that impressed me the most is that I would swear to you that those words just came from the top of his head as he spoke them.'

O'Carroll looked like she'd just enjoyed a spiritual moment, and McCusker imagined her seemingly quixotic search would continue with vigour anew. But, as was becoming his habit, Professor Vincent Best wasn't quite finished yet.

'The point I'm making to you two fine members of the Royal Ulster Constabulary is that Bloom was indeed a passionate man. He was not the type of man to live his life in a loveless marriage. No, Bloom would have sought out *Love* and that is what got him into trouble. Period.'

Now the professor was finished.

Well, he did say that he would bet his final years that Bloom's murder had nothing to do with money, property, politics or anything other than love, or the lack of it.

He also had the perfect alibi for the previous evening – he had gone to a concert at the Waterfront Hall with two old friends. He qualified that by confirming that both his friends were of a ripe old age and that they had all known each other for a long time. The concert had featured Christy Moore on the second of his three sold-out nights at the venue. McCusker had gone to the venue on the first night to see the same artist, who wasn't just his favourite artist but also a genuine national treasure of the island of Ireland. After the concert, Best and his two friends had finished off a bottle of whiskey in his humble (his words) accommodation, his friends calling for a taxi at 2.30.

'The other great thing about getting old,' Professor Best started, 'is that you get so many more hours out of your day, as the need for sleep greatly decreases. Period.'

CHAPTER TWENTY-TWO

DS WJ Barr was always so on the case that McCusker instinctively knew, as he walked up the stairs of the Customs House, he'd have some valuable information waiting for him.

'Mr Bloom withdrew £340 from a cashpoint at the Ulster Bank on University Road, just opposite the Whitla Hall yesterday afternoon at 1.11,' Barr offered breathlessly, suggesting there was more.

McCusker wrote the time and the activity down on his page titled Louis Bloom's Day.

'He drew a similar amount out most days.'

'Two grand a week in cash?' O'Carroll noted for her book. 'That's a lot of change.'

'How much money was found on his body?' McCusker asked Barr.

'Forty quid.'

'Any other credit card activity?'

'A lunchtime bill for two people, of £38.00 including a £5 tip, at Cafe Conor,' Barr replied, checking his summary.

'Did Louis have any other credit cards?' O'Carroll continued.

'One MasterCard credit card and one Visa debit card,' McCusker voiced, remembering their first interview with Elizabeth Bloom.

'Any activity on the debit card?' O'Carroll asked Barr.

'Nope, none at all, in fact he seemed to have never used it.'

'What about his mobile phone?' O'Carroll continued.

'His wife said he didn't have one,' McCusker offered.

'I found one in the back pocket of his trousers, when we searched him up in the graveyard,' Barr offered.

McCusker wondered how he'd missed that piece of valuable information, and what would Louis Bloom need to keep from his wife that would have necessitated him having a secret mobile phone.

Barr, being the organised man he was, carefully closed his "Bloom credit card" file, moved it to one side of his desk and opened his "Bloom mobile phone" file, which had been waiting underneath the credit card file.

'Let's see,' Barr started up again, as he flicked through a few pages, 'he rang his office number at 15.50. The call lasted 2 minutes and 10 seconds and he rang the same number again at 17.33 for 4 minutes and 3 seconds. He rang Mariana Fitzgerald at 15.55. That call lasted 3 minutes. No other activity on this phone.'

'Did he have just the one mobile?' O'Carroll asked.

'Yes,' Barr said, and then added, 'that we know of.'

'Let's check that with Leab David,' O'Carroll instructed, clearly taking the DS's point.

'Good work, WJ,' McCusker said. 'Did you speak to Belfast's answer to Billy Connolly?

'You mean our esteemed pathologist, Mr Anthony Robertson,' Barr replied, tidying and closing Bloom's mobile phone file, and placing it on top of the credit card file, revealing his autopsy notes, 'yes… Anthony said the single stab wound was either a complete fluke or delivered by someone who knew exactly what they were doing. He leans towards the later, in that multiple stab wounds would tend to suggest someone who didn't know what they were doing and wanted to make sure they killed their target.'

'Either that or they really wanted to hurt/punish their victim,' McCusker suggested.

'Quite.'

'Any other marks about the body?' McCusker asked, thinking that surely couldn't be it.

'Just some superficial scratches along the arms. Anthony thought that the body must have been cleaned up at the scene, which tends to tie in with the scene of the crime.'

'How so?' McCusker was totally intrigued.

'Well, when we found the actual point that Louis Bloom was murdered, in the avenue formed between the hedge behind the bandstand

and the hedge that runs along the road, Colenso Parade, just opposite Louis' house – it's quite a tranquil avenue, far from the madding crowd, with a tarred path with several wooden arches, and with trees, flowers and park benches on both sides–'

'Please stop there,' McCusker said to Barr, and then turned to O'Carroll. 'Can we go down there again and walk the site with WJ giving us this new information?'

'Okay, you and WJ skip along there and go through it, so you're comfortable with it,' O'Carroll replied, while looking like she was seriously thinking about joining them, 'I'll stay here – I'm still trying to get the Vice-Chancellor on the phone to fix up a time to visit him. I'd like to do that today, so I'll keep on at it.'

Ten minutes later McCusker and DS WJ Barr were walking along the same herbaceous borders off the tranquil avenue in Botanic Gardens where Louis Bloom lost his life.

About halfway along on the side facing Colenso Parade, and just behind a park bench, was the taped-off scene of crime.

'What I was about to say back at Customs House, but now can *show* you, is that it appears that the murder was carried out here on the soil and away from the plants and grass, so that there would be no–'

'Tell-tale blood. Great, WJ, well done,' McCusker said, as he saw Barr's point.

'Not just that, Sir,' Barr said, being the only person in the Customs House who always addressed McCusker as "Sir", 'but if you look there, where the soil seems fresher, it seems that the soil has been recently dug, maybe even to *hide* the blood.'

'But how did you even find it then?' McCusker asked, in genuine awe.

'Oh, it was easy, Sir; Bloom's New York Yankees baseball cap was caught there on the thorns of that rose bush. Obviously, as Bloom and his assailant cut off the main path and into the bushes, his cap came off. I imagine the assailant searched for it on the ground and saw the markings on the soil over there, but never thought to look above him. There was just one thing a wee bit odd about the baseball cap…'

'Oh?'

'Well, it may be something and it may be nothing. But it smelled of perfume.'

'Really,' McCusker said, more amused than inquisitive.

'I've asked the lab to check it.'

'Are there any footprints then?'

'Sadly not; the assailant covered his shoes with some kind of variation on our plastic crime scene bootees. Maybe even just a plastic shopping bag around each foot and taped at the ankle.'

'So how did Louis' murderer get him to come here with him?' McCusker asked, himself as much as Barr. 'There were no signs of any marks around Louis Bloom's person?'

'Nope.'

'So that means he didn't feel a need to protect or defend himself, which means…'

'Which means that he knew his assailant?' Barr offered, finishing off McCusker's sentence for him.

'Any fingerprints around the park bench?' McCusker asked, and then said, 'No, of course not,' before Barr could answer.

'I have to say, you don't seem overly concerned about that, Sir.'

'You know what, WJ, to be honest I've never set much store by fingerprints, or even footprints, for that matter, but please don't tell the superintendent that. No, I've always felt if a criminal is stupid enough to leave their fingerprints or footprints then they're certainly foolish enough for us to catch them… eventually.'

McCusker left Barr examining the scene and went to sit on the park bench, opposite the murder scene. There was a bit more activity as directed by Barr. Two suitably kitted-out Crime Scene chaps started to dig out the topsoil, down to about 9 inches, in the spot that Louis Bloom had died. They placed the soil carefully in plastic sacks for shipping back to the lab for particle-by-particle examination.

McCusker viewed the scene of the crime and as ever he was just as much preoccupied with what was missing as what was present. He tuned into this and try though he did, he couldn't come up with a single missing thing. It was certainly a very clever location to pick; it was in a public place, yet it was probably to be avoided in the darkness. Which means the murderer would have been left alone to do their evil work. But during the day there would have been numerous footprints around and about the area, contaminating the site. So even if the murderer had left any clues, they'd have been neutralised by unwitting members of the general public.

Yes, evil had been committed on the previous evening, just a matter of a few feet from where he now sat. McCusker felt that evil was always around. It might change its course, or find another way to spend its force, but it most certainly never just disappears.

Over the hedge opposite him, McCusker could hear people out for a stroll in Botanic Gardens and he imagined the parts of the conversation he missed out. He was saddened by the fact that, just a few feet away from them, a man – a good man, by all accounts – had lost his life, and the world, with the exception of a few, was both unaware and unconcerned by his passing. He could hear the infrequent traffic on Colenso Parade on the other side of the hedge behind him. How had the murderer arrived here, at this location? What time had he arrived at the scene? How long had he lain in wait? McCusker started to assume that the murderer was indeed a male due to the physicality of the murder, and the fact that there must have been a certain amount of *man*-handling of the body in order to get Bloom to this location from wherever he'd been hijacked. Next, he would have had to transport the body up to and over the graveyard wall. Then he would have had to carry the body from inside the graveyard up to the Lennon Mausoleum.

Bloom left his home at around 8.55. He'd got as far as being able to dump his garbage. That would have taken him to 9.00 to, say, 9.05 at the latest. So McCusker knew where Bloom was at that point. Okay. Did the assailant allow Bloom to start his walk home before accosting him? So somewhere between 9.05 and, say, 9.10 the assailant met up with or accosted Bloom. McCusker assumed, due to the lack of any marks on or about Bloom, that Bloom went willingly. Did they both head off to this location? McCusker looked around the quiet avenue, which would be much quieter during the night. What happened here when Bloom arrived? Was there a third person lying in wait for them? There would have to be some logic to that, in that it would be clearly easier for two people to get Bloom's corpse from here, up and over the eight-foot high wall that separated the graveyard from Botanic Gardens and across Friar's Bush graveyard to Lennon's Mausoleum.

'So we're dealing with a professional?' McCusker asked, himself more than anyone else, 'someone whose aim was true and who had planned every minute detail?'

McCusker thought of Bloom in his final moments. Did he know what was ahead of him? Did he position his favoured baseball cap above him in the bushes to serve as a clue perhaps? What other evidence was there on or about the cap? That was down to the good people in the forensic department.

'When you get a chance, can you have someone check all the local CCTV footage?'

'There are no cameras in Botanic,' Barr replied, offering what McCusker had learned since yesterday – that some locals referred to the Gardens as simply "Botanic".

'No, sorry, of course not – I meant the streets around here. I was thinking about how the assailant arrived here. I'm wondering if he's local. Did he walk here or did he drive here?'

McCusker then shared with Barr the thoughts he'd just had about Bloom and his final moments.

'That would make a lot of sense,' Barr said, as they headed off back to the Customs House, 'you know, that he knew his murderer, that there was someone else, an accomplice, waiting up here for them both. They murdered Louis Bloom and then the accomplice helped the assailant take the body over to the graveyard.'

'Yeah, I find myself favouring that, but only because I can't come up with a plausible alternative. But that's never a great starting point for a suspicion.'

'Oh yes, I nearly forgot,' Barr said, 'I was about to tell you up at the office and then you said hold off until we were at the scene of the crime. But the other important thing Anthony Robertson said was he felt sure that the murderer would have cleaned some blood away from Bloom's back. He said there wouldn't have been a lot of blood, because the knife would have done its damage immediately and the heart would have shut down and stopped pumping blood pretty quickly, but there would have certainly been some spillage that would have disappeared into the soil. There most certainly would still have been some spillage around the wound. Apparently the wound was very clean and there were no blood stains on Bloom's shirt, so the murderer appears to have cleaned his back.'

'That's very interesting, WJ,' McCusker replied, but still deep in consideration. 'Did you ever notice, Willie John, that a tiger has markings on the fur just above its eyes? These markings tend to make it look like its eyes are actually above its real eyes. This is quite a dangerous distraction, because it can make it appear as if the tiger, cowering in the long grass or among the bushes, is not even looking at you as it prepares to pounce.'

'Meaning our assailant must have managed to misdirect Louis Bloom's attention?'

CHAPTER TWENTY-THREE

They finally got to meet the man referred to by all as the Vice-Chancellor. Just *the* Vice-Chancellor. Not the Vice-Chancellor, Joe Bloggs, but… the Vice-Chancellor. McCusker wondered if he should address him as Vice? Was that being too familiar with someone he was just meeting for the first time? Maybe he should call him Mr Chancellor.

McCusker knew he was acting a bit giddy, but he also knew that it was partly because he had the privilege to once again see the interior of Lanyon's red-brick cathedral of culture. Leab David, for it was she who had set up the meeting with the Vice-Chancellor on behalf of DI O'Carroll, met them at the information desk in the university shop, where she was busy, as ever, working on the screen of her iPhone, the fingers of her ring hand doing their impression of a bird's wing at the end of each message. She took them across the stunning black and white checkerboard-tiled floor of the entrance hall where Galileo, deep in marble thoughts, sat beneath a large wall clock, which in turn was set immediately under a spectacular stained-glass window. They travelled on in silence, along darkened, wood-panelled corridors, until Leab opened a door on their right, nodded to a secretary on her left, but instead of waiting to be shown through, or announced, or even knocking on the inner door, she opened it and strode straight in.

'Vice-Chancellor, this is Detective Inspector Lily O'Carroll and Mr McCusker from the PSNI.'

Whereas the Vice-Chancellor seemed ambivalent about the detectives, McCusker noticed that his eyes totally lit up when he first saw Leab David. He shook hands with both McCusker and O'Carroll and rested his free hand on Leab's back briefly, in a proud parental way, as they all small-talked.

The Vice-Chancellor, was well groomed, down to his manicured fingernails – perhaps even his toenails as well, McCusker guessed. The detectives' host had a clean-shaven, weather-beaten face, and his hair was fashioned in an "old man trying to look young" American-style crew cut. He had the Brooks Bros look off to a tee: dark blue blazer, blue button-down collar shirt, red tie, cream chinos and perfectly polished, classic light brown leather shoes. McCusker figured, due to the absence of a wedding band, that the Vice-Chancellor was either divorced or his wife had passed. He had big ears, bushy eyebrows and a habit of hooding his eyes with the forehead above his eyebrows, as though he was being cautious, on guard, or maybe merely protecting himself from things he didn't want to see. But equally, when he opened his eyes fully, as he did when he spotted Leab, the contrast in his facial expression was a revelation.

But now Leab was gone, and the Vice-Chancellor seemed more at ease with the two detectives and invited them to sit down at a large formal table positioned in the middle of yet another wonderful room in Lanyon's building. McCusker looked through the window to his left and realised that the room was probably exactly the same as it would have been on the day the university first opened. It had been designed – and the window positioned – so that the inhabitants could view the exterior of Lanyon's majestic entrance hall; the entrance hall McCusker and O'Carroll had just passed through. The autumn sunlight, the blue sky, the students milling around in various degrees of solemnity and laughter, the contrasting greens of the privet hedge and the perfectly manicured lawn, the decorative fawn and red brickwork painted a picture so satisfying that McCusker would treasure it vividly for the remainder of his days.

'Well, I can tell you, I must apologise to you, in advance, if I don't have my wits totally about me – I have to admit that I'm feel totally cast adrift at sea, if you will, since I've lost my very best chum,' was the Vice-Chancellor's first address when they were all comfortable at the table.

'We're sorry for your loss,' McCusker felt obliged to offer although, on reflection, it seemed quite a weird thing to say, given the circumstances.

Either way, the Vice-Chancellor didn't seem to register Mc-Cusker's words, because he continued, 'We must do all we can, all that *you* can, to track down and bring to justice the perpetrators of this crime.'

'You use the plural to describe the perpetrators – does that mean you have an idea of who it may be?'

'Just a figure of speech, if you will,' he replied, in a crisp, easy-to-understand voice. 'But at the same time, don't the PSNI say: when someone goes missing, think first of the in-laws and not the outlaws.'

'I think McCusker and I much prefer to spend our time ruling people out in an effort to discover who we are eventually left with.'

'Ah yes, the Sherlock Holmes approach, he said as he smiled warmly, 'I will admit, I do subscribe to that approach myself. So how can I help you?'

'How long had you known Louis Bloom?' O'Carroll asked.

'Twelve years?'

'How did you meet?'

'I knew of him before I met him,' the Vice-Chancellor replied. 'He came to see me. He introduced himself and said he hated to be a bother, but he needed better office space, please.'

'Really?'

'And we just hit it off immediately.'

McCusker saw a bit of a pattern developing, whereby if the VC didn't like a question, he just totally blanked you and ignored it completely.

'There are some people who you meet and know right from the start that you are going to get on with. Louis Bloom and I were two such people.'

'Professionally and personally?' O'Carroll asked.

'Most certainly both.'

'So you talked about everything?'

'Yes, of course,' the Vice-Chancellor replied and looked out of the window wistfully at the jewels in Lanyon's crown. 'My wife, Loraine, passed away six years ago. She suffered a long but dignified battle with cancer. You know, I can honestly say, had it not been for my friendship with Louis, I would never have survived the loss myself.'

'You were close,' O'Carroll said, more in sympathy than as a question.

'Oh yes.'

'Were you technically his boss?'

'No.'

'Really? I would have thought–'

'No. If you want to put it in simpler terms, Louis looked after the pupil's brains and I looked after their environment.'

'Nonetheless, every ship needs a captain,' O'Carroll persisted.

'And ours would be *the* Chancellor, Sir Patrick Bryson.'

'Let's return to the in-laws,' O'Carroll offered, as McCusker mentally returned to an earlier theme of even the Chancellor had a proper name, while the Vice-Chancellor was still always *the* Vice-Chancellor.

'Yes, let us.'

'We know that Elizabeth and Louis, although they were not exactly estranged, were no longer man and wife in the true sense of the word.'

'That would be correct.'

'Do you think that Elizabeth and this fellow Al Armstrong had anything going on?'

'Louis believed they were friends, nothing more, nothing less. Don't get me wrong, he still liked Elizabeth, but he believed she needed something more out of life than he was able to give her.'

'Is that to say Louis felt he too needed something more out of life?'

'I will answer direct questions that deal with the things I know for sure. I will not volunteer information, nor speculate, if you don't mind.'

'But you said you wanted to help us?' O'Carroll said.

'All you need to know, if you will, is what questions to ask.'

'Miles... let's talk about Miles?' O'Carroll suggested.

'Okay.'

'Miles felt that his father had cheated him out of his inheritance, by leaving all his property and money to Louis,' O'Carroll offered, in summary.

'That's not the problem as I see it,' the Vice-Chancellor replied, 'Miles felt that his father owed him a life. He was incapable of working for a living and he believed his father owed him his life and the wherewithal to live it without the daily inconvenience of having to find the money for that particular week's provisions from. Every penny that the father made during his life, Miles felt he was making it for the both of them. But even worse than that, he believed that after his father died, he should get the estate. All of it. He felt he was entitled–'

'But if he wasn't entitled to the entire estate,' McCusker ventured, 'then surely he could have at least expected to receive *some* of his father's estate?'

'It's an interesting dilemma, isn't it? Who owns the father's estate: the father or those who feel they are entitled to be the heirs? The other important point, not to be forgotten here, is that Miles had berated his father for years about money. As I said, he really felt the money was his and his father was merely an obstacle in the way to him getting his hands on it.'

'And Louis? Did Miles feel Louis was entitled to any of the money?'

'That right there, just might be a spotlight on the main part of the problem. As far as the father was concerned, he felt – no, strike that. Let's say their father knew the money and the estate were his and he could and *should* do with it as he wanted.

'Miles wanted the money, because a) he believed it was his and b) he didn't want to work himself. His father believed, and I would agree with him 100 per cent, that if he had given any funds to Miles he would have squandered it away and the estate the father had worked towards all his life would quickly disappear. Sidney was a proud man. He was proud of his achievements, of the businesses he had built up, and he wanted them to continue to be successful. He did not want them sold off to the highest bidder just to satisfy Miles' need for more money to furnish his lifestyle.

'Sidney and Louis discussed this subject at length over the years. Louis explained that he was very happy with his life and work here at Queens and he didn't want to give that up. It was Louis' idea that his father set up a trust in the name of all his main employees, in order to continue to run his business interests. His father was to serve on the board as non-executive Lifetime Director and on his death Louis would take over that seat/directorship as an unpaid role, mainly for his father's peace of mind.'

'Was it still not a bit mean of the father not to leave Miles anything at all?' McCusker pushed, as he noted the slightly different slant on the Miles, Sidney and Louis Bloom conundrum.

'Well, that's certainly what Miles felt, particularly as he was the oldest sibling.'

'Yes of course, Miles is the oldest. I'd forgotten about that,' O'Carroll admitted. 'So no wonder Miles was so pissed off Louis.'

'More than you'll ever know,' the Vice-Chancellor offered, sadly. 'And that's the reason Louis wanted it kept very quiet. He was advising his father on how to set up the estate.'

'Okay,' McCusker offered, as much in acknowledgement of the conflicting information they'd been hearing on the subject.

'But the father's point was,' the Vice-Chancellor continued, totally ignoring McCusker, 'as I said, leave any of it to Miles and it will all be squandered. Leave him nothing at all and it might shock him into getting his life together and going out and earning a living. That's all that Sidney was trying to do: get Miles off his backside and working.

'The funny thing is, if Miles had channelled but a quarter of the energy he'd squandered on anger over all of this, on constructive applications instead, then he'd be a very rich man by now.'

'What time did you meet Louis yesterday?'

'He dropped in to see me here at 2.45.' The Vice-Chancellor looked directly at O'Carroll. 'In fact, he sat in the exact same seat you're in.'

This declaration spooked O'Carroll to the degree she hopped up out of her chair.

'What did you talk about?' McCusker asked when he saw O'Carroll was okay.

'Yesterday we were discussing whether QUB should re-name one of the campus buildings after Seamus Heaney. Louis was all for honouring the former QUB student, but some in our midst felt that we could make a lot of money by offering the naming rights to AIG or Santander or Ryanair, even. Louis' priority was for us to get a head of steam up before the money-boys knew what hit them. He even joked that Ryanair would want to charge extra for priority seating.'

'How long did he stay for?' McCusker asked. O'Carroll still seemed distracted at been spooked about sitting in Bloom's chair.

'About twenty minutes.'

'How did he seem?'

'Louis was always pretty much up.'

'Do you know if he was seeing anyone?'

'Seeing anyone – as in dating?'

'Yes,' McCusker replied, feeling the time for beating about the bush was over.

'I believe so.'

McCusker was relieved at the Vice-Chancellor's reply – the fact that he, out of all of them, was prepared to address what could have been a taboo subject in respect of Mrs Elizabeth Bloom. But here was someone willing to discuss it at last.

'A certain person or several?' McCusker pushed on.

'Definitely a certain person.'

'Do you know who...' for a split second McCusker hesitated, trying to decide whether to go for "they" rather than "she". In the end he just let the words spoken stand as his question.

'No.'

'Did you discuss her?'

'Only in that he said he didn't want me to get tied up in it. There was a husband.'

'Did Louis' friend Mariana know who she was?'

'She never told me that she did.'

'Did Louis ever discuss where they met or anything like that?'

'No, he said he didn't want to – he said it was complicated. Apart from anything else, if you will, due in respect to his own wife, he was very happy to keep it all quiet. In fact, he might even have invented the husband in order to have the excuse of the cloak of secrecy.'

'When–' McCusker started.

'What I will say is that Louis wasn't in any way down about it. If anything he seemed very happy and in a good space, if you will.'

'When he left you yesterday how did he seem?'

'Yeah, all good. We were going to go out for a meal tonight in fact.'

'Can you tell me what you were doing on Thursday night between the hours of 9.00 p.m. and 1.30 Friday morning?' McCusker asked.

'Yes, the "ruling people out" question,' the Vice-Chancellor said coyly. 'Can I just say, I was with someone and I'd prefer not to give you her name, but if, at a later date, I have to then I will.'

'I'm afraid that doesn't work for us Vice-Chancellor,' McCusker replied, and he had thought so much about the name issue that he very nearly addressed him as Vince Chancellor. 'We will of course endeavour to be very discreet about it.'

The Vice-Chancellor seemed to consider all the issues and balance it up. He seemed very troubled about it.

'She's not married or anything like that,' he claimed, 'it's just that...

she works here at the university, and we're trying to fly under the radar.'

'So how long have you and Leab David been dating then, Vice-Chancellor?' McCusker asked.

Chapter Twenty-Four

McCusker and O'Carroll arrived at Louis Bloom's office just in time for the 15.00 appointment with Miles Bloom.

The look on Leab David's face betrayed the fact that the Vice-Chancellor had already tipped her off that he'd told the detectives that, whereas Leab might just have been "washing her hair" on the night in question, but even if she had, she had been washing it in the company of the Vice-Chancellor.

As Miles Bloom was already waiting – Leab, it transpired, had already refused to allow him to enter Louis' actual office until the members of the PSNI were present – they didn't have time for a discussion with her.

Miles seemed to have calmed down since their last meeting; equally, he did not appear to be a brother grieving over his younger sibling.

McCusker took stock of Miles as O'Carroll directed the witness where to sit, successfully steering him away from his preference behind Louis' desk.

Miles Bloom carried himself with his head back and his chin forward, much the same as a boxer who did not suffer from a glass jaw. If you wanted to be unkind, McCusker thought, you could say he was continuously looking down his nose at the world. His grey-silver goatee defined the line of his jaw rather than his actual jaw defining the line of his jaw. He was dressed in matching blue denim shirt, with mother-of-pearl snap-buttons, and jeans. His shirt was out over his jeans and under the shirt he wore a black T-shirt. His American-flavoured outfit was completed with a pair of expensive-looking moccasins. He'd a full head of silver-white hair, and the parting, if there had been one in the morning, had been lost to the autumn winds and his earlier hissy fit up at his brother's house. He frequently swept his right hand – fingers first, from forehead to crown – through his hair. He had a habit of announcing this movement by hiking his shoulders slightly, as if he was lowering his head to accommodate the passage of his hand. McCusker figured that Miles Bloom had recently had a drastic haircut in that he was forever fiddling with phantom hair on his left shoulder. His silver stubbled face looked like it might be two stages this side of puffy.

'Do I need a lawyer?'

'We just want to ask you a few questions, Miles, but if you feel you'd like a solicitor present you're most certainly entitled to one.'

'I know my rights,' he snapped.

McCusker and O'Carroll just looked at each other with an "Okay, here we go then" look.

'What football team do you support Miles?' McCusker started, throwing in his own curve ball.

'What? What the eff?' Miles started, and immediately went into a rant that made Gordon Ramsey sound like a choirboy. 'Let me tell you something: I don't have time to sit here with you discussing effing football teams. Let me tell you something: I am a very busy person. Do you realise I have four – that's one, two, three, four – lawsuits going on at present...'

Mid-rant, McCusker turned to O'Carroll and in a quieter, yet audible voice continued to speak even as Miles ranted on: 'How many lawsuits have you currently in your life, Detective Inspector?

'...I know what's going on here, I know that Louis...'

'That would be none, McCusker, that's N, O, N, E,' O'Carroll answered.

'...disappeared, just so that he could put my money beyond me...'

'Yes, I'm the same as you, Detective Inspector; I find I can sleep better without them.'

'...I'm on to him. I'm on to all of you...'

'I mean, my solicitor is nowhere near as happy as he'd like to be,' O'Carroll ping-ponged.

'...I know for a fact it wasn't Louis' body that was found...'

'But you know what they say?' McCusker returned.

'...if he thinks by disappearing he's going to avoid our day in court...'

'What do they say, McCusker?'

'...that money is mine – he knows it, I know it...'

'They say that a happy solicitor is as strange, yet acceptable, as a dog walking about with a lampshade around his neck.'

'What the eff are youse two on about?' Miles finally conceded, as he banged his brother's desk loudly with his right hand, which immediately rose – stinging deeply, McCusker felt – to enjoy a wee, cooling-off dander through his hair.

'Well, we've heard that you do seem to like a wee rant every now and then, so we thought we'd just chat among ourselves and let you get it out of the way before we started the questioning proper,' McCusker replied, turning to face Miles Bloom for the first time in ages.

'But we'd also like to tell you this, Mr Bloom: question you we will, and we've got all night to do it if we need to. Equally, if we need to take you down to the Customs House to do it officially with your solicitor then we can do that too, it's entirely up to you,' O'Carroll stated.

'What do you want to know?'

'Miles,' O'Carroll continued, 'I feel I should also advise you that the body we found has been positively identified as the body of your brother, Louis Bloom.'

'What do you want to know?'

'Did you and your brother ever get on?' McCusker asked softly.

Miles signalled he was about to allow his hand another cruise through his hair, by hiking his shoulders.

'Let me tell you, even before I was aware of what "brothers" meant I never felt he was close to me. I never felt close to him. We didn't fight; we just didn't really get on. You see other brothers – and, yes, they would scrap a bit – but if anyone else picked a fight with one of them they were always picking a fight with both of them. I never went to Louis' rescue.'

'Did he ever come to yours?' O'Carroll asked, when it was apparent Miles wasn't going to add that caveat.

'You know, I'd really like to be able to say no,' he admitted, 'but when I think about it now, I'd have to admit that, yes, he did, he came to my rescue in a few scraps… and he'd help me out and try to cheer me up when it didn't work out with a girl.'

'So why all the bitterness?'

'My father was never on my side and he should have been.'

'But don't you think your father was just trying to prepare you for the world?' O'Carroll offered.

'Oh please!' Miles' voice rose again. 'Don't try and psychoanalyse me, sister.'

'It's none of our business, Miles, but a man's estate is his to do with as he pleases,' McCusker offered.

'Yes…' Miles appeared to agree, but then added, '…it's none of your business.'

'Well actually, it might be,' McCusker replied, firmly but not aggressively.

'How so?'

'Well, let's look at the facts,' McCusker continued, 'you're in dispute with your brother over the estate your father left him in his Will.'

'Let me tell you this,' Miles said, 'where there's a Will there's a… lawsuit!'

'That may very well be the case,' McCusker admitted, 'but you lost your lawsuit. As we're led to believe it, you lost several of them, so it would appear that as far as the law of the land is concerned, your father's Will is valid and you have no case. But for some reason or other you continued to hound your brother, way beyond what would be considered reasonable.'

'And your point, if there was ever going to be one?'

'My point is that you've tried every possible way to get your father's estate back again and you failed at every turn. Your father legally left the estate to your brother. Then your brother is murdered, and within hours you turn up at his home claiming that now he's dead, you are entitled to the estate. Most certainly this establishes a motive as to why you might have murdered your brother.'

'Holy Mary, Mother of God man, what were you thinking?' O'Carroll chipped in. 'She'd just recently lost her husband in such a tragic way and yet within hours you're round at the house, banging on her door, screaming and shouting like a spoilt child.'

"I've learnt to my cost that you can't win an argument with a lion – so you shoot first and then they don't talk back,' Miles declared proudly.

'Really? *Really?*' O'Carroll hissed in disbelief. 'That's what you want to say to us?'

'Let me tell you something about the precious door you said I was banging on,' Miles continued, completely unfazed, 'those doors were bought with my money. She is living under the roof of a house that was bought with *my* money.'

'Miles, just listen to yourself,' O'Carroll pleaded. 'Louis, as well as benefiting from your father's Will, was a very successful man. He bought Landseer Street with his own money, long before your father died.'

'You don't know what scheming Louis and my father got up to before my father died,' Miles shouted. 'Look, it's now part of the official record that he advised my father about how to pass the businesses on to the workers, just because he didn't want to run them himself.'

'Miles, the reality is different,' McCusker reasoned, trying once again to calm him down. 'The reality is that your father feared you would run the business into the ground.'

'That's your reality, brother,' Miles spat, 'it's certainly not mine. I think we're done here.'

'Miles, we're not done here,' O'Carroll advised him, 'not by a long chalk and if you force us to arrest you in order to question you further, we will most certainly do that and continue this down at the Customs House. Your call?'

'What else do you want to know?'

'Are you self-employed, Miles, or do you work for someone?' McCusker asked.

'What does that have to do with anything?'

'Well, it's like you mentioned earlier: you have one, two, three, four court cases currently running, and the legal system as we know it is very expensive, so I'm assuming you must have a job of some kind to fund your cases.'

'There's always legal aid.'

'Do you get legal aid, Miles?'

'No.'

'So are you going to tell us what you do for a living?' McCusker persisted.

'I'm a house husband,' he admitted.

'So your wife pays the bills?' O'Carroll said.

'Our *family* pays the bills.'

'I see,' O'Carroll said, betraying exactly what she saw.

'We'd like you to tell us what you know about Louis' life,' McCusker began, 'we're getting a picture from his friends, but I'd be really interested in your perspective.'

'Am I my brother's keeper?' Miles started off, surprising McCusker. Usually this was misquoted as "I am not my brother's keeper", which would have been more apt in the current circumstances. But interestingly Miles had quoted it correctly. Miles seemed to think better of what he had been about to say and eventually continued with, 'Louis was unhappily married to an unhappy wife who hangs out with a pot-head. Louis was the darling of the students on campus and the majority of his peers. He was a natural at public speaking. In his defence, he didn't seem to have an ego. He was the perfect child, youth, young man. He caused my parents no stress. He knew what he wanted to do and he knew what he had to do to do it; he just got on with it. He even willingly worked in my father's business to pick up pocket money. More fool him; I received the exact same pocket money without having to work and mix with humans.'

Guess which of the teenage brothers won that round, McCusker thought, uncharitably.

'He has a subject he is passionate about: love, which is kind of ironic considering the state of his own love life. He has a book he's been trying to get published for a few years. I tried to get a copy of it just in case it contained anything inflammatory about me. Our claim was rejected on the grounds that as there was currently no publisher, there was no need for justification. My lawyer did get an assurance from Louis' solicitor that I'm not even mentioned in the book. This in itself is quite interesting, in that if it's a book about his life, how come he doesn't even mention his brother in it?'

'Aye, it appears he's damned if he does and he's damned if he doesn't' McCusker said. He was thinking it, so he said it, then he thought perhaps he shouldn't have.

'But all in all,' Miles started, completely ignoring McCusker, 'apart from a disastrous marriage, hedid well for himself.'

'How's your father's businesses been doing since he passed?'

'Very well actually, no thanks to those fools he left to run it.'

'Is Louis involved?' McCusker wanted to continue with this line, if only to see where it would go.

'He had an honorary seat on the board, I believe.'

'He must do quite well out of that,' McCusker said, knowing in fact that Louis hadn't taken a salary from his father's business.

'Most likely raking it in from there as well.'

'Actually, Miles, he doesn't take a penny from your father's business,' O'Carroll started, seeming to have had her fill of Miles Bloom, 'and you know that very well, being such a litigious man. It is my opinion – and I should qualify that by saying it's not necessarily the view of the PSNI – that Louis behaved very honourably in all his dealings with his father's business and estate. He probably could have dumped you behind bars in court several times over the years with your outrageous claims and lawsuits against him.'

'*Really*, sister?'

'Yes *really*, Miles. And I can't understand your behaviour towards your brother. I have a real sister, Grace, and if she was ever left lock stock and barrel of my parent's estate, I would be nothing but over the moon for her.'

McCusker hoped it wasn't noticeable that he was absolutely beaming with pride, because he was.

'And tell me this, Detective Inspector O'Carroll: is this bitch, the one you refer to as your sister, is she really your sister or was she, just like Louis, an interloper and adopted?'

McCusker found himself involuntarily rise from his seat, and the seat swiftly flew back from him. O'Carroll simultaneously rose and reached across to him and put her hand on his shoulder in a vice-like grip, exerting such force on McCusker as to render him stationary. She mouthed rather than whispered the words, 'Leave this to me.'

Chapter Twenty-Five

'God forgive me,' O'Carroll hissed as they left Louis' office, 'but there is a part of me that would really like it to be him.'

'And it still might be,' McCusker chipped in, as they passed Galileo for the second time that day.

'I'll tell you, I was just this much away from arresting him,' O'Carroll admitted, showing a space of about an eighth of an inch between her forefinger and thumb.

'Yeah, I noticed you were as keen as a sheep in search of the shade on a hot day.'

'He'd just upped his own motive ratio with that bombshell about Louis being adopted,' she said, while still looking at McCusker and shaking her head from his last statement. 'But then I figured, we weren't quite there yet and I was scared of botching all of it up and being responsible for him getting away with murdering his brother.'

'Good call,' McCusker replied, trying a more conservative approach.

'We need to put a 24-hour surveillance on him until such time as we have enough to take him into custody,' she said, as they strode into their office, 'DI Cage – can I have a quiet word with you? I've a very important job for you.'

McCusker was impressed at O'Carroll's powers of delegation. It was so seamless, he never even noticed the join.

'We have a suspect – Miles Bloom – and I need you to–'

'I thought he was missing,' Cage said.

'No, that was his brother, Louis.'

'So have you found Miles?'

'Yes, sweetie, we have found Miles. It's Louis who is dead.'

'And you suspect the brother?'

'Yes.'

'And this is the case that the TV people are interested in?'

'Jarvis, it's going to be a big local case.'

'That's genocide isn't it, when a brother murders a brother?'

'It would need to be a very large family of brothers before it would qualify as genocide, so you're going to have to settle for fratricide on this one.'

'Can we title it the Fancy Fratricider?'

'They might think that's a drink from the West Country, sweetie. Why don't we just leave it to the TV people to pick the name?'

'Good point, DI O'Carroll,' Cage agreed, not even feeling the hook now deep in the roof of his mouth, 'no matter what we call it, they're probably going to pick their own name anyway. Right? So, what do you need me to do?'

'I need you to monitor Miles Bloom, 24/7.'

'Like a stakeout?'

'Not *like* a stakeout, but *a* stakeout.'

'I knew it, I just knew it,' DI Jarvis Cage hissed.

'What did you know, Jarvis?'

'I just knew when I woke up this morning that I was going to start working on my name-making case today, I just knew it!'

O'Carroll gave DI Jarvis Cage Miles Bloom's address and sent him on the way with the strict instruction to make sure that Bloom never spotted him.

* * *

Earlier, as McCusker was leaving Louis Bloom's office after the interview with Miles Bloom, Leab David handed him an envelope. The envelope contained the names of the four members of Magherafelt High School currently enrolled at Queens University, Belfast. McCusker read the four names aloud to himself as he sat down at his desk.

Sammy Bruce

Michael Lamont

Thomas Chada

Derek McClelland

Where to start? Barr was already busy checking if Al Armstrong had a criminal record. He also had Louis Bloom's journal on his desk, ready to go through it. He was also working on discovering the monies Louis Bloom and Ron Desmond had raised on their joint funding ventures, in order to ascertain whether all of those funds had reached their designated accounts.

O'Carroll was getting ready to leave the office, on another of her blind dates, McCusker reckoned. It was probably Mr Niblock's turn today. McCusker was quite sure her hairdresser had recommended him, but it was difficult to keep up with her industrious progress. She had even taken to using five-by-three cue cards, for heaven's sake.

Leab David, recently revealed as the Vice-Chancellor's true love, had kindly included street, email addresses and mobile phone numbers for the four former pupils of Magherafelt High School. So now McCusker had his starting point. He rang the numbers, one by one.

Sammy Bruce was both polite and friendly, and advised McCusker that he hadn't actually been in Botanic Gardens since September. Michael Lamont was in a hurry to leave his room to meet with someone, so he answered questions as he walked along. He said that he didn't currently have a girlfriend but that if there were spare kissing partners in Botanic Gardens, he'd make sure he visited there at the first available opportunity. Thomas Chada had his answer phone on and McCusker left a message. Derek McClelland was studying and was annoyed by the interruption – obviously not studying so intently that he had turned his mobile phone completely off, mind you. Perhaps he was scared of what calls he might miss. McCusker found himself wondering what calls McClelland was keen to receive. McClelland assured the detective that he'd also been studying the previous evening.

McCusker then began to try to convince himself that this – trying to track down the boy spotted kissing in Botanic Gardens last evening, just as Louis Bloom was murdered, or at the very least, kidnapped – was a foolhardy idea. To prove his point, he mentally listed all the reasons why his idea was a weak one, at best: the boy – well, more like young man, really – might have borrowed the scarf from someone in his accommodation; he might have borrowed it from the girl he was kissing; he might have found it; it might have been the scarf of an old girlfriend; he might have bought it at a jumble sale; he might have inherited the Magherafelt High School scarf in his current student accommodation.

McCusker paused work on his mental list when his desk phone rang.

'Is this Mr McCusker from the PSNI, Belfast?'

'Yes, I'm McCusker.'

'You just rang this phone a few minutes ago.'

'Yes, Thomas Chada is it?' McCusker asked, thinking that the caller sounded more like a mature student than someone who'd be out snogging with a girl in Botanic Gardens. He had to admit this was an option he'd failed to consider and was about to add it to his mental "bad idea" list when the voice in his Bakelite earpiece replied:

'No, this is his father – Harry, Harry Chada. Is Thomas in trouble?'

'No, no, not at all, not in the slightest,' McCusker continued, more than necessary, hoping to reassure the father. 'I believe he was in Botanic Gardens yesterday evening with…' McCusker was just about to say, "with a girlfriend" when he pulled himself up instantly in his tracks, not wanting to get Thomas in any more trouble, '…and he might have witnessed something. If you could just put him on, I'm sure it won't take more than a few minutes.'

'Oh, he's not here, I'm sorry,' Harry Chada said. 'He arrived back home here in Magherafelt this afternoon, and his friends picked him up about half an hour ago. They're headed off to Donegal for the weekend.'

'Oh I see,' McCusker said. 'But he was in Belfast last night?'

'Yes, he was in Belfast last night. Anyway, as I say, he's away for the weekend and he rushed off without his mobile. Normally I'd never answer his phone, you understand, but I thought it might have been Thomas checking to see if his phone was here or had been stolen. I didn't get to it quick enough, so it went to message, and then I got your message and thought the worst. It's so difficult; this is the first time Thomas has been away from home for any period of time and it's been very distressing for his mother and me. We're missing him every day but, even worse than that, he seems to be totally happy in his new environment and seems to barely spare us a thought.'

'Oh, you'll be okay; Belfast is very close to Magherafelt, so he probably doesn't even think he's left home yet,' McCusker replied, trying
to put a spin on it, fully aware of the leaving-the-roost syndrome.
'Could you maybe get him to give me a ring when he arrives in Belfast
on Monday?'

'Oh I will, Mr McCusker.'

'And please warn him that he's not in trouble.'

'I will and thank you.'

CHAPTER TWENTY-SIX

Just after 7 o'clock, McCusker was (genuinely) busy at his desk when he received a telephone call from Station Duty Sergeant, Matt Devine.

'There's a young lady down here called Le…' Devine struggled to get his tongue around the name.

McCusker heard a voice in the background saying, 'Leab, tell him it's Leab David, Louis Bloom's PA and–'

'I assume you got that,' Devine took over again. 'She says she's got something for you – she needs to hand it to you in person.'

'I'll be straight down.'

Leab David was on the way home, she didn't want to go back up-stairs with McCusker; she didn't want to go into the warmth and then have to go back out into the cold again. She was well protected from the cold evening anyway, with her black hoodie, hood up, black trousers and Ugg boots.

'I wanted to hand this directly to you,' she said, as she removed a DVD in a Perspex jewel case from her canvas bag. Someone (perhaps even Leab, McCusker reckoned) had written in large letters with a Sharpie: "L. Bloom, Emeleus Lecture Theatre Oct 2016, Love Lec-ture," on the front of the case. The same legend was also written on the DVD itself.

She handed it to McCusker. 'This is a copy of a video recording I made of Louis two years ago. It's pretty much the basis of the first lec-ture he gives to his students each year. The content might float around a bit, but then not really. I thought it might help you get to know Louis better.' Her voice was breaking up a bit. 'I wanted to try… to help you... to... you need to catch this person... please catch this person and punish them for what they did to Louis, Inspector.'

McCusker started off to explain that he wasn't an inspector.

She cut him off near enough immediately with, 'You and I are the only people who have a copy of this, so if it gets out... I'll know where it came from.' Leab turned on the heels of her Ugg boots and walked across the lobby.

'Thanks Leab, I'll be very careful with this!' McCusker called after her. Leab didn't turn around; she walked on and out of the door of the Customs House into Belfast's cold, blustery, autumn night.

McCusker immediately rang O'Carroll.

'Where are you?' he asked, once they connected after what seemed forever.

'What McCusker...' she started.

He could hear a lot of noise in the background. 'No it's okay,' he said, 'I'm sorry for disturbing you, I'll... it'll do in the morning.'

'No,' she said, clearly having walked to a quieter area, 'I can hear in your voice that it's something serious – what is it? Please?'

The detective explained what had happened with Leab.

'I thought we should view it together,' he added. 'But look, you're out for the night, so I'll save it until tomorrow.'

'No we won't,' she said firmly, 'on top of which he didn't even shower and shave for our first *and* final date. You've just given me the perfect excuse to cut it short and not have to pretend to be sociable and waste another couple of hours of my life.'

'Okay, if you're sure?'

'See you there in ten minutes. And get the DVD set up in the conference room so we can have a bit of privacy.'

Before she'd even disconnected the call, he could hear her say to someone 'Look, I'm really sorry. Something has come up...' before the line went dead.

Twenty minutes later, when this stunning looking woman walked into the office, McCusker had to blink twice before he realised it was Lily O'Carroll. He'd never, ever seen her with a skirt on before; she always wore trouser suits while on duty. He couldn't take his eyes off her. He couldn't believe how perfect her legs were, or how her subtle make-up softened up her look somewhat.

McCusker was quite literally left speechless.

'I appreciate the popping eyes, McCusker, and dropped jaw, but you're spoken for already,' she said, as she swished past him over to her side of their partner's desk.

McCusker apologised for interrupting her date.

'As I said, it was never going to work out. I will always forgive a man for maybe... well... let's just say, not turning out in the best of clothes. That's okay just as long as they're clean and his shoes are shined – but a bar of soap and a packet of razor blades cost nothing. I think it's written in the Bible somewhere: "For what shall it profit a man if he has a shiny brand new Jaguar F-Type in the driveway, yet he can't afford to wash behind his ears".'

'And what exactly was it you were doing behind his ears?' Mc-Cusker risked asking, before considering the wisdom of such an inquiry. 'No, no, sorry, I really don't want to know. TMFI.'

'That's a relief,' she said, laughing.

'What did he say when you told him you were bailing out?'

'That if I left, he'd cry.'

'No!'

'Yes!'

'How embarrassing! What did you say?'

'I said I'd make his tears my souvenirs.'

'Pass me the bucket. Do people really say this kind of stuff?' Mc-Cusker spluttered. 'It was a great line to come back with, though.'

'Not mine sadly,' O'Carroll admitted quickly, 'Charles Aznavour got there before me in his song 'She'.'

All the time, McCusker was tapping the DVD jewel case on the back of his hand. O'Carroll stared at his slow beat.

'But thanks again,' she said, 'for holding off watching this until I was around.'

And without further ado, they headed off to the damp-smelling conference room in the basement. The basement actually smelled of a combination of the damp and the air-freshener it was regularly sprayed with in an attempt to disperse the mustiness. Though all such thoughts were instantly forgotten the second McCusker placed the DVD in the machine, pressed the "Play" button and the wall-mounted screen flickered to life. O'Carroll jumped up and switched off àll the horrible fluorescent lights, focusing both their attention on the images developing on the screen.

The cameraperson – Leab David, McCusker figured – started off positioned by the entrance door to the Emeleus lecture theatre. She panned around the regal, original polished benches, which were fixed in gentle arcs across the room and inclined down in mini steps to a herring-bone-wooden-floor which was fitted right up to the platform. The room was side-lit by two tall single-bay windows, one either side of a four-bay window, all with red velvet curtains opened to their extreme to steal maximum light for the dark, woody room. The six inch high platform housed an in-situ antique desk-cum-lecturer's station containing several drawers and cupboards on the lecturer's side. To the lecturer's left, on the desktop, were a computer, keyboard and mouse, and to the lecturer's right was a large screen fixed to the wall. The camera actually caught the full extent of the excitement and the anticipation of the packed house of students, keen for their first lecture from the renowned Louis Bloom.

Louis himself appeared from out of nowhere and made his way, past the camera position, straight to his platform. McCusker was not prepared for his first look at Louis Bloom. Not because he had a dynamite presence, and not because he didn't, but more because of the contrast of the moving images on the screen and the corpse he had witnessed the previous morning up at the Lennon Mausoleum in the nearby picturesque Friar's Bush graveyard.

'Good afternoon, I'm Louis Bloom,' he began, pronouncing the silent "e" to his Christian name very positively. 'The majority of you are here, I assume, because you feel this course, The Politics of Love, will show you the way to true love.'

Louis Bloom allowed the resultant muttering from his students to grow for a few seconds before silencing them again with, 'It's not going to happen. You're all most definitely on your own with that one.'

McCusker wasn't sure, but he thought he could hear a sigh of disappointment from O'Carroll.

Louis Bloom looked even younger on the screen than he did in the photograph McCusker had seen earlier, up at his Landseer Street house. He was wearing tan chinos, black blazer and a white shirt. McCusker couldn't see what kind of shoes he wore. The droopy moustache in the photograph was missing, and he looked all the better for being clean-shaven. His copper-coloured pageboy hairstyle was very evident and healthy. He seemed totally comfortable, at home even, in the old-world, library-look of the Emeleus lecture theatre.

He paused for another beat before adding, 'And, if in your time here, any of you manage to discover such a path, if in fact such a path does exist, then perhaps you could share your secret with me. It'll come in very handy for next year's students.'

More laughing, and McCusker noted that the entire class visibly relaxed a little at this point.

'So, what do we mean by the word "love"?'

'It's a cliché to describe a deep feeling,' a girl in the front row could be overheard saying.

'It wasn't a question,' Bloom stated to friendly laughter, 'and I always find it's good to note that we have the word "cliché" in our language for a reason and, unlike this, it was never meant to be used as a put-down.

'But don't be discouraged... sorry, what's your name?'

'Eileen Rea,' the lone voice sheepishly replied.

'Eileen Rea – I was going to say that you shouldn't be discouraged,' Louis Bloom offered in a very friendly voice, 'even the dictionary can't properly define the word "love". One such tome states: "Babies fill parents with a sense of love." Yes, but what is this thing called love that babies fill their parents with? Is it truly just the affection a parent feels for a baby? I really don't think so. John Lennon wrote and sang "Love is asking to be loved", and later in the same song "Love is needing to be loved." But once again we have to repeat our question: "What is love?" We're still none the wiser.

'Another brilliant writer, Mike Scott – in one of his incredible songs, 'How Long Will I Love You' – wisely chose not to tackle the problem of *describing* love by opting instead to answer the question of his title and, in doing so, perhaps better than most, he captures some of the essence of love.

'Maybe that's the route we should choose to explore in this year's studies. Not to try to define the word "love" but to try to *show* love,' Louis said and then paused, paused just enough to change gear, 'I love movies,' he stated confidently as the cameraperson focused in on his face for the first time, catching him in a large, warm smile, one Mc-Cusker had never felt Bloom would be capable of from studying the photograph. 'I *love* to go to the cinema. I love to get lost in a movie. In order to successfully get lost in a movie the environment has to work. For me, the cinema needs to be quiet, clean and dark. I feel I should point out at this stage that I never feel the need to say "*very* quiet, *very* clean or *very* dark". To me a cinema is either dark or it's not dark; it's either clean or it's not clean; it quiet or it's not quite. Neither should a cinema be too warm or too cold. How many of you have seen the movie *All the President's Men?*'

The majority of hands were raised and there seemed to be a general muttering of approval. McCusker wondered how many of the students picked up Louis' switching from "quiet" to "quite" in that previous sentence. Was the play on words just for the students, or did he just throw it in there to amuse himself? Every time the camera panned to the students, hardly any of them were taking notes.

'That's one of my absolute favourite *filums,*' Bloom continued, fully pronouncing one of the Ulsterisms McCusker was frequently accused of using himself, 'in that when I watch it, I am not aware of a great screenplay, or great camera work, or great lighting, or how brilliant Robert Redford, Dustin Hoffman or Jason Robards are. I'm not even aware that there is a screen. I am right there in the newsroom of the *Washington Post* and I don't see Jason Robards' Oscar-winning performance – no, I see Ben Bradlee and I believe it *is* Ben Bradlee. I see Woodward and Bernstein, not Redford and Hoffman. I am not hearing lines from William Goldman's Oscar-winning script; I hear the words spoken by Ben Bradlee, Bob Woodward and Carl Bernstein. I don't see or hear actors pretending to be Messrs Bradlee, Woodward and Bernstein. I'm able to suspend disbelief and be transported to the scene, totally, and, more importantly, I am not even aware that I am being transported. To me that is a successful movie: a movie where no pretending exists.

'Love is another place where pretending doesn't exist.

'Perhaps when you're in love, you don't even know it.

'When you're in the state of love, you are not preoccupied with it, with love that is. You just *are.* You don't play or *pretend* at being boyfriend and girlfriend. Sometime later, however, when it's over, you may come to realise that, yes, *what* you'd just experienced was in fact love. The only sound advice I was ever offered was: nothing stays the same – everything, but everything, including The Glee Club, changes, so enjoy it while you can.

'If you ever find yourself wondering are you doing the correct thing in the right order, are you saying the right thing at the right time, have you left it long enough before ringing back, is it too much time or too little between dates; if you find yourself preoccupied with you or your partner's pleasure, or doing anything for effect rather than just doing them from the heart, then perhaps you have to accept that you are not in love.

'I frequently wonder at what age we form our preferences of attraction. Have our preferences been there, somewhere in our psyche, all the time and we just grow into becoming aware of them and accepting them at a certain age? And here's another important thing to think about: is it at all possible to change your preferences? Or, is there such a thing as a simple universal beauty that everyone will be attracted to? We'll discuss this again in a few minutes.

'We instinctively pursue love from an early age, even though we don't really know what it is. We may not know what it is, but we certainly quickly learn how cruel it can be.

'When we're younger and cheated on, it's devastating, and it most certainly kills a part of us. But of course we will get over it. Or at least we reach a stage where we *think* we've gotten over it. The reality is, deep inside, we feel that there is still something wrong. Something will have hijacked our natural momentum and feeling of wellbeing. Knowing that our relationship didn't work out the way we dreamed/needed/thought it would, manifests itself in our acceptance that fundamentally our lives are not the work of perfection we thought them to be.

'Yes, there will be other people, potential partners and our earlier disappointment will be well hidden, but rest assured it will never, ever go away completely.

'It is very important to be aware of two vital pieces of information here:

'1. Take heart from the fact that even if your life had continued with your ideal dream-partner, it would still never have turned out to be perfect. Perfection doesn't exist, and if it did, it would be incredibly boring. Struggling, striving, fighting for it, for your love, for your life, is the real nirvana.

'2. You'll also find the people who leave you will rarely just fall for someone else. No, initially before that stage comes for them, they will also cheat on you. What's more, they will cheat on you with someone you already know – like an ex-partner of theirs, someone who they know you hated, or even a friend or a relation of yours. A brother or a sister scores highest points, followed closely by someone they knew you'd be sure to be jealous of. Their cheating will have been skilfully manoeuvred to cause you the greatest hurt possible. They didn't really have to do that to you, did they? So clearly they *needed* or *wanted* to hurt you.

'Why?

'Is this also part of this mysterious thing called love?

'Are they doing it to you just to get their own back on someone, a third party, who has already done the same to them, or are they just trying to chalk one up, in advance, to even up the score for when it (surely) will happen to them?

'I'd like to stay with this theme for a while longer if you don't mind. It will certainly have been painful, probably even devastating at the time, but hopefully enough time has now passed that it's now going to be fun to look back on.'

He pauses to look around at the faces of the students.

'Okay maybe not, but if only in the name of further education we should still examine our feelings. So, you're lucky enough to be dating a girl or a boy you're happy to be with. Initially he or she seems happy to be with you. A bit of time passes and you instinctively feel something is wrong, but you can't quite put your finger on it. Couldn't we have all saved ourselves so much pain if we'd only listened to our instincts? It appears, apparently, that he or she has come to the conclusion that you're not the right girl or boy for her anymore, and so she can't be with you. Unlike Phil Collins, she can't dump you by fax – maybe by texting, but certainly no longer by fax.'

Louis paused shortly to allow the resultant hissing from the girls to die down

'No, he or she has to take you out to tell you. And wouldn't you know it, but it's to a very expensive spot. I started to turn down invitations to very expensive spots, not because I was mean but because I felt I knew what was coming. Over dinner, she'd claim she loves you, but she doesn't *love* you. So she dumps you but not until after the only dessert of the evening. Yes, she splits up with you. She masterfully breaks your heart in so many different ways. But she doesn't let it rest there. No, she can't. She finds a new boyfriend, as you knew she would. But that's not what really hurts you. What really hurts you is that she takes her new boyfriend to the places she used to take you. You're forced to imagine she's doing all the things she used to do with you, with her new boyfriend. And then you pick up the courage to ring her one night. When you ring her you get her answer machine and her voice says: "Jean and Louis (meaning *you* of course) can't come to the phone right now, because we're having *so* much fun." Of course, you know it's not you she's currently "having so much fun" with, and either she has forgotten to change your name on the answer machine, or she's found another way to hurt you by leaving it there.

'And you're forced to remember what it was like when you first got together. In a way, getting together with someone new is a lot like the feeling of enjoyment you experienced with a new toy when you were younger. Unlike the chemical induced highs of drugs and alcohol, this new toy is safe and free and available each and every day. You both enjoy this new toy immensely and when you are apart you imagine and plan for the great fun you're going to have with this new toy when you get together again. Perhaps neither of you is ever brave enough to declare what you'd really like to do with this new toy. And maybe you should have. Could that have progressed this new toy to love? Probably not, but you'll never know. Now she was sharing this new toy with someone new and "having so much fun", *so* much so she couldn't possibly answer the telephone.

'What you're now feeling, as the great song goes, "can't be love, so it must be influenza".'

Again, more laughter from the audience, and maybe, encouraged by Bloom's approach to the lecture, McCusker thought, the raucous laughter was no longer polite.

'Even more surprising in the game of love, you will find yourself doing things you never thought yourself capable of. Maybe even devious and spiteful things, but we can all leave the remainder of that topic to our imagination, if only because I don't want to be accused of giving any of you vengeful notions.

'When love goes bad, or sour, always try to remember and take heart from the fact that at the time you declared your love, as you made love to your beloved for the first time, that you really meant it, and that they, in turn, really meant their physical and vocal reply. What comes later, when love is lost, in no way diminishes what you both felt and what you both said and did in those initial days. In those special days the power of the words far outweighed the power of the physical coupling.

'But equally we should beware, because love and sex are never, ever the same. Sex might very well be a part of love. However, it's also worth remembering that no matter how passionate you are and no matter how sound your back may be, you will still need something else to do to occupy the remaining twenty-two and a half hours of each day.'

Louis paused as the laughter gathered up a head of steam.

'This year, we'll also need to consider relationships where the *love* of our course topic will neither be sought nor discussed. In those relationships we discover the joy of a true partner is the lack of agenda. Even though the relationship may never break the borders of carnal, it's enjoyable because the priority of the pleasure is mutual. Yes, just two people gleefully taking sensual advantage of each other, and where you will find yourselves grow quite fond of each other. So, consequently all the other "stuff" – where "stuff" equals all you would cite in a divorce – is so much easier to take.

'In today's society so much stock is set by looks, or maybe *the* look might be a better way to describe it. You can't get hung up about it. And mostly people don't. Generally speaking though, people do take their assets for granted – that's *physical* assets, of course. I mean, there is no reason whatsoever in the world why one person would have a beautiful body or face or, even more annoying, both, and the next person doesn't. I'm referring here to male *and* female assets of course. I kind of hanker back to the days when we were all encouraged to count our blessings, and one by one at that.

'I know this is a cliché – another cliché,' Louis said and paused to look at Eileen Rea, 'but in matters of love, beauty really is in the eye of the beholder.

'Let's take an example. A man talks to his friends about his partner – and really, we're all guilty of this, aren't we? That *was* a question this time, Eileen.' Louis Bloom refrained from looking at Eileen as he said this. To McCusker, it looked like Eileen Rea was keenly doing what she'd do in every Louis Bloom lecture thereafter – keeping quiet. McCusker hoped that wasn't really the case. Perhaps Louis Bloom had hoped that as well.

'So, we're out with friends and we go on about how magical, spiritual and special our partners are. We'll go on and on about just how beautiful they are, how stunning they are with their perfect figure – yes, well fit and totally dope, or whatever the words we use nowadays to describe how perfect and cool your partner is.'

Chuckling was heard on the sound-track from various parts of the lecture theatre.

'Through time your friends will end up with this incredible picture of your partner, even though they've never met them. Well eventually your friends do get to meet your partner and... well... but of course they are going to be disappointed. I mean, grossly disappointed. And this disappointment is going to be very evident in their eyes. At the same time, you will be equally disappointed in their partner after all the bigging up your friend has done on their partner's behalf. And of course, if you've got your own eyes open you will also be able to observe the same look of disappointment when the partner meets *you* for the first time, proving your friend has also been equally generous in their compliments about you. So the question is: how can we all get it so wrong? Unless of course we add the "love factor" into the equation, and then maybe we're not getting it wrong at all.

'I mention this not to comment on people's looks or physiques but more to see if this phenomena is a clue to one of the secrets of what love is.

'Let's throw another cliché in here for our friend Eileen,' Louis Bloom continued, and this time Eileen laughed as much as her fellow students. Yes we all say, "Beauty is only skin deep." And it surely is... however once you're intimate with someone, they change. They lose their air of mystery. But be prepared for the fact that you are also losing your own air of mystery. You will realise that the Spanish hat they were wearing when you met first them in a wine bar, the one you thought was very cool and set them apart from the crowd, well, you'll start to think that they only wore the Spanish hat because they wanted to appear as sexy as Penélope Cruz. So, you'll eventually discover that your new acquaintance was more interested in sweating the small stuff. Yes, most definitely you'll discover she's more than preoccupied with the small stuff, such as avoiding the aforementioned sweating like she would the plague; or keeping a mental list of those places that have the longest waiting list for the latest hoodie; or where to get the best Spanish hats; or which anti-aging cream really defies both science and decay and actually works; that she has spent considerable time – and even more money – trying to come across as alluring and beautiful for men as she can, yet she doesn't want to be treated as a sex object. Whereas you thought she was the real deal, the only real woman you'd ever met in your life. A woman, you might have thought, was way beyond the word 'love' and all its human imperfections. At the same time she was most likely equally disappointed in you, because you couldn't drink multiple shots; or you didn't wear Nike; or perhaps you weren't on Facebook – actually, even I know Facebook is no longer your version of Glee Club, so maybe we should now be talking about Tinder, Twitter or Snapchat. Yes, disappointed in you just because you refused to grease and spike up your hair...' and here Louis paused once more, this time to borrow a mirror from a student to puff up his hair a bit and view with disgust the reflection.

'I can't believe this guy,' O'Carroll said, 'he's hilarious and so on the nail.'

McCusker couldn't be sure, but he thought he saw her wipe some tears from her eyes.

'So, we will look at what it means to really love someone. We'll also consider what happens when the one you love dies and they're no longer in your life – what exactly will that change? It's easier to assess what it changed in their life, in that they sadly no longer exist. Certainly you can no longer converse with them, but you can still *talk* to them or, at least, to the memory of them, and, depending on how well you knew them, you can guess their reply. So what else is different? I mean, no matter how tight you were with someone, you still couldn't have been in their lives 24/7 or even 12/7, for that matter. What were they doing for you that you miss – that you not only miss, but that you can't do without? Surely the reality is that no matter how much you think to the contrary, time will sadly prove that you *can* do without them. Does love linger on or does love expire as well?

'Is love a necessity? Is love merely the glue that holds the success of mankind's future through its shortcut to procreation?

'The animals elect for an easier route: they eat; they fertilise the jungle; they do the deed; they sleep; they wake up; they eat; they fertilise the jungle some more and they do the deed again. Admittedly they don't get to dress up in their finest and head down to the Europa with their true love to see Sir Van Morrison do his thing. But is that really all that separates us from animals?'

'What, love?' a solitary voice asks.

'No,' Louis Bloom replied, right on cue, 'our ability to pretend.'

'A lioness, when confronted by a lion from another pride, keen on eating one of her cubs, will initially fight like crazy to scare off the lion. However when she sees she's about to lose the fight she will become all coquettish. She'll turn her neck to the ground, roll around in the dust and submit to his amorous advances, knowing perfectly well that he's going to kill her at the end of their tryst, but in the meantime her cubs will, hopefully, have been cute enough to escape. Now *that* sounds like real love to me, perhaps a different kind of love, but love nonetheless. The lioness isn't pretending; she's just doing what she has to do.

'At this stage I feel I should also point out to you that if you're ever close enough to observe the above, the lion has another noticeable trait. Just before he is about to attack his prey he licks his paws – the jungle equivalent to nipping into the bathroom to wash your hands just before you eat. The lioness does this too. So I'm suggesting to you that if you see a lion lick its paws, then you get the heck out of there as quickly as possible.'

More laughter on the soundtrack, this time even more relaxed.

'I'd like to conclude our chat with a line from the pens of Mr John Lennon and Mr Paul McCartney, which we will definitely debate further during the term:

"And in the end the love you take is equal to the love you make."

Louis pauses and makes his best effort to look each and every student directly in the eye.

By their silence and attention, they acknowledge that is exactly what he is doing.

'Thank you,' he announced after a minute, with a slight bow of his head.

Louis Bloom took the students' applause for a few minutes before adding above the din, 'No need for any more applause, thanks – it won't better your grades.'

That was it. He was off, past the camera and out of the room. The camera kept on recording the hustle and bustle of a large class of students breaking up.

McCusker thought that the secret to the success of Louis' pubic speaking was that he had really found a technique where he could stand on a stage - this time on a platform raised but a few inches from the floor, in what would be McCusker's favourite type of space - and talk to roughly 140 people, yet make each and every one of them believe that he was having an intimate and personal conversation with them, on a one-to-one basis.

CHAPTER TWENTY-SEVEN

'Can I drop you anywhere? O'Carroll asked, as they walked out of Customs House.

'Where're you off to?'

'I was going to head home.'

'Let's go and drop in on Elizabeth Bloom and see how she's doing,' McCusker started, 'then Grace and I were going to go out for a bite and before you say a word, when we were setting it up, she did ask me to also invite you.'

O'Carroll accepted immediately – she admitted to feeling "all dressed up with nowhere to go" and looked happy for the company.

McCusker wondered about the dating game. He knew so many people out there looking and yet here was a woman of immense beauty and understanding, finding it difficult to make the connection she so clearly sought. He loved her dearly for never, ever feeling sorry for herself over it. McCusker also liked the fact that even though Lily O'Carroll was keen to find her life-partner, she just wasn't prepared to accept just anyone, and was holding out for the right one.

Elizabeth Bloom looked equally happy for the extra company, and studied O'Carroll up and down closely before saying, 'Are youse two out on a date?'

O'Carroll laughed and then said, 'No – sure, he's already spoken for.'

'Is Mr Armstrong here?' McCusker asked, as Elizabeth Bloom led them through to the living room.

'No, he was here earlier but he scarpered when Angela and Superintendent Larkin dropped in about an hour ago.'

'I bet,' McCusker said, under his breath, wondering how WJ Barr was getting on checking if Armstrong had a criminal record. Out loud the Portrush native said, 'How have you been getting on?'

'Oh you know,' she said through a large sigh. 'I find myself talking to Louis, then I realise it's not him answering me; it's my imagination and I'm just being a silly moo. Angela and Niall, and even Al, have been great to me, trying to support me while equally trying not to crowd me.' She looked like she was about to have another moment but then she snapped herself out of it and said, 'Right, who's for tea?'

'We're going on for supper from here so we're okay thanks,' McCusker, a man rare to turn down any chance of a nibble, replied.

'So youse *are* on a date?'

'We're joining his girlfriend – my sister, Grace – for a meal,' O'Carroll offered, in hope of clarity.

'Augh but sure you'll have a wee cup of tea in your hand, please?'

Arm sufficiently twisted, McCusker said, 'Oh go on then.'

'There was a letter that came for Louis this morning. I opened it. I hope I wasn't doing anything wrong. It's on the mantelpiece there, have a look,' she said, as she disappeared into the kitchen.

O'Carroll walked over to the fireplace and lifted the letter that had been opened cleanly with a letter opener, rather than being ripped open by someone's finger.

The letter was from Random House Publishing, now officially listed as Penguin Random House UK and based at 155 Oxford Street, London. Basically, the publishers were acknowledging that they had received Louis Bloom's manuscript, *The Politics of Love,* that they had read it and were very excited by what they had read, and that they'd like to offer him £210,000 against a royalty percentage to publish the book in the following autumn's list. They noted Louis didn't have an agent and asked him to contact them immediately to finalise details.

McCusker felt himself getting very excited on Louis' behalf, much the same way he did while willing Rory McIlroy on to greater and repeated successes.

'That's amazing news, isn't it?' Elizabeth said, as she returned with a tray, with three cups of tea, already poured and milked, and a few scones.

'That's brilliant news, Elizabeth,' O'Carroll agreed.

'Just incredible,' McCusker chipped in, finding himself welling up a bit.

'The silly bugger worked on it for ages. He never showed me a word of it, of course, but I do know he was very proud of it. I think he'd pretty much given up on anything happening with it.'

'Can you imagine how happy he would have been if this had just arrived 24 hours earlier,' McCusker said.

'Do you think they won't publish it, now that he's... he's passed?'

'I think they made their offer based on how great they think the work is – they'll still publish it,' McCusker enthused.

'How can I make sure this whole thing goes through properly? Someone like Miles would have been green with envy if he'd known Louis was going to have a book published. Mind you, I always thought Miles had a great book in him – I'd even picked out a title for him: *Fifty Shades of Mean*. Even Al wasn't as excited about Louis' book deal as I was when we read the letter... if you know what I mean.'

'I'd say you should have a chat with the Vice-Chancellor about it,' McCusker volunteered, 'he was a very good friend of Louis', and due to his status at QUB he'll have a certain amount of clout and I imagine prior knowledge of publishing deals.'

'What a great idea, that's what I'll do,' Elizabeth gushed.

'Talking of Miles, we chatted to him earlier this afternoon,' McCusker said.

'Had he calmed down?'

'Somewhat,' O'Carroll offered, 'but he claimed that Louis was adopted.'

'Oh right.' Elizabeth sighed the sigh of a woman who'd been haunted by a sensitive matter for years, but now she'd finally reached the point where she could enjoy the sheer pleasure of the large white elephant balloon in the room being completely deflated. 'Did he go on and on about his mother always playing Hank Williams' 'My Son Calls Another Man Daddy' record around the house to rub all their noses in it?'

At that, Elizabeth Bloom actually broke into a verse:
"My son calls another man Daddy
He'll ne'er know my name nor my face
God only knows how it hurts me
For another to be in my place."

'Louis' mother had a son (Louis) with another man,' she continued. 'She'd just turned twenty. Miles' dad, Sidney, had already been happily married to Miles' mother, who died in childbirth. Miles survived.

'Louis' mother worked for Miles' father in his shop. Actually, it was Miles grandfather's grocery shop at that time. Louis' mother helped Miles' dad raise Miles as a baby. Miles was a year older than Louis.

'Eventually Louis' mother also helped keep Mr Bloom's bed warm, if you get me drift,' Elizabeth said, as McCusker and O'Carroll sat mouths agape. 'Then Miles' father and Louis' mother married and Miles' father became Louis' father and Louis' mother became Miles' mother.

'Miles and his father were always arguing over something or other – that's where he took it from. Miles' father never even had a single argument with Louis in his life.

'Miles felt his father owed him everything, including a life. He continued arguing all his life. He wanted to be like his dad. He argued about everything with everybody. The big problem is, he really doesn't *think* he's arguing, he thinks he's just putting you right. He knew he was going to end up like his dad, but not as rich, because he'd never work as hard as his dad had. Deep down, though, he'd always wanted to be Louis, if only because he felt that his dad always favoured Louis. And that's what made him so bitter.

'Louis never agreed this with me, but I always thought that Miles's dad was never ever going to leave Miles a penny, if only because the father thought Miles was responsible for the death of the only person auld man Sidney Bloom ever loved: his first wife.'

* * *

McCusker, Grace and Lily's dinner in Deanes at Queens absolutely flew by. McCusker loved the fact that Lily looked good, so good in fact that neither he nor Grace had to actually say so. He loved to see the sisters together; they were great company to be with in that they didn't go all cliquey on him with non-stop in-jokes. He also felt somewhat spoilt in that he got to see a side of each of them that the other never witnessed.

They closed Deanes at Queens, in that they were by far the last ones out. Without asking, Lily O'Carroll dropped them both off at Grace's apartment.

Ten minutes later, Grace and McCusker were enjoying what was fast becoming their favourite shared moment; Grace stripped down to her undies, McCusker more discreetly attired, both lying on top of Grace's made-up bed, talking, occasionally caressing. Surprisingly they didn't discuss the intensity of their shared moments from the previous night.

Grace asked McCusker what his childhood was like.

'I didn't have rich parents but we had a rich life,' he explained.

'You just never know do you?' she replied. 'I mean, about people. Our Lily figured you came from a rich family.'

'Really?' he asked, trying to figure out when he would have given her that impression.

'Well, she thought you always wore fine suits and shirts but she's never been able to work out if they're expensive or not.'

McCusker considered this for a few moments.

'Oh, don't be going all self-conscious on me,' Grace said. 'Lily said that to me long before you and I met. Since we started dating, she hardly says a word about you. The fine suits conversation might have been the only one we had about you. Just so that it's all on the table, she also said you had smiling blue eyes, you were about forty-seven ish, you love your food, but you burn the cals by walking a lot – and she'd never known anyone who walked so much. She also said you didn't like scruffy coppers and you have an eye for a beautiful woman.'

'That was you,' McCusker admitted, excitedly. 'I kept seeing you in McHughs. Every time I went in there, it was you I saw, but I didn't know it at the time.'

McCusker had never felt this comfortable with a woman before. It hadn't always been like that with Grace. They'd gotten off to a very slow start, as it were. While walking her home on their first date though, they'd found each other's hands. Their fingers touching for the first time was one of the single most electrifying moments of his life. They hadn't even kissed that night. There had been no need to. After that it went pretty slow, as in very slow. Then eventually they had kissed. Then a month later, they had come together. He felt, he said, the delay was her trying to decide. Afterwards she said she knew from the first moment their fingers touched that they were going to be to-gether, but that *he* wasn't quite ready for them to be together. She also said that for them to have a proper chance it was vital they took the first steps carefully.

'Lily knew that she wanted to be a detective when she read *In Cold Blood* for the first time,' Grace started. 'When did you know?'

'My mother always said she knew from the time I was six that I was going to be a detective, because I told her I didn't believe in Santa Claus anymore. She protested, and asked me why I thought that. She said I claimed I recognised the kind hands, and the wedding ring, of the white bearded man in the red suit giving out presents at Sunday school to belong to a friend of the family. She thought my early powers of deduction set me off on the road to the RUC.'

'McCusker, what can you do, that you have never, ever done before? That you will do for me now to seal our union or, to put it another way, to get you laid?'

He thought about this long and hard, and again about the previous evening's encounter. 'I know,' he said, quite nervously, 'I can do a headstand.'

'You can stand on your head?' Grace said, through a fit of giggles, 'and you've never done it before in front of anyone?'

'Correct!'

'Okay, McCusker I'll take that as a worthy gesture,' she said, even though she was still finding it difficult to stop laughing.

McCusker hopped off the bed, went to the middle of her bedroom and placed his forehead on the carpet. Using his hands, palms upon the carpet, to support himself, he raised his feet shakily up towards the ceiling. He steadied himself, but was finding it difficult to retain his position because Grace's laughter and applause was distracting him. She was leaning over the end of her bed in her full glory and his inverted view of this wonderful, full-bodied woman was enough to make him collapse in a heap on the floor, which also helped to spare him carnal blushes.

She rolled onto the floor beside him and they both fell into a hysterical, tear-inducing fit of the giggles. Then they climbed back into bed and every time they tried to get close, one or both of them would break back into a fit of the giggles, to the extent that McCusker's headstand turned out to be in vain.

CHAPTER TWENTY-EIGHT

DAY THREE: SATURDAY

Superintendent Niall Larkin had okayed overtime for as many of the team as DI Lily O'Carroll deemed necessary, which is how Barr, McCusker and O'Carroll were all at their desks by 9 o'clock that Saturday morning. The first thing they needed to do was to update the noticeboard. They were at the board when Larkin walked in.

'Perfect timing,' he said, as he strolled over to them, 'where are we up to?'

McCusker nodded to Barr's to-do list and general case updates:

<u>Current Issues:</u>
1. Awaiting Leab David's email of L. Bloom's email nutter file.
2. Louis journal to be read. McC.
3. Thomas Chada will phone Monday a.m.
4. CSI soil inspection results.
5. 4 rubbish bags inspection results.
6. L Bloom's email account.
7. Where was L Bloom on Thur p.m. 16.00–17.30?
8. What was L Bloom's £2G a week for?
9. Cage on Miles Bloom's stake-out.
10. Armstrong's criminal activity?
11. Funds raised by L Bloom and Ron Desmond?
12. L Bloom asked Harry Rubens to analyse his wife's energy drink – results?
13. Review CCTV footage of the surrounding Botanic Gardens, Colenso Parade area.
14. Scent on L Bloom's baseball cap?

Alibis:
1. Leab David – in alone, washing hair.
2. Vice-Chancellor – with Leab David. Both now agree.
3. Miles Bloom ?
4. Al Armstrong – in alone, writing songs.
5. Ron Desmond – in Dublin, alone, back in Belfast @ ???
6. Prof Vincent Best – with 2 chums until 2.30 a.m.
7. Harry Rubens – in office, working alone on Stranmillis Road.
8. Sophie Rubens – Eric Bibb blues concert at MAC, alone, confusion over layout?

Outstanding Interviews:
1. Mariana Fitzgerald
2. Francie Fitzgerald
3. Muriel??? MURCIA!!! Friend of Mariana
4. Al Armstrong (again)
5. Sophie Rubens (again)
6. Thomas Chada (potential youth in the scarf at scene)
7. Miles Bloom (again – with solicitor)

Rubbish bag Owners:
1. Elaine Gibbons, Elaine Street. Addressed envelope. Black bag (8.00 p.m.)
2. George Divito, Stranmillis Gardens, Indian takeaway Green bag (8.40 p.m.)
3. L Bloom, Landseer Street. Blue bag (9.00 p.m.)
4. T Husbands, Landseer Street, Amazon packaging. Grey bag (9.20 p.m.)

McCusker wasn't even aware that Wee George's family name was Divito until he saw it listed on the Perspex noticeboard. The ever-efficient DS Barr must have asked his full name on the way out.

'Okay, well, there's no questioning the approach – all seems very sound and thorough to me,' Larkin started. 'Is there a reason why we still don't have the rubbish bag's inspection results? I thought they'd all been examined and that was how you discovered the identity of the other three owners?'

'Yes exactly, Sir,' McCusker started, 'but we were mainly looking for information on the owners, the first time round, but then we thought, what if Louis Bloom's priority on Thursday night hadn't been getting the rubbish out of the house? What if his priority was to get rid of something he just didn't want in the house? What we haven't been able to find, so far, in the house is anything… well, anything revealing. So we started to consider what might be missing from the scene and then maybe how did whatever might be missing, go missing.'

'Good, good thinking,' Larkin said. 'Mariana Fitzgerald is next on your witness list? They're just outside of Bangor, aren't they? That's a bit of a drive for you?'

'Mariana volunteered to come in and meet us in Belfast, Sir,' O'Carroll offered.

'That's handy; you might even get to enjoy a bit of your Saturday, DI O'Carroll. Right, I'll leave you to it. I'll be upstairs if you need me for anything.'

Barr continued with his chores and O'Carroll and McCusker set off to meet up with Mariana Fitzgerald at the Merchant Hotel in Skipper Street. The former bank was now considered to be a very hip and cool hotel. McCusker figured that hip and cool must mean having a lack of light. In fact, it would have been much easier for them if they'd brought a couple of flash lamps along. Eventually they discovered Mariana in a secluded annexe, trapped in the darkness of one of the hotel's complicated labyrinths.

Mariana Fitzgerald's signature dark hair was even longer than McCusker had expected. There were a few, a very few, hints of grey specks starting to creep through her hip-length hair and it was to her credit, McCusker felt, that she wasn't trying to hide them. She rose from her seat when she saw they recognised her, and walked towards them. She was tall, slim, and sultry, with hints of an Eastern European look. Her accent, however, was pure, unadulterated Belfast. She had very big, round, sad eyes. She wore an expensive-looking cream blouse, loose-fitting black trousers and black ankle-length high-heel boots. Her movements were extremely laboured and she appeared to help herself back into her seat by supporting herself on the arms of the black leather chair.

From nowhere, McCusker found himself wondering if her husband had hit her. There were signs of pain in her eyes, yet at the same time there was always a hint of a smile present.

'We wanted to thank you for coming in to see us,' O'Carroll started, getting the etiquette out of the way and ordering a "do not disturb us again" supply of tea, coffee and mineral water from a passing waiter.

'I can't believe it; I spoke with Louis on Thursday afternoon,' Mariana said. She spoke very quietly, gently even, a couple of decibels above a whisper.

'What time would that have been?' McCusker asked, knowing from Barr's research that it was at 15.55.

'It was in the afternoon, 4 o'clock, maybe a little earlier,' Mariana replied.

'How did he seem?' O'Carroll asked.

'He was Louis, no?' she replied, meaning, McCusker assumed, that he was like just like Louis Bloom always was. She pronounced the name "Louis" with the slightest hint of a French accent. 'I mean, he was good. Louis was never down, he was a good friend, a great listener, he was – yes, he was always supportive.'

'You'd known each other for a while?'

'Oh a good while now.'

'Sophie Rubens introduced you?'

'Sophie Lawson, sorry, sorry, but of course you know her by her married name,' she replied. Sometimes she spoke so softly that McCusker had to really strain to hear what she was saying. 'Yes, Sophie introduced us and we became great friends.'

'You dated for a while?' McCusker felt she was maybe flirting with him a little with her eyes, so perhaps it was best he continue asking the questions. O'Carroll, with her recent silence and scribbling in her pink book, seemed to concur.

'We dated? But no, I mean we went out to dinner on certain dates, we had good fun, yes, but there was no funny business, nothing romantic...'

'Did, you...' McCusker started to ask his next question when he realised that she might not have finished her answer. 'Sorry, you hadn't finished?'

'No, I mean, I was only going to say that we weren't "just" good friends, you know, as people sometimes say to maybe suggest that it was a less intense or, shall we say, *inferior* relationship.'

'I see.'

'Louis Bloom was such a wonderful man and such a great friend,' she positively gushed, for her at least. 'You have to realise... for instance, when I had trouble with Francie...'

'Francie?'

'My husband.'

'Yes, of course,' McCusker said.

'Well, I really needed someone like Louis,' she started hesitantly. 'You see, girlfriends can sometimes be too anti-men to give good councel in such instances. Louis could always see the big picture in matters of the heart.'

'What was the problem you were having with your husband?' McCusker asked, innocently.

'But he didn't want to get married,' she protested, 'Mariana can only wait a certain amount of time for you men to make up your mind.'

'Oh.'

'You say "oh" as if that is okay behaviour,' she protested again, 'are you married Inspector McCusker?'

'I'm not an inspector,' McCusker explained, as the PSNI insisted he do, 'I'm a freelance agency cop, attached to the PSNI.'

'So you're not even a proper cop,' she said, giggling. 'But why should I even talk to you?'

McCusker waited for O'Carroll to come to the rescue, only she didn't. She continued taking notes. McCusker, in the awkward silence, wondered what exactly it was she was writing; there certainly wasn't much conversation currently. McCusker hadn't realised that immediately after Mariana had said "you're not even a proper cop" that she had winked at O'Carroll. O'Carroll advised McCusker of this after the interview as they walked back from the Merchant Hotel to the Customs House. O'Carroll also mentioned to McCusker that she didn't think it was so much that Mariana was flirting with him, as it was that she was such a ridiculous flirt that she was even trying it on with not just the waiter but also the leg of the table. 'But in the nicest possible way, you understand,' she'd added.

'Well now, let's see,' McCusker started back up, when he became aware that O'Carroll was not in fact going to take over the reins of the interview, 'well, we are here to try and find out what happened to your friend, Louis Bloom, and as his friend we feel you might have some valuable information, which might help us apprehend the person who killed him.'

'Of course. I see.' She smiled, her big, sad eyes betraying the extent of her personal loss. 'But you still haven't answered my question?'

'Mrs Fitzgerald asked you if you were married,' O'Carroll said, pointedly, reading from her notes.

'Oh but please, call me Mariana,' she said, 'I hate being called Mrs Fitzgerald; it makes me sound like a really old, Irish washerwoman, with my shawls gathered about me, down at the riverside.'

'Yes,' McCusker eventually replied, 'I was married.'

'But no longer? No longer?' she repeated.

'No longer,' McCusker confirmed.

'Divorced?

'Not... so far.'

'So you are hoping?'

'No, not possible.'

'Your fault or hers?'

'When a marriage fails, I think both sides must share the blame and I'll certainly admit to my fault in it not working,' McCusker replied, as honestly as he knew how. He normally wouldn't be so open to strangers about his personal life but he hoped that by being candid with her she would return the favour. On top of which, he was under a certain degree of scrutiny from O'Carroll, if only on her sister's behalf.

'And you?' Mariana asked, shining the spotlight on O'Carroll who had most certainly been guilty of hiding her light under a bushel, deep in the shadows of the Merchant Hotel's lounge.

'No, I'm not an agency cop, I'm a detective inspector with the PSNI,' she replied, and McCusker acknowledged with a quiet nod that she had shown great restraint by not using the oft-quoted line: "I'm a proper cop."

'But no,' Mariana persisted, perhaps showing she was happy that the attention had been drawn away from her for the moment, albeit temporarily, 'I meant are you married, DI O'Carroll?'

'No,' O'Carroll replied immediately, 'but I am looking,' she added through a laugh.

'Perhaps I can help you with that,' Mariana replied, in not much more than a whisper, as McCusker continued.

'You were telling us about the difficultly Louis helped you through.'

'Oh yes. So he supported me; I was talking a break from Francie when I met Louis and he was the perfect remedy for a relationship on the rocks. You know, if anything, I had Louis to thank when Francie came calling again. Before Louis, I had dreaded, that if a man doesn't marry me, that's it, I'm on the scrapheap. After I met and had started a friendship with Louis, I was more "if you're not going to marry me, your loss! I'm off to find someone worthy of me!"'

'How did your husband feel about your new friendship with Louis?'

She gave McCusker a devilish wink and said, 'I've found it's not a bad thing if your man is aware he shouldn't take you for granted. Did he think I slept with Louis? He probably did. I certainly did deny it – not too energetically, you understand, then you might start to give off a "methinks you do protest too much" vibe.'

'And Louis and Francie met?'

'Oh yes, they seemed to get on okay but they were never best buddies.'

'What did Louis think of Francie?'

Mariana laughed and thought for a few seconds. 'You know,' she started, 'I asked Louis that very question when they met for the first time. Louis said, "You know what, Mariana, a man can never own a woman the way he owns a classic car or a grand house – the house or the car will never, ever answer back – but Francie, well, Francie certainly has the wherewithal to finance your lifestyle. I've always found that to be one of men's greatest qualities."'

'But Louis never had any trouble with Francie?'

'Louis didn't really do trouble – either he really liked you, and was interested in you, or you pretty much didn't exist. He didn't waste energy hating people.'

'What about Al Armstrong?'

'Good case in point: an unexceptional man who proves the rule. I don't believe Mr Armstrong ticked any of Louis boxes of interest. He was a friend of Louis' wife and so Louis was polite to Mr Armstrong but never over-friendly.'

'Did Louis ever discuss the situation with his wife?'

'Elizabeth was like a sitting tenant in that marriage,' Mariana said, 'but he'd never discuss leaving her, let alone think about it.'

'Do you think Louis was the type of man who felt, "I've made my bed, so I'll lie in it"?' McCusker asked, trying to mould the conversation around to extra-matrimonial relationships.

'Most certainly not. He was not a man to shirk his responsibilities. But, no, Louis most definitely would never have felt or said that.'

'Do you think Louis had other relationships?' McCusker asked, hoping, she wasn't going to say "no" and close this topic down totally.

'This is very difficult for Mariana,' Mariana admitted, 'I know this could be very important for you but...'

McCusker could feel both himself and O'Carroll not breathing out for fear any movement in the universe might cease further discussion on the topic.

It certainly turned out to be a breath well held.

'...you see, they were both friends of mine.'

'Louis' girlfriend you mean?'

'...I keep thinking if I hadn't introduced him, he might still be alive. Now he's dead and she's petrified.'

Chapter Twenty-Nine

'It's probably going to be more helpful to you if Mariana starts at the beginning,' Mariana began, as she breathed out for the Island of Ireland, the resultant pain etched across her face. 'I was attracted to Louis – I mean, it was impossible not to be – but I took an oath to myself that I wouldn't get involved with anyone else until the situation with Francie had fully resolved itself one way or the other. As I might have mentioned to you earlier, at that point I was equally happy to commit to Francie, or content to let him go. Louis helped me to get to that point.

'He was charming; while in one breath he would say he would never leave Elizabeth, in the next he would admit that he was attracted to me. But for Louis it was no biggie that I shouldn't or couldn't. I couldn't even work out which of those two it was. If he liked you, then he didn't suddenly stop liking you, just because you wouldn't get physical with him. But more importantly, we had great fun as we were growing to be friends.

'At the same time this was happening – or not happening, if you want to look at it that way – between Louis and I, another friend of mine, Murcia, a friend I used to work with, was trying to extract herself from a very bad marriage.'

'O-kay,' McCusker said, as Mariana seemed to have reached a full stop of consideration.

'Maybe I need to go back even further,' Mariana said.

O'Carroll and McCusker both nodded at her to continue.

'I used to work as an escort,' Mariana admitted, 'it was a top-class escort service… oh my goodness,' she said, sighing through a large exhale, 'I don't think I should tell you this but I've thought a lot about it and feel it would be better for your investigation that I should, so I will.' She sighed again, took a deep breath and whispered, even quieter than normal, 'for Louis.'

McCusker nodded his agreement, or acceptance – he couldn't really work out which, but he prayed she wouldn't lose her nerve and he made a promise to himself to stay quiet until she'd reached the end of this.

'Cards on the table, here,' Mariana continued, looking like she was mentally taking the plunge, 'when I say "escort service" I don't mean that as a euphemism for a high-class hooker. However, in the course of full disclosure, I will admit that we... well, at least *I* would go on some of these dates and if the gentleman behaved well and took me out a few times and was well-mannered and I was attracted to him, well, then I would do what any girl would do on an ordinary date with a man who ticked all those boxes.

'And yes, I will also admit that on those dates, my escort fee would be increased accordingly. So far so good,' she whispered, and paused to refresh her coffee.

'Is that when you met Francie Fitzgerald?' McCusker asked, risking the wrath of his colleague.

'Yes,' she admitted, 'and I always felt that was why it took him a time, quite a time in fact, to get his head around marriage. The real crux of the matter was that Francie had to reconcile himself with marrying an escort girl.

'The money I earned was absolutely amazing and I put the majority of it away to secure my independence. That was also when I met Murcia. She was great fun and we became firm friends. She met someone she was escorting who fell for her hook, line and sinker. He was rich, and he chased her and chased her, until she eventually agreed to give up the work and marry him. Noah Woyda – he's a self-made Belfast-based businessman. I've never been able to fully understand what business he's in, but believe me, he's rich. He's so rich. Poor Francie is a pauper in comparison. I bet there's no noisy plumbing in Mr Noah's house.

'Mr Noah didn't want Murcia associating with any of her former colleagues, even Mariana, so I lost touch with her for a few years.

'Then, late one night my phone rings and it's poor Murcia and she's crying saying, "Please help me, I just had to get out of there". She'd run away and was ringing me from George Best Airport. I drove on out there and picked her up. The poor girl was black and blue. I have to tell you something here about Murcia. She's the spitting image of a smaller version of Marilyn Monroe. She's very quiet, doesn't say much, but, and without even knowing it, she's very sensual and extremely sexy. She was very popular as an escort. All the boys wanted to sleep with her. Again, like me, she would only sleep with people she liked. The men she liked would just keep on offering more and more money until she would eventually sleep with them, then she would admit to them that she would have slept with them for free because she liked them. But that night she was in a bad state and it turned out that Noah had beaten her up just once too often. Why would a man beat up his woman just because she looked like Marilyn Monroe?'

'Most likely,' McCusker suggested, 'he beat her up because she *wasn't* Marilyn Monroe.'

'You know, you might be right, agency cop. Murcia told Mariana that Mr Noah wanted to better himself through the things he owned, to show people he'd made it. She figured his successful businesses, big house, big cars, big paintings – the bigger and more expensive these things, the better Noah thought it showed him to be. Yes, Murcia would say, "Big, big, big. This big, that big, everything big and then me, little wife who looked like a movie star", and we'd both fall about laughing.

'Anyway, long story short, we'd a lot of false starts, a lot of help initially from my husband, who was a real trooper when this all blew up. Eventually, with the help of a restraining order, we managed to get her away from Mr Noah.

'Time passed, Murcia had started to pick up the pieces of her life again and Francie and I were looking after her and she started to fancy an ever so tiny bit of independence. Mr Noah is ensuring divorce proceedings are going nowhere, and fast, and Murcia said she wouldn't mind doing a bit of escort work again, but she doesn't want to do it with the agency in case she bumps into Mr Noah again. So Mariana thinks about Louis, and I introduce them and, surprise, surprise, they hit it off. They are very discreet for lots of reasons but eventually they're… well, I'm just so jealous because they're bonking each others brains out while Mariana appears to have grown into an old woman.'

McCusker thought, but didn't say, 'And?' As in "And then what happened?" But nothing more was forthcoming. That seemed to be the end of the story, as far as "Mariana is concerned", as she would say, in her confusing manner of frequently referring to herself in the third person.

'So do you know how often Louis and Murcia saw each other?' he offered instead.

'No, I wasn't involved in setting it up, apart from…'

'Apart from?' McCusker coaxed.

'When Louis needed to get a message to Murcia, but he wasn't sure where she was, or if Mr Noah was around, he didn't want to land her in any trouble and he didn't want to phone her at an inopportune moment.'

'Like yesterday, for instance?'

'Yes, like yesterday for instance,' she replied.

'Where did they meet?'

'She would book a room in the Dukes Hotel on Botanic Avenue and pay for it in cash, give her postal address as mine. He'd meet her in the bar and if the coast was clear, they'd hook up and retire to her room. To ensure they didn't raise the suspicions of the staff, she'd always stay there overnight. Louis would discreetly leave after their adventure. Sometimes I'd join her afterwards for a meal and a girl's late night.'

'And he rang on Thursday because…?'

'Because she wasn't in the bar and he was checking to see if there was any change to their plan.'

'And was there?'

'No, Louis was just early, that's all.'

'Did Noah Woyda know about Louis?' McCusker asked.

'Well, even when there was nothing happening in Murcia's life, Mr Noah believed there was.'

'But did he know it was Louis this time?'

'Mariana and Murcia believed he did; that's why Murcia and Louis were being ultra-careful.'

'Did Al Armstrong ever sell you any drugs?'

'He tried. But Mariana had seen too many beautiful young women in the escort agency destroy their bodies, you know, where once they proudly wore tight-fitting jeans, the jeans no longer fitted them tightly in all the right places. And that's before you consider what the horrible stuff does to their minds. So it's always been a no-go area for me.'

'Where were you, Mariana, between 9.00 on Thursday night and 1.00 on Friday morning?' McCusker asked.

'Francie and I were at home having dinner with two friends of ours, Ross and Samantha Wallace.'

McCusker and O'Carroll looked at each other.

'Sorry, what? What is wrong?'

'We know them.'

'Really? No! How?'

'They were also friends of two of the suspects in another case we worked on…'

'Oh, of course,' she gasped, 'Ryan and Larry O'Neill. That was such a tragedy.'

'What time were you with Mr and Mrs Wallace?' McCusker asked.

'They arrived at our house just before 8 o'clock and left way past midnight.'

'How can we get in contact with Murcia Woyda?'

'To be honest, I don't know. She was staying at an apartment I have here in town but she wasn't there all day yesterday, nor last night. Mariana thinks she's gone to ground because of what happened. I'll try and get a message to her to give me a shout, and I'll put you in touch with each other.'

It was a very unsatisfactory arrangement. Mariana said that she (and she actually referred to herself as Mariana again) was happy to give them Murcia's mobile number, which she did, but as predicted it went straight to voicemail.

'She'll get in touch with me a lot quicker than she'll get in touch with you. I promise I'll give you a shout.'

She asked for O'Carroll's number, but not McCusker's, and 57 minutes after they first met her they were getting up to go when she rose unsteadily to her feet with a look midway between shock and surprise.

'Oh my goodness, and here is the very husband I was talking about, Mr Francie Fitzgerald! He can confirm Thursday night's arrangements for you.'

'I thought I might find you here,' Fitzgerald said, with a soft, Free State accent. 'I thought we might have a bite of breakfast together,' and then without waiting for a reply, continued, 'Where's Murcia?'

Mariana just glared at her husband before saying, 'This is DI O'Carroll and Mr McCusker – they're working on Louis' case. Perhaps you should also have a chat with them? You knew Louis quite well. Sorry darling, I've another appointment I have to dash off to. See you at home, sometime in the afternoon.'

Mariana Fitzgerald was gone – gone as quickly as she could hobble out of there, leaving her husband quite speechless.

'Must have been something I said,' he muttered, as he took over his wife's seat.

Francie Fitzgerald had a bushy red beard and matching long red hair, which he had done up in some elaborate system that concluded in a bun towards the rear of the crown of his head. McCusker felt that someone should take a photograph of the back of Fitzgerald's head; he was convinced that even Fitzgerald himself would agree the resultant spaghetti junction was not an attractive sight. Fitzgerald was tall and heavy-set. He removed his long, flowing, dark blue button-less coat with a buckle-less belt of the same material. The belt had been tied in a half-reef knot, as in the left-under-right-and-over section. Underneath the coat he was wearing what looked like a pair of Virgin first-class black pyjamas, matching top and bottoms. Surely he must have something warmer, McCusker thought. Fitzgerald's outfit was completed with a pair of black laceless Dr. Martens.

'So how's the case coming on?' Fitzgerald asked, rubbing his hands together, perhaps to regenerate some of the heat his body was losing through Sir Dickie Branson's jim-jams.

'We're collating information at this stage,' McCusker admitted. 'Just for the record, what were you doing on Thursday night?'

'I know the routine, Inspector,' he interrupted, with his voice booming all over the place, 'I imagine Mariana has just told you we had the Wallaces over for dinner. They arrived around 8 o'clock and they left when it was way past midnight. Is it true Louis was murdered with a single shot between the eyes?'

'DI O'Carroll is a DI, I am not – I'm an agency cop, freelance,' McCusker advised, for the record, because he had to.

'Great, you mean just like Pinkerton's Assorted Colours?'

'Pinkerton's Assorted Colours was a 1960s pop group who were a one-hit wonder with 'Mirror, Mirror',' McCusker replied, quickly correcting what was becoming a very common mistake. Nine out of ten times when McCusker mentioned the words "agency cop", Pinkerton's Assorted Colours was thrown back at him, but thanks to Barr's mysterious Google, McCusker now had all the correct information at his fingertips. 'I believe what you meant is: Pinkerton's Detective Agency.'

'Okay,' Fitzgerald shot back at him, clearly ignoring the information. 'What does a man have to do to get a cup of coffee in here?' he continued, smiling just too sweetly at O'Carroll.

'Asking politely is always a good place to start,' she said, as she very conveniently caught a waiter's attention.

Francie Fitzgerald ordered not just a short cappuccino, but also a round of bacon sandwiches: 'Fat cut off, bacon done crispy, sandwich packed, soft bread – the kitchen knows how I like it done.' No please or thank you.

'Did you spend a lot of time with Louis Bloom?' McCusker asked.

'Well he was a good friend of my wife's, and we'd occasionally bump into him at QUB fundraisers and social events, but like, I'd never go to a game of rugby with him – you only do that with your mates, don't you?'

'Have you any idea who might have murdered him?'

'Of course not!'

'Did you know any of his other friends?'

'As I say, I only really knew him because he was friends with Mariana, and they liked to have a good old gossip every now and then. But like, neither his wife nor I were ever invited to those. Was he in trouble with the PSNI? It was always my understanding he was quite well-off. I mean, he never flashed the cash, but I'd heard that he was well set up. How did he make his money, do you know?'

'Do you know Noah Woyda?' McCusker asked, ignoring Fitzgerald's questions.

'Well, I knew him as the husband of Murcia,' Fitzgerald replied, 'is there a connection to Louis?'

'When was the last time you saw Louis?'

'When was the last time I saw Louis,' he said, pretty much mimicking McCusker's accent perfectly. He looked to O'Carroll for approval, and finding total indifference, he continued, 'probably last month – Mariana will know the date for sure.'

'Mariana looked like she was in pain,' O'Carroll said, flatly. 'What happened to her?'

'What did she say happened to her?'

'We know what happened to her, we'd like to hear your version,' O'Carroll continued. McCusker willingly played along with the bluff.

Fitzgerald looked like someone whose coke confidence had just worn off very quickly. He glanced around the room, either to check who else was in there or if the waiter was about to rescue him with the delivery of his customised sandwiches. No waiter. No rescue.

'Listen, like I told her,' he whispered as he leaned towards them, 'not to mess with him. I warned her she was on her own. I warned her not to cross him. She's seen what he'd done to Murcia.'

'Why don't you press charges?' McCusker asked.

'Are you fecking crazy altogether?'

McCusker sighed.

'I told her: anyone asks me, she walked into a door.'

'Well, if your wife walked into a door,' O'Carroll said loudly, 'then the door in question was attached to a car and the car was breaking the speed limit.'

Something twigged in Fitzgerald's eyes.

'You haven't a clue what happened to Mariana, do you?' he said, looking scared.

McCusker could see Fitzgerald mentally re-running everything he'd said, desperately searching for something, anything that might have got him into trouble. Only the detective could see that it wasn't getting in trouble with the PSNI that was worrying his interviewee.

'I know nothing, absolutely nothing,' he hissed, 'you want a statement from me, that's exactly what it will say: "I know nothing."'

'What about Murcia,' McCusker asked, 'from your point of view, what exactly is going on there?'

'As far as I can see, her husband loves her, worships her in fact…'

Just then, Fitzgerald's bacon sandwiches arrived.

He greedily took a bite, a large bite – half of one sandwich, in fact – and munched away as he held a thumb of approval up to the waiter. He pointed to his chomping jaws, hopefully as a sign that he didn't want to speak with his mouth full.

'You know,' he said, licking his lips, 'that was exactly what I needed.' He then proceeded to tuck into the next one. Fitzgerald repeated the same routine of pointing to his munching mouth. When he finished his second sandwich, he wiped off his mouth with the napkin. McCusker was still convinced there was enough food lost in his beard for a satisfactory "afters" session.

'Tell you what, DI O'Carroll and Mr McCusker, if you want to talk to me any more we need to do it in the company of my solicitor.'

With that, he stood up, pulled on his coat, gathered it about him by securing the belt –this time in a full-reef knot – and strode off purposely as if he thought (or maybe hoped) that there was a camera following his exit.

'Excuse me a moment, DI O'Carroll,' McCusker said, and casually strolled off after him.

McCusker waited until Fitzgerald was literally 3 feet from the front door of the hotel – and freedom. The detective reached out and firmly put his hand on Fitzgerald's shoulder.

'Excuse me, Sir,' McCusker said, quite loudly, as Fitzgerald turned around, literally bricking it. McCusker let him sweat for a few moments, wondering why exactly Fitzgerald looked so nervous and so worried. 'Do you realise that it is an offense to leave an establishment without paying for the food you ordered, and consumed, on the premises?'

McCusker felt he was guilty of behaving a little childishly himself, but it had been worth it, for in the moment after Fitzgerald had turned and his initial shock of being stopped had dissipated, he dropped his guard, and the gentle-giant image had quickly been replaced by a look of sheer, unadulterated, liquid hatred.

CHAPTER THIRTY

'I've got something I need to do this afternoon,' McCusker started, as they walked back to the Customs House.

'You have some PB with your wife, Anna Stringer, don't you?' O'Carroll said, sounding nervous.

'You'd be the detective then,' he replied, more amused than upset. 'How'd you know?'

'I figured she'd have suggested a weekend day so you wouldn't have an excuse to say no to her. You told me she's very religious, so Sunday was out.'

'I feel like I've taught you all I know, Grasshopper,' McCusker said, his feeble attempt at aping David Carradine's Kung Fu's wistful voice falling flat on its face, and deservedly so.

'Holy Mary, Mother of God, McCusker, please, for my sister's sake at least, try and give me something from this millennium.'

They walked on in quietness for a few minutes.

'I really don't know why my sister is with you,' O'Carroll said eventually. 'I really don't – you're so… grand-pappy. Why is she still with you?'

O'Carroll looked at McCusker. McCusker looked back at her with just the slightest hint of a grin.

'Oh, you – dirty – dog! You dirty dog, you. That's way, way too much information, McCusker. For heaven's sake, man, stop your smirking or I'll never be able to look my sister in the eye again.'

'"For heaven's sake",' he repeated, 'surely that's a very grand-mammy thing to say?'

'Grand-mammy, McCusker? Don't you mean Grannie?'

'Okay, surely Grannie is a very *grannie* thing to say.'

'Right, Mr Yellow Pack, it's back to work for you. Before you leave for this big meeting with your wife, it's my job to ensure the PSNI gets our shilling's worth out of you.'

McCusker was going to make reference to the fact that even he knew that a shilling was no longer legal tender, but he didn't want to push his luck too far; after all, there was a big puddle coming up at the edge of Customs House Square.

Inside their office, McCusker added a few details to the notice-board. He talked DS Barr through what they'd discovered during the meeting with Mariana Fitzgerald.

'Any sign of any form yet on Al Armstrong?' McCusker asked, at the end of the briefing.

'He was on the Drug Squad's – as it was – radar but he never really got himself in trouble with them. A few warnings, a few seizures of assets, but grass is so low priority these days, they just laughed at me when I asked.'

McCusker was visibly deflated. He didn't mean to show it, but he kept thinking that people like Armstrong always seemed to get away with stuff, the jammy barstewarts that they were.

'However,' Barr continued, 'a few years ago Armstrong ended up in the Royal Victoria Hospital...'

'Goodness, he wasn't pregnant was he?' McCusker joked, honing in on one of the grand hospital's specialities.

Much to O'Carroll's chagrin, Barr shared McCusker's sense of humour. McCusker wasn't sure that was entirely true – that O'Carroll was that annoyed at his humour - because she derived so much of her own humour at their joint expense, so her faux protests were most likely part of her rap.

'I'll check the Guinness Book of Records, but no, I don't think so,' Barr replied. 'But apparently the then RUC was called in as routine by the hospital, because he'd been beaten up so badly. It turned out that Armstrong had been set upon by some of the casual labour he'd been using for work on one of his refurbs. All of this five-man team claimed, to a man, that there had been a disagreement over payment. They said in their statements that Armstrong had short-changed them by two weeks' wages. Armstrong had maintained that as it had been in cash, they'd just been confused. Armstrong, the RUC files recorded, had raised the "cash" angle in the hope that his team, in fear of the taxman, would walk away from the dispute. He'd been wrong. The boys had also blatantly said that Armstrong had attacked them and they'd been forced to defend themselves. Armstrong refused to press charges, claiming it had all just been a misunderstanding, and wisely settled the disputed amount with the team before he was discharged from the hospital.'

'Street justice,' McCusker claimed, and took a certain amount of pleasure out of the story, but nowhere near as much as he'd been hoping for. 'How are you getting on with the Nutters Email File?'

'Slow work,' Barr said, not as a complaint but more a statement of fact, 'it's mostly boring people with an email account who have no one to communicate with, so they seek out people like Louis, or politicians or celebrities, to vent their spleen on. I eventually managed to get into Mr Bloom's own email account and trawled through that for a couple of hours just using key words, and it's just normal day-to-day work stuff. Either he had another private, personal email account or he didn't communicate with his friends by email. I'll broaden the search just in case he was consciously hiding stuff behind coded words.'

'It's all a process of ruling out both people and stuff at this stage.'

'But do you think this recent development with your discovery of a girlfriend could be thing behind all of this?' Barr asked.

'At this point I'm leaning towards Thomas Andrews.'

'Thomas Andrews?'

'Thomas Andrews. Aye, I'm leaning towards Thomas,' McCusker said, sighing, 'if only because he's blamed for everything else.'

'But surely he went down with his creation in the Atlantic on April 15th 1912?'

'Is that a fact, Willie John,' McCusker replied. 'In that case you can remove him from our suspect list immediately. Progress at last!'

'Have youse two ever thought of going on the stage?' O'Carroll asked, rolling her eyes.

'No,' McCusker replied, 'do you really think we should?'

'Yes, definitely,' she offered sweetly, 'I believe the next one for over the Glen Shane Pass leaves the Crown at 1.00 p.m. so you've got five minutes to get there.'

'You're kidding,' McCusker gushed, in genuine horror, as he jumped up from his chair and swung his coat on, 'that means I've only got five minutes to get to the Fitzwilliam.'

He wasn't sure, but he thought he heard O'Carroll call out 'Good luck' after him, as he crashed out through the doors of the office.

* * *

McCusker was nervous about meeting his wife. He couldn't really call her his ex-wife because they'd never legally separated. Anna Stringer, because that is how he always referred to her, both vocally and mentally, had just one morning upped and left him. Thinking about her name, he'd referred to her so much as Anna Stringer than eventually after a few years she also slipped into the habit of referring to herself by her maiden name until eventually, without informing McCusker she was doing so, she changed the name on her passport from McCusker to Stringer. But anyway, be that as it may, one morning Anna Stringer just upped and left him. Well, actually it wasn't quite as simple as that.

In the months before, she'd accomplished a very fine impersonation of Amelia Earhart (or a re-enactment of Agatha Christie's 1926 Theresa Neele/Harrogate adventure); she'd quietly and secretly busied herself with liquidating all their assets – mostly properties they'd purchased for rentals in the lucrative Portrush area. She'd been so effective in her efforts that McCusker hadn't even noticed she'd sold the very house they were currently living in and had rented it back from the new owner. Then one evening McCusker came home from work (late as usual) and she'd gone. All her stuff with her, and the only evidence was a postcard of Barry's Amusement Arcade with the note "Goodbye Brendy, Anna", scrawled in the back in her spidery handwriting. McCusker hadn't a clue where she'd gone. He'd guessed, but never checked, that she'd done a midnight flit to America where she had a sister. Later he discovered the full extent of her pre-departure pilfering.

McCusker didn't entirely blame his wife for her actions. He'd realised, especially since he'd met Grace, that he'd never, ever been in love with his wife. He had been very naïve way back then. There had been an intense – non-consummated – teenage relationship with jet-black-haired Adelle Hutchinson, but Anna Stringer had been the first person he'd slept with and, consequently, he felt he should marry her. You couldn't really say they'd grown apart, because they'd never been together. They lived two separate lives under the same roof. They enjoyed what could be called a "static-free co-existence". He went about his life enjoying being a detective and hanging out with his mates as they pretended to play golf.

Then, at the time of the Lord Patten scheme and, due to the fact that he'd been promoted to Detective Inspector but had found himself doing more desk-work than investigating, McCusker had decided to take Patten's lucrative early retirement package. The idea was that he and Anna Stringer would sell all their nest-egg properties and slide off into a Primark- or Apparel-dressed retirement, mainly composed of golf jumpers. Clearly the lure of golf widowhood had not appealed to Anna Stringer, and so she took matters into her own hands and set her sights on a more Ralph Lauren-sculptured landscape.

McCusker didn't really begrudge her, her drastic, and final, approach. His logic was that the reality of their situation was their property portfolio existed solely through her efforts and his Patten handshake (minus the gold watch) was his, and all's fair in the absence of love. O'Carroll had frequently argued that he was entitled to at least 50 per cent of the net results of the property sell-off. He had noticed that her arguments had become more frequent and fierce since he'd met Grace.

Apart from all the predictable problems Anna Stringer's departure had caused, and there were many, there were two that particularly troubled the detective. The Patten pay-off, generous though it was, was by itself certainly not sufficient to finance the remainder of McCusker's days. The downside was that once you took the early retirement package, you could never join the ranks of the PSNI again. McCusker thought long and hard about what other work he could do and came to the inevitable conclusion that the only thing he was capable of doing, the only thing he wanted to do, was to solve crimes. So he'd visited his former boss, Superintendent Thomas Davies, in Portrush. Davies had put him in touch with a good friend of his, Superintendent Niall Larkin, who was stationed at the Customs House in Belfast.

Larkin came up with a solution for McCusker, and it was based on the strength of Superintendent Thomas Davies' unreserved recommendation. If McCusker would register with the Grafton Agency in Belfast, then Larkin would be able to hire him in on a freelance basis, as what was affectionately known as a "Yellow Pack", Yellow Packs being an reference to the inferior in-house supermarket brands.

That is how McCusker moved down to Belfast and found himself partnered up with DI Lily O'Carroll.

Now just when he'd settled into enjoying his Belfast life, Anna Stringer was back in Ulster and he was on his way to the Fitzwilliam Hotel, to see her for the first time in two years. He'd discussed the invitation with Grace, who had encouraged him to go and see her. Even Lily, who was never backward about coming forward, had said, 'Holy Mary, Mother of God, McCusker – she's your wife, you know, and I'm just saying,' as she directed McCusker's eyes to her sister, 'maybe it would be a good idea if she wasn't your wife anymore. I'm just saying.'

That was of course if DI O'Carroll ever *just* said anything.

As he made his way up to the suite that some of the hotel staff had nick-named the Frank Lampard Suite, he wondered about the sense of visiting Anna Stringer in her rooms. He also wondered why she wanted to see him. As he knocked on the door in the dark corridor he found himself quietly whispering one of his mother's many famous phrases. "Wonder in one hand and wee in the other, and see which one fills first."

* * *

Forty-seven minutes later he made the journey back along the shadowy corridor, into the lift and down into the lobby of the Fitzwilliam, where the very first person he spotted was DI Lily O'Carroll, non-nonchalantly reading a local daily newspaper.

She was visibly shaking when McCusker sat down beside her by the lobby's faux fireside.

'Your *Tele* is upside down,' McCusker offered in jest.

For a split second he had her, and she quickly squinted back at the page. She was still shaking as she untidily folded the day's early edition of *The Belfast Telegraph*.

'Does my sister have anything to worry about, McCusker?'

'Only that one of her sister's blind dates is going to get her whole family in trouble someday soon.'

'McCusker!'

'Lily,' he said, and he rarely called her Lily, 'I love you dearly for caring about your sister so much, but can I just say that Grace and I are both totally okay with each other. In fact, she had me at "Hello", and I haven't looked back since. She knows that there is nothing Anna Stringer could say or do today, or ever, that is going to change what is between your sister and I.'

'So what did she want?'

'She wanted to tell me that her sister in America died eighteen months ago, shortly after she went over to America, in fact. She also told me that she and her sister's husband are going to get married and she's going to settle in America permanently. She wants a divorce.'

'And that was it?' O'Carroll asked, snapping back into her usual upbeat spirit. 'And that's all?'

'Yeah, I think that was all. Let's think, was there anything else? McCusker hammed, playfully, 'oh yes, I knew there was something else. She brought me a cheque for my half of the sale of our properties.'

'Holy Mary, Mother of God!' she involuntarily said, with a loud gasp.

'She apologised – she wanted to make her peace with me. She and her husband-to-be want everything settled so they can get on with their new life without having to look over their shoulders. I told her about Grace and she seemed genuinely happy for me.'

'Can I just say,' O'Carroll said, as she sidled up to him as they departed the Fitzwilliam ten minutes later, 'don't ever used the word "cheque" in public again, particularly in somewhere as public as a hotel. People, cool people, don't do cheques any more. That's just so old-fashioned, McCusker. Financial transactions are concluded by swift or electronic transfers these days.'

'Oh okay,' he said, appearing to take his chastisement on the chin. 'In that case, I won't be "uncool" and show you how much my cheque is worth.'

Neither gave way to the other as they scrunched tightly together through the swinging doors. She playfully elbowed him in the ribs.

CHAPTER THIRTY-ONE

DAY FOUR: SUNDAY

The morning after his meeting with Anna Stringer, McCusker woke up alone, feeling like he was back in his childhood house up in Portrush once more. He could hear all of the familiar sounds and voices outside his bedroom window, just like it was yesterday. The Booths were fighting; the Morrows were bawling; Mary Rose Porter was leaning on her gate gossiping with a shop boy; the Smiths were mowing the lawn; Papa Hepburn was chasing the daughter and the McCuskers (no relation) were washing and shining their fleet of cars.

McCusker hadn't seen Grace O'Carroll on the Saturday night because he'd gone to relieve DI Jarvis Cage for a late shift. DS Barr had done his shift the previous night, but Cage liked to be considered as the point-officer on the stake-out, and be there the majority of time.

Miles Bloom hadn't received any visitors, no personal callers at all. The only movement was his wife frequently coming and going, just like a wee red-robin busy nipping in and out of her nest, in case she'd miss some food for the family or another twig to feather the nest. But there was absolutely no sign whatsoever of a denim-clad Miles.

McCusker got to his bed at 5.00 a.m. and was awakened by the neighbours – the sounds he mistook for his childhood neighbours – at 10.30. He felt like lying on, but that would only serve to give him a sluggish, wasted day. So he jumped out of bed, ran straight into the shower, and seventeen minutes later he was sitting in his comfortable easy chair (which he'd brought from Portrush) with a fresh cup of coffee and two croissants stuffed with hot scrambled eggs. Crumbs dispensed with, because that was all that remained, he topped up his coffee and took out the journal of Louis Bloom.

The professor had written in very neat, rectangular or square boxes, or blocks of lettering. It appeared that he'd always used tidy, printed letters – never joined-up writing – in his journal. McCusker read it all twice to see if he could pick up any secrets that weren't being covered elsewhere.

Bloom had used yellow post-it notes to earmark several notes, diary entries, blogs, doodles, springboards for his book, ideas for lectures – call them what you will, but they all appeared to be notes that said something to him. Maybe he even felt there was some relevance deep within. McCusker had, in the end, to admit – if only to himself – that the journal was disappointing in providing clues, but otherwise it did contain some interesting ideas and thoughts. Having felt that, he knew he needed to read it another time, particularly the following extracts, to check if they made some connection with him when he was of a different frame of mind.

> *Extract I. The thing about Marilyn Monroe is that in some of her photographs (not all) but the ones where she is staring directly at the camera lens (i.e. you, the viewer) she has the look of someone who would have shared her soul with you – it's like it is far beyond the fact that she was willing to make a physical connection with you.*

McCusker wondered if Louis had really been referring to Murcia Woyda, or Mrs Noah, as Mariana had referred to her, in this first extract.

> *Extract II. Sometimes I go through my day thinking about all the things that I do as I am doing them, knowing that this might just be the last time I do these things. Mundane tasks gain so much more significance when they are known to be the final actions of a man or woman. I wonder: what if you knew it was the last time you cleaned your teeth? What would you do differently that day as you cleaned your teeth? Would you think, feck it, it doesn't matter anymore, it'll be over soon? Would you think, with what's about to happen, no amount of*

showering and deodorant was going to keep the death smell away from me? Or do you have the full spoon of sugar in your tea and an extra Kit Kat, because being good in order to protect your end-game (the last lap as it were) is no longer a concern? Would this revelation be a relief or a great concern? Then I think that just because I've had the thought, i.e. that this could be the last time, it means that it won't. And then I wonder if there is a subconscious trigger that activates the initial thought, just so I could bask in the relief of the second thought, i.e. just because you've thought it, means it's definitely not going to happen. Finally, to balance this out, sometimes I think it would be great if say, for instance, I was offered a deanship (or honour) out of the blue. Then I accept that just because I've had that thought, it's never going to happen. Then I wonder why, grammatically, "finally" rarely means "finally". I wonder what will people talk about afterwards.

McCusker wondered if this one suggested Louis feared for his life, or, to put it another way, was preparing himself for his expected demise?

Extract III. *You've drunk too much and you need to be sick. You want to stand up, you want to sit, you want to lie down, but you can do none of the above. You want a cold towel on your brow, you want to be warmed by a comforting blanket, hot water bottle or body, but you know that deep down all you are really going to do is to be sick. And then you break out in a cold sweat, next a shiver descends and then you are sick, and then it calms down and goes away and in the relief period you try to fall asleep and then you wake up again. This time the process happens much more quickly but you always hope the relief after being sick is going to last this time.*

Extract IV. *John loves Mary, does anyone love John?*

McCusker wondered was there a John and Mary. Could Louis be John, and if so who was Mary? Alternatively, he accepted that these seven words together just might be the saddest story he had ever read.

Extract V. *Really it seems to me that we're paid to sit around and have these great thoughts. But the sad reality just might be that the majority of us here have had no greater thought than this one.*

Extract VI. *Death, this thing called death is a bit like an alligator lying deep in the swamp, slowly, lazily sloughing around, waiting for prey to come to him. Suddenly from out of nowhere the alligator scents a helpless victim passing close by. The alligator will shed its bored, lethargic, listless air and will dart, as fast as a F1 racing car; as agile as Usain Bolt; as vicious as a lion, and as deadly as any assassin, in the hunt of his prey.*

Extract VII. *I always find that when I'm praying I can never keep my mind on the prayer. My attention always wanders off on other, sometimes several, tangents. No matter how much I focus on the prayer it's always the same. Sometimes one of the tangents may be how much I'm focusing on trying to have a single-thought prayer. One ruse I've managed to come up with is to rest a fist on my head and point my forefinger to Heaven. More often than not, I start to think of my fist, my head, my forefinger, but, strangely enough, never, ever of Heaven.*

Extract VIII. The Drug of Love. Recently while watching a docudrama, The Secret, on the infamous Coleraine Case, where two lovers were found guilty of planning and executing their own respective wife and husband in order to be together, I glimpsed a real sense of the drug of love. I know it was an actress, Genevieve O'Reilly, and she was acting the part, brilliantly it has to be said, but the look of sheer ecstasy on her face as her partner entered her was so powerful, so revealing. She really looked like a junkie who was totally blissed out as her particular drug flowed into her bloodstream. I felt guilty, as though I was eavesdropping on a scene so physically intimate. This was without the camera revealing anything to you other than the look on the actress's face. I felt that a woman who reacts so might, just might do anything – including murder the father of her children – yes, anything at all, just as long as she was allowed to continue to get a fix of her own personal drug: physical love.

Extract IX. What is it about humans' make-up that has us programmed to need to keep repeating our pleasures? It's accepted that the first time is usually the best, and surely it would be even better in our memory if we knew it was going to be our only time. Okay, okay, maybe there is an excuse to indulge yourself and your partner twice, or even thrice before the cock crows. But do I hear calls for more? Of course I do. Okay, I'll agree to seven, but only on the condition that we all know our ration runs out on the seventh heaven. Please just remember the pleasure of the joy and freedom you used to feel at the start of a school holiday – it never goes away, but it's equally important that we acknowledge that it is but a memory, and that we can never reclaim the original feeling!

Extract X. *They say school prepares you for university and university prepares you for life. But on reflection, perhaps that should be: school prepares you for university; university prepares you in the noble art of avoiding life. Only life prepares you for life.*

Extract XI. *Sometimes I really wonder if dying might feel like committing suicide. Not that I have any wish to. No, it's never been a thought I've entertained. But I wonder where my comparison between dying and suicide comes from. Surely with dying you have no control over the process and it is so much more painful? Having said that, I keep remembering that when you cut your hand, or finger, with a knife by accident, the initial feeling is so deceptively painless and so eye-openingly enlightening, as in a feel-good kind of way, that it totally stimulates you. That's of course until you realise it's just too late, you've cut yourself and you're actually bleeding. Maybe it's just a way of fearing death less.*

Extract XII. *Days are a bit like pages, so it's vitally important you don't flick through one just to get to the next one.*

Chapter Thirty-Two

McCusker walked from his apartment in University Square Mews, up to the leafy end of Botanic Avenue, stopped at the French Village – his favourite bakers in Botanic Avenue – picked up four Paris buns and walked back through Botanic Gardens, out of the gate that led into Colenso Parade, past Louis Bloom's house on the corner of Landseer Street, on past Elaine Street, then Pretoria Street, before turning right into Stranmillis Gardens, passing all four streets with their neat, tidy, matching, red-bricked houses, and knocked on the green door he remembered as belonging to Mr G Divito.

Once again the door was opened with a bit of grumbling and groaning from within.

'Mr Divito', McCusker announced, 'do you remember me?'

'I do,' Wee George said, as he looked past McCusker, 'where's that clever young partner of yours?'

'He's not with me today, but I brought you something else,' McCusker said, offering his warm bag. 'I seem to remember we ate you out of house and home last time.'

Wee George accepted the bag, and as he opened it, a very large grin spread across his face.

'Come on in, man, sure you can help me with them?' George said. 'I thought you'd be back. You look like a man who is as good as his word.'

They chatted away through to the thin end of half an hour and between the two of them made short work of the Paris buns.

'I'm always here,' George said, when they were back on the doorstep again, 'you're welcome any time, particularly when you're prepared to share your stash.'

Wee George Divito was just about to close the door when he appeared to have a second thought about doing so and opened it fully again.

'Oh goodness, I almost forgot,' he started up, 'last night, when I was out for my evening constitutional, as I walked back to the Botanic end of Landseer, I notice this woman behaving suspiciously near the Bloom's house. The closer I got to her the more I realised she was crying. I figured she must be a student of Louis Bloom's. I went over to her and asked if I could help. She was wearing a dark duffle coat, with her hood up.'

'Did she look like Marilyn Monroe?' McCusker asked.

'How did you know?'

'We're looking for her,' McCusker replied. 'Did you talk to her for long?'

'Not long… she was in a hurry to get away and she kept looking around and over her shoulder.'

'Did she go up to the door of the house?'

'No. The only thing she said, as she was weeping, was that she needed to be near his house. She thanked me for stopping for her and she left.'

'Did she have a car? Or was she walking?'

'Definitely walking; I watched her walk up Landseer Street and she turned right into Stranmillis Road.'

'Do you remember anything else about her?'

'When I was up close to her I saw what a stunning looking woman she was but I also realised she was a little older up close than she looked from a distance, but not in a bad way. Initially I thought she looked like one of those crying girls you see on the telly outside a dead pop star's house, but then, as I say, when I got up close, I realised she was too old for that.'

Even with his stop-off, McCusker was still in the Customs House by 9.00 a.m., and on foot at that.

He had thought about calling in to see Sophie Rubens again, to see if he could get to the bottom of her confusion about the location of her alibi. But it might be better to pick up more information first. That was the main problem: before they spoke to anyone, apart from Murcia Woyda and Thomas Chada, they really needed more information.

'I think we might have something here,' DS WJ Barr said, as McCusker walked through the door.

O'Carroll, who was already at her desk, and McCusker walked over to Barr's corner of the office.

'This is the report from the forensic accounting department,' Barr started, laying down three foolscap pages on his desk in front of his two colleagues.

'Okay,' McCusker said, searching the pages of figures. He wasn't connecting the dots. Neither was O'Carroll, it appeared.

'Okay,' Barr started, 'for each fundraising project, Ron Desmond, on behalf of QUB, opens a separate bank account.'

'Good so far,' McCusker said.

'So this page shows the current balances on the different accounts.'

'Wow, that's a lot of change,' McCusker said, as his eyes ran down the various balances.

'This page lists the summary of the donations on each account,' Barr continued.

'And this other page,' O'Carroll guessed, 'is the outgoings so far for each account or project.'

'Still with you,' McCusker said, if only to get to the next stage.

'Now,' Barr continued patiently, 'all of these amounts, raised on the separate accounts for the various projects, minus outgoings so far, tally with the balances currently on the accounts... except for...'

'...except for the Holywood House project, which is £480,000 short,' McCusker added.

'Holy Mary, Mother of God,' O'Carroll gushed, 'that's a heck of a lot of money to go missing.'

'And Ron Desmond is one of the people who doesn't really have an alibi,' Barr added.

'Okay, McCusker, you're expecting your scarf-man to get in touch this morning, so DS Barr, you and I will skip on up to QUB to have a chat with Ron Desmond and confront him with this evidence.'

McCusker knew that O'Carroll's skipping would only be as far as her Mégane. It didn't make him being left behind any easier, particularly when O'Carroll returned – solo – just over an hour later, and Thomas Chada still hadn't contacted him.

'So, how did it go?' he asked his partner.

'He was brutally honest. He said he "Didn't have a fecking clue",' O'Carroll started, sounding like this was not going to be a happy tale.

'He checked with the bank, was left on hold for twenty-three minutes while various people checked out various things with various departments, which ended up where we all were, which is still none the wiser. Desmond made repeated calls to the QUB accountant in charge of these accounts. He got really aggressive with this accountant when he eventually rang Desmond back. The accountant put the phone down on him, so he rang him back to tell him he was a wee... I believe this particular substance is very effective when spread around the roots of rose bushes, yes, that's it... he was a wee one of those. The accountant put the phone down on him again. Ron Desmond did what most people in his position, but no members of the public ever have a chance of doing: he rang the wee attachment to a rose bush's senior and played the old boy's act, for... oh, about three or four sentences, before saying, "Ah that would be a no to that one.' Which O'Carroll took as a reply to Desmond being asked if everything was okay with him? He then proceeded to get to the crux of the matter. Very shortly thereafter Desmond set the phone down, totally satisfied, and announced: "You'll be happy to hear that your query is now being dealt with as a matter of great urgency."'

'And that's it?

'No, McCusker,' O'Carroll continued, 'ten minutes later Desmond's phone rang again and this time he remained quiet and said "Okay, that'll be a yes to that one. I'm coming right over with the members of the PSNI – please have everything ready for an inspection."'

'And you left Willie John to accompany Ron Desmond to the accountants by himself?'

'Yes, of course – I felt I'd already watched enough paint drying this morning already,' O'Carroll replied, sounding rather pleased with herself.

'Don't get too excited about leaving him to a brain-numbing hour, it's not like you're ever going to win a *Crackerjack* pen over your fancy footwork.'

'You don't say things like that when you're around my sister, do you?' O'Carroll whispered, as she thumped him playfully on the arm. '*Please* say you don't. I thought you were getting better, but then you go and say something like that!'

Just then O'Carroll's mobile chimed its 'Chariots Of Fire' signature, 'it's the only exercise I get,' O'Carroll said, when anyone's eyebrows questioned her choice. 'Yes… yes… right now… was that a two or a three? We're on our way.' She turned to McCusker. 'That was Mariana Fitzgerald; she's with Murcia Woyda. They're both in Mariana's Belfast apartment in Opel Tower waiting for us.'

CHAPTER THIRTY-THREE

When Mariana Fitzgerald had originally told McCusker and O'Carroll that she had an apartment in Belfast that her friend Murcia was crashing in, she had made it sound like a student's dive. But on the twenty-sixth floor of Northern Ireland's highest building, the luxury apartment in question was anything but a dive. It was so luxurious that McCusker felt too self-conscious to sit down on any of the furniture in the grey, black and silver themed décor.

As they waited for Murcia to come out of her bedroom (Mariana said she'd been crying all night long) the two detectives both strolled over to the window to gain a better look at the majesty of their favourite city. So clean was the glass, both unconsciously took a quick pace backwards, in-step with each other, feeling they might fall off the edge. They could see the Customs House far below them and close enough that if this building ever fell down, in a certain direction, it would collapse right on top of their office. McCusker tried to pick out several landmarks with which he was familiar: the Europa Hotel, the City Hospital, the Waterfront Hall, Napoleon's Nose and the tower of the Lanyon Building at Queens came easiest.

They both turned at the same time as they heard Mariana's voice behind them.

'I'd like to introduce you to Mariana's best friend, Murcia.'

As both friends made their way across the generous-sized living room, Mariana was still very laboured in her movements.

Murcia Woyda really did look like Marilyn Monroe. McCusker felt that when people said so-and-so really looks like so-and-so – say

George Clooney – and you finally got to meet the supposed Clooney lookalike, you'd usually be thinking, well, they are similar – in that they both have two eyes, two hands and two feet, but that's where the likeness ends. However, not with Murcia – she looked like Marilyn Monroe's sister. Yes, Murcia most certainly worked and cultivated her look. Like her bottle-blonde hair was cut in Marilyn's style, and, yes, she was also wearing Ferrari-red lipstick on her permanently pouting lips. But there was something else as well… that look Louis Bloom had described in his journal, where a subject of a photograph hints that she might be prepared to share her soul with you. The deceased QUB lecturer had hit the nail right on the head.

For someone who had supposedly meant to have been crying all night, Murcia looked a million dollars. She didn't appear to need a lot of make-up, apart from her lipstick, that was. She was smaller than Mariana – a bit, but not a lot. She had a more feminine figure than Mariana but didn't flaunt herself or flirt as much as her friend did. McCusker guessed that Mariana wasn't even aware that "Mariana" was doing it.

'Right, I'll leave you to have your chat,' Mariana said, 'if you need Mariana, Murcia, just ring me and I'll be back.'

'Can I make you tea or coffee?' Murcia offered, with a hint of a French accent.

'Let's have a wee chat first,' McCusker said, knowing the start of an interview always dictates if it's going to be a difficult or an easy one.

As they were walking over the spacious room to the section with a low glass coffee table, guarded by three large grey sofas and a massive TV screen (fixed to the wall) on the fourth side, O'Carroll, following McCusker's lead, quickly said, 'So, you saw Louis Bloom on Thursday at Dukes Hotel between 4 o'clock and 5.30?'

'Yes – Mariana told me she'd mentioned that I was there with Louis and, yes, that is the last time I saw poor Louis.' Murcia sat down on the sofa to the left of McCusker and O'Carroll's choice of sharing the central sofa.

O'Carroll took out her pink notebook and started to write, usually a signal to McCusker that she wanted him to take the majority of the questions.

'You were seen outside Louis' home on Friday night,' McCusker said – again, like O'Carroll's, it wasn't really a question, but he thought confirmation would be good for the record.

'Oui, sorry, sorry, I mean yes,' she replied, seeming surprised. 'The kind man, he told you?'

'Yes,' McCusker returned a confirmation.

'I don't know why I went there. I… I was upset, very upset – I didn't know what else to do.'

'Were you going to go into the house?'

'Non, certainly not,' she shook her head violently, so much so that her hair umbrella-ed. 'I do not know the wife. I have no wish to upset her. I just felt a need, a separate need, to be near his house. I needed to be close to him. I was drawn there beyond my wishes.'

'Had you ever been there before?' McCusker asked, as O'Carroll recorded the words.

'Non, certainly not, ah… we, Louis and I, we were not… shall I say, what… we were not jealous lovers.'

'Did Louis speak French?'

'Oui, and Mariana, too. My English will grow the more we talk.'

'Thank you for speaking in English for us,' O'Carroll added.

'*Pas du tout,*' she replied, the slightest hint of a smile breaking her lips, 'not at all.'

'I met the man you talked to outside Louis' house,' McCusker started back up, trying hard to find common bonds. 'I visited him this morning. In fact, we shared Paris buns.'

'Ah yes, I also know this bun! They are very agreeable, yes?'

'Why yes,' McCusker agreed, as O'Carroll tutted not so subtly.

Murcia didn't seem upset to McCusker. He wondered if Mariana had said that Murcia was upset in order to make it appear that she cared, and therefore, that she couldn't be involved in Louis' murder.

'What did you and Louis discuss when you met on Thursday?' he asked, and regretted the question the moment it had left his lips. They had a room in a hotel they shared for ninety minutes – talking might not have been their priority.

'We talked about my situation with Mr Noah,' she replied. 'Mariana calls my husband that – Mr Noah – and she calls me Mrs Noah. I'm afraid it stick.'

'Stuck,' O'Carroll involuntarily offered, in correction and, just like McCusker, appeared to regret it the moment she did.

'Stuck, yes good,' Murcia continued. Like Mariana, Murcia had a quiet voice, maybe a bit more gentle than her friend's, and to ears like those of McCusker's, very sensual.

'Have you spoken to your husband recently?' he asked.

'Oh no, no – bad for me, no more,' she gushed. 'He leave message on my phone, I never answer.'

'Does he know where you are?'

'Non,' she spat, 'he mustn't.'

'We need to ask you some personal questions?'

'It is good.'

'Mariana introduced you to Louis as an escort?'

'Oui, but it is true.'

'Did he pay you?'

'Why yes, but of course, but that is how we met,' she replied, sounding as if it was the most natural thing in the world.

'How often did you meet each week?'

'As often as we could, but never on Thursdays or Sundays.'

'So maybe as many as five times a week.'

'Perhaps say four,' she offered, 'Ah sorry, I see, I see, you mean that's a lot of times to pay?'

'Well...'

She smiled at McCusker again. 'He pay when we first meet, because that was how we meet, but then we became friends and lovers and of course he doesn't pay then.'

'Oh,' McCusker said.

'But as friends and lovers, well, of course he gives me an allowance to live... but that was only until I get my divorce settlement.'

'Do you see anyone else as an escort?'

'Non, but of course not – I have a husband *and* a lover,' she shot back indignantly.

'Of course...' McCusker replied, only to be interrupted with:

'But now poor Louis, no more, no lover,' she added. 'Are you a husband?'

McCusker struggled, feeling something must have been lost in the translation.

'He has a wife and a lover already,' O'Carroll offered, coming to McCusker's rescue, after a fashion.

Murcia looked at McCusker with fresh eyes.

'What does Mr Noah do?' he asked, ignoring O'Carroll's dig.

'He is a business man.'

'Yes, but what is the nature of his business?'

'Oh, I don't know.'

'But you're his wife.'

'But I didn't care.'

'But still, you must have... he must have told you something?'

'I met my husband when I was an escort, he was obsessed with me. He wanted me to stop being an escort, to only be with him. I said no. He kept making better proposals until I agreed. And I agreed. I agreed because when Mariana and I work out the deal, it was the same as being an escort for several years – more money, less work. I never feel our marriage was emotional or romantic. I was doing a business deal.

'But I make a big mistake; I never consider the complications of such a deal. Like when a man buys something, he needs it to be his. He wants to make a statement, saying, "This woman is my wife and she is mine". But that is just not possible. Louis understood. Louis knew that could never be.'

She laughed sadly to herself.

McCusker and O'Carroll allowed her the moment.

Her eyes welled up.

'Oh my Louis,' she cried out, 'my poor Louis. He left me when I needed him most.'

Neither McCusker nor O'Carroll could find the right words to say.

'Louis knew that a man could never own a woman. He'd say, "Forget all that *bulle merde*, let's get our clothes off!"'

O'Carroll and Murcia laughed heartily, but McCusker didn't. He figured it must be a girl's thing.

'So, Mr Noah wants you back?'

'He thinks he bought me. He thinks he is better than me. He thinks I cannot be alone and be happy.'

'Why not just get a divorce?' McCusker asked.

'Mr Noah is not a nice man when he gets angry, he hurts people.'

'Sorry?'

'He hurts people when he gets angry.'

'You've seen him hurt people?'

'Oh yes,' she admitted.

'When? Where?'

'If I tell you that, my life will be over.'

'He's threatened you.'

'He has done more than that. He has beaten me,' she said.

'He can't do that; you can go to the courts.'

'It is no use being in the right, having the courts on your side, when your bones are broken, or worse still, you are in the graveyard.'

'Do you think Mr Noah is involved in Louis' death?'

'I can't think how. Louis and I… we were both so careful.'

'Did youse always meet at Dukes?'

'Yes. Mr Noah, he know this is Mariana's apartment. So we assume he's watching here.'

'So Louis has never been here?'

'No never, I wouldn't do that to Mariana.'

'You never, ever met anywhere else other than Dukes?' McCusker repeated.

'We would only meet… oh… sorry, I just remember one time it was different… with Louis we couldn't get back to the hotel quick enough, if you see what I mean, and so we had a moment or two in Botanic Gardens, in the bushes over by the sports centre. But nobody would know about us then.'

'If Mr Noah wanted to get in touch with you, how would he do it?'

'He would assume I pick up the messages he leaves for me. I don't read them. I delete them all immediately. He needs to know I'm out of his life for good.'

'Do you have a solicitor?'

'Yes, Mariana found one for me. She asked him to write to Mr Noah's solicitor and say he would be acting for me in the divorce proceedings.'

'Did Louis ever meet Mr Noah?'

'I don't know, maybe – something happened, but Louis wouldn't talk about it. He certainly became more cautious over the last few weeks. It was more "I don't want to talk about it" rather than "it didn't happen". This leads me to think that perhaps something did happen. But we were careful. We were very careful.'

'When Louis went on his talking engagements did you ever go with him?'

Murcia seemed at first bemused by McCusker's question and then seemed to accept something. Perhaps, McCusker thought, that they hadn't been as careful as she'd first suggested.

'Well, I wouldn't actually travel with him. And I wouldn't stay in his hotel room. I would book into the same hotel, and he would come to my room.'

'Did you ever attend any of the events?'

'Mostly no, but if there were tickets available to the public I would buy one and slip in. But he would never ask the organisers for a ticket, or for a seat at his table for me. No one would have known about us.'

'Would you ever go for walks around the city when you went to the talks?'

'Sometimes he would arrive at the hotel a day early. Or stay on an extra day, and we'd have more time together. We would never leave or enter the hotel together, but we'd meet outside and have lovely walks and go to quiet hotels or bars.'

'What were your plans?' O'Carroll asked.

'Plans? How do you mean?'

'Had you talked about being together? Did you ever consider what you would do if you managed to secure a divorce from Mr Noah? Would Louis leave his wife? Would you get married?'

'With Louis, he was so preoccupied with enjoying today that he never worried about tomorrow. He was married to Elizabeth. Louis would never leave Elizabeth. He thought when you marry you should be like wolves, you should mate for life.'

'Did he think that Elizabeth...' McCusker started.

'Look, I can see in your eyes, you are thinking, "okay, he wasn't considering marrying her, so it was a certain kind of a relationship, it wasn't really serious." But that was not how it was with Louis. He was so loving, but he never discussed love. He was my friend, my lover, my mate. We weren't together forever but we were *together*. Louis believed jealousy was an incurable disease. He... we had no time or need for jealousy. What was there to be jealous about? He said we shared ourselves with each other. There were other circumstances and considerations in both our lives that had to be accommodated. I do know he shared, what he shared with me, with no one else, and I, in return, honoured that. And now he is no more.'

'I am sorry if you thought we misjudged your relationship, but please believe me, we most certainly didn't mean to – we just need to uncover all we can about Louis to try and figure out what happened to him,' McCusker said. 'What I was going to ask you was, if you, or Louis, ever thought that perhaps Elizabeth might leave Louis?'

'That was Louis' main point. He thought you can't leave your brother or sister or parents, you can't leave your husband or your wife...'

'But you're leaving your husband,' McCusker said, as an image came to mind, of Louis passing a sample of the energy drink Elizabeth Bloom had prepared for him to Harry Rubens for analysis.

'My marriage, it was but a business arrangement, it was nothing, it was not emotional, it was not spiritual.'

At that point they heard someone trying to open the door. Murcia nearly jumped out of her skin and was petrified until she heard Mariana say, 'It's only Mariana.'

Mariana noticed immediately how upset Murcia appeared, so she explained to O'Carroll and McCusker that once when Murcia had been at the flat by herself she heard someone turn the door handle several times. She feared Woyda had found her. Murcia froze in silence and eventually whoever had been at the door went away.

'A few more minutes please?' O'Carroll said, 'and we'll leave you both in peace.'

'Of course, I will shut myself in the kitchen and make us all some tea and coffee to go with these fresh croissants I've just bought. Just give me a call when you're ready.'

'*Merci, mon ami*,' Murcia called out to Mariana.

'Could you tell us please, Murcia, where you lived with Mr Noah?'

'But of course, I will write out the address for you in your little pink book,' she offered.

O'Carroll gave her a clean page at the back of the book and her pen. Murcia scribbled for a time and handed book and pen back over the table.

'Can you please tell me what you were doing on Thursday night between the hours of 9.00 and 1.00 on Friday morning?'

'But non... surely you don't think that I... this is... *pas bon*... it is terrible.'

'It's not that Murcia,' O'Carroll explained, 'in our investigation it is equally important for us to identify those we can definitely rule out; it means we can concentrate on fewer people.'

She smiled her thanks.

'On Thursday night... I saw Louis in the afternoon, he left at 5.30. Mariana had friends over for dinner. She invited me over but I stayed in Dukes. I had dinner in my room. I watched a TV programme called *The Fall* and went to sleep at 10.30.'

'You didn't see anyone?' O'Carroll asked, for the record.

'No one.'

'You said you had food in your room,' McCusker said, 'what time would that have been?'

'Just after *The Fall* had started,' she replied.

'So someone brought your food to the room just after 9 o'clock?'

'Yes, yes, but of course! A waiter, a waiter saw me in my room,' she said, offering McCusker a heart-warming smile. 'Wait... I have a receipt in my bag. Mr Noah taught me to keep all my receipts. Mr Noah said receipts are better than cash.' She fished around in her Bobi leather Jérôme Dreyfuss shoulder bag and eventually pulled out a receipt with all the joy of a woman who felt she had just saved her own life.

McCusker examined the receipt. It was for a mushroom risotto, a glass of Chablis and a tarte Tatin. The bill was printed out by the kitchen at 21.08, for an amount of £34.60, and according to the waiter's signed "Paid" scribble, she paid £40.00, including tip, in cash.

Mrs Noah most definitely could not have been in Botanic Gardens when Louis Bloom was delivering his bag of rubbish to the bin.

As the three of them walked across to Mariana's kitchen in silence, O'Carroll thanked Murcia for her patience.

'*De rein,*' Murcia said, smiling as they opened the kitchen door.

'You're welcome too,' Mariana said, slightly confused.

Chapter Thirty-Four

Back at the fort, also known as the Customs House, DS Barr was back in residence. Ron Desmond and he hadn't quite cleared up the issue of the missing £480k, but Barr felt they were not very far away from doing so. The bank had confirmed that they had received the money but, due to the fact that there was "an error with one of the digits" on the transfer request, the funds had not been credited to the actual account.

'Not an error you'd get if the business had been conducted by cheque,' McCusker proudly claimed.

O'Carroll made a great fuss of totally ignoring him.

The bank confirmed that the minute the donor's bank provided the correct digits for the recipient's account, the full funds would officially be transferred over. Ron Desmond was very grateful and had officially contacted Superintendent Niall Larkin to praise the superintendent's team, claiming that if DS WJ Barr hadn't been so diligent and brought the discrepancy to the university's attention, the funds could most certainly have disappeared forever into the banking equivalent of a black hole.

McCusker wondered if there was such a space and, if there was, how much had accumulated there; where it had come from; how long would it stay there; and, most importantly, where would it end up?

Perhaps they needed Detective Sergeant Willie John Barr over there to keep an eye on things for them. Then again, perhaps they didn't; he was much too invaluable where he was.

Thomas Chada, the former Magherafelt High School pupil, had rung in for McCusker and politely said he would ring again after his 4 o'clock lecture.

Before he and O'Carroll left the office again, McCusker asked DS Barr to pull all the records he could on Noah Woyda.

'What does a woman like Mariana ever see in a man like Francie Fitzgerald?' O'Carroll asked, when they were on their way back to Queens University. McCusker was keen to walk but O'Carroll insisted on taking her car, reasoning that they could get over to Queens and clear up the couple of things they needed quicker than McCusker could tie up his shoe laces.

'His chequebook,' McCusker replied. 'Seriously, though, didn't Murcia pretty much admit as much in our interview?'

'But Mariana could do better for herself?'

'So could Murcia?'

'So you like the Marilyn Monroe look?' O'Carroll said, and shot him a glance to catch his reaction.

'No, I mean, yes, of course,' he agreed, 'but with Mariana and Murcia, both of them have clearly accepted that they aren't going to get the man of their dreams.'

'I find it sad that they feel that imperfection is actually okay,' she said.

'Maybe neither of them wanted the lifestyle they felt they would achieve with the people they were dating?' McCusker suggested.

'Well, I must admit, I wouldn't want to be living hand to mouth. But to some degree, even in marriage, you have to take responsibility for your own preferred lifestyle choices. It's hard to get it right, but I'm not sure I agree that you have to compromise.'

'You mean like Mariana and Murcia did, where they opted for financial stability over happy ever after?' McCusker said.

'Well yes,' she agreed, 'you have to wait until you find the right person. Maybe waiting is the only compromise we should tolerate. Waiting to get it right.'

'Sure, in all our lives there will always be something that is wrong,' McCusker said, 'something we need to fix; maybe even something we can't fix and so we have to own up and accept our situation and find a way to move on.'

'My worry is that if women like Mariana and Murcia can't find Mr Right, there's very little chance for me,' O'Carroll admitted.

'Well, Grace found me, and I found her–'

'But neither of you were looking...'

'Maybe so, but I still think it's much too early for you to give up on
Jenson and Gary,' McCusker said, referring to O'Carroll's preference
for the perfect, English gentleman types in general, and Jenson Button
and Gary Lineker in particular. Both were very English, polite, good
looking, friendly, personable, all-round good guys, and world-champs
in their chosen sports.

'And pray tell, how do you figure you're in the same league, McCusker?
Can you play football better than Gary? Drive faster than Jenson?'

'No,' McCusker replied, pulling a packet of Walker's Smoky Bacon
crisps out of his pocket, 'but I can eat these a lot quicker than either of
them!'

By which point, luckily for McCusker, they'd reached Harry
Rubens' office in the David Keir Building on Stranmillis Road. The
previous day McCusker had felt that the building - named after a previous and celebrated Vice Chancellor, Sir David Lindsey Keir - was
drab and more like a 1950s style hospital than a hall of knowledge.
But today's sunlight had totally transformed the building and the twin
cylindrical towers guarding the regal entrance were now quite majestic. In this illuminating light, McCusker found it difficult to believe
the well documented ghost stories about the underground tunnel that
connected this building to the Ashby Building next door, on Stranmillis road.

Harry surprised O'Carroll and McCusker by not dismissing tales
of hands on shoulders but nobody being there, or several anonymous
reports of a member of staff's hand that had been taken hold of, for
them only to find, once again, that no one was there. Rubens' theory
seemed to be that some of the ghosts of the neighbouring (directly
across Stranmillis Road) Friars Bush graveyard were trapped on a different spiritual plane and couldn't find their way back to the graveyard. Hence the ghosts' reason for taking hold of people's hand was in
the hope todays visitors might help the ghosts return to their natural,
if somewhat nonphysical, habitat. McCusker was shocked that an academic, such as Harry Rubens, was prepared to give such tales credence. Perhaps he was just trying to spook the two cops.

'I won't ask you how the case is going,' he continued, changing
gear flawlessly and getting down to business, offering them some Cold
Zero as per last time, 'I know you wouldn't tell me anyway and like

everyone else, I will wait to find out in the *Belfast Telegraph* once you've solved the mystery.'

'I'm happy you have that confidence in us,' McCusker admitted, 'but it's very difficult, don't you see, when people who claim to be Louis' friends don't tell us the whole truth.'

'Sorry,' Harry said, looking shell-shocked and visibly taken aback, 'what exactly do you mean?'

'Well,' McCusker started off, the way you would when you were trying to be patient with a child, 'you didn't tell me that your friend Louis was dating a married woman by the name of Murcia Woyda.'

'And I didn't, because she's married to Mr Noah Woyda,' Harry replied, and smiled nervously.

'How on Earth would he even know that you'd shared that information with us?' O'Carroll asked.

'Because Mr Woyda makes it his business to know these things.'

'Do you know Mr Woyda?' McCusker asked.

'Sophie is good friends with Mariana. Mariana is also good friends with Mrs Woyda.'

'I still can't figure out how it would get back to Noah Woyda that you talked to us about his wife and Louis,' McCusker said, noting how genuinely scared Harry Rubens looked, but then McCusker remembered this was a man who apparently believed in ghosts.

'Oh yes he would, oh yes he would. It's a small town, the campus is even smaller and, word does tend to get around,' Harry Rubens admitted, with the air of a tired man. 'Look, I knew you would find out elsewhere and I simply preferred you just didn't find out from me.'

When it looked like neither O'Carroll nor McCusker were buying into that, Rubens continued, 'Look, Mariana rang Sophie and said Noah wanted her and me to know that he didn't want *anyone* babbling about his wife to the PSNI.'

Okay, McCusker thought, a threat, and not even a veiled threat. Now his reluctance certainly made more sense.

'But worse than that, Sophie said that Mariana was crying and sounded absolutely petrified,' Harry added.

'But don't you see, it could be important for us to know this?'

'Surely you don't think that Noah is involved in Louis' death?' Rubens said, and sounded like he never considered that to be an option.

'Sophie and I thought Mr Woyda was just a proud man. We figured he was trying desperately hard to win his wife back and it was clear to us he didn't want the police minding his business.'

McCusker just stared at him blankly, maybe even challenging him.

'Yes we did,' the lecturer claimed, 'yes we did.'

'Well it now turns out that he might have had a motive,' McCusker claimed.

Harry Rubens laughed. 'That's just crazy! Noah Woyda is not going to murder Louis!'

'Someone did,' McCusker said.

'Hagh!' Another laugh from Harry, this time more self-conscious.

'So you knew Louis was seeing Murcia?' McCusker asked.

'Yes, we did,' he conceded, 'yes we did.'

'Did you ever see them together?'

'No.'

'Do you know where they met up?'

'No.'

'Did you know that she occasionally went along and met up with Louis Bloom on his speaking engagements?'

'Did she?'

'Did you and Louis ever discuss Murcia?'

'Only in general terms – he liked her, she wasn't needy, they had fun.'

'Never about her being in trouble with her husband because she'd left him?'

'Absolutely not.'

'Okay,' McCusker said, knowing he wasn't going to get much further on this, 'on a totally different matter, Sophie's friend Mariana…'

'Yes?'

'Tell me this: does she suffer from a bad back?'

'Not at all,' Rubens replied, without hesitation.

'A bad leg?'

Rubens shook his head to the negative.

'Okay, Harry,' McCusker said, hoping it sounded on a lighter note. 'I believe that Louis Bloom handed you a sample of a drink his wife was mixing up for him regularly.

'Yes she did. And I know Sophie told you so.'

'Louis wanted you to analyse it?'

'Yes.'

'And?'

'And… yes, I did,' Harry stuttered, 'yes I did. It contained: almond milk, banana, peanut butter, maca powder, turmeric and a generous helping of cinnamon.'

'And nothing else?' McCusker added, somewhat relieved that he wasn't going to have to advise his boss that his wife's sister had, in fact, poisoned her husband.

'Nothing else,' Rubens confirmed, appearing as if his dark moment had passed. 'Elizabeth really cares for Louis – she also used to spray a little perfume on his scarf before he went out in the morning, and he also reported that his favourite baseball cap always smelled of the same scent.'

Ah, McCusker thought – yet another mystery solved.

'Also,' Harry Rubens offered, through a very large sigh, 'Sophie believes she might have made a gaffe when she was telling you what she was doing at the time Louis was murdered.'

'Oh yes?' O'Carroll said, looking up from her notebook.

'Yes. She thinks you thought she was lying about where she was because she mistook the layout of the MAC lobby.'

'Yes, I remember the confusion,' McCusker replied.

'My wife suffers from a rare condition called Aphantasia. Most people don't even know that they have it. It isn't really debilitating physically, which is why, mostly, it goes undetected. It's like she really doesn't have a mind's eye. She can't recall the layout of a building, or road layouts – when she's there, fine, but when she tries to recall them she just can't.'

'Wow, that's a new one on me,' McCusker admitted.

'Sophie also wanted me to tell you that she has the ticket stub for the Eric Bibb concert at the MAC and she can tell you the titles of the majority of the songs he played on Thursday evening.'

CHAPTER THIRTY-FIVE

According to DS Barr's research, Mr Noah Woyda was involved in all sorts businesses that turned over money. Money, as in real, old-fashioned, folding money. He wasn't one to nurture and develop his enterprises. When they stopped producing fast cash he would asset-strip the business to the bones and dump the carcass with the highest bidder. This clearly hadn't sat well with some of his partners, who came to discover that they weren't really his equal, but rather would-be entrepreneurs still clinging to the dream that had got them thus far. When they found the paperwork to prove they *were* still legally binding partners with a say in their business, Noah Woyda wasn't above intimidating them until they saw *sense*. In hindsight, none of his partners spoke favourably about Woyda in private. Most who discussed their dealings with him in public lived to regret it.

His businesses ranged from escort services to coffee houses, taking in mini cabs, bakeries, public houses and hotels in between. Police had confirmed one of his hotels to be a high-class brothel. In that case, Woyda had avoided prosecution by producing, at the last moment, a lease, which he maintained put an acceptable legal distance between himself and the illicit enterprise. The last man standing in the firing line took the rap and the prison time, while all the time claiming that he was nothing more than Noah Woyda's in-house manager. In a bid to earn his freedom, the "manager" had offered the PSNI what he claimed to be proof that Woyda was using the hotel as a means to catch politicians, lawyers, judges, accountants, dignitaries and celebrities "on camera" in extremely compromising positions. According to "the manager", Woyda's priority was not to blackmail his clients but to encourage them to keep using his premises and services. He'd then have them in his back pocket for a later date, when he needed to call in a favour. Apparently, you only had to check the launch-night guest lists for any of Woyda's new projects to discover the names of those he'd caught on camera.

However, "the manager" had a last-minute change of heart and had decided to withdraw his accusations, claiming they'd been nothing more than sour grapes on a deal that went bad. The hotel in question had allegedly cleaned up its act. But of course it hadn't really. It had merely been redecorated, increased its official (and unofficial) rates, and become even more successful after all the publicity from the case. According to Woyda's spin machine, he had well-advanced plans to open three other hotels in the chain: one more in Belfast, and one in both Derry and Dublin. It had also been reported, but never proven, that a PSNI senior infrequently checked into Woyda's hotel. In PSNI circles the chain became known as S & C Hotels, as in Short & Curlies.

Woyda, it transpired, always refused to be involved, either directly or indirectly, in drugs of any kind. In fact, anyone caught dealing or using on his premises received a full, sharp shock before being handed over "on a plate" to the PSNI. Apparently these actions had gained Woyda substantial Brownie points in certain PSNI stations. Noah Woyda's file also maintained that he had no known paramilitary connections.

He'd often flirted seriously with the letter of the law but was extremely careful about remaining on its correct side, and only once had he crossed the boundary. On that particular occasion, he was working without the safety net of a local powerful connection. He went down for three years and got off just after fourteen months. His file showed that he was a model prisoner, who was preoccupied with working out, behaved properly and always keen to help his fellow inmates. What the file didn't show, but a friend of Larkin's maintained, was that Woyda was flashing the cash on the inside and was absolutely living the life of Riley. The only inmates he was helping were "contacts" he was nurturing and cultivating for when he was released.

It was unclear who did Woyda's intimidating for him, or if in fact he did it himself. DS Barr assumed that if it was him, he'd have been in more trouble with the PSNI than had been recorded. Equally, he conceded that Woyda could have been relatively trouble-free due to his connections with judges, lawyers, police and politicians. Sometimes the likes of Woyda didn't even have to have such connections; it was more than enough to just claim it.

CHAPTER THIRTY-SIX

'On line 409, McCusker,' O'Carroll said across their partner's desk, 'an American.'

'Hello, I'm Joe Long, New York,' the upbeat voice at the other end of the phone announced. O'Carroll had batted it over to McCusker, she later said, because initialled foreign secret services interfering in PSNI cases made her far too impatient.

'Okay,' McCusker replied, 'how can I help you?'

'I believe from the doll who put me over to you that you're working the Louis Bloom case?'

'That's correct, how can I help you?'

'It's more how I can help you – meet me in the Lanyon Quad in ten minutes – hang on a second, yes, I've got you on my screen now. Okay good, I'll recognise you. Password, Surf's Up.'

O'Carroll laughed at McCusker as he went off for his meet. 'If you're really lucky, it's only DI Jarvis Cage getting his own back on you,' she shouted after him. 'Shit, I better check in and see how he's doing.'

Ten minutes later McCusker was walking through the front door of the Lanyon Building out into the Lanyon Quadrangle. He felt so privileged to be able to so. Well, truth be told, McCusker had a wee bit of a problem with the rectangle in question. The main problem – the *only* problem, really – was that it wasn't all in fact the work of Sir Charles Lanyon, as half of the rectangle – on the left-hand side as you walked through the front door, aka the Peter Froggatt Centre, and the entire opposite end to the front door, the Administration Building –

were modern carbuncles, which had somehow attached themselves to Lanyon's perfection. Nonetheless, this was such a tranquil place to pause and sit – certainly with your back to that section which resembled a multi-storey cricket pavilion – so that it would cease to exist and you could view another elevation of the worthy jewel in Lanyon's uncontested crown. McCusker wondered how a space with so many students, with their daily worries and pressures, criss-crossing it non-stop, could remain so tranquil. Wouldn't it be nice to be able to just sit here in the warmth of the sun, a pleasant autumnal sun, and enjoy this for the rest of the afternoon.

'Surf's Up,' an American voice behind him called out. McCusker turned to be greeted by a man with his hand extended.

'I'm Joe Long, New York. You must be McCusker. Do I call you Mc or Cusker?' he said as he shook his hand firmly.

'Great to meet you too, Sir,' McCusker replied. 'Do I call you Joe Long or New York?'

If he was, as O'Carroll had suggested, a secret agent, he was more Tom Hanks than Sean Connery, the one and only true James Bond. It was just before lunchtime, yet Joe Long was dressed in a tuxedo, a starched-white shirt with black bow tie and black patent-leather shoes.

'I can see in your eyes that you're stressed over what they've done to the Lanyon Quad. Certainly it's a bit of "Look what they've done to my song, Ma." But listen, I'm reliably informed that somewhere in these hallowed buildings they discovered Charles Lanyon's original plans for the complete rectangle and plans are afoot to bulldoze and rebuild. Be true to your school. So speak to me: what's your interest in my Noah Woyda?'

'Sorry?'

'Woyda's been on my radar for a while; hints of a bit of arms dealing, I'm led to believe. But I think he mentioned gun dealing just as a way of bigging himself up. The GCHQ facility – *the watchful eye* facility – picked up some static, chatter, that the PSNI is also interested in him. We believe he likes to pretend that he doesn't know what he's really doing, but we're not so sure. So, speak to me: what's the story? Please tell me he's nothing more than a wooze so I can get back to the two dolls I left in Tangiers; it's a three-hour flight away and I promised them I'd be back for supper.'

McCusker told Joe Long what he knew. Maybe it was just that the American had such an honest face.

'Okay, we can leave him to you then. We hear you and your partner know what you're doing. My only tip for you is this: find out where his money comes from. That'll help you with your particular case.'

Joe Long New York looked around nervously as if he'd just been spooked. 'I'm out of here,' he said, as he headed back to the safety of the crowded university shop.

The last thing McCusker heard from him was 'Surf's Up!'

CHAPTER THIRTY-SEVEN

McCusker and O'Carroll met Noah Woyda on the doorstep of his grand house on Malone Road, south of Queens University. The property had been cleverly landscaped into the acre-and-a-quarter site to ensure no part of his home was visible from the Malone Road's traffic. Although the house had double-doored garages on each side, two vehicles (a Merc 4x4 and an Alfa Romeo) were parked at the end of the curvy drive, very close to the front door where Woyda greeted them as they poured themselves out of O'Carroll's Mégane.

Woyda made no sign of inviting them into his stone-faced house. In fact, he was chomping at the bit like someone who needed to be on the move. He looked as happy as a bulldog that'd just eaten a wasp.

'We've come to talk to you,' O'Carroll said, as they both flashed their identity cards, 'about Louis Bloom.'

'Which nick are you from?' Woyda asked, as he continuously sucked on a mint flavoured boiled sweet.

'The Customs House,' O'Carroll replied.

'Is Superintendent Murray Wilson your gaffer?'

'No, Superintendent Niall Larkin is our immediate boss.'

'Don't know him,' he grunted, as McCusker thought that could only be a good thing. He made a mental note to check out which branch Superintendent Wilson was with. 'I knew youse were coming through.'

Woyda made a dogs dinner over pronouncing "youse" – the unique Ulster pluralised version of the singular "you" – showing that, no matter how hard he was trying to pretend otherwise, he was not from these parts.

'Can we go inside?' O'Carroll asked.

'Look am… that's not convenient just now – why don't you ring my office and fix an appointment? The number is in the book under XTC Holdings UK.

That's not going to happen Mr Woyda,' O'Carroll said firmly, 'either we have a chat here or, I'm afraid, we're going to have to ask you to accompany us to the Customs House for a more formal chat.'

'Unfeckingbelievable,' he hissed, 'whatever happened to a man's castle is his home?'

Noah Woyda wore an expensive-looking grey three-piece suit, when, in McCusker's opinion, a black one would have looked much better, since it would have shown the wrinkles less. He had a blue shirt with a pure-white collar, the top two buttons undone and exposing a hairy chest. Woyda's footwear were a black canvas affair, more like outdoor bedroom slippers. He had darkish, dead eyes chiselled into his grey-black bushy eyebrows. Veins spread out like a spider's web all over his red nose. His head and face were both clean-shaven but the monk's shadow on his crown betrayed the fact he was bald apart from the "back and sides". He was solid, but not overweight, and he looked like he still worked out a lot – he looked good for his probable early fifties.

'You better come in then,' he said, as he back-heeled the door open. When he spoke, there was a slight whistle through his teeth.

Perhaps it was just the contrast from the cold, stone-wall exterior but inside his castle was certainly warmer, more inviting – homely even. A woman's touch was in evidence, particularly around the entrance hall with the dramatic sweeping oak-wood staircase splitting it in half. It seemed as though Woyda had hijacked Elton John's weekly supply of multi-coloured flowers and stuffed them all into this one space. Woyda positively beamed with pleasure as the detectives' stood in obvious awe at the sight of his pile. 'Is Gene Landy in the Customs House?' Woyda asked.

McCusker figured he was working his way through the list of people he could call on for favours, striking out on both occasions. He'd be out on the next negative call.

'No, Sir,' O'Carroll replied. 'Your house is very beautiful – it's a credit to you and your wife.'

Maybe Woyda figured that out as well, because he seemed to completely change character and tact mid-stream.

'Yeah, we were very lucky; we bought at the bottom of the market – you wouldn't get a house with this amount of land for anything under 2 mill these days,' he said, as he showed them into a smaller meet-and-greet reception room, with three packed bookcases and four more vases bursting with flowers. But pride of place went to a ginormous framed photograph of his wife Murcia, pulling off a Marilyn Monroe-lookalike pose 98 per cent successfully.

McCusker played dumb. 'You're a fan then, Sir?'

'I should be,' he replied, with a louder than normal whistle, 'she's my wife!'

He lifted a phone, ordered some tea, coffee and nibbles, and set it back down with neither a please or thank you.

'Sorry, I thought it was Marilyn,' McCusker said, because he felt he should, if only to hide the fact that they'd already spoken to the woman in the portrait.

'Common mistake,' Woyda laughed, 'you can only tell the difference when you're signing the cheques for her jewellery.'

Meanwhile O'Carroll was browsing the bookcases in search of rare editions, only to find mostly large-format paperbacks.

'I love a great book, don't you?' Woyda asked.

'Of course,' O'Carroll said as McCusker said, 'Yes, me too. I've never been one for reading a book right, through,' he continued glancing to O'Carroll before saying, 'the only thing I get from reading a book right through in one sitting is a sore ar… rear end.'

Woyda and O'Carroll were still laughing when the door to the room opened and a tray appeared. This in itself was not surprising for McCusker. What was surprising was the fact that it wasn't a maid or a housekeeper who carried a tray but a red-faced Ulsterman who looked like he was down from the country for the day. He was dressed in one of the loudest jackets McCusker had ever seen. It was plastic in appearance, this particular one being a blue plastic zip-up number with a yellow, green and red trio of stripes that ran across the chest from armpit to armpit and circled around the back. It was the kind of jacket a film director chooses for a character because it creates immediate identity-cum-recognition. It was also the kind of jacket one would find in an unsolicited, unaddressed catalogue dropped through the letter-box, but one which nobody would ever buy – nobody, that was, apart from Woyda's man-Friday here.

'So how long have you been here?'

'Did you hear that Sammy?' Woyda replied, addressing his man-Friday rather than O'Carroll, 'she's asking how long we've been here.'

Sammy grunted.

'But we all know that she'd have checked my PSNI file long, long before she came here, so she knows all about me, chapter and verse, now doesn't she?' His eyes had a habit of indicating that his sentences were coming to an end before his voice did.

Sammy grunted and darted off, looking as though he wanted no part of an argument with the PSNI. As McCusker watched him speed away, he thought clearly Woyda had no time for a housekeeper or maid betraying the secrets of his house, or castle, as he called it.

Once again, in the matter of a split second, Noah Woyda's mood swung back to the friendlier version of himself.

'Right, you be mammy,' he instructed O'Carroll, 'we'll play the parts,' he continued, nodding at McCusker, 'of the good children.'

O'Carroll did as bid, and milked and sugared the tea for Woyda and the coffee for herself and McCusker.

'Is your wife around?' O'Carroll asked, joining in with McCusker's earlier charade.

Woyda studied her very carefully for close to a minute, all the while stirring his tea, until he eventually said, 'She's staying with friends just now. Look, I really am very busy at the moment; can we please get down to business?'

O'Carroll took her time returning her cup to her saucer, and getting her pen ready for her notebook again.

'We wanted to talk to you about Louis Bloom,' O'Carroll started.

Woyda muttered something that sounded like 'Progress at last'.

'You knew Louis Bloom?'

Noah Woyda thought for a few seconds and replied, 'I knew Louis Bloom.'

'How did you know Louis Bloom?'

'I was introduced to him by Mariana Fitzgerald, a friend of my wife's,' he offered, after consideration.

'When was the last time you saw Louis Bloom?'

Again a pause before, 'The last time I saw Louis Bloom was at a fundraiser at Queen's in September.'

'Did you know him well?'

'He wasn't someone Sammy and I would go down the pub with,' he eventually said with a snigger, following the longest time for consideration so far.

'Did you have any business with him?'

'None, that is apart from both of us contributing to a few of the same charities.'

'Were you on any boards with him?' O'Carroll continued in the hot-seat, looking like she was trying very hard not to betray her annoyance at Woyda's continued attempts to slow the pace of the interview way down.

To McCusker's mind, it looked like Woyda had been well briefed by a solicitor who worked under the theory that the less you said, the less likely you were to incriminate yourself.

'No,' Woyda replied, after a very long break, confirming McCusker's hunch.

'Did you have any business dealings with him?'

Woyda appeared as though he was about to say something several times. He smiled at O'Carroll, not in a friendly way but more as a way of trying to unsettle or disarm her. Eventually he proved that his searching for an answer was just another ploy by saying 'No'.

'Did you see Louis Bloom on Thursday last?'

Woyda removed a very small diary from his inside pocket. He flicked through several pages before declaring 'No'.

'What about the early hours of Friday morning?' O'Carroll asked, trying a different approach.

Woyda, who had returned his diary to the inside pocket, pulled it out again, and with very deliberate and exaggerated Marcel Marceau signature movements flicked through the pages one by one, licking his forefinger after each page before eventually declaring 'No'.

'Have you any information you can give us on Louis Bloom?'

This time Woyda afforded himself a different smile; the smile of someone who thought that even if they hadn't already won, they were certainly on the way to winning.

'No,' he replied, after his Cheshire grin had run its full course.

O'Carroll visibly rolled her eyes as if she was about to give up.

McCusker, right on cue, remembered something Joe Long, New York had said to him. 'Do you have any business dealings with Francie Fitzgerald?'

The detective's ruse worked.

'We're developing his manse into a high-end country hotel.'

'I thought that was Mr and Mrs Fitzgerald's home?' McCusker continued.

'What can I tell you,' Woyda replied, adopting a very superior attitude, 'old money is not what it once was. There's a recession, and owning one of those old houses is like having a large hole in the ground that you continuously have to pour money into.'

Woyda had just broken his record for the duration of his replies.

'Could you please tell us what you were doing between the hours of 21.00 last Thursday evening and 02.00 on Friday morning?' McCusker asked.

Noah Woyda looked like he was going for his diary again but instead he stood up, walked over to the phone, lifted it and said 'Come in'. Once again, no please or thank you.

Sammy returned to the room, looking a little less comfortable than his last visit.

'Tell the officers what we were doing from 21.00 on Thursday night until 02.00 on Friday morning.'

'We were driving around looking for poster sites in and out of the city.'

'Did you meet or talk to anyone?' McCusker asked.

Sammy looked like he was about to answer when Woyda offered a very firm, 'No.'

'Was Mr Woyda in your company the entire time during those hours?' McCusker continued.

'Yes,' Sammy replied.

'Sammy, please write down your full name and address for me in my notebook?' O'Carroll asked.

Sammy looked to Woyda, who nodded "yes", and Sammy did as bid.

'Tell me this, Mr Woyda,' McCusker began, as Sammy continued writing, 'did you know that your wife had been sleeping with Louis B–'

That was as far as McCusker got.

Because right at that moment, he experienced first-hand the most controlled ballistic fit he'd ever witnessed.

Woyda took his white china saucer and flung it into the fireplace with all his might, smashing it to smithereens. The half-filled matching cup wasn't too far behind. These were the only outwards signs of displeasure Woyda displayed apart from his face, which was violently contorted, and his body, which physically shook with rage. He took some time to compose himself again. Eventually, when he was extremely calm and collected he said, 'You come to my house, you accept my hospitality, you drink my coffee and you insult my wife in front of witnesses. I have to advise you, I will be making an official complaint to your seniors.'

All the time he spoke, it was as though he was discussing the weather with his best friend.

'If you were thinking of making that complaint with either Superintendent Wilson or Superintendent Landy, then I feel I should warn you, Sir, that both of them were fired from the force earlier this year when they were discovered trying to sell off PSNI assets for their own benefit. '

McCusker, nostrils busy twitching away, appeared to offer to shake hands with Noah Woyda as they were leaving. Woyda refused.

'He's in good company,' McCusker claimed later in the car, as they drove back to the Customs House, 'George Washington would never shake hands either.'

CHAPTER THIRTY-EIGHT

By the time McCusker and O'Carroll were back in Customs House, McCusker had missed Thomas Chada's 4 o'clock phone call. According to DS Barr, Thomas Chada was very polite and apologetic. He left a message that he would call the detective again just after his midday class the following day.

Also, Barr advised them that the CSI team might have discovered something in Louis Bloom's rubbish bag – the rubbish bag that had been responsible for concluding the final day of the 20,000 (give or take) days in Louis Bloom's life.

'They wouldn't comment on it any further,' Barr stated for the record, 'until they conclude their tests.'

'Did they even give you a clue as to what it might be?' McCusker asked, hoping he wasn't sounding desperate.

'I get the feeling that they didn't want to tempt fate by spelling it out. However, it's usually a positive sign when we get such a call.'

'I doubt you were ever disappointed with what Santa Claus left you, Willie John,' McCusker offered, 'you're my kind of man; your cup is always at least half full, isn't it?'

'Talking about praise, McCusker, I wonder how DI Nicholas Cage is getting on,' O'Carroll asked.

'The last I checked he was fine,' McCusker replied, 'nothing to report, happy with the relief shifts, but says he wants to ensure he remains the point person. He's convinced that this is his big chance to make it into the movies.'

'Holy Mary, Mother of God bless him – but not a lot,' O'Carroll said, sighing.

McCusker and O'Carroll seemed to hit the wall at the same time, running out of steam while DS Barr seemed to ride off into the sunset. He was one of those annoying types that towards the end of a marathon who, just as you'd expended all your energy trying to get past them in the home straight, would move into another gear when they sensed you at their shoulder, and fly off into the distance, showing that they had been toying with you all the time.

The Portrush detective knew that to be able to enjoy and appreciate his day there certainly had to be those things he also resented having to do. Perfection only came with contrasts and compromise. He wished, though, that he could get to a stage where he could embrace everything, the way Willie John Barr seemed able to do.

He mentioned this to O'Carroll as they were driving out towards Springwell Road, Bangor.

'Aye, and he wishes he could be one of the Brownlee brothers. And I wish…' She paused, and then changed topic mid-thought, as was her wont. 'Actually, an early boyfriend's family lived out on Springwell Road – a very well-to-do family.'

'Really? And how did that go for you?'

'The pranny claimed that I couldn't get pregnant if we didn't like each other,' she announced, 'and then, when I clearly wasn't buying into that approach, he said if I'd like a 100 per cent guarantee, I should go on top, that–'

'Ah jeez, Lily' McCusker protested, 'stop right there, please! TMFI!'

* * *

'Well, here we are – the home of the B&B.' O'Carroll offered, as they pulled onto a small laneway off Springhill Road.

'I thought they were going for more of an exclusive country house, high-end hotel, rather than a B&B?' McCusker said, as he unfastened his seatbelt.

'No, no, I didn't mean the house. I meant the *B&B* – you know, the man with the beard-and-bun look,' she said, sniggering. 'I mean, if you're a man and you're going to grow your hair, then why hide your vitality in a spinster's bun?'

Mariana and Francie Fitzgerald both came to meet them in the forecourt. She looked much happier than he did to see the PSNI officers, but neither seemed any more comfortable in the other's company than they'd been earlier at the Merchant Hotel.

Their manse was indeed an impressive house, if looking a wee bit sorry for itself. McCusker figured Woyda's idea of turning it into a country house hotel was most likely based on the availability of numerous stone outhouses about the property. The back of the house had a very generous-sized courtyard, which was completely surrounded by stone buildings, broken only by a double-gated carriage entrance, with more room for accommodation above.

'We'd like to speak to Mrs Fitzgerald first, if that's okay,' O'Carroll started, as they were led in from the courtyard to a warm, family-style kitchen.

'But of course,' Mariana replied, in her whispery voice, without consulting her husband, 'he can bring us some tea and scones.'

In fact, much to McCusker's annoyance, neither tea nor scones appeared, as Fitzgerald disappeared into some other part of the house.

The inside of the house – a kitchen, through an antique-laden hallway, into a living room, and all generously peppered with various-sized paintings – showed signs of damp and was in a visible state of disrepair. McCusker felt the manse was going to need more than a facelift before it could be opened to the public.

'What has happened since this morning?' Mariana asked, as she, McCusker and O'Carroll took comfortable seats by the log burning fire. She seemed more comfortable now that her husband had peeled off.

'Well, there are a couple of things we need to talk to you about,' O'Carroll said.

'Okay, Mariana is ready.'

'When we interviewed you at the Merchant Hotel, you told us that you didn't know where Murcia was,' McCusker said.

'Yes?'

'She was in your apartment all the time, wasn't she?'

'Yes,' Mariana admitted, 'but she was absolutely petrified. Mariana just wanted to give her a bit of space and time to deal with losing Louis. I knew if we just gave her a little time, she'd be happy to talk to you.'

'So when you told us you didn't know where she was, you were lying to us,' McCusker continued, softening up his accusation with a mellifluous voice.

'There is an old Polish proverb, which says "a lie is only a lie if it's malicious",' Mariana whispered back, equally sweetly.

'You see our problem is, if you lie about that, malicious or not, what else might you be prepared to lie about?'

'But surely you check out our alibi with Samantha?'

'No, I didn't mean that – I meant maybe the details about how close you and Louis were?'

'Ah, Mariana sees where you're taking this, sir,' she said, still appearing unconcerned. 'If Louis were my lover, then perhaps that puts my husband in the frame?'

'Perhaps,' McCusker replied, but that hadn't actually been what he meant.

'Well, Francie has a solid alibi. What would be the point fibbing about an alibi while knowing it would take you a mere five minutes to check it and catch him out?'

'There is that,' McCusker agreed.

'But maybe you could have also meant that if Louis were my ex-lover, and he was now with my best friend, Murcia, then perhaps I too would have a motive. And the motive would be jealousy.'

'But, as you say, you'd still have an alibi.'

'Exactly, Mariana would still have an alibi,' she confirmed, as she flicked her long hair away from her shoulder.

'Okay.' McCusker decided to let this sit, for now at least, and move on. 'Yesterday you seemed to move as though it caused you great pain to do so. You appear to be in the same position today.'

She actually winced as McCusker made his observation.

'Was that a question?'

'Yes.'

'What exactly is your question, Mr McCusker?'

'Have you been hurt recently?' the detective asked, still circling the topic.

O'Carroll simultaneously took the more direct approach, and jumped in feet first with, 'Who beat you up, Mariana?'

Mariana's eyes immediately looked to the door, which was slightly behind her to her left, and the movement appeared to cause her even greater pain. She looked back at the detectives and laughed.

'Who said Mariana was hurt? Could I not have been in a car accident, or fallen in the yard?'

'Or walked into a door?' McCusker added. 'We don't think so.'

'Why did Noah Woyda beat y–'

'Noah?!' she gasped, as she looked back to the door.

'It wasn't Noah Woyda, was it? It was your husband who hit you, wasn't it?' O'Carroll suggested, in a whisper.

Mariana Fitzgerald broke down, not from the humiliation of having been beaten by her husband, but through the continued pain of the hiding.

Fitzgerald's earlier reaction in the café, to McCusker's bluff about his wife suffering at the hands – or fists, more like – of Woyda, now made so much more sense. He'd obviously thought that McCusker really believed Woyda had beaten his wife. He'd then wasted little time in spinning the facts to fit the story.

'Please, just check where Francie is,' Mariana pleaded with McCusker.

O'Carroll blinked her eyes slowly, signalling she too felt this was a good idea. Maybe even trying to get across to her colleague that longer would be better.

McCusker eventually found Fitzgerald in one of the outhouses off the courtyard. He was clearly not in the process of preparing tea or scones, but rather was studying plans spread out before him on a workbench. Fitzgerald appeared nervous when McCusker walked in on him.

'I just wanted to advise you, Sir, that we'll need you in about thirty minutes,' McCusker offered. Before McCusker had fully closed the door again, Fitzgerald said, 'No worries, I'm not going anywhere. Please shut the door properly after you, there's a wild draft coming up the glen.'

The detective stepped back into the courtyard and did as he was bid, and in a gesture of just how much he wanted to help keep the draught away from Mr Fitzgerald, he very quietly turned the large key sitting in the door lock.

Ten minutes later he re-entered the sitting room, with a tray full of tea and nibbles he'd managed to rustle up.

'Where was he?' Mariana asked.

'In the outhouse, working away on plans.'

'Phew, really?' Mariana seemed totally surprised at this. 'He won't come back in on us, will he?'

'I can guarantee he won't come in until I go fetch him,' McCusker said, with a hint of a grin.

'Mariana here was showing me the results of her beating,' O'Carroll started. She was still shaking with anger, 'I took photos on my mobile of each bruise – look, all of them can be hidden behind clothes. Very clever. I assured Mrs Fitzgerald that I'd keep the photos only as a record, but would be happy to use them if in the future she chooses to press any charges against her husband. I advised her not to talk any more to me about it until you returned to witness the conversation.'

Mariana didn't wait for a second prompt.

'Noah Woyda had no need to beat me,' she started, 'he got my husband to do it for him. Woyda knew I would be in touch with Murcia. He wanted Francie to find out from me where Murcia was. I wouldn't tell him.'

'But did Francie not know Murcia was at your apartment?'

'No. I told him, as I told you, that I didn't know where she was. I also told him that I had left a message for her. Some she returned, some she didn't. I told you the untruth not as a lie but as a way of protecting her. Were you to interview him, you might let it slip that she was at the apartment because you assumed that, as my husband, he would already know. Mariana apologises.'

'We understand,' McCusker said.

'Murcia was convinced that Noah would do something terrible to her if she didn't return to his house. She was equally convinced that he might even do something worse to her if she did. Noah was putting on the pressure to find out where she was.'

'But could Francie not just go and check out your apartment?'

'He doesn't have keys,' Mariana admitted.

'Sorry?' O'Carroll said, in disbelief.

'It is my private apartment. Mariana bought this apartment off plans with my own money,' Mariana offered, by way of explanation. 'My husband had no involvement in this apartment. The lease or, purchase agreement, as our friends in America would call it, is safely locked away in my safe deposit box. The apartment and the nest egg I told you about earlier are my independence. You can see, with the trouble Murcia is currently experiencing, just how important it is to have your independence.'

'So Francie has no keys?' O'Carroll said.

'No, he rarely goes there, and only with me.'

'Do you think Woyda knows about your apartment?' McCusker asked.

'I'd bet money on it, but he's not going to go there, is he, with all the security and the cameras.'

'So he was trying to get Francie to persuade you to tell him where Murcia was so that he could… what… go and get her?' McCusker suggested.

'Yes.'

'And then?'

'And then when Mariana refused, he told my husband to persuade me. Francie said I was making him into a, how you say, laughing stock. He said, Mr Noah said "She's your wife, you're the husband, and she has to do as you say and if she doesn't, be a real husband – make her!"

'And so Francie puffed himself up and said I'd better tell him where Murcia was or I'd regret it. He said a woman has to go back to her husband, that's what marriages were all about: "in sickness and in heath, to love, honour and obey, YOUR HUSBAND!"'

'I laughed at him, told him that he and Noah should realise that it's 2018. He took a half-hearted swing at me, I brushed it off.

'He laughed at me. He said, "You've been asking for a good hiding for years and now it's time for Mariana to get what she deserves." He changed before me, yes. He looked like he became physically charged. A bit like he does when he becomes amorous, but this was different. I got the feeling that it didn't matter what I said or did, the devil was in his eye and he was going to beat me.

'I started to run away from him. He tripped me up from behind. I fell badly on my hip. He jumped on top of me. He started to bombard me with punches; all below my shoulders and all above my waist. It was like someone had coached him on how to beat someone up without leaving any tell-tale marks.

'My first fall onto my hip is what did the most damage. The bruises I hope will disappear but I am sure he has done more lasting damage to my hip and back.'

'How did you get him to stop?'

'Mariana pretended she passed out. I found his punches were less effective when I wasn't tensed up in preparation for them. I relaxed and thought of playing with my father in our garden when I was young. I thought I was going to die and Mariana wanted to die with good thoughts. Francie must have thought I was unconscious, because he stopped.'

'Then what happened?' O'Carroll asked.

'I pretended to come around again,' she said, 'for the first time since I met him, Francie looked like an old man. I got up to get away from him but I fell down again. My hip and back felt like they were broken. I told him to ring for an ambulance. He kept asking where Murcia was. He kept getting phone calls and he kept replying, "She won't tell me".'

'Why was he doing Noah's dirty work for him?' McCusker asked.

'Apparently Mr Noah had agreed to put up some money to help finance converting the manse into a top-of-the-range hotel. Francie needed the deal to go ahead. Mr Noah was clearly calling in a favour.'

'But, sorry; I thought your husband was well off?' McCusker said.

'Just an illusion, Mr McCusker, nothing but an illusion,' she claimed. 'Around the time we married, he was very well-off with his family money, old money. But although he clearly had no idea how to make money, Francie certainly knew how to spend it. There was one hare-brained scheme after another. Non-stop. He was always coming back from these long, boozy lunches were he'd have met someone who just needed "a few grand" to start up one of these "can't-fail companies". Someone even sold him on the idea of running an Elton John concert here in our back garden. He parted with £25,000 for a feasibility study on how to best stage the concert. They spent ages working out where the stage would go, where the seats would go, where to get the PA and lights from, where to get the toilets from, where to sell the tickets, where to advertise the concert. I have to admit I was totally in on that one. We were to retain FAB rights.'

'What's FAB rights?' McCusker asked, for it might be important to know.

'Food and beverage, darling, food and beverage. Anyway, Francie said I could take charge of, and pocket the profits from that.'

'And what happened?'

'Everything was going great, the plans were all coming together. I believe that, including the £25,000 for the feasibility study; £20,000 advance to secure toilets, tents, stage, turnstiles; £20,000 advance to secure PA and lights; £5,000 advance to a social network guru; £5,000 advance to a production manager; £1,000 advance to a stage manager; £7,500 advance to solicitors; £6,000 advance to a firm of accountants to ensure we didn't pay too much tax on our profits, we – or, should I say Francie – paid out around £90,000.'

'Ninety grand!' McCusker cried out involuntarily.

'What happened?' O'Carroll asked.

'Oh, someone forgot to figure in Elton's fee.'

'And how much was that?' McCusker asked.

'Well, it seems our "well-connected fixer", a contact of Francie's from Cheltenham, never got that far. All he would tell us was that Elton's people had already turned down £2 million for a similar event.'

'And that was the end of it?'

'No, it was decided to scale it back a bit for the first year, you know, not be quite so ambitious. What is the saying? Oh yes, "learn to creep before you try to walk". Well, we eventually settled on a rave in the big lean-to out the back. We ended up selling 78 tickets and it was completely washed out.'

'Unbelievable,' McCusker said.

'Then Francie said we had to sell my apartment to pay for the manse conversion. I said but "we" didn't own my apartment: Mariana alone owned that. Anyway, he kept on about that for a couple of years and then eventually it appears that he persuaded Mr Noah to come in with him on making Mariana's manse into a hotel, and they were plotting and scheming away, always sneaking away like two schoolboys behind the bike shed for a ciggy. At least Francie wasn't bugging me any more about selling my apartment. Eventually Murcia left Mr Noah and initially Francie was very supportive of Mariana and Murcia, but then Mr Noah put pressure on Francie and Francie beat the crap out of Mariana. When I was at my meeting with you - at the Merchant Hotel and he stormed in on us - that was the first I'd seen him since he beat me. I refused to stay here. I left and went into Belfast. I'd just come back here about an hour ago to pick up some things. He started up again – not with the beating, just the shouting. He went berserk – just *crazy* - about how he had to find Murcia for Mr Noah or there would be hell to pay for everyone. He kept screaming that everything was at stake. So I ran out of the house to get away from him and that was when you drove up.'

'I recommend you leave while we're still here,' O'Carroll advised her.

'Don't you worry, I'm out of here,' she replied, touching her still-sore hip as she did so.

CHAPTER THIRTY-NINE

'He's been out here a long while, McCusker,' O'Carroll said, as they walked across the courtyard, 'after what Mariana's told us, are you sure he's not just scarpered?'

'As the bishop said to the actress, I took a precaution…' he replied.

'Oh jeez no, McCusker, please save those quips for the *Antiques Roadshow,*' she mocked, in good humour.

'I locked him in his office,' McCusker said, as they reached the door and he turned the very large rusty key.

'Oh okay, go on then, I will make an exception, but only in this one instance,' she whispered to McCusker, as he turned the antique key and pulled open the door.

It turned out that Francie Fitzgerald was so engrossed in his plans that he wasn't even aware he'd been detained at the PSNI's pleasure.

'Look, I'm sorry about earlier, when I ran out without paying,' Fitzgerald said, addressing McCusker, 'that was unforgivable of me. I really thought Mariana had a tab going at the Merchant and they'd just automatically add my sandwich to it. But on another matter, I really meant it when I said that if you wanted to talk to me again, it needs to be in the presence of my solicitor.'

'This is about a different matter altogether,' O'Carroll said, as she produced her warrant card. McCusker followed suit because he felt he should. 'We're here to talk to you about domestic violence.'

Francie Fitzgerald fell back down into the seat he'd just risen from as they walked into his office space.

'We are led to believe that yesterday you beat Mrs Mariana Fitzgerald, contravening Act–'

'I already told McCusker here that she walked into a door?' Fitzgerald replied, when he'd managed to get some wind back in his sails.

'Then her head would be bruised as well as the entirety of her upper torso,' McCusker replied.

'I've taken photographs,' O'Carroll began, 'it's disgraceful, totally disgraceful. Holy Mary, Mother of God man, how could you do that to any woman, let alone your wife?'

'I think you'll find my wife will admit she was careless and walked into a door.'

'I think you'll find she won't, besides which, there is another person involved,' McCusker said.

'A witness? There were no witnesses!'

'I think you'll find your correct answer just there, should have been: "There was nothing to witness",' McCusker said.

'Gone are the days when you'll get away with this kind of behaviour,' O'Carroll offered, every single word betraying the utter contempt she had for this excuse of a man.

'Is Mariana really going to press charges?' Fitzgerald asked, visibly shocked.

McCusker and O'Carroll both just glared at him and shook their heads from side to side slowly.

'Oh look, don't give me that crap – you weren't there, it was the heat of the moment. She was giving as good as she got. Do you want to keep this fair and take photographs of *my* bruises?'

It was O'Carroll's experience that wife-beaters went into denial and usually always managed to find a way to rewire their brain to re-script the event. O'Carroll was having none of that with Fitzgerald.

'Please – take off your top, sir,' she said, as she pulled out her phone.

'Sorry?'

'You've just made a very serious charge, so we have to treat it as a complaint,' O'Carroll continued. 'We'd like to take photographs of your bruises.'

Of course, she knew there'd be no bruises, but she wanted to get it on record, so that he couldn't make that claim again.

'No – it's my right to refuse.'

'In which case we can arrest you and take you to the cells in the Customs House, where you'll be given a full physical examination in front of your solicitor.'

Fitzgerald's face was growing redder by the second.

'The choice is yours, sir,' O'Carroll said, after a few minutes of in-activity.

Fitzgerald slowly and reluctantly started to remove his black top, followed by a black short-sleeve T-shirt underneath.

Of course there were no marks or bruises about his person – nothing but flabby skin, in fact. O'Carroll snapped furiously away, though, capturing invaluable evidence; evidence that would hopefully loosen a tongue.

'They must have worn off?' he complained.

'Your wife's bruises haven't worn off, Sir,' O'Carroll stated.

'Look,' Fitzgerald started, focusing on McCusker, 'you know how it is: things get out of hand, they egg you on, don't they… one thing leads to another…'

'We know *exactly* how it is, Mr Fitzgerald,' McCusker replied, 'that's why the courts deal with it accordingly. That is of course when they're allowed to; when the husband doesn't contribute a very generous settlement in order to remind his wife she walked into a door. We're hoping that such bribing eventually becomes illegal as well.'

'Chance would be a fine thing,' Fitzgerald mumbled.

'Sorry?' O'Carroll said.

'Look, we don't have a pot to piss in,' he admitted, 'that's why I tried to do a runner on paying for my bacon sandwich this morning. We've run out of money. I can't even claim it's a cash-flow issue, we've plain and simply run out of fecking money.'

'But surely,' McCusker started, looking around the premises. 'But surely the manse is worth a lot?'

Fitzgerald studied both detectives in silence for a moment.

'You just don't understand, do you?'

McCusker wanted to say, "No we don't understand, we've had to work all our lives to pay for our lives." But he realised now wasn't the time to be patronising and smug and antagonising a potential valuable witness.

'It's all gone…'

'The manse?' McCusker asked, seeking clarification.

'Everything. The money my father bequeathed me, the manse, everything. I can't get credit anywhere. Look at my clothes for heaven's sake! Virgin fecking freebies!'

'But this house, the manse?'

'My wife is the only one of us with any assets. She owns the apartment in the city. It's probably worth three-quarters of a mill. I've tried to persuade her to sell it. That would have been more than enough to pay for converting the manse and the outhouses to hotel accommodation and we'd still be left with a good few bob. Then we'd be set up for life. Eventually maybe we'd even be able to also have a getaway in Barbados. We could've had a very comfortable life. But it appears to me that what's mine is *ours*, whereas what's hers is most definitely *hers*. I also believe she's got at least a quarter of a million squirreled away, but I've never been able to find it.'

McCusker couldn't believe that this guy was actually trying to make out that his wife had caused all of his problems. No doubt that was the real reason he'd beaten her.

'So anyway; I meet up with Noah Woyda, through Mariana and Murcia, and he's big on the hotels and properties, and so I showed him my plans.' Fitzgerald paused as he flicked through the actual plans on the Λ frame pine trestle table in front of him. 'Noah got it immediately. He was in – hook, line and sinker! So we did a deal. I would put up the property, he would put up the cash and we'd go 50/50 on it.'

Oah oh, McCusker thought as he felt the sting in the tail coming.

'All was good, we signed the contract. The contract agreed with the details I mentioned earlier. I signed the freehold of the manse over to the company. For tax reasons it had to be a company Noah Woyda already owned. My share would be governed by a separate trust, and would be totally tax-free. Leanne Delacato, Woyda's solicitor, took care of all the paperwork.'

'Here comes the good bit,' McCusker said to himself under his breath.

'Things took a lot longer than I thought,' Fitzgerald claimed, 'I hate to have to admit all of this to you. Although Woyda was responsible for putting up the money for the building works, I was responsible for half of the start-up money for planning permission, solicitors, surveyors etc. I started to fall behind with my half. Can you believe, my wife had her apartment and nest egg all along and we were so close? All we needed was a couple of hundred grand maximum and we'd have been set for life.

'Once Woyda saw that I didn't have a pot to piss in, he immediately clicked into another gear, citing all these penalties I'd missed in the small print. He threatened me – said that if I didn't produce my share of the start-up costs, then the project would fail and his company would own the manse. They'd have to sell it off to cover their losses on the investment.'

'Was the manse in your name or jointly with Mariana?' O'Carroll asked.

'Our joint names, although I did have power of attorney to sign on our joint behalf.'

O'Carroll scribbled away in her book.

'Does Mariana know you no longer own the manse? Does *she* know that she no longer owns it?'

'No,' Fitzgerald admitted.

O'Carroll made it perfectly clear she was also recording that answer in her book. McCusker wondered what language she was using that took a complete minute to write the word "no".

'When Murcia walked out on Woyda, he moved into another gear,' Fitzgerald continued, appearing to brush his very recent revelation under the carpet. 'He heard Mariana and I were helping her and all hell broke loose. He said he wanted that stopped immediately. He hinted that there may be a way to resurrect the manse hotel project, but only if I played ball. He wouldn't spell it out, he just kept saying if I played ball he'd think about it and try to work something out.'

'So you felt that if you spied on Murcia, you'd get back in Woyda's good books?' O'Carroll asked.

'Well yes,' he replied, sounding like someone who was thinking "at last, the PSNI get it, the penny has finally dropped". He looked like he was searching O'Carroll's eyes for even just the smallest sign of sympathy and on finding absolutely no forgiveness nor understanding he continued, 'That's probably why I really lost it with Mariana. I swear to you, I'd never laid a finger on her before, you can ask her.'

'That's never an acceptable excuse, Sir,' O'Carroll replied, 'you know you could have just as easily killed her. As it is, I do believe you've done very serious damage to her back and hip.'

'I was under so much pressure from Woyda,' were his final words of justification.

'I think Murcia and Mariana, and possibly yourself, could still be in danger over the next day or so,' O'Carroll said, sternly. 'It goes without saying that we expect you to have no contact whatsoever with Mr Woyda.'

'I won't, believe me I won't.'

'Do you think that Woyda had anything to do with Louis' death?' McCusker asked, as they were about to leave.

'He'd too much to lose,' Fitzgerald replied, breaking into a weak smile. 'I was just thinking there that I'd be a much more likely suspect; I've got absolutely nothing to lose. Woyda has much too much going on in his life to risk that. Woyda is convinced that the batty brother Miles is to blame.'

As an afterthought, Fitzgerald felt it necessary to add, 'Of course, I should point out, as you already know, that at the time of Louis Bloom's demise I was in the company of my wife, and Samantha and her husband.'

* * *

'Have you any regrets, McCusker?' Grace O'Carroll asked when they were both in his favourite stage of undress later that evening. He had to sacrifice a few garments of his own to persuade her to lie on top of the sheets. It was such a small price to pay for his own personal Heaven.

McCusker, when it started to get serious with Grace, had sworn to himself that he was never going to take his work home with him into their "space". Clearly Fitzgerald's treatment of Mariana had greatly upset both he and DI O'Carroll, and he was obviously coming across a bit more pensive than usual, hence Grace's question. He thought for a while longer, discreetly using his own silence to examine Grace once again in her natural beauty.

'I have but two regrets in my life,' he started, breaking the hallowed silence.

'Only two?'

'Yes, only two if you rule out George Best never leading Norn Iron into a World Cup final. Or Eddie Irvine being greeted by three, and only the three, replacement tires as he pulled into the pits in the

Nürburgring, Germany, on Sunday September 26th, 1999. He was clearly in the lead at that point. But the Ferrari crew allowed McLaren's Mika Häkkinen to pass Eddic in both the race and the F1 World Championship with their "misunderstanding".'

'I can't believe that you still haven't told me your two regrets yet, McCusker.'

'Okay, okay, sorry about that wee diversion – that was the beginning of my Ferrari soapbox moment. They had him parked in the pits for 48 seconds, Grace, that's two lifetimes in Formula One!'

'Okay, okay,' she said, laughing, 'it's nearly twenty years ago now – don't you think it's about time to let it go? '

'Right,' he agreed, and let it go. 'Okay, so my two regrets. 1) I never learned to ride a horse. 2) I never moved to the USA like I always dreamed I was going to.'

'So Anna Stringer got a chance to do what you wanted to do,' Grace offered slowly. 'Does that make you feel bad?'

'No, not at all. The time I could, probably should, have gone to the States was when I was younger, and it was no one's fault but my own for not being brave enough to take the plunge. Apart from anything else, America then was a much younger country when the "land of the free and the home of the brave" afforded equal opportunities for those brave enough to take said plunge.'

'Anna Stringer didn't really resist taking the plunge, did she now?' Grace offered, without sounding judgemental.

'In her defence, she wasn't as much going somewhere, as she was getting *away* from somewhere... or someone. She was getting away from a failed marriage and that's what really took a lot of courage.'

'True,' Grace agreed, 'but if she hadn't then I'd never have met you!'

'Exactly!'

'What would you have done if you had gone to America?'

'My dream was always to become a detective over there.'

'And you've never ridden a horse?' she said, in total disbelief.

'Well, for a couple of summers I worked part-time in the West Strand, up at the Port. I used to lead the ponies or donkeys up and down the beach taking the kids for a ride. The ponies were pretty docile – they needed to be docile, to accommodate some of the screaming kids, whose parents wanted nothing more than a respite from the non-stop give-me's. We'd charge 10p a time and I used to take an occasional go myself when business was quiet. The owner drummed into us "Ponies with riders are our best adverts, so when business is slow, mount up yourself". Business was always slow when it rained and so we spent our time as drenched human adverts.'

'Why did you not take lessons?'

'It was always something I was going to do at a later date, and sadly, I just never got around to it.' McCusker lifted himself on to an elbow. 'Here's me blethering away ten to the dozen, but what about you? Do you have any regrets?'

'Just one really,' she said quietly, 'and it's that my mum and dad never got to see what a brilliant detective my sister is.'

'Hmmmm.'

'Lily told me that you both watched that DVD of Louis Bloom's lecture. Apparently, in the lecture he talked about when you meet someone, someone special, and you start to have a relationship with them, sometimes you reach a point with them that it is so special and so new. Lily said Louis said it was like having a new toy to play with and you spend some of your time planning what you're going to do with this new toy next time you meet. That's really what it's like with you.'

McCusker grimaced. He wasn't really great at taking compliments, and he couldn't fake it. He would admit himself that he did like people to think well of him, he just wasn't great when they showed it.

'I was wondering,' she started up again, perhaps sensing he'd been having a bit of a moment, 'if we could maybe play with our new toy a wee bit more tonight?'

He looked at her and felt his entire being shudder with a mixture of anticipation and delight. He didn't like to talk about doing things; he just liked to do them. He did, however, feel like this moment called for *something*, if only because he was caught up in the thought that this woman appeared to be as attracted to him as much as he was to her. Now surely that just wasn't possible?

He cleared his throat in preparation for his great delivery. 'Aghahuragha!' he offered, in his best impression of Johnny Weissmuller's Tarzan.

CHAPTER FORTY

DAY SIX: TUESDAY

First thing, 06.45, on the Tuesday morning, O'Carroll had Noah Woyda picked up and brought into the Customs House, to "help the PSNI with their enquiries". The three of them had to wait until 14.28, so that his solicitor, who was on her way to Dublin, could be contacted and persuaded to make her way back for the interview. They'd expected her back earlier and if they'd known they wouldn't have been able to able to start the interview with Noah until after lunchtime, they most certainly would have used their time better, but, McCusker figured, that was usually the way with life.

In the meantime, a freshly showered and shaved DI Jarvis Cage called in to update O'Carroll on the stakeout at Miles Bloom's house. Miles hadn't once set foot outside the house since the stakeout began. His wife would leave each day (Sunday excluded) around 07.10. She would return at the earliest at 17.00 (Saturday) and at the latest at 19.00. They had no visitors apart from the postman, the pizza delivery man and takeout food delivery of an undetermined type.

The elusive Thomas Chada was still elusive, but due to report in that afternoon.

Furthermore, Barr's boys were still not ready to give up their discovery from Louis Bloom's rubbish bag, so generally it was a day for kicking one's heels. McCusker had one little experiment, and he required one of Barr's boys and an independent witness to undertake it for him. Apart from that, the only business attended to was taking official statements from Mariana and Francie Fitzgerald, and Murcia Woyda. In fact, McCusker and O'Carroll were getting so frustrated waiting that at one point they were actually thinking of paying Miles

Bloom a visit to see if they couldn't infuriate him into doing something. But just as they were about to leave the Custom's House on their ruse, Woyda's solicitor walked into the reception.

By 14.30 and after McCusker's missed lunch, the two detectives, Woyda and his solicitor, Leanne Delacato, were all in the interview room as O'Carroll pressed record, and announced that proceedings had officially started. She'd asked Superintendent Larkin to attend the interview, because that is what she believed she should do. But Larkin had declined. This had worried McCusker; if Larkin didn't want to be attached – directly or indirectly – to the proceedings, maybe he wasn't 100 per cent confident of the outcome.

'I would like to go on record,' Leanne Delacato stated, spelling out her name and pronouncing it – Del-a-cat-o – for the digital recorder, 'to protest about my client being brought into custody at 06.45 this morning.'

'We interviewed Mr Noah Woyda, 59 years old of Malone Road, Belfast, yesterday,' O'Carroll started, in a very controlled voice. 'Mr Woyda himself terminated the interview and suggested if we needed to speak to him further, it had to be in the presence of his solicitor. You, Miss Delacato, were on your way to Dublin.'

'You could have released my client until such time as I had returned to Belfast. It was very inconvenient for me to have to return to Belfast 48 hours early.'

'We are investigating the murder of Mr Louis Bloom. We needed to speak with Mr Woyda to help us with our inquiries. Your client has a criminal record. He has done time in prison. In my opinion he was a flight risk. I am sorry to inconvenience you, but it couldn't wait.'

'I have my complaint on the record,' Miss Delacato replied, in a high-pitched, school marm tone – one hardly befitting a woman in her mid-thirties. She theatrically ticked off the first note on her legal pad.

That was one of the reasons McCusker was happy working with DI Lily O'Carroll – she kept her cool about all the official stuff and never reacted to the bait spouted out by those who made a living defending professional criminals.

'You know the procedure by now, all complaints to PONI,' O'Carroll replied and turned to address Woyda directly. 'What were you doing between the hours of 9.00 last Thursday evening and 2.00 the following morning?'

Woyda leaned across to his solicitor and, with his hand protecting his mouth, whispered something to her.

'My client says he has already answered that question,' Delacato replied, on her client's behalf.

'Agreed,' O'Carroll replied, 'we just need it officially on the record.'

Woyda leaned across again and whispered to his solicitor. This time she raised her hand and whispered something back again. Woyda whispered to her again. This time she audibly snapped back, 'Just tell them yourself!'

Noah Woyda's face registered shock at his solicitor's reaction. He continued staring at her as he replied, 'I was out driving around Belfast, and the countryside and towns around Belfast, looking for poster sites for a new bill-posting company I'm setting up. Samuel Brice, my associate, was with me the entire journey. Mr Brice confirmed this to be a fact at our previous meeting. Can I go now please?'

'Please just humour us a little longer,' McCusker said, taking over at the pre-agreed spot, 'did you stop anywhere on your journey for a bite, a newspaper, a pizza, fish and chips, even a wee sit down? I mean, specifically somewhere you would have used your credit card?'

Woyda looked at his solicitor who nodded at him that it was okay to answer the question.

'No. We brought some lemonade, crisps and chocolate with us,' Woyda replied.

'Did you buy those items at the start of the journey?' McCusker continued, trying to give the impression he was after credit card receipts.

'No. I have a stash in the house.'

'Did you maybe fill the Merc up with petrol before you set off on your journey and used your credit card to pay for it?'

'No, afraid not – it was already on full.'

'So you were driving from at least 9 o'clock until 2.00 the following morning?' McCusker continued.

'Just to be safe, let's say from at least 8.30 until 2.30.'

'So that's a long journey – six hours?'

'Yes, you see I need lots of sites for the posters to make this billboard company a viable business concern,' Woyda replied, the length of his answers growing at the same rate as his confidence. 'The more prime sites I have the more I can charge.'

'Yes, that makes a lot of sense,' McCusker replied, 'and we don't have a problem with any of that. No not at all. What we have a problem with is your mpg.'

'Sorry?' Woyda said, looking like he'd been thrown off his rhythm a bit.

'Well, you see, earlier today we hired a vehicle – same model and year as yours, a Mercedes-Benz G-Class, G55 AMG a 4x4, nicknamed a G-Wagen because of its cross-country abilities. So we filled it up to the brim with fuel. We discovered the tank takes just under 21 gallons. We had one of our officers and an independent witness drive around. Some of the journey was in the city and some was out in the country and the surrounding towns and villages, and do you know what happened, Mr Woyda?'

Leanne Delacato's eyes betrayed that she did, even if the penny still hadn't dropped with Mr Noah Woyda.

When no reply was forthcoming McCusker continued with: 'Well, the thing about the G-Wagen is that it was originally recommended to Mercedes as a military vehicle, by one of their major shareholders, the Shah of Iran. Turned out to be a brilliant idea in fact and it became a very successful military vehicle. So successful in fact they eventually made it available to the general public. I've always thought of this SUV as Mercedes' version of a Land Rover. It was developed mainly for rough terrain consequently it does guzzle the petrol. It gets about 12 miles to the gallon. So that's 252 miles on a full tank. We found that, running inside the speed limit of course,' McCusker said, and checked on a report-like page he'd brought in to the interview with him, for effect, 'that the said vehicle ran out of fuel after three hours and forty-two minutes of continuous driving.'

'Yeah, and so what does that prove?' Woyda said, sniggering.

'Well, what that proves, Mr Woyda,' O'Carroll offered, taking the reins back again, 'is that you and Mr Samuel Brice were both lying to us about what you were doing last Thursday evening and Friday morning.'

McCusker wondered why Woyda didn't come up with something on the spot. For instance, he could have tried "we always carry a spare five-gallon can of fuel in the boot", or "we called out the AA", or "we stopped another car and paid them to syphon off a couple of gallons". It was as if Woyda really didn't care that he'd been caught lying. Not only that, but he'd also persuaded his colleague to subscribe to the very same lie. No, Woyda looked like he'd been caught out because he had been concentrating so hard on *not* being caught out. He'd been preoccupied thinking that having to produce a credit card receipt would betray him. Either that, or he had something else up his sleeve and he was so confident with his play that he was prepared to give O'Carroll and McCusker the first spoils.

'Mr Woyda: could you please tell us what you were doing from 9.00 on Thursday evening last to 2.00 on Friday morning?' O'Carroll asked for the second time that afternoon.

'You know what, I really can't remember what I was doing but whatever I was doing it was with my colleague, Mr Samuel Brice.'

'Very cosy I'm sure,' McCusker whispered, low enough that it wasn't audible for the digital recorder, even though McCusker was convinced Woyda picked it up nice and clear.

'We've been advised that you arranged to have Mrs Mariana Fitzgerald beaten up in order that she'd reveal where your wife was hiding out from you,' O'Carroll said, moving on as though it was the most natural thing in the world.

'My wife isn't hiding out from me!' he spat back at the detective inspector.

'Well, we also have a sworn statement from her, stating that you beat her up and she had to flee the matrimonial home in fear for her life,' O'Carroll continued.

'That's just a wee misunderstanding between husband and wife,' Woyda said, laughing, 'it's the same the whole world over, the strife between husband and wife, isn't it? But you know what they say: "The best part of breaking up is when you're making up." I can tell you here and now, no matter what you say my wife will not stand up before me in a court of law and say those libellous things.'

'You deny you subjected your wife to mental and physical violence?' O'Carroll asked.

McCusker figured they both knew the answer but that O'Carroll wanted it on the record.

'I've already told you, it was just a wee misunderstanding – we'll work our way through it. She'll come back, we'll go to expensive counselling, I'll buy her the new car she wants and everything will be rosy.'

'So you're saying your wife is lying?' O'Carroll continued relentlessly.

Woyda just glared at his solicitor.

'I believe we've covered this topic fully,' she replied. 'Let's move on, shall we?'

'Miss Delacato,' O'Carroll said, 'is it true that you've received notification from Mrs Murcia Woyda's solicitor that she's filing for divorce?'

'That's covered under client privilege, I believe,' Miss Delacato replied smugly.

'I believe you'll find it's not. It's not a confidential communication between you and your client, its a notice of a public filing by a third party, a solicitor, on behalf of his client, Mrs Woyda, of her intentions.'

'I'll check the ethics on that when I get back to my office,' Miss Delacato replied, successfully deflecting the issue. 'Now, let's move on here. Please! My client is a businessman and he's been stuck in here all day, being forced to neglect important issues.'

McCusker's eyebrows tried unsuccessfully to play ping-pong with each other.

'Mrs Murcia Woyda has made a statement claiming she was having an affair with Mr Louis Bloom for the past several months and up until the time of his death.'

'She's just saying that...' Woyda started, and pulled himself up short.

'So you're saying that even though your wife, and Mr and Mrs Fitzgerald, all state your wife was having an affair with Mr Louis Bloom, she wasn't?'

'Did my wife accuse me of having an affair?' Woyda asked, innocently.

'No she didn't,' O'Carroll replied.

'Because I wasn't,' Woyda offered, to the slight concern of his brief, who clearly didn't know where he was taking this. 'If she had made such a claim to you then I would have defended it forcefully. But I'm not accusing my wife of being unfaithful, so why would I need to defend her?'

'Here's the problem, Mr Woyda,' McCusker said, 'Mr Bloom was murdered in Botanic Gardens last Thursday night. Your wife admitted that she was having an affair with him. She also admitted that she's scared of you, that you beat her, and that she had to run away from your matrimonial home in order to protect herself. She said she fears for her life. You, Sir, don't have a credible alibi for the time of Louis Bloom's death.'

'Most likely at least half the male population does not have an alibi for the time of Mr Bloom's death,' Miss Delacato claimed, 'but I did-n't see a queue of them in the lobby of the Customs House awaiting their interrogation.'

'But half the male population of Belfast do not have a beautiful wife who had been sleeping with the deceased,' McCusker replied.

'Nonetheless, you have shown absolutely no reason nor proof as to why you have the right to detain my client any longer, so unless you have anything else, we're out of here.'

'Here's the thing,' Woyda started up again, clearly sensing the momentum was with him, 'every second I remain in here does untold damage to me, my marriage, my standing in the community and my numerous businesses, and any claim we make against the PSNI will reflect that.'

McCusker could see in O'Carroll's eyes the wheels turning through various scenarios, none of which she seemed to love, or even like, for that matter.

'Let's take a break here,' she announced for the benefit of the recorder. She confirmed that she and McCusker were leaving the room, turning off the recorder and leaving Woyda and his brief in the company of the constable, who had been waiting just outside the door of the interview room. All of the above had happened so quickly that neither Leanne Delacato nor her client had a chance to protest.

* * *

'So you don't really have enough evidence to detain him,' Superintendent Larkin said, not so much a question as a statement made to O'Carroll and McCusker in his office three minutes later.

'But we're both pretty sure it's him,' McCusker offered.

'Yes we are,' O'Carroll agreed.

'Innocent men would want to know about the victim,' McCusker claimed, 'but your man downstairs seems to only be concerned about how his arrest would impact his job, his marriage and his standing in the local community. The suspect displayed no concern for or interest in Louis Bloom. In my experience, this makes the suspect seem very much like a guilty man. Surely an innocent man would seek more details about the victim whose death had led to his questioning? Surely he'd want to know how the murder had been committed, and where and when, so that he might be better furnished with information with which to clear up the misunderstanding? Woyda's not even concerned that we've caught him out in the blatant lie on his alibi. The suspect was behaving in a very suspicious manner. If you ask me, he's behaving like a man who felt he'd left neither clues nor a direct connection back to himself... well, either that or he's 100 per cent innocent. We don't feel like that is a possibility.'

'I hear you, McCusker,' Larkin said, 'but from where I sit, if we detain him any longer without anything more solid, we're just giving them the ammo to walk later.'

'But–' O'Carroll started, only to be stopped in her tracks by the palm of her superior's hand.

'If we try to succeed with what we have now,' Larkin announced, 'I predict it will be as unsuccessful as a musician at the controls of his stereo system trying desperately hard to make his music sound the way he needs it to sound while he only has the bass, treble and volume knobs available to him. Let him go and let's get what we need to make it stick.'

While disappointing, neither detective felt their boss was being unreasonable. They both agreed that they'd taken it to Larkin in the first place because they knew instinctively that they didn't have enough.

'But what was all that stick at the end, about a musician and his bass and treble knobs?' McCusker asked.

'Haven't a clue,' O'Carroll replied, 'probably something he picked up at a dinner party and he was trying it out on us for size.'

'Sounds to me like he needs to do a bit more fine-tuning on it,' McCusker said, as O'Carroll returned to the interview room to advise Woyda and his brief that they were good to go, but that they weren't to leave the city, as Mr Woyda would be required for more questioning in the very near future.

'Be careful how you proceed,' Delacato, clearly hoping for the last word, warned the detective.

'You too,' O'Carroll replied, managing to pip the solicitor at the post.

CHAPTER FORTY-ONE

Remarkably, neither McCusker nor O'Carroll felt down about developments, or the lack of them.

When they returned to their office, DS WJ Barr was sitting with a student; a very well turned out student, in grey flannels, black blazer, white shirt and QUB tie. His jet-black hair seemed long, clean and all over the place, in a cool sort of way. He kept having to flick his fringe to the right and out of his eyes. McCusker couldn't make out if he was either clean-shaven or hadn't started shaving yet. The ultra-important thing for McCusker was the aforementioned scarf: it sported long, yellow stripes on a black background, the very same colours of Magherafelt High School.

'You must be Thomas Chada?' McCusker said, stretching out his hand.

'And you must be Mr McCusker?' the student replied in a broad Mid-Ulster accent, accepting the detective's firm handshake with one just as firm.

'Have a seat,' McCusker continued, as O'Carroll gave them both a polite smile and swerved directly to her own seat.

McCusker had second thoughts about conducting the interview in the office with all the others buzzing around within listening distance. Part of what he'd called Thomas Chada in for could be sensitive, and probably difficult for him to talk about in front of a lot of people. At the same time he didn't want to conduct the interview in the formal settings of the interview room.

'I don't know about you but I've been talking all day and I'm parched,' McCusker started, as O'Carroll shot him the evil eye, clearly thinking he was going to suggest a trip to McHughs. 'I fancy a good old cup of tea and a few nibbles – let's nip down to our canteen and see what we can get them to rustle up for us, eh?'

On hearing the word "canteen" O'Carroll reached into her top drawer and produced a couple of white fivers, also known as luncheon vouchers, and handed one each to McCusker and Thomas Chada. McCusker seemed the more pleased of the two.

'So,' McCusker started up, when he had Thomas Chada's undivided attention. The PSNI canteen was empty apart from the staff at the other end. 'I hear tell you had a great night in Botanic Gardens.'

'Ah no, Siobhan's not your daughter is she?' Thomas gushed, in red alert.

'You mean you didn't even get to know her second name?' McCusker replied, feeling that a little more uncertainty could favour the brave.

'Honest, Sir, all above board as it were. Nothing Australian, I assure you.'

'Nothing Australian?'

'You know, nothing Down Under,' Thomas Chada said, through a wicked smile.

'Ah jeez, Thomas – you're very lucky Siobhan isn't my daughter and if you do ever get to meet her dad, for goodness sakes, man, do yourself a big favour and don't ever mention any of the auld Australian carry on.'

'Point taken, Sir, but it's all good… all good… and in fact I'm seeing her again tonight,' Thomas Chada confessed.

'So this is a new relationship, this one with you and Siobhan?'

'Yeah, I met her on Thursday at a lecture. She's really cute. Afterwards we just kept on walking, talking – she's very funny. Totally holds her own. She doesn't take any of the boy shit. We went down Botanic Avenue for a pizza, we walked, we talked some more, and we ended up in Botanic Gardens, not by design. I didn't realise that we were heading anywhere. I'm quite sure we weren't. We seemed to be looking as much at each other as to where we were going. To be honest, I was happy just to hang with her. She's so clever – can talk about everything and rabbits away as much as I do. And, to top that, she's so beautiful. Really! I just usually see girls like her from a distance. I never dreamed anything was going to happen. I just thought if I hung on to her coat-tails, I'd get a lot further than I ever dreamed was possible by just talking to a stunning girl.'

'Wow,' McCusker thought, and said. He hoped he wasn't sounding patronising, because he wasn't meaning to. He was just thinking 'Wow!'

Thomas Chada smiled, agreeing entirely with McCusker's sentiment.

'Tell me this, Thomas: what time did you get to the Botanic Gardens?'

Thomas made the sound of expelling air through not-quite-closed lips.

'I'd say, maybe about 8.00-ish, not later, maybe 8.30, because we stayed there until about 9.30. I know this only because Siobhan said, "We've been sitting here for nearly an hour."'

'Sitting where, Thomas?'

'You know, the shelter just over from the bandstand; it has a coni-cal roof, no sides and bench seats,' he replied. 'What happened there?'

'You tell me?'

'Really?'

'Why yes,' McCusker added, a little confused.

'Well, I suppose it's a little embarrassing.'

'Oh, yes, I mean no, I see what you mean – there's no need to go into those types of details,' McCusker said, 'save those for Siobhan's father.'

Luckily Thomas got the joke. In fact, he thought it was hilarious, or maybe his echoing laughter was sheer relief after a possible troubled few days thinking he was in trouble with the PSNI.

'So do you mean from the moment we entered Botanic Gardens?'

'Well, for the minute let's just focus on your time in the shelter.'

'Well. We were chatting away, still,' Thomas said, laughing, 'and just as we were passing the bandstand, she asked me if I thought we'd been together long enough to consider it to officially be a date. I said, as you do, that as we were coming up to just over 50 per cent of avail-able waking hours then, yes, we could now officially consider it to be a date.

'She seemed to consider the full implications of this while I was en-thusing away about Otis Redding – my dad's a big fan and turned me on to him. When I next paused for breath, she said, and get this, it's her exact words: "How do you feel about kissing on a first date?" Wow, that just blew me away. Here was this intelligent, beautiful girl and she'd asked me a) if we could consider we were on our first date and b) would I kiss a girl on a first date.'

Thomas stopped talking.

'What did you say?' McCusker asked, slightly worried he might be more interested in how Thomas's first date with Siobhan turned out than what Thomas actually saw while he was on it.

'Well, I didn't say much, if anything, but I thought a lot; I mean, all this shit flies through your mind in a microsecond. I thought this just doesn't happen to the likes of me – this surely happens to the class studs, but not to me. Then, did you know what I thought next?'

'No.'

'I thought there is something very wrong with this picture. I wondered if I was being set up? Was there a sting in progress? Could she be another Anna Chapman who thinks I have some vital information? And then do you know what I thought?'

'No?'

'I thought, I don't give a fig, I don't care about the consequences. She's pretty much invited me to kiss her, so damn the consequences; I'm going to kiss her. So I kissed her!'

McCusker could swear he heard the bells of St Mary ringing somewhere in the background. He felt like jumping up and cheering for the little guy for winning the intelligent, beautiful girl against all the odds, just like he had done himself. Then he suddenly remembered why he and Thomas Chada were in the canteen drinking tea, a tea that was so weak it had trouble passing the spout of the teapot.

Before McCusker could formulate his next question, Thomas said, 'And it was just the most amazing kiss of my life so far. Her lips were so soft and responsive and I realised... I just realised, right there, actually, that this stuff is really not what you're interested in. The fact that I shared an earth-moving moment with Siobhan has nothing to do with why you needed to talk to me.'

'Well, in a way it has,' McCusker started, really happy to have an opportunity to get the chat back on track again. 'When you were in the shelter with Siobhan, did you notice anything odd?'

'No, not really.'

'Okay, Thomas, we're all a little more observant than we think,' McCusker started slowly, hoping his disappointment wasn't transparent.

Thomas looked like he was concentrating, deep in thought trying to recover something, anything, from the night in question.

'Okay, well there was something that I missed mostly, because I was facing away from it, but at a point about twenty minutes after our kiss started when we'd come up for air, I felt Siobhan tense up all of a sudden. I thought I'd maybe done something wrong. I asked her if she was okay. She said she'd just seen something weird. One of her lecturers was out walking in Botanic and a man had approached him. I turned around to have a look but by that time, both the men she was referring to had their backs to us and were walking away.'

'Why was Siobhan troubled by it?'

'She said that although the man didn't touch the lecturer, he'd apparently snarled at him – she said the man's face had transformed from being another man in the park to a man so sinister it scared her. I asked her if she wanted to do anything about it. She said no, she didn't want to interfere in the lecturer's business, and he seemed to be walking away of his own free will with the evil man – they were both talking, apparently.'

'But you only saw them both from the back?'

'Yes, they were walking away from us before I'd a chance to turn around.'

'Did Siobhan recognise the lecturer in question?'

'Yes she did, she said he was her favourite lecturer, she just mentioned his name once but it was so distinctive a name I remember it. Louis Bloom.'

'And the other man – did she recognise him?'

'No, she said she'd never seen him before.'

'And he'd his back to you at all times. Anything else about him you can remember?'

'I was kind of distracted with Siobhan,' Thomas Chada admitted.

'I know, but anything at all?'

'Well, he had one of those loud car jackets on. I remember thinking that's the kind of a jacket you'd never be caught dead in. It was a blue plastic one and just below the shoulders across the back there were yellow, green and red strips, which were each about 2 inches deep.'

Chapter Forty-Two

Just before O'Carroll and McCusker were about to leave the office for the day, DS WJ Barr came to them with potential good news. As Mc-Cusker knew O'Carroll was off to another of her blind dates, he told her to go and he would deal with whatever it was Barr had discovered. He'd give her a shout later to bring her up to date. She tried to give him an affectionate pat on the arm but she caught Barr's eye at the last moment and so she turned it into a full-blown thump.

'Don't you two go messing it up on me,' she said, as she winked at her partner.

Barr took McCusker back up a floor to a suite of three rooms, which the forensic boys and girls had recently commandeered.

The biggest of the three was an open-plan office and at its centre was a very large table with what McCusker assumed was the contents of Louis Bloom's final rubbish bag. A person's rubbish is never a pretty sight after the fact; plastic bottles, lettuce leaves – there always seems to be an abundance of lettuce leaves and tea leaves too. There was also stained, crumbled newspapers, toast remains, opened vegetable tins, broken glass, various past-their-sell-by-dates food cartons, take-away remains and all manner of containers. McCusker didn't want to imagine any deeper than that, but all of Mr and Mrs Louis Bloom's waste was here, on the table, betraying their domestic secrets.

'So,' Barr started, quoting the most-often used word on factual television, 'the first thing the team noticed was among the rubbish a 10-inch by 8-inch brown manila envelope, addressed to "L Bloom". On first inspection they couldn't see anything that might have been the contents of said envelope.'

'Okay so far, WJ,' McCusker said. Some of the technicians seemed to be wetting themselves in anticipation for the big reveal they knew was coming.

'Then they started to notice, mostly among the newspapers, small pieces of something they couldn't exactly make out. They separated these similar pieces from the rest of the rubbish. Some of them had torn edges, some had straight edges, as though they'd been cut. At first they thought it might be some photo pages from a colour supplement. But on closer examination they discovered the pieces were too glossy and too thick to be from a magazine. Then they realised they were pieces of a real photograph.'

'O-kay, guys and gals, now you've really got my attention.'

'Then they stopped work on it immediately. Although they were only picking out and examining the pieces, they realised there could be valuable fingerprints on this photo. So they set up a system, of taking a 4 inch x 4 inch photo of each section of the photo from the bag. Then they endeavoured to complete the jigsaw puzzle using the new photographs they'd taken. That was when they realised the reason it was taking them so long to complete the puzzle was down to the fact that they had in fact discovered three separate photographs, of a lesser number of pieces, in the bag.'

'Now I know what it must feel like when the mysterious voice announces on *The X-Factor* "And the winner is…" and then they keep the contestants, and the audience, dangling on until they *finally* announce the winner,' McCusker offered, involuntarily taking large breaths.

'Okay, well we're not going to do that,' Barr announced. 'Let me show you the first part of their completed work.'

Barr led McCusker, with the rest of the team following closely in their wake, over to a smaller table.

'Oh my…' McCusker stopped mid-sentence and couldn't find any words to describe the three scenes in front of them. In any other situation the photographs could have been labelled as porn – maybe soft porn, but porn nonetheless. But these images before McCusker and the rest of the gang were images of pure beauty. The three photographs showed Louis Bloom and Murcia Woyda undressed in their room in Dukes Hotel, giving themselves to each other, both clearly totally lost in the moment of their mutual pleasure.

McCusker felt 100 per cent confident that not one person in the room with him was titillated by the images – envious perhaps, but mostly just acknowledging the exquisiteness before them. McCusker felt guilty, staring at the images, but no one around him was even aware that he was, so intent were their own gazes. 'And the second part?' he eventually asked.

'Well, the second part was even more difficult, because by attempting to place the originals together in order to complete the photos, they risked smudging the fingerprints, and the main problem we had was we had to accept that a percentage of the fingerprints would be on the rear of the photographs. So they placed the original pieces on a clear, non-sticky sheet of Perspex roll. Then they dusted the photos with fingerprint powder and lifted the prints, turned it over, sprayed it again and lifted the prints.'

'Did you get a match?' McCusker felt scared to ask, but he did anyway.

'Yes, we found Louis Bloom's prints on both sides of the photo,' Barr replied.

'Right,' said McCusker, unable to hide his disappointment.

'Oh yes,' Barr grandstanded, 'sorry – there was one other clear set of prints on the photograph, remind me whose they were again?'

No one offered any help to Barr, and McCusker, once again, had that awful X-Factor sinking feeling.

'Oh yes, the other prints we managed to find were in the police PSNI computer system. They belonged to a certain Mr Noah Woyda.'

'You're kidding?' McCusker said automatically, but accepted that he'd feel a terrible fool if Barr said "Yes sir, I was kidding".

But no need for McCusker to worry, because Barr said, 'They checked and re-checked, Sir, and they are 100 per cent confirmed as being the fingerprints of Noah Woyda.'

'Amazing job, the lot of you,' McCusker offered in praise of the entire team, and silently ate his "anyone who leaves fingerprints is a fool who we'll eventually catch anyway" words.

He eventually tracked down DI O'Carroll. Once again she sounded like she was in a noisy bar. She was as happy about the news as he was. Both agreed that they'd still a way to go to join all the dots, but they were a lot more excited than they had been earlier when Leanne Delacato had managed to walk her client, Noah Woyda, out of the Customs House uncharged.

'Just tell me this, McCusker, before you go,' she shouted, 'on a scale of one to ten, just how hot were the photographs?'

'Oh, I'd say,' McCusker offered, in a large exhale, 'on a scale of one to ten they'd be about one...' and he paused '...hundred and ninety-nine!'

CHAPTER FORTY-THREE

McCusker felt it only fair he take Barr and the forensic team out for an after-office drink at McHughs.

At first he was preoccupied with the numerous types of body noises about the pub, repeated as signatures. The man who wheezed; the lad who coughed; the girl who cried; the man who sneezed; the woman who sniffled; the man who snocked (a McCusker, pig-like word for the noise of someone drawing snotters back up their nostrils, causing sounds like a death-rattle in the back of their throats). They all reminded McCusker of a street rhyme from his youth and one that Elizabeth Bloom claimed her husband had often used: "Coughs and sneezes spread diseases, so trap your germs in your handkerchiefs." Maybe the word "handkerchief" should be replaced by "Kleenex" in O'Carroll's modern version. It made him realise that you didn't see many handkerchiefs around these days. He agreed with himself that perhaps that may not be the best topic to bring up with the DI right now.

The above distraction was but a fleeting one and before long he and DS Barr got into quite a conversation about forensics and firearms.

'Don't forget, we are living in a society where we're always working on ways to kill one another, and we and other police forces are working on ways to, hopefully, prevent said crimes – not only to prevent them, but *catching* the criminals after the crimes,' McCusker said, following on from one of Barr's accounts of how the forensic team were becoming more and more successful. 'But what we seem to ignore is that it is well within the PSNI's power to cut out some crimes completely. Say firearms, for instance. We could just ban all firearms and save ourselves and the public so much pain and anguish. Stop all this madness overnight.'

McCusker felt that Barr's eyes betrayed "That's just too simplistic a view", but in respect of McCusker, the DS abstained from saying the actual words.

'So tell me this, WJ: why are they even legal? Why are people even allowed to buy guns?'

'Oh, I wouldn't worry too much about guns, Sir,' Barr replied confidently, 'the guns themselves aren't the problem we need to address. If guns *were* illegal and someone wanted to kill someone, you can bet your bottom dollar they'd soon find another method.'

'Yes, yes of course, I get that,' McCusker offered, sincerely hoping he was debating more than arguing, 'but don't you see that with a gun, the assassin removes part of the actual murder process out of the kill? If you seek to kill someone with a gun, you're once removed from the actual killing. Whereas with Louis Bloom, his murderer got up close and personal with him. Louis' assassin was close enough to smell Louis' deodorant, his sweat. The murderer was close enough to his victim to hear him breathe, to feel him gasp for his final breath. That certainly takes a different kind of resolve than someone who just pulls a trigger, maybe even from a distance, maybe even while hidden in the bushes, or from a window high up in Dealey Plaza in faraway Dallas, Texas.'

Then the head-turning, conversation-stopping vision that was Grace O'Carroll walked into McHughs, and the two colleagues' debating stopped immediately. As McCusker enjoyed every single microsecond of her walk towards him, he remembered that it was in this very bar that he first spotted Grace, or French Bob, as he had christened her then. He didn't know at that point that she was DI Lily O'Carroll's sister. Nor did he know that his many daydreams about her would one day become a reality. Before she was close enough to him to say hello to, he wished with all his might that Thomas Chada and Siobhan might one day themselves enjoy a similar reality.

CHAPTER FORTY-FOUR

DAY SEVEN: WEDNESDAY

The Wednesday was only a matter of one hour and forty-seven minutes old when McCusker was awoken from his slumber. He tried ever so gently to disentangle his and Grace's limbs from each other. In the process, he disturbed her but didn't awaken her.

Ten minutes later he was in her sister's battered, metallic yellow Mégane, racing towards Miles Bloom's house up on Cyprus Avenue.

'How did your date go?' McCusker asked his partner.

'Well, it was all going okay, not great, but okay, that is until he asked me back to his place,' she said, as she jumped a red light at Newtownards Road and Holland Drive.

'Yeah… and it's 2018, surely that's permitted on a first date?' McCusker offered in surprise.

'Agreed,' she conceded, 'but then that was when he told me he still lived with his mum…'

And that was when McCusker and O'Carroll pulled up outside Miles Bloom's house at the bottom of Cyprus Avenue.

By the time they arrived there was already an ambulance, two Battenbergs, three Blues and Twos, DI Jarvis Cage's vehicle, lots of flashing lights and lots of people milling around behind the taped-off "Do Not Cross" police lines, trying to steal a better view of… well, all of the above, really. Mrs Miles Bloom – the other Mrs Bloom - was not in attendance. She was over in Brighton at a conference. She had been contacted and would make her way back first thing in the morning.

McCusker, for some reason or other, had not been expecting what was waiting for them inside Bloom's house. Even when O'Carroll had rung him, all she had said was there had been an incident of some kind or other up at Miles Bloom's house and that DI Cage, who was on his third day staking out Miles Bloom, had been hysterical, just screaming at her to get over there immediately.

The first thing that shook McCusker and shattered his happy-go-lucky mood was the copious amount of blood splattered on the walls of the living room.

That was before he even saw the denim-clad remains hidden behind a rose-patterned sofa.

Miles Bloom was dead!

The only two surviving members of the Bloom family had died within a week of each other.

DI Jarvis Cage seemed to have settled down somewhat since his phone conversation with O'Carroll.

'Just after 1.00 a.m. a large, black 4x4 pulled onto the corner of North Road, just on the corner of Cyprus Avenue and close to the Bloom residence.' Cage's eyes darted from O'Carroll to McCusker, as if seeking some kind of approval. 'Before I actually noticed the vehicle, they'd turned off their lights. I wasn't concerned about this. I initially thought it was just a few neighbours returning after a night on the tiles.

'Then when two men got out of the SUV, walked diagonally across Cyprus Avenue to Mr Bloom's, I thought I'd better record them on my iPhone. They stopped at the front door for a few seconds before going around to the back of his house. I didn't hear anything else, but I felt it best to turn off BBC Radio Ulster, which had been getting me through this stakeout for a few nights now, just in case.

'Next thing I know, the light goes on in what I've always assumed was Miles' bedroom. Then a few seconds later the hall light goes on. Another few seconds passed before the light in the front room went on. Then nothing at all happened for several minutes.

'Then I heard some screaming and shouting from the living room. I called it in at that point, asking for back-up and started filming with my iPhone again. The screaming and shouting stopped for a couple of minutes then it started back up again. It was louder the second time. I saw a flash and a pop, then another flash and a pop.

'Then I repeated my call for back-up. I didn't know what was going on over there in Miles Bloom's house but all hell seemed to have broken loose. The front door burst open and those same two men ran out and back to the black Mercedes SUV. A few seconds later, the car sped off without switching on its lights, so I didn't have a chance to record its number plate.

'I did get a great clip, on my mobile phone, of them running towards the car. I also shot some footage of them jumping into the car and driving off,' Cage offered eagerly, as he produced his mobile and replayed the scenes he'd just described.

Mostly the images were too dark to make anything out but the street lamps, but part of it, with the two men high-tailing it, backs to the camera, clearly showed that one of them was wearing a blue plastic car-coat with tell-tale red, green and yellow stripes across the back of the shoulders.

McCusker and O'Carroll just nodded at each other.

DI Cage then took them over to the body.

Miles had a piece of white paper stuffed in his bloody hand. But there was no blood on the paper. DI Cage had waited to remove it until O'Carroll had arrived, although all, in their own way, noted the fact that Cage hadn't actually said "I wanted to wait until DI O'Carroll and McCusker arrived".

O'Carroll had the fist and the crumpled paper photographed from every possible angle. Then, gloved up, she carefully removed the paper.

She unfolded it.

It was half of a foolscap page with the typed words "i'm sorry for what I done to my brother. didnt solve my problems. this is my only escape". A large handwritten "M" was signed beneath the typed lines.

'And you're sure you heard two shots, DI Cage?' McCusker asked.

'Yes, of course,' Cage hissed back, indignantly.

'It was just a question, Cage,' O'Carroll said, her warm fuzzy feeling for Cage over his stellar work disappearing fast. 'And where did the second shot go?' she continued, as they all searched the body.

There was one clear wound right between the eyes. A sickening lot of blood and brain matter were sprayed all over the walls around the sofa. There were no other wounds about the body.

McCusker eventually found the second bullet. It was at the opposite end of the room from the blood-spattered walls. McCusker's first thought was that this, the living room – the good room – was not the usual room in which to commit suicide. There was also the theory, which McCusker believed held a lot of water, that suicidal people were considerate to their survivors and usually picked a garage or even a forest to do the deed. Certainly, somewhere that would cause minimum stress to those left behind. Most certainly some place away from the window and the front of the house.

The lack of blood on the suicide note, compared to the hand in which it was found, indicated that the note had been stuffed into Miles Bloom's fist after shots were fired.

Furthermore, McCusker knew that Miles Bloom would never have referred to Louis as "my brother". He also surmised that surely such a man of letters and writs would have used proper punctuation and wouldn't have restricted himself to only nineteen words. He most certainly would have had a well-practiced, flamboyant signature, and not just a single initial.

On top of which, two shots were fired in opposite directions, in the company of two strangers... that was stretching the imagination just a wee bit too far.

A few minutes later, O'Carroll found McCusker out in the hallway, sitting on the second-to-bottom stair.

'Are you okay?' O'Carroll asked him, quietly.

'Yes. But now and again I'll get a flashback to a smell, a fond memory of a treasured smell from my childhood that I'd long forgotten,' McCusker replied, pulling himself out of his thought. 'It might be a sweet or a cake I'd enjoyed. Even the smell of a comic, a new comic, you know: *Superman* or *Batman* or a *Commando* comic. They all had very different, distinctive smells. When I catch a whiff like that, I'll try, sometimes for weeks, to match the smell up to the item that had once brought me such immense pleasure.'

'Yes, and...?'

'Well, just there I got a whiff of that there again, and I got it yesterday when we were interviewing Woyda, and that's why I tried to shake his hand, you know, to try to get closer to him to pinpoint the smell. I couldn't get close enough – he wouldn't shake my hand. Then when we were entering this house I experienced the smell again in the hallway; it was just for the briefest of moments, and then my nostrils were filled with the smells of gunpowder in the living room. But then I came back out here – well, the same smell hit me again. This time I got it. It's sweets, hard-boiled sweets, and that smell is so powerful and so evocative. I always felt the smell was so pungent because they used to keep hard-boiled sweets in those large sweetie jars and then the absolute explosion of aromas on the nostrils when the top was screwed off…. just now when I came out here again, I recalled all this, and it was the same smell that hung on Noah Woyda, as strong and as distinguishable as any talcum powder, aftershave or deodorant. It is the joyous smell of black and white mint humbugs.'

O'Carroll just smiled.

'If we needed any more proof that he was here, that was it,' McCusker claimed.

'Let's go and get our man before he does any other harm,' O'Carroll said, helping her partner up from the step.

CHAPTER FORTY-FIVE

Noah Woyda was born in Katowice in Poland, on March 4th, 1959. When Noah was three years old his father – a dentist, also named Noah – decided to move the family, lock, stock and barrel, to Antrim in Northern Ireland. He chose Northern Ireland because as a volunteer for the Polish FA he had worked as a medic (or the man with the magic sponge who ran onto the field in times of injury) when the Northern Irish team visited the Chorzow Stadium on the October 10th, 1962, to play Poland in the first round of the European Championship Qualifier. Northern Ireland won 2-0, which was the same score when Poland (with volunteer Woyda) visited Windsor Park, Belfast, on November 28th, the same year, for the second leg. Following the monumental fixtures, Noah Senior told anyone who would listen that he was moving the entire family (himself, wife, Noah and Noah's two older sisters) to Northern Ireland, simply because he thought the Ulstermen in the Northern Irish FA party were the nicest, funniest and friendliest people he'd ever met in his life. The Woyda family moved to Antrim Town in February 1963. Noah Senior bought into a local, and very successful, dental practice at the perfect time.

Noah Woyda (Junior), unlike the rest of his family, didn't settle well in Antrim. He fell behind in school because he was so slow learning to speak English. The older Noah got, the more he never forgave his father for moving the family from his native Poland. He didn't make friends easily; he claimed he didn't want to be friends with the locals. He blamed them for him not living in Poland. With the passing of years, he became more and more romantically attached to Poland, although, strangely, he never returned to his native land. When he was eighteen years old he refused his father's invitation to become an apprentice in the dental practice; Noah Junior claimed he didn't want to serve the Ulster people. He didn't want to serve anybody.

He worked as a labourer on the roads until he was twenty-seven. He wasn't scared of hard work and was happy to work all the overtime he could get. Then he got a job as a lorry driver. He met his first wife, Maureen, at the Flamingo Ballroom in nearby Ballymena, dancing to the legendary Billy Brown & the Freshmen. Maureen Wallace, aged 32, and her three friends were from Belfast, and dedicated fans of the Freshmen. So Noah Junior moved to the city and married Maureen in 1986. But Maureen still wanted to continue going out with her friends, to see the Freshmen and hang out with the band. That wasn't what Noah expected his wife to do. So he just up and left her and, in fact, he didn't divorce Maureen until he met and decided he wanted to marry Murcia in 2014.

By the time he left Maureen, he had his own lorry and was doing very well as a haulage contractor, which is how he got into trouble with the RUC for the first time. Noah was transporting lorry-loads of tobacco and liquor across the border.

He soon realised the shippers had been taking advantage of him. He was the one taking the risk by crossing the border with the contraband; he believed that, logically, he should be the one making the lion's share of the money. So he started doing his own bootlegging, and in 1992, the RUC lay in wait and caught him red-handed. Some said the RUC had been tipped off by an ex-associate who wasn't happy that Noah had started up his own "business".

Noah claimed that the RUC made an example of him because he was a foreigner, rather than arrest the locals, the real organisers. He was found guilty and sentenced to three years in Crumlin Road Gaol, which coincidently was also designed by Sir Charles Lanyon, opened in 1846 and is the only Victorian era prison still standing in Northern Ireland. Noah took great pleasure in working out, beefing up and learning how to handle himself while in prison. All the time he was incarcerated he was very careful to keep his nose clean. With good behaviour, he was out in fifteen months.

Noah Senior died in 1996. With the money the father left the son, he bought his first business – XTC Ltd., a thriving, yet bankrupt, pub with a strip-club upstairs. The bank was happy to get rid of the troublesome property at a greatly knocked-down price. And the recent cash from his father's Will greatly assisted Noah's cause. Once the pub was officially his, the first thing he did was to contact Samuel Brice, a fellow Crumlin Road Gaol inmate he'd done time with. He brought Brice in as his "enforcer". And Noah Woyda hadn't crossed the line of the law, nor looked back since then.

* * *

When McCusker and O'Carroll pulled up outside Mr Noah Woyda's stone-walled house, quite literally just off Malone Road, all the lights were still on, even though it was just before 3 a.m. Furthermore, the master of the house was up and about and as wide awake as if it was the crack of dawn.

There was the black Mercedes, G-Wagen, and the red Alfa Romeo, Giulietta, parked in their normal positions.

'Can you confirm that both these vehicles are yours?' McCusker asked, as Woyda came out of the house without being summoned and approached the detective.

'Yes, of course they are, bought and paid for,' Woyda boasted, as Samuel Brice, in his trademark blue plastic car-coat with its tricolour of hoops, joined them.

'Were you and Mr Brice out for a drive in either of these vehicles this evening?' McCusker asked, as he appeared to concentrate on the red one.

'No, of course not, they haven't moved all night,' Woyda claimed. 'Isn't that right, Samuel?'

'Of course, that's correct, Mr Woyda,' Brice offered, in confirmation.

'That's very funny,' McCusker declared.

'And why's that?' Right on cue, Woyda took a black and white mint humbug from his pocket, unwrapped it and popped it in his mouth.

'Well you see, Sir,' McCusker replied, as he took several photographs of the bonnet of the black Merc G-Wagen on his mobile phone, 'dew forms on a car when the temperature drops below a certain level – I believe it's 50 degrees, but we can check the exact temperature for you. Of your two vehicles in the drive here, one – the red one, the Alfa Romeo Giulietta – has dew on it, and one hasn't – the black Merc G-Wagen. You've just claimed that both cars weren't used all night. However, when a car is driven, the heat from the engine makes the dew on the bonnet evaporate. Therefore, if the car hadn't been driven, the dew would still be on the bonnet of the Mercedes G-Wagen, as, in fact, it is on the red Alfa Romeo's bonnet.

'Something we can have a wee chat about next time we meet with Leanne,' Woyda said, as he offered a threatening look to McCusker.

'No need to wait, Sir,' O'Carroll said. 'We're arresting you both for the murder of Mr Louis Bloom. You do not have to say anything. But it may harm your defence if you do not mention when questioned something you may later rely on in court. Anything you do say may be used in evidence.'

Woyda was so shocked he didn't even notice that O'Carroll had secured him in handcuffs, while McCusker did the same to Samuel Brice.

* * *

Proceedings resumed at 9.00 a.m. the following morning when O'Carroll and McCusker, freshly showered and, in McCusker's instance, shaved, met Mr Samuel Brice in the company of his solicitor, Mr Victor Savage. Savage was a junior – and consequently less expensive – member of Leanne Delacato's company. He made it clear from the very start that he wasn't singing from the same hymn sheet as his boss and clearly really wanted to do what was best for his client.

Brice was either in his late forties or his early sixties – for a faceless, mortgaged man, the in-between doesn't exist. He wasn't exactly what you would call overweight, but as McCusker would say, and frequently did, "He'd leave pretty deep footprints up on the West Strand at Portrush."

As Brice confirmed during the interview, he'd met Noah Woyda when they were both doing time. It appeared to McCusker that Brice didn't really have a life outside of Woyda and was on call, quite literally, 24/7. According to Brice, he was paid well for his efforts and loyalty, plus he received generous bonuses and assistance with his mortgage. It was difficult to work out who was taking advantage of whom – probably easier to say it was a relationship of mutual inconvenience. His loyalty extended to not completely selling out his boss. But, where there was a direct conflict with his own potential liberty – as there was with Woyda borrowing Brice's famous blue car-coat on the previous Thursday night – he erred on the side of his own, personal interests.

McCusker, O'Carroll, Victor Savage and Samuel Brice sped through the interview and statement pretty quickly, so the detectives felt well prepared when they reconvened with Noah Woyda and Leanne Delacato in the same interview room at 11.00 a.m.

Delacato was all business and behaving as if she was confident that pretty quickly – like their previous meeting – she'd be walking out of the Customs House with her client a free man.

The two detectives, and not to mention DS Barr and Superintendent Niall Larkin, all had other ideas. McCusker was relieved to hear that the Super, pragmatic as ever, was taking the philosophical view that Miles Bloom would still have been a marked man, with both a target and a price on his head, even if he had detained Woyda yesterday with the insufficient evidence they had at that point.

O'Carroll switched on the digital machine and announced for the record all those who were present.

'Mr Woyda we better get started; we've a lot to get through,' she began.

'First,' McCusker continued, 'we'd like to show you three photographs.'

The two detectives had discussed the tactic of producing the photographs right from the start. She favoured keeping them up their sleeve until they hit troubled waters and needed them. McCusker felt that it was always best to start off with what you hoped would be your winning hand – in other words, what you felt was your unbeatable hand. It gave you a bit of momentum and hopefully carried you through the first couple of hands. O'Carroll was happy to follow her partner's lead on this particular occasion.

McCusker dealt what he felt was his best three-card-hand on to the desk between them. The photos were the right way up for Delacato and Woyda, but McCusker still edged them even closer to the accused and his brief.

Mr Noah Woyda let his mask drop for ten seconds. Right before the detective's eyes, yet unseen by his brief, Woyda's face physically contorted into a mask of hate personified. McCusker believed that if they'd been by themselves, Woyda would have done his very best to kill him in that instant. He also looked like he was absolutely bursting to say something.

'These photographs–'

'What could these photographs possibly have to do with my client?' Delacato shot in, beating McCusker to the punch. She looked like she felt her client expected her to say something, anything. She too was behaving like her client, in that they both appeared to know something that the PSNI didn't. Although, McCusker had to admit that apart from Woyda's anger and Delacato's discomfort, neither of them seemed overly concerned.

'These photographs,' McCusker repeated, 'of Mr Woyda's wife and Mr Louis Bloom sharing some intimate moments were secretly taken on behalf of Mr Woyda and delivered to Mr Louis Bloom in this envelope.'

McCusker paused to take a soiled and stained brown envelope, sealed in an evidence bag, from yet another file. The envelope bore the legend "L Bloom" hand-printed on the front in blue felt-tip.

'Mr Bloom cut and tore the photographs into little pieces and discarded them in his rubbish bag. Perhaps *that* was the reason he was so keen to be out dumping his rubbish so late that night. Maybe he didn't want to risk anyone else seeing these images. Maybe he just didn't want these photographs in his house.'

'I've certainly nothing to do with those photos,' Woyda barked. 'I've never seen those disgusting photos of my wife before and if the PSNI release them to the press… I'll… I'll… put you out of business!'

'Before we move on,' McCusker started, freezing his face to avoid a smirk, 'if you've never seen these photos before or had nothing to do with them, could you please explain why your fingerprints are all over them?'

Leanne Delacato looked like she'd just been sucker punched, not to mention betrayed.

'Would you accept that you and Mr Brice were not in fact driving around looking for poster sites last Thursday night?' O'Carroll continued, not waiting for a response from either Woyda or his brief.

'That must have been a different night,' he conceded slowly, but still seemed generally unconcerned.

'We know you borrowed Mr Brice's distinctive blue plastic car-coat with the three stripes across the chest and the back last Thursday night,' McCusker started.

'Is that what Samuel said?'

McCusker was heartened by his response; at least it wasn't a flat-out denial.

'Yes,' McCusker confirmed, as he patted the file in front of him, 'it's all in here, in his statement.'

'Well, I've always said that Samuel had the better memory, so that must be correct,' Woyda conceded, very well humoured.

'We also have another statement,' McCusker continued, shuffling his files and taping the new one on top, 'this one is from a witness who was in the Botanic Gardens at the same time Louis Bloom was delivering his garbage bag to the rubbish bin, close to the shelter in the bandstand section of the Gardens. This witness saw you approach Mr Bloom–'

'Correction, Mr McCusker,' Delacato offered in interruption, 'your witness saw *a man* wearing a jacket similar to the one my client borrowed from his colleague.'

'Yes,' O'Carroll conceded, 'that's what we also thought, but our DS Barr went to work on that issue for us and do you know what he discovered?'

'I have a feeling I'm about to find out,' Delacato replied, clearly still basking in the glory of her earlier victory.

'He discovered that those jackets are not in fact sold over the counter in Ireland,' O'Carroll continued, appearing to lay down one of her trumps, 'but through Dobens, a mail-order catalogue, the suppliers of which state that they only managed to sell one of their blue plastic coats in Ireland, and that was to a certain Mr Samuel Brice, of Seaview Drive, Fortwilliam, Belfast BT15 4QU.'

'Oh come on, Detective, surely you can do better than that!' Delacato said, tutting away as her client basked in the sunlight of her glory.

'We're talking about the campus of Queens University, ranked in the top 1 per cent of universities in the world! There are around 25,000 graduates or post-graduates who have arrived in Belfast from all over the world. Surely it would not be out of the question to assume that out of those 25,000 students at least one – and maybe even as many as ten – might have also purchased one of these rare jackets in their homeland through the Dobens catalogue?'

McCusker thought Woyda really wanted to high-five his brief right at that very moment. The detective barely managed to hide his disappointment, as he reluctantly agreed that was possible. In fact, Constable Ian McKay, a bright young protégé of DS Barr's, had made a similar point during the process of Barr's research.

'That'll be a matter for the Director of Prosecution to decide,' O'Carroll offered, sacrificing her trump. 'Let's say for now that our witness saw a man in a *distinctive* blue plastic, striped jacket approach Louis Bloom. They had heated words and Mr Bloom and Mr Wo–'

'Uh-uh!' Delacato offered, with a negative shake of her forefinger in chastisement.

'Mr Bloom and a gentleman in a unique blue plastic, striped jacket,' O'Carroll offered, to a nod of approval from Delacato, 'walked off together. Mr Bloom was never seen alive again.'

'Come on! Is that really all you have to throw at us?' Leanne Delacato said, as she stood and started to pack her papers into her expensive but old-fashioned brief case. 'Really? I'm shocked and very disappointed by the calibre of the officers currently in the PSNI.'

Noah Woyda also stood up, seeming shocked that proceedings appeared to have reached a conclusion in his favour so quickly.

O'Carroll and McCusker let them both put on their coats and pack away their paperwork. Just as brief and client reached the door the constable on duty failed to move out of their way.

'If you'd just like to indulge us for a wee while longer, please,' O'Carroll asked.

Client and brief looked at each other in false amusement.

'Yes,' O'Carroll continued, 'we wanted to talk to you about Mr Miles Bloom.'

'Yes,' Delacato said, sitting down again but keeping her coat on. 'I did hear through the grapevine that he committed suicide,' she continued, revealing the reason for her and her client's confidence. 'That was so tragic. Apparently he left a note saying he was sorry for what he did to Louis.'

'Well, not exactly,' O'Carroll said, 'you see, what actually happened, and I know you're going to have trouble believing this… but we had an officer on duty outside Miles' house for the last few evenings and not only did he see a distinctive black Mercedes 4x4 G-Wagen pull up outside Miles' house in the very early hours of this morning, but he also recorded two gentlemen exiting the vehicle – one of them, in fact, wearing the infamous blue with tricolour strip, plastic car-coat. The officer in question, DI Cage, also caught Mr Woyda and his colleague, Mr Brice, on an iPhone camera, leaving their vehicle and entering the house. On top of which, DI Cage witnessed the lights go on, heard two pops of a revolver and then your two boyos swiftly leaving the house in a hurry, jump in their Mercedes and drive off without turning their headlights on. DI Cage also caught their exit on his mobile phone.

'Mr Brice has already made a statement confirming that he was the gentleman in the blue with tricolour strip, plastic car-coat, who last night had entered Miles Bloom's house. He has also confirmed that he was accompanied by Mr Woyda. They entered the house by breaking in through the back door. They climbed the stairs to Miles's bedroom. Mr Brice confirmed that he and Mr Woyda forced Miles Bloom down to the lounge by gunpoint. Mr Woyda, while threatening Miles Bloom with his gun, tried to get Miles to sign a suicide note, which Mr Woyda had earlier prepared on his home computer. Miles pretended he was going to sign the note, but then at the last moment he rugby tackled Mr Woyda, spinning him and the gun around. Mr Woyda's first shot missed Miles, hitting the wall in the opposite corner of the room. Mr Bloom scarpered back over across the room, dived over the sofa but landed on his head and knocked himself out. Mr Woyda leaned over the sofa and instead of shooting Miles up through the underside of his chin and into his brain, the way most suicides would go, he shot his second bullet right between Miles Bloom's eyes.

'Mr Woyda then scribbled an "M" at the bottom of the suicide note, rammed it into the fist of the corpse, and he and Mr Brice made their exit.'

Miss Leanne Delacato removed her coat and started to unpack her briefcase again.

Chapter Forty-Six

Mr Noah Woyda surprised McCusker by not protesting his innocence. He accepted that he'd been caught fair and square, but still, he didn't show any remorse.

'Tell me this, Mr Woyda, how did you manage to persuade Louis Bloom to accompany you when you met him in the Gardens? According to our witness, although there looked to be a bit of "static" between both of you, you didn't use any force to get him to walk away with you.'

'Very simple: I told him that my associate had Murcia in another part of Botanic Gardens and that he would hurt her if we didn't join them in the next five minutes.

'Of course, neither Samuel nor Murcia were in the Gardens that night. When I got Bloom as far as the secluded lane, I pointed to the hedge and said she was in there. When he went to look, I came up behind him and rammed the knife into his back and straight up and through his heart. It's a wee trick I learned when I was up in the Crum. It was all over very quickly.'

'But without Mr Brice to help you, how did you manage to get him up to, and over, the Friar's Bush graveyard wall?' McCusker asked, as ever intrigued by the minutia of the murder method.

'Well, first off, when I knifed him, he fell into the hedgerow and I pushed him in even deeper so that he was out of sight,' Woyda continued, clearly proud of what he considered to be his handiwork. 'It's a quiet laneway in the hours of darkness. I hid him in the hedge and then waited until after midnight, when there was no one around. I snuck back into the Botanic Gardens, pulled Bloom out of the hedge,

put him in a fireman's lift and carried him over to the wall. I'd two
wheelie bins waiting over there. I put one tight up against the wall
and put the other one on its side and in front of the first one, using it
as a step. I climbed up on the one on its side, then on up onto the one
against the wall. I'd enough height to just slide Bloom down on the
graveyard side of the wall, dropping him down onto the ground. I
hopped in after him, lifted him up in a fireman's lift again, carried
him up to the Lennon Mausoleum and spread him out in front of it.'

'Why by the Lennon Mausoleum?' O'Carroll asked.

'Because he was a Beatles fan,' Woyda and McCusker replied simultaneously, one more proudly than the other.

'You've got to understand, it's *all* about doing your recce,' Woyda
boasted. 'It's all about doing your recce. I discovered through my own
recce that Louis Bloom used to take out his rubbish every Thursday
night just before 9 o'clock. I knew every nook and cranny of the graveyard and the Botanic Gardens. I knew where to get the wheelie bins
from. I knew they had to be taken back to where I got them. I knew
where I could hide the body and not risk being caught red-handed
with the corpse. I knew when the Gardens closed. I knew the easiest
way to get into the Gardens when they were officially closed.'

'That's *how* you did it, Mr Woyda, but *why* did you do it?' Mc-
Cusker asked.

'Plain and simple,' Noah Woyda offered, 'he stole something of
mine and it was something I could never get back.'

'What, you mean your wife?' McCusker asks.

'No, no, not at all,' Noah spat, shaking his head furiously, 'nor even
her love, for he surely stole that as well. No, the unforgivable thing he
stole was my *respect*. I couldn't let him get away with that.'

'But you'll go to prison,' McCusker said, not prepared to just let it
go.

'Prison? No biggie! Easy peasy,' Noah said, laughing. 'I'll plead
guilty, I'll be an ideal prisoner and I'll be out in six years max. My
business will run itself, so I'll enjoy putting my feet up and having a bit
of break from the rat race. It'll do me the world of good.'

Right there, just right there, McCusker thought – that's the big
problem.

Woyda genuinely believed Louis Bloom's end justified the means.
Bloom's murderer clearly lacked a conscience. Nor did he seem to

have battled with *the* big issue that had troubled McCusker since he first became a member of the RUC: how does one human take another's life?

McCusker also recognised that Noah Woyda wanted to come across as a bit of a "bloke" and if you didn't know what he had done, you might even think he was a "decent bloke", in a salt of the Earth kind of way. In a different world he might have tried to network himself into a friendship with the detective. McCusker had always felt that in order to take someone's life, you needed to have a dark side. But Noah Woyda didn't have a dark side, an inner conflict that the successful businessman side needed to fight with. So now McCusker wasn't quite so sure. In fact, in this case a distinct lack of any conscience at all made so much more sense.

This thought, this realisation, of the modern criminal was the scariest concern the detective had ever hosted. The brutal ordinariness of the modern murderer was frightening in a way McCusker never thought possible. The lack of intelligence, coupled with this whole sense of entitlement – the "I can do what I want, when I want" attitude and ultimately the idea that modern life was cheap – was truly unbelievable.

McCusker had always thought that a murderer would wake up in the middle of the night in a cold sweat, haunted by ghosts of the dead or by their own conscience. They would surely re-trace all their steps, all their movements. In the resultant examinations, their victims would come alive again and stand as their judges.

But Noah Woyda most definitely wasn't worried about burning in Hell. In the first place, he probably didn't even believe that Hell existed. Woyda would most likely have claimed that Hell was a place invented by parents to scare their children – when the children were at an age that they would believe them – just so they would be good.

McCusker said as much to O'Carroll after they'd finished their work in the interview room and Woyda had been led away to be processed.

'That's your problem, McCusker,' she said, 'you and he both think you know that he's not going to burn in Hell. In your case, so much so in fact that you've made it your vocation in life to make sure that he's going *somewhere*, even if it's only to be detained at Her Majesty's pleasure, and for no matter how little a period of time it turns out to be. Yes, your priority will be to try to ensure that for as long as humanly possible, his lack of conscience doesn't cause anyone else to lose their life.'

CHAPTER FORTY-SEVEN

About six weeks later, DI Lily O'Carroll received a call from Mariana Fitzgerald. She told O'Carroll that her hip and leg had mended quite well and there were no after-effects. Mariana had remembered her promise to O'Carroll to introduce her to a few decent men. With that in mind she invited the detective to a social event at Queens. Independent of this, McCusker received an invite to the same event from the Vice-Chancellor. His invite included a "plus one". Angela Larkin *also* received an invite for her and her husband, from her sister Elizabeth Bloom. This was how, on the first Friday of December, DI Lily O'Carroll, Superintendent Niall Larkin and his wife Angela, and McCusker and Grace O'Carroll all joined the good and the great of Belfast in the spectacular wood, brick and glass Canada Room in the eaves of the Lanyon Building, QUB.

The event had been organised to celebrate the life and times of Louis Bloom. Louis, in his Will, had ensured that both his wife, Elizabeth, and his lover, Murcia Woyda, would be comfortable for the remainder of their days. However, he had left the bulk of his estate to Queens, some of it to be used to build a new building (in the style of the Lanyon), beside the McClay Library. The new building would house three new lecture theatres. The majority of the endowment would go to seeking out deserving students and financing their academic lives at Queens. Both the building and the endowment would be in the name of The Bloom Family Trust, citing Sidney, Miles Bloom and Louis Bloom. Each of the three new lecture theatres would, in perpetuity, take one of the Bloom names.

In addition, Mrs Elizabeth Bloom – minus her normal croaky plus-one for functions – announced that she was donating the advance and all future royalties on Louis' book to the university, insisting all funds were to be used to directly benefit students. She claimed, barely able to contain her tears, it was what Louis would have wanted.

As the O'Carroll sisters and McCusker arrived at the Lanyon Building and made their way through the entrance hall in the direction of the staircase, Lily was distracted once again by the statue, still deep in thought.

'I used to think that Galileo was just a character Brian Kennedy sang a song about,' she admitted.

'It's okay,' Grace, in turn, said to McCusker, 'of course my sister is not that dumb and she knows full well who Galileo is – she's just trying out a new chat-up line for later.'

When they entered the classic old world styled Canada Room, they were hit with a wave of sights, sounds and scents of the buzzing masses. All those in attendance were rushing around with their wine glasses and dainty canapés. As a voice and volume of one, they sounded like they were speaking in foreign tongues, but to McCusker, they were all merely seeking the same nirvana, the look of love from someone, from anyone.

'All these wonderful boys and girls just trying to find the right boys and girls,' was how Lily O'Carroll succinctly put it. 'We're all people just out looking for someone to come home to.'

'It's been a while since any of us could be termed as boys and girls,' Grace quipped back.

Pretty soon they came upon Mariana Fitzgerald at the centre of a group of people, which included her husband. She happily broke away to join McCusker and the O'Carroll sisters.

'Murcia is getting on okay. Elizabeth Bloom was enlightened enough to invite her to tonight's event, but Murcia was too shy to attend, I think she's only come to realise just how much she loved Louis,' Mariana offered in her quiet voice, which was difficult to hear due to the volume of the chatter in the room. They all instinctively drew in closer. 'The jury is still out on my husband,' she explained, when Lily asked how they were getting on, now that she had discovered his and Woyda's plans for the manse. 'I can't work out if he's a good man who had a temporary lapse of playing the fool, or if playing the fool is a terminal issue. Either way, I've decided to delay a decision until after our hearing. I'm contesting Noah Woyda's right to the freehold of the manse, on the grounds that I was the joint owner and I wasn't consulted. In light of what just happened, my solicitor…' she stopped dead in her tracks, 'Oh look, Lily, it's Oisin … or maybe Darragh… Toal! I can never tell them apart! Either of them would be a perfect catch, let me introduce you!' And just like that, she whisked Lily away.

Grace and McCusker walked a few circumferences of the room and in the course of doing so, they met and chatted briefly to Leab David, the Vice-Chancellor, Professor Vincent Best, Angela and Niall Larkin, Gary and Eilish Mills, and Harry and Sophie Rubens (who apologised once again for not being able to recall the layout of the MAC). Grace was convinced that every time McCusker bumped into her from then on, Sophie would always apologise.

They even bumped into Thomas Chada and his date, Siobhan. Thomas took great pains to introduce McCusker to Siobhan and then, as he stared at Grace, unconsciously nodding his approval, he offered 'I can see now why you knew exactly what I was talking about.'

Later again they sought out Lily to say goodnight, before heading off for a quiet supper at their favourite eatery, the popular Café Conor, so that they could continue their discussion about their search for a new home – together.

Before they left they eventually found Lily, still with Mariana, and they were deep in what sounded to McCusker dangerously like a golf conversation with three men. As he and Grace drew closer to the quintet, McCusker could very clearly hear Lily O'Carroll say:

'When Rory talks about his game of golf before and during a match, you know, when he tries to justify his play, well then eight times out of ten he will lose the game. When he keeps himself to himself before and during the game and doesn't get drawn into anything deep, during his contracted interviews, well, that's when he wins. That's because he's playing pure golf and not preoccupied with fulfilling his own sound-bites.'

This is not the end of the story; it is just where we leave it.